Reviews

"The Witness"

"*The Witness* shifts gears into high-stakes suspense. Raina, whose act of selfless courage turns her into a target, is thrust into a nightmare of trauma and pursuit. What follows is an emotionally gripping narrative where action and tenderness coexist in perfect balance. The pacing remains taut, the stakes high, but Standridge never lets the heart of the story fade. Through Detective Channion Scott's devotion and his growing feelings for Raina, the novel becomes less about survival alone and more about endurance and human connection.

"Standridge's prose is vivid yet unpretentious, the dialogue authentic, and the pacing perfectly tuned...She brings both the ache of grief and the promise of healing to life with quiet emotional precision." ~ **The Prairies Book Review**

"Raina is a vivid presence throughout *The Witness*, filled with urgency from the very first page. Author Jordan Standridge does a very good job of convincing the reader that this woman is the sort who would instinctively intervene to save someone's life. Her recovery from her injuries and developing relationship with Channion as he strives to protect her both emotionally and physically are compelling and authentic... The sense of danger as Raina slowly recovers her memories and the police close in on the criminals is convincing... *The Witness* is buoyed by its core character relationship. Channion and Raina's burgeoning romance set against the backdrop of danger is consistently interesting and engaging." ~ **IndieReader Review**

"HEA!!! Wow. A page turner for sure. Just about the time you think you know where the story is going, there is a twist and turn I was so not expecting. It's impossible to stop reading once you start." ~ **Amazon Review**

"Fantastic book! Best book I have read this year. It has it all...courage, strength, laughter, romance, suspense, friends, and family." ~**Amazon Review**

"This book was an amazing book. I got intrigued by all the characters and could easily relate to them. Once I started reading the book, I could not put it down. I would recommend this book as a great read. I read Jordan's first book also and can't wait to read the next book." ~ **Amazon Review**

"Great mystery (Police FBI). Best 'free book' ever! Little did I know that I would get into reading a free book this long. Words to describe: RIVETING, PAGE TURNER, CLEAN, SUSPENSEFUL, GREAT CHARACTER DEVELOPMENT, WELL WRITTEN AND MORE!...WILL BE READING MORE of this author's books, and they don't have to be free!" ~ **Goodreads Review**

"Phenomenal book. Jordan Standridge is a new author for me. Man, am I ever glad that I read this book! I started this morning before going to work, was almost late to work because I didn't want to stop reading, came home from work and read non-stop until the book was finished. I connected with the characters. The descriptions in the book were so well written, I could visualize what was happening in my mind." ~ **Goodreads Review**

"...If you enjoy a strong female protagonist, thrilling action, and a sprinkling of romance, then this is an excellent choice of book. The author balances the internal emotions and external action of the plot well and creates likeable, believable characters." ~ **Amazon Review**

"I'm a huge fan. This book [*The Witness*] has incredible character development, making it easy to get attached to everyone. [Jordan's] attention to detail truly brings the story to life, immersing you in the world they've created. It's a fun journey to go on with the characters, and you can't help but feel invested in their adventures." ~ **ARC Reader**

"…An inspiring and really emotional story that captures the strength of a woman who refuses to be broken. From the very first pages, I was drawn into Raina's world. I believe the author did a wonderful job showing her physical and emotional recovery. This makes her courage and determination shine in every chapter. In my opinion, this book is about re-discovering oneself after tragedy. The relationship that develops between Raina and Detective Channion Scott adds warmth and hope to the story." ~ **Amazon Review**

"The book is full of suspense from one page to the next. Just when I would go to put it down, something else would happen and I would have to keep reading to see what happened next. The book held [my] complete interest from beginning to end.

"The main character fights hard for her life, her loved ones, and for what she believes in. She never gives up, but holds on to her values along the way. Can't wait to see more from this author. Well done!!" ~ **ARC Reader**

"The Secret"

"Standridge introduces Morgan O'Connell, a woman clawing her way out of grief to rebuild both her life and a sanctuary for others. Harmony Hills is more than a horse facility—it's the heart of Morgan's recovery. Standridge ties Morgan's emotional recovery to the daily work of restoring trust, both in herself and in others. Though the story's suspense heightens the stakes, it's Morgan's self-discovery and the authenticity of her connections that give it real depth." ~ **The Prairies Book Review**

"…A truly heartwarming story of strength, resilience, and second chances. Morgan O'Connell's journey after a personal tragedy is inspiring…It's a beautiful tale of love, trust, and finding peace after hardship. A truly enjoyable read!" ~ **Amazon Review**

"Jordan has a gift for bringing characters to life. Her writing is passionate, vivid, and flawless in my eyes. I could imagine everything so clearly… The emotional depth felt real… Highly recommend!" ~ **ARC Reader/ Amazon Review**

"This book is fire! The characters will draw you in, and make you feel like you're there. It is so good, I even read it in the bath tub! Must read!!!!" ~ **Amazon Review**

"Jordan is really great at making the reader attached to the characters. You can feel the soul behind them. She brought every character to life with the passion she's invoked! It's absolutely going to be a book I buy and re-read as a comfort.

"The humor has been amazing as well! I haven't laughed out loud reading a book in a long time. And I'm a stone, so to actually cry while reading it was amazing. This one book really was able to touch all of my emotions and made me tap into them as a reader. Reading certain chapters definitely had me on the edge of my seat. I feel such an attachment to the characters and I need more! I'm hooked!" ~ **ARC Reader**

"[*The*] *Secret* was such an amazing book, it kept me in suspense from one chapter to the next. I am not an avid reader, but could not put the book down until I had it read. Such courage by the main character Morgan, that it would give anyone hope and courage to move on with your life. The love that grew between Morgan and Josh was so real and very uplifting…You will not be disappointed in buying and reading this book. I look forward to more books by this author." ~ **Amazon Review**

"Just finished *The Secret*. Loved it. Jordan writes so you can relate to the characters. You can feel their ups and downs. You felt what they were going through, and the courage they had to reinvent their lives and move on. The book completely held your interest so that you did not want to put it down but to keep reading to see what happened next. There was a surprise twist at the end that I didn't see coming. When reading the book, you actually feel what the characters feel. Can't wait for her next one. So far loving what I've read from her." ~ **Goodreads Review**

"The Rescues"

"*The Rescues* brings the series full circle, returning to Harmony Hills with a story that hums with quiet strength. Ripley Capilano's chance arrival at the ranch and her bond with a traumatized horse set the stage for one of the series' most emotionally nuanced romances. Her relationship with the guarded and steadfast Ty Stanton unfolds with slow-burning depth. Their journey from cautious strangers to soul-deep partners mirrors the horse's recovery—pain yielding to trust, and fear to faith." ~ **The Prairies Book Review**

"*The Rescues* is a heartfelt exploration of love found through healing rather than perfection. As Ripley helps restore a traumatized horse's trust, she and Ty slowly confront their own fears and past wounds. Standridge's writing is immersive and compassionate, blending emotional growth and quiet romance into a cozy yet powerful story about learning to begin again." ~ **NewInBooks.com Review**

"For some years now, I've been looking for stories that have meaning, that are captivating but also offer a lesson. In *The Rescues,* I found everything I was looking for in a novel: a strong and determined protagonist, a gripping plot, and compelling characters... This is undoubtedly a story to fall in love with, to return to what we left forgotten, and to relive." ~ **Amazon Review**

"This captivating story had me glued to every page. I found the use of a horse as both a connection and a mirror to be absolutely brilliant; it reflected exactly what the protagonists needed to face in their lives things they had been avoiding until that moment...It's a journey that helps you not only discover the true reasons behind your actions but also work through them to lighten the emotional load. I highly recommend this book to anyone looking for a story full of hope, where the great quest to find true strength and courage within oneself is at the heart of a beautiful narrative." ~ **Amazon Review**

"It left me feeling like I had actually been to Harmony Hills, breathing in hay, silence, and second chances. Seeing Ripley heal an injured horse while, almost without meaning to, letting Ty get close to her own emotional wounds, feels genuine, tender, and not at all forced. It's one of those romances where the process of learning to trust again is almost more enjoyable than the inevitable." ~ **Amazon Review**

"I was captivated by this moving story from beginning to end...This book left me feeling good and gave me the knowledge that there is always hope for another chance and a better future." ~ **Amazon Review**

"The Guardian"

"...Themes of resilience, healing, faith, loyalty, and second chances are woven naturally into the narrative. This volume succeeds as both a suspenseful conclusion to a larger mystery and a heartfelt exploration of what it means to truly love someone through uncertainty, loss, and change. A thriller fueled as much by emotion as mystery." ~ **The Prairies Book Review**

"...*The Guardian* is a book that makes you just want to keep reading to see how it will all turn out, and when you think you may have guessed the ending, well, let's just say Jordan has a way to keep you trying to figure it out until the very end." ~ **ARC Reader**

"Book Four, *The Guardian,* is definitely a must read. The riveting twists and emotional turn of events show strength, compassion, and honor—all of which truly make this an inspirational story. Love this series! Way to connect the dots, Jordan!" ~ **ARC Reader**

"The Women of Strength, Courage, and Hope" Series

"Standridge's heartfelt trilogy traces the intertwined journeys of three women overcoming loss and danger, each uncovering that the path to healing runs through connection as much as endurance.

"Rooted in the heart of Arizona, the stories feel authentic and alive. The expanse of the desert and the quiet pulse of ranch life anchor the emotional intensity of each story. Read together, the three novels form an emotionally cohesive trilogy that celebrates endurance, compassion, and second chances. Standridge's prose is vivid yet unpretentious, the dialogue authentic, and the pacing perfectly tuned to the rhythm of each story's emotional stakes. She brings the ache of grief and the promise of healing to life with quiet emotional precision. Harmony Hills feels real and lived in; a refuge where pain meets possibility and where the land itself seems to mirror the characters' longing for peace. Fans of Debbie Macomber's *Cedar Cove series* and Nicholas Sparks' *The Rescue* and *Safe Haven* will find much to admire. A page-turning, emotionally charged trilogy that blends suspense, romance, and redemption in equal measure." ~ **The Prairies Book Review**

"Jordan's work has genuinely inspired us. Each narrative resonates deeply, exploring profound themes of faith, resilience, and the transformative power of the human-animal bond. Her storytelling captures universal messages of hope and personal growth, making her work truly special.

"Jordan's work is captivating with its emotionally resonant themes and interconnected narratives. The layered storytelling not only keeps readers engaged but builds anticipation between books. Her stories on faith, resilience, and hope also make them ideal for book clubs and online discussions. "She has a genuine, emotional storytelling that distinguishes her." ~ **ARC Reader**

Also by Jordan Standridge

<u>The Women of Strength, Courage, and Hope Series</u>

The Secret *

The Secret, Large Print

The Witness **

The Rescues

The Guardian

The Guardian, Large Print

*2025 *Global Book Awards Gold Winner- Women's Fiction*

2025 *Global Book Awards Silver Winner- Romance Suspense **as well as*

**2026 *Next Generation Indie Book Awards -Gold x2- Suspense & Second Novel*

The Witness

Book Two

The Women of Strength, Courage, and Hope Series

Jordan Standridge

HAPPY TRAILS PRESS

The Witness

The Witness:

ISBN: 978-1-967457-02-1 (KDP ebook)

ISBN: 978-1-967457-03-8 (KDP paperback)

ISBN: 978-1-967457-08-3 (non-KDP ebook)

ISBN: 978-1-967457-09-0 (non-KDP paperback)

www.JordanStandridge.com

Happy Trails Press

Cover Design by Damonza

Formatting Software: Atticus

To all law enforcement officers (LEOs) and First Responders everywhere who serve with honor, integrity, and compassion when needed: Thank you. Be safe out there. May you have a brave witness of your own if one is ever needed.

And thanks also to their family members, who often sacrifice as much as the officers themselves. The long hours and the never-knowing-what-could-happen can be stressful. Stay strong.

And last, but not least, to the dispatchers who never know what's happening on the other end of the line. I've been there myself—on both sides. You got this.

Prologue

GROWING UP IN THE Midwestern Bible Belt, young Raina Stewart repeatedly heard that old preacher man say everyone has the choice of going to either heaven or hell. How many times had she heard his sermons, threatening salvation or damnation? How one lived their life, and the choices they made on a daily basis, would determine whether his or her eternal roommates would be angels or devils?

By the time she was in her teens, Raina had begun to dismiss that old, bitter preacher man and his tales of woe and fiery trials. But a few short years later, she liked to believe there really was a heaven because that way she knew exactly where her sweet mama was.

And hell? Who knew hell was actually located here on Earth?

She bet not that old preacher man.

Chapter 1

What lies behind us and what lies before us are tiny matters compared to what lies within us. ~ Ralph Waldo Emerson

IT WAS A PERFECT day. Miles-long sunbeams shoved their way through the cumulus clouds in the sky and the shady pine trees on the ground. It looked magical... Heaven on Earth.

Raina always enjoyed this part of the wide two-lane road because of those towering pine trees that lined both sides. Although they didn't crowd the road, their slippery, yet sticky, needles did litter the shoulders.

Humming as she drove her truck down the country road, she thought about the concert in Paducah, Kentucky she was performing in next week. She already had her clothes hanging in her closet, ready to go at a moment's notice. The music was selected, rehearsed, and locked in her mind.

She just needed to get back-up strings for her autoharp from the studio. She was excited to be playing it for the folk song selections. She felt it helped to keep the instrument relevant and the show fresh.

She was feeling both confident and comfortable with the schedule. She'd spend three days at a great venue with, if the past two years were any indication, a highly enthusiastic crowd. The event coordinator, Jason Charles, was her biggest fan.

Coming up on a sharp curve, she began to coast to take it within the posted slower speed limit. It was one of those curves that was sharper than it appeared. Being new to the area, Raina wondered if people ever wrecked there because they lost control due to speeding—or those slippery pine needles.

She then wondered if police ever patrolled this far out because of these curves and possible wrecks. As soon as the thought entered her mind, she got that old, familiar feeling of forewarning.

Cops and deer. Her mama always said if you want to avoid either of those two things, take Raina with you. *"She knows they're there before they do!"* How many times had she heard her mama say that to people? Oddly enough, her mama was usually right. It didn't matter the season or the time, Raina would suddenly get this feeling of deer or cops around... and there they'd be. Sometimes, she even spooked herself.

Her mama told her that sixth sense of hers had saved her a few tickets—and more than a few deer their lives. She'd always told her daughter to never ignore it. When her gut feeling kicked in, Raina was to listen to it and act accordingly. Mama described her gut feelings as her very own angel's warning system. And no one should ignore an angel.

As Raina came out of the curve, she saw a marked county sheriff's car with its flashing red, white, and blue lights pulled behind a car. That answered *that* question! she thought, smiling.

Slowing down as she neared them, she also moved over into the oncoming lane to give extra room for safety. Glancing over quickly, she noticed the officer in his car looking down. Probably writing a ticket, she thought. She couldn't help but give another quick, curious look at the offender. A dark-haired man, he was also looking down.

Raina moved back over into her lane, slowly picking up speed again. About two miles farther down the road, she saw another car pulled over on the shoulder of the opposite lane. Automatically, she began slowing down. Based on her gut instinct, she'd sometimes stop to offer help to stranded motorists.

Her instincts went on alert when she noticed a man standing beside the car, looking at his phone. Calling out or reading a text? Looking for a signal? He should have one since there were towers that provided pretty reliable service out there, even in the hills. His brows were furrowed, his mouth pulled tight. His body looked tense and rigid.

Coasting, she assessed the scene, careful to not give any indication she was going to actually stop. The trunk lid was up, so she assumed he had a flat. As she was passing the rear of the car, she caught a glimpse of another man reaching into the trunk for something that looked long and black. Not believing she saw it correctly, she immediately looked again while her heart skipped a beat. Was that a *rifle?*

The man shut the trunk lid. She glanced at the road to make sure she didn't drive off it before quickly looking into her mirror. She didn't dare put on her brakes. She continued to coast to give her more time to look. Raina saw the men get in the car and saw the taillights flash red as the car was put into gear.

Going around the next curve, Raina's gut instincts were churning. *Had* she seen a rifle? She'd only had a second to look... Surely she was wrong. She pulled over and stopped so she could think. *Why* would someone pull over during the day on a deserted country road to get a gun out of their trunk?

The random answer that came to her mind was a sickening one. No. That'd be preposterous. But try as she might, she just couldn't think of any other reason.

What if she turned around to just check? She didn't know them. They didn't know her. She might feel like an idiot, but who cared?

Raina bit her lower lip as she thought it through. She had to know for sure. Checking her mirrors and looking around to be sure the road was clear in both directions, she turned her truck around.

She already felt like an idiot, but her *gut*... Her gut was telling her something was off. It was churning more than usual, and it'd only worsen if she didn't do something about it. Her mama said to always listen to it. And anytime in the past when she hadn't, she'd always wished she had.

Her hands clammy, she wiped them one at a time on her shorts. Why was her heart beating so rapidly? Taking a couple of deep breaths, she told herself she hadn't seriously seen a gun being taken from that car.

But still, her gut prodded her on. Turning off her headlights to avoid being noticed as easily, she took the curve. She noticed right away that car she'd seen was nowhere in sight. She turned down the air conditioner to give her hands something to do besides sweat. A second later, she turned it back on.

Feeling foolish, Raina reached into her truck's middle console and pulled out her pepper spray. And with her cellphone in its case on her hip, she felt better. Still foolish but better.

Thinking quickly, she pulled over to the side of the road. She was close to where the cop had pulled over that car, but she couldn't see him with the slight curve in the road. Turning off her truck, she checked her mirrors before opening her door and sliding to the ground. Running across the road into the thick line of pine trees, she breathlessly jogged closer.

Peeking around a tree, Raina got a clear view of the road. Her heart skipped a beat before it began beating so furiously she could barely catch a breath. The blood rushing through her head made her feel dizzy, and she put a hand against the tree for support.

The second car she'd seen, the one with the imagined rifle, was pulled over in front of the first car. And that imagined rifle was anything *but* imaginary. It was being pointed at the officer who was standing beside his car. He was helpless. He couldn't run, get in his cruiser, or even try to get off a shot as his gun was still in his holster.

The three men were arguing... probably about murdering that defenseless deputy in cold blood. She noticed one of the other men held a pistol. Raina felt frozen to the spot. What was she supposed to do? No way was she just going to stand there!

She quickly grabbed her phone and turned on the camera feature. Zooming in the best she could, she took pictures of everyone. She even got the license plate of the second car. Her hands shaking, she tried to take clear pictures... just in case. Just in case the absolute worst happened, and she couldn't do anything in time. She quickly switched from camera to video mode and recorded what she was seeing. She wished she had her other camera!

What should she do? Call 9-1-1 immediately, a voice in her head screamed. But they'd never get here in time! another voice screamed back. That officer was in peril and needed help *now!* Her internal argument raced through her mind in seconds... Precious seconds before her gut, her heart, prompted her to act.

Raina ran as fast as she could toward her truck, sliding on the pine needles as she rounded a tree. She skidded to a stop at her truck's door and barely missed hitting herself with it as she yanked it open. Jumping in behind the wheel, she started the engine even as her door was slamming shut.

Snapping on her seatbelt, she floored it and drove straight toward hell.

Chapter 2

TIME WAS A LUXURY she didn't have. She couldn't waste what she had of it to think. The way she saw it, *she* was that officer's only chance of hope... And maybe even survival. She had the element of surprise. She fervently prayed it'd be enough of one to give that officer a chance of either defending himself or getting away.

In her heart, she *knew* they were going to kill that deputy. He'd seen all three of their faces, hadn't he? He was breathing his last breaths even now, and she was positive he knew it. If she were in his shoes, the one thing she'd be doing at that moment would be praying for a miracle. She may not be his miracle, but she *could* be his divine intervention.

She'd once read that if one but looked, they'd find a weapon to be used in self-defense. A lamp, a chair, a book, a pen, hot water, dirt, a hot curling iron. *Anything*.

Raina figured she had a cellphone, pepper spray, and a truck.

As she neared the scene, Raina saw everything in slow motion... The falling officer, the shooter walking closer, aiming his gun at the man lying motionless on the ground. He was going for either the kill shot, or to make sure the officer was indeed dead. One of the other men was shaking his head and angrily waving his arms. Raina heard more shots, and the fallen officer's body twitched.

There was no stopping, no turning around, no just driving on by now. She felt like she was driving in molasses. Could she get there in time? Was she already too late? Raina saw the three men jerk around. They tried to get out of the way of the speeding vehicle aimed directly at them.

She screamed as her truck rammed directly into the nearest car, shoving it into the other one. She sensed her airbags deploying and felt the punch of the impact as she was caught by her seatbelt. She was mercilessly jerked back to the seat before she saw nothing but black.

She came to her senses. Did she black out? If so, for how long?

In a daze, she looked out the cracked windshield and window. What had happened to everyone? Where were the men with the guns? Was the officer dead, or nearly so?

Her head fell back against the headrest as she fought to clear her blurry vision. She managed to unfasten her seatbelt and slid it away. Pushing at her airbag, she gasped in pain. Her chest hurt, and her right hand was numb.

Clenching her teeth against the pain, she shoved at her door. It wouldn't budge. Gingerly climbing over her front seats, she was able to open the passenger door. She quickly looked around. Raina saw the fallen policeman beside his cruiser, blood pooling around him. Sliding to the ground, Raina reached back inside her truck and grabbed her pepper spray. She was turning around when her head was violently yanked backwards by a strong grip in her hair.

Yelping in pain and terror, she desperately tried to fight off her attacker. Whether it was an innate instinct to survive or pure adrenaline, Raina fought like an enraged wildcat. She felt the blows hit her body and doubled over in reflex and in pain. When her head made contact against her truck, she saw stars and a blackness flash over her.

Somehow, she held onto her only weapon—her pepper spray. She struggled to bring it around but felt it knocked from her grasp. Feigning complete weakness, she made herself fall limp. Her attacker, apparently surprised or thinking she fainted, let her drop to the hard ground.

Seizing the opportunity, Raina saw and grabbed her pepper spray with both hands. Rolling over quickly, she sprayed her attacker full-on in his face just as he was leaning over her. She instinctively turned her face and tightly closed her eyes to protect them from the spray. She kicked and screamed as he bellowed in rage and pain. Aiming her kicks toward his knees and groin, she lashed out with what strength she had. Staggering backwards, he fell against her truck.

Scrambling to her feet, she kicked him again in the groin and kneed his face while he was doubled over. His screams, mingling with her own, rang in her head. She scrambled to get away in that split second of opportunity.

Her shoes slipped on the pavement and pine needles, and she fell against her truck. Just as she was getting a grip with her shoes, she felt herself being shoved to the ground. She landed with a grunt and felt the pavement tear into her face and arms as her head was pushed down. Her pepper spray went flying from her grasp. Screaming and bucking to get the weight away from her, she fought with all she had.

Raina felt herself being turned over. She felt, rather than saw, two large hands grab her hair and slam her head onto the unrelenting pavement. She saw stars again. This time, they were followed by a blinding light.

She tried to fight, but she simply couldn't seem to move. She felt her head being raised again by those hands. Was she even holding onto the man's wrists? Could she scrape his skin with her nails?

Instinctively, she turned her head and sank her teeth into his arm. Vaguely, she heard an enraged yell. She felt her head hit the ground again, and then she couldn't feel anything.

The last thing she remembered was hearing a loud popping sound. It even seemed to echo in her head.

Oh, dear God, she'd been shot.

In her mind, Raina saw a wave of black rolling toward her. She was helpless to fight it back.

Chapter 3

RAINA CAME TO AWARENESS slowly. Her head, her body, *everything*, felt detached from anything that should've been there to let her know she was whole. There was an odd sense of blessed numbness.

She remained motionless as she tried to get her bearings. Where was she? In a flash, she remembered and her breathing sped up, making her aware it hurt to breathe. Not knowing whether or not she was alone, she dared to move only her eyes.

She vaguely smelled the scent of pine as well as the musty smells of the asphalt and dirt she was lying on. She heard the wind softly whistling through the pine trees. But she didn't hear anything else. Not even a bird.

Taking a chance, she moved. Tears sprung to her burning eyes as she forced herself to turn to her side to get up. She could only make it to her knees before the pain made her stop. Through sheer will, she half-crawled, half-stumbled to the officer. Her knees felt stiff and were protesting her every move.

Avoiding the pooled blood around him, she felt for a pulse. As tears ran freely down her face and burned her open wounds, she prayed he had one. She finally felt it in his wrist. It was faint, but it was a pulse. She barely saw his chest slowly rise and fall. She sobbed in relief at his being alive.

Looking around again for the armed men, she didn't see them anywhere. She noticed the deputy's gun was out of his holster. Had her collision given him a chance after all?

She again listened intently. Nothing but the wind.

She read his badge. "Mitchell? Deputy Mitchell? Can you hear me?" She felt like she was yelling, but her voice was barely above a strained whisper. She shook him with one hand.

Certified in First Aid, AED, and CPR years ago, Raina remembered only parts of her training. She knew he was breathing, had a pulse, and had bad injuries judging by the amount of blood. She gingerly got to her feet and stumbled to her truck.

She yanked open the back door of the quad cab. She quickly looked around herself again, anticipating another attack. She always kept spare clothes in the truck in case of emergencies like her mama had taught her. She lifted up the backseat to get to the storage compartment underneath it, yelping in pain the jerky motion caused. She grabbed her bag of clothes and her First Aid kit.

Making her way back to the fallen officer, she carefully knelt down beside him. She cried out when her bloodied legs touched the rough pavement. Her hands shaking almost uncontrollably and her breathing labored, she opened his shirt. She saw drops of her own blood land on him as she leaned over before she looked around for the men again. She was terrified they were still there, somewhere, but she needed to render aid first.

She saw the two embedded bullets in his Kevlar vest. Where was the blood coming from? She finally traced the blood to his lower abdomen just below the vest and also to wounds in his upper right arm and shoulder. She fumbled open the First Aid kit.

She used the sterile gauze and antiseptic to clean around the wound, using another piece of gauze to cover it. Holding it in place, she used her teeth to tear the tape. When the tape broke away from the roll, she swore her head was going to fall off. The pain was searing. When she needed more tape, she stopped just short of it breaking.

Would she be removing evidence? She couldn't worry about that right now. Her priority was the policeman's life. Did he flinch? She hoped so because if he was feeling pain, that meant he was alive.

Raina looked around again for the men. She sobbed as she pressed a feminine hygiene pad against the bleeding wound in his abdomen, taping it down. She stuffed a clean shirt over it, tucking it under the vest. The other end she pulled toward his back, shoving it under the waistband of his pants, using his belt to help hold it in place. She grabbed another sanitary pad and pressed it against the bloody hole in his shoulder. She used the last of the tape to keep it in place. She saw blood seeping out from his arm and wrapped the hand towel around it. She knew the man could die from blood loss and shock.

Where was her phone? She needed to call 9-1-1.

Looking at the officer, his face white, she slapped him to try and keep him awake, aware. His eyes were closed, but she thought she caught a reaction from her slap. She didn't want to be out here by herself. She'd never felt as alone in her entire life as she did at that moment.

Where were the other men?

She grabbed the gun from the ground beside him. Too heavy for her to carry in her numb right hand, she dropped it with a gasp of pain. Awkwardly, Raina picked it back up with her left hand. It wobbled in her hand. She tried to get used to its weight and feel as she carefully made her way around to her truck. What she saw made her stomach heave.

Partially sandwiched between her truck and the car was one of the men. He was dead.

Reaching inside her truck, she put the gun on the seat and grabbed her digital camera from the console. She took pictures of the cars: the makes, models, and license plates. Feeling sick, she made herself take pictures and video of the dead man. What if they returned and took the body? Dropping the camera inside her truck, it bounced out of sight. She grabbed the gun again. Her mind was on pure survival mode, but she was thinking clearly all the same. For now, anyway.

Looking around, she made her way back to the cruiser. She heard nothing coming from the radio inside. Did the dispatcher know the traffic stop had gone horribly wrong? Could they hear? Did they think it was over, and the officer was simply driving back to the station?

Trying to think through her pain and shock, she knew she had to drive the officer's car since the other cars were wrecked. She opened the back doors. Slowly, painfully, she dragged the unconscious officer onto the back seat, scooting out the other side as she pulled him. Her salty tears ran down her face, mixing with her blood, dripping onto the officer's tan shirt. Worried about his rolling onto the floor if she drove too fast or wrecked, she rigged the seatbelts around him. She tried to be gentle, but she knew she herself wasn't going to last too much longer. This adrenaline rush was going to make her crash any moment. She needed to hurry!

After tossing her bag and First Aid kit onto the floorboard, she shoved at his legs so she could close the door.

Still holding the gun, she returned to her truck again, grabbed her keys, cellphone, and purse. Knowing it was probably foolish, she automatically held up the key fob to hopefully lock the doors and set the alarm. Would it even work? She didn't know.

Before she got into the cruiser, she painfully made her way back to the cars and took pictures of them and the man with her cellphone's camera. Just in case.

She tossed her purse, keys, and phone onto the passenger front seat of the deputy's car. She put the gun on the dashboard before she got in so her hands were free. She cried out in pain as she lowered herself into the driver's seat, her bloody hands slipping off the door frame.

She feared she had a broken nose as she realized she was breathing through her mouth. Blood was still running in little streams down her face and neck. She used her shirt to dabble at it, wiping her hands on her shorts. The salty tears still flowing from her eyes burned like hot branding irons as they landed in raw flesh. Automatically, she wiped at the tears and trickling blood, rubbing the peeled skin, the raw wounds in her own flesh. The burning sensations she now felt were excruciating.

After closing her door and locking all of them, Raina realized her feet couldn't quite reach the pedals. She had to take the time and effort to figure out how to adjust it. Where was the handle that allowed her to move up the seat? She couldn't find it. A wave of panic, surging through her veins, riding the crest of adrenaline, spurred her to hurry.

Knowing she wasn't going to last much longer, Raina gave up and turned her attention back to driving out of there. Thankfully, the car was still quietly running, the colored lights still flashing. Putting the gun on the passenger seat, she clipped on her seatbelt and pulled out onto the road toward town.

"Deputy Mitchell! Can you hear me? Please don't die on me! I'm going to get you to the hospital, okay? You hang in there!" Her voice hoarse, Raina kept talking to the cop laid out across the back seat.

She heard the dispatcher using a number and a ten code. Raina didn't know what she was saying, or if the dispatcher was even talking to *this* officer. Not knowing how to use the police radio, Raina ignored it. She was terrified she'd wreck if she tried to figure it out while she drove. And there simply was no time to try to figure it out now.

Instead, she grabbed her cellphone. With numb, bloody fingers, she dialed 9-1-1.

Chapter 4

"9-1-1. WHAT'S YOUR EMERGENCY?"

Raina almost cried in relief at the mere sound of another human's voice. She was so overcome with emotion, she couldn't make a sound come out.

"This is 9-1-1. Do you have an emergency?"

Raina forced out, "An officer has been shot, and I'm driving him to the hospital." Raina had to stop talking to take a breath. Her chest felt like it was on fire.

"Ma'am? I'm having a hard time understanding you. Did you say an officer was *shot?*"

"Yes. I tried to save him. I'm driving his car into town."

"Ma'am, stay where you are. Where are you exactly? We're on the way as soon as you tell us where you are."

"No. They might still be out here. It's not safe."

"Who's 'they'?" The dispatcher kept her own voice calm as she quickly waved for her supervisor to join her. "Where are you?"

Raina slowed for another curve. The phone was hard to hold onto, and she could barely handle the steering wheel with her other one. What'd the woman ask her? Her mind could only focus on one thing right now so she concentrated on the road. Finally, she replied vaguely, "Outside of town."

The dispatcher relayed the information as Raina paused. It was hard to talk as she was breathing through her mouth, tasting the coppery taste of blood. "His badge name says 'Mitchell' and... *Oh!*" She dropped the phone to keep control of the wheel as she sped down the road.

"Ma'am, are you there? We can get officers and an ambulance en route toward you. Which highway or road are you on? They can meet you." The dispatcher waited for an answer, but none came. "Are you there?"

The dispatcher could hear white noise, so she knew the call hadn't been discon-nected. She said softly to her supervisor, "I think she put the phone down. I can still hear background noise like she's driving."

Inside the dispatch room, all were silent as they waited anxiously to hear a reply, any reply, from the caller. Since only the dispatcher could hear on the phone through her headset, all eyes were locked on her. Another minute went by. And another. Still nothing from the caller.

"Ma'am? Are you there? Can you hear me?"

Her supervisor stood beside her, his face as anxious as hers. They were trying to get a location fix.

After another few minutes, Raina put the phone on speaker and laid it on the console. It promptly slid off when she took another curve. She tried to catch it, thankful it fell in her lap. Crying out at the sharp pain in her wrist, Raina blinked away the fresh tears welling in her eyes. Gaining control of her breathing again, she picked it up. "Are you still there?"

"Yes! Are you okay? Can you tell me your name?" The dispatcher worked to keep her tone calm while her heart pounded furiously in her chest.

"Raina Stewart. I need to get to the hospital, okay? There were three men. One will be there. I'm sure he's... he's dead. I don't know where the other two are. They could be following me, so I can't stop." Struggling to think straight, she thought to describe them. "Three men. Two white, one black. Medium builds, all dark hair. Kinda tall. They have guns. Okay? Did you hear me about the guns?" She felt she needed to stress that important fact.

"Yes, ma'am. Three men with guns. Where are you now?"

"We're crossing the blue bridge. There's more traffic now... I don't know how long I can talk to you."

The dispatcher and her supervisor were now relaying the information to the responding units as Raina talked. Was the driver's voice getting weaker? Her words were slurring together even worse than before. The dispatcher was scared the woman driving was going to pass out.

"Raina? You stay with me, okay? Where are you hurt?"

"I... don't know. I can't really talk to you, okay? But he's shot. I saw two bullets in his vest. He's got other shots too. He's lost blood." Raina's voice cracked. "I'm heading toward St. Joseph's Hospital. It's the only one I know. Can you let them know we're coming? Please?"

Her words were soft and hard to understand. The dispatcher caught something about lost blood. Apparently the policeman was suffering from more than one shot, outside of his Kevlar vest. She added what she could on her screen as she tried to understand the caller. When she heard *St. Joseph's Hospital*, she quickly typed it into her computer, along with *multiple shots*. Reading her screen, her supervisor picked up a phone. Straining her ears, the dispatcher concentrated on the caller's fading voice.

Raina dropped the phone and blared the horn as she passed a slow car who didn't notice the flashing lights. The little blue car swerved quickly to the shoulder as the cruiser zipped by. She was getting dizzy. She *had* to hold on! Frantically, she reached over to get the phone. "We're almost at the elementary school now."

Town meant even more cars. Raina called into the phone, panic in her voice, "How do I turn on the sirens? *Oh no!* They don't know to get out of the way!" She barely avoided hitting a car in front of her. Her reflexes were slowing down.

The dispatcher told her supervisor what was happening, and he quickly got on the line. He could only hope this squad car was like the others he knew about. Calmly, he said, "There should be a big black knob in the middle of the console to your right. Turn it one click, clockwise. You should be seeing the other officers any minute. They'll escort you all the way to the ER."

Raina dropped the phone, quickly looked at the console full of knobs and labels. Looking back and forth at the road as she drove, she turned the biggest knob she saw one click to the right. The siren blared over her, louder than she expected.

The supervisor heard the siren turn on and nodded to the dispatcher, giving the call back to her. She stayed on the line, listening intently for anything else that could help.

Raina could feel her brain beginning to shut down, and she fought hard to stay aware. Leaving the phone in her lap now, she focused like a laser on just driving. Her back felt like it was on fire. It was now cramping on her as she couldn't lean back against the seat and still reach the pedals.

She thanked God every time the traffic pulled over to let her pass. One car whose driver wasn't paying attention almost hit her as she went through an intersection. Thankfully, they swerved and slammed on their brakes in the nick of time. Raina didn't even notice.

Up ahead, she saw two squad cars pull out in front of her, lights flashing. Once she got closer, she could hear their sirens blaring. One slowed to let her catch up to them before accelerating again. Both were clearing the way for her.

Her head was throbbing something awful. Her vision was blurring again, and she fought hard to fight through the fog. She screeched around the corner behind the escorting officers, faintly aware of another one now behind her. They made a tight turn around another corner with cars hastily pulling over.

She kept praying and talking to herself to stay awake. "Stay with it, Raina. You're almost there. Officer Mitchell! Can you hear me? Please, God. You've been with us so far. Just a little while longer... Please help me get him to safety. You must have put me there for a reason, so You've got to guide me a little while longer..."

Raina saw the hospital up ahead on her right. She sluggishly applied the brakes... almost too late to make the turn into the hospital's entrance. She knew she was going to pass out any moment, but she was *almost* there.

Hospital staff were waiting at the ER doors as the police cars in front of her pulled to screeching stops. She barely got her car to stop before hitting the squad car that she'd followed, passing the ER doors. She felt the slight impact of her car hitting the other one, but her speed was slow enough it wasn't too jarring. Her brain couldn't seem to control her legs and arms anymore.

With fierce determination, Raina shifted the car into *park*. She heard the faint clicking of the door locks releasing their grips. She tried to shut off the engine, but her wrist and hand hurt too much. She realized the siren was still blaring overhead, so she tried to turn it off. Focusing on the little black knob and turning it counterclockwise, she finally heard blessed silence.

She slowly scooted backwards until her back was supported by the seat now that she didn't have to worry about reaching the pedals. She flinched at the additional pain touching the seat brought on, but she simply had to lean against something. *Anything.* She had to let out a sigh, which turned into a gasp as a sharp pain pierced through her. Fresh tears rolled down her cheeks, over the drying blood on her raw, torn cheeks and chin.

Raina barely even registered the cops looking through the windows or the back doors being opened. She barely noticed Deputy Mitchell being checked before he was carefully pulled out and gently put onto a gurney. The hospital staff raced through the sliding doors, calling out orders while a few remained behind for her. She didn't even notice them.

When the driver's door opened, Raina offered a tiny smile and closed her eyes. "Thank you, God. We made it. Thank you. Thank you. Thank you."

HEARING IN HER HEADSET now the sounds of people talking rather than the road noise from before, the dispatcher breathed out a huge sigh of pent-up relief. She rested her forehead in her sweaty hands. She could now make out who she figured were either nurses or other policemen talking and barking out orders.

Looking up at her supervisor, she nodded. She proudly proclaimed in a whisper, "*She made it!* She's at the hospital!"

As she heard her co-workers clapping, she wiped the tears of relief from her eyes as she slowly disconnected the call.

Chapter 5

AN OFFICER OPENED HER door after looking through the window for any possible threat coming from the driver. When he swung the door all the way open, Raina looked over. He tried to keep calm as he surveyed the damage done to her face. What had she gone through? he wondered as he took a moment to assess her.

He saw blood trails and pieces of what looked like dirt and asphalt embedded in her skin. Some of her skin was scraped away. Her hair was a mess. He could already see faint bruises beginning to form on her cheekbones, unless it was actually pavement residue. Her glazed eyes were looking into his now. He noticed one of them hemorrhaged as the white was beginning to turn red from the invasion of blood. The left side of her face looked to be swelling up already. Her shirt was ripped, showing even more blood, gouges, and debris in her shoulders and upper chest.

Blood was also slowly trickling down from her nose, making a narrow red river that spread out into a few red tributaries to under her chin. His glance transferred to her bare arms and legs. They were as torn up as her face. Fresh drops of blood plopped down on them from her chin. The officer's own body hurt just looking at her. She looked like she'd been in a war zone.

Not being fully sure of the situation, the officer checked again to make sure there wasn't a gun or weapon within her reach. He saw a gun on the floorboard on the passenger side, but there was no way she could get to it.

Looking directly at her again, he asked calmly, "You're Raina? You did good, Raina. There are some people here who are going to take you inside now, okay?"

Raina let her head fall back against the seat, closing her eyes. She felt someone else's presence now. A new voice called out softly, "Oh, man... Roll that gurney around here, Lynnette." She felt someone gently tapping on her shoulder. "Ma'am? Can you get out on your own, or do you need some help?" Since she didn't answer, he reached over her, releasing the seatbelt before stepping back a little. He carefully pulled the straps out of the way without touching her.

She slowly opened her eyes. He saw they were glazed and unfocused.

"Do you need help, ma'am?" Raina heard him ask. After a moment, she began to turn to exit the vehicle. Oddly enough, she felt pretty comfortable in it and didn't want to leave. It'd become her safe haven. She was fully content to stay right where she was. But at his urging, she decided she had to get out.

As she twisted her body, sharp pains radiated through her. Gasping loudly, she stopped and tried to grab the steering wheel for support but couldn't seem to grasp it. She took gulps of air and fought back the tears she could feel burning in her eyes when she did that.

The nurse noticed. He was betting she had some broken, cracked, or badly bruised ribs. Was there internal bleeding? If she had broken ribs, she could puncture an organ. It was best she didn't turn or bend, if possible. Her right wrist seemed to be giving her problems too. As the battered woman slowly got out, he gently supported her. With help from Lynnette waiting beside him with the gurney, they had her lie down before clicking the safety straps around her.

They quickly wheeled her through the doors as the officers took over the car, now part of a crime scene.

"*Miss Stewart? Can you hear me?*"

The sound seemed to be coming from far away. She didn't recognize the voice at all. Too exhausted to open her eyes, she tried to listen. In another moment, she passed out again.

"Doctor, she might be coming out of it again." The female voice had a Southern accent Raina liked.

"Miss Stewart, can you hear me?" She felt someone gently grab her left hand. "Squeeze my hand if you can hear me, okay?" She gave a weak squeeze. "Good! That's good. Can you open your eyes, Raina? Come on, open your eyes for me."

Her eyes fluttered, opened a slit before they quickly shut again. Concentrating on opening her eyes scared her spitless. How could someone not even be able to open their own eyes? Wasn't that supposed to be a natural thing even a baby could do? Her breathing began to come in shallow gasps. Somewhere in the background, she heard some beeps begin to sound louder and more rapidly.

"Doctor, she may be going into a panic attack..." The Southern charmer was talking again.

"It's okay, Raina. You're safe. Take your time, but try to open your eyes. Take a deep breath, and let it out slowly. It might hurt to breathe deep, but give it a try. You're safe, Raina. That's it, nice and easy." She felt a hand running up and down her left arm in a soothing motion. "That's it. We turned off the lights, but you let us know if the light in here is still too much for you, though, okay?"

Raina struggled and finally got her eyes to open and stay open. Actually, she could only see out of one so she wasn't sure if both were open or not. She'd already noticed taking a deep breath hurt her ribs so she took smaller ones. Her back didn't seem to hurt as much now, but her vision was still blurry. It took her a moment to get her eye to focus on the faces looking down at her. An older man she assumed to be the doctor was smiling at her. A middle-aged nurse was looking at her with concern on her face.

"I'm at the hospital?" Her voice was low and scratchy. She tried again. "Am I at the hospital?"

This time they made out her slurred words. Her battered face had swollen up rather quickly, making it hard for her to speak clearly. "Yes, you're at the hospital. I'm Dr. Benson, and this is Nurse Carter. Can you tell us how you're feeling?"

Raina tried to look at them closely, but they were slightly blurry. They must've taken out her contacts. Her heart sped up thinking maybe they were stuck behind her eyes. It'd been a fear she'd always had since she began wearing them in junior high school. Both the doctor and nurse tried to soothe her as she took her time answering. Both listened to the monitor beeping in time with her rapid heartbeat.

"My contacts..." she slurred out. "In my eyes?"

Dr. Benson understood. Reassuring her, he said, "We got them out earlier. If you're seeing blurry, it's natural." He hoped it wasn't anything worse.

Lifting her right arm closer to inspect it, she almost hit herself in the face when she couldn't control it. Dr. Benson thankfully caught it just in time. He laid it gently at her side again. She saw her wrist was wrapped in bandages and in a splint. Her fingers looked like sausages. Her entire body ached, and her head felt like it was going to explode with the tiniest movement. Her torso was so sore she was scared to breathe. Careful to keep as still as possible, she mumbled, "I'm hurting something fierce. Not one particular spot... It's all of me. My head... It really hurts. All of me really hurts."

Dr. Benson and Nurse Carter nodded at each other. The nurse reached over to dab at her cuts again. Her Southern-belle voice was soothing as she said, "You'll feel tired, Raina, and that's normal. It's going to take some time to heal here, okay? You have a bad concussion and some badly cracked ribs. Your wrist is sprained, but it's not broken although your nose was. But you'll be fine, just fine."

The nurse figured that was enough information to give her new patient. If she heard more, or saw anything of her face, she'd probably end up having a full-blown panic attack. "What you need now is rest. You've been through a lot, but it sounds like you're a strong woman. We'll help you..."

As Nurse Carter spoke, both she and Dr. Benson checked Raina's vitals, working quietly and efficiently. The nurse helped her drink some water she poured into a little cup with a straw. As Raina became more aware of her surroundings, the reason she was there filtered through the grogginess she felt. She didn't remember anything specific but...

Raina had to try twice before she could make her voice loud enough for them to understand. "The cop? Cop... Okay?" Her heart rate sped up in her chest, the beeping monitor keeping pace as she waited for their answer.

Dr. Benson looked at her solemnly, laid a hand gently on her shoulder. "Yes, Raina. You got him here in time. You saved his life! There are a lot of very appreciative people who want to talk to you. You are a heroine, Miss Stewart!" He smiled at her, watching the tears roll from her right eye. Her left eye was too swollen even for tears.

Nurse Carter gently dabbed at her tears with a Kleenex. She imagined the saltiness of those tears had to be burning in those raw skin spots.

"I was so scared... We were so far away..." Raina tried to stop crying, but her relief was too much to control. Crying made her hurt even more, but she simply couldn't stop. The doctor added a little more painkiller into the tubes connected to his patient. Now that she was awake, her pain would be a conscious thing causing her extreme discomfort. They needed to keep in front of it. He turned and typed notes into the computer.

Nurse Carter tried to soothe her. "You did a great thing, Miss Stewart. You can be proud of what you did! Now, time and rest are what you both need." She wiped away more tears from Raina's cheeks. She changed the subject to help distract her patient. "They found your purse in the squad car. And your phone was given to us for a moment for contact information. Right now, the police said they're both going into evidence. We wrote down a few numbers first, but did you want us to call anyone specific for you? Anyone to come here to be with you?"

Raina groggily thought about it. Finally, she answered, "No."

Dr. Benson and Nurse Carter looked at each other. Softly, he asked their patient, "There's no one you want us to call? Family or a friend? Surely someone would want to know you're in the hospital."

Raina spoke slowly through her swollen lips, "No. But ICE numbers... in my phone."

Dr. Benson nodded his head slowly. "We saw them. It was smart of you to be prepared like that. We did call and left a message with two of them to let them know you'd been in an accident and were in the hospital. We left our number so they could reach us."

Raina closed her eyes, which were feeling heavy again. She felt disoriented and wondered if she was going to pass out. She mumbled, "And they didn't call back?"

Their silence was her answer.

Chapter 6

"Miss Stewart, are you awake?"

Raina's mind registered someone's soft voice, but it took a moment for the question to sink in. She struggled to open her one good eye before painstakingly turning toward the source of the voice. Raina would've studied the man with her usual interest if only she could see. With one eye swollen shut, the other without a contact, and her head too swollen to wear the glasses she didn't even have with her, she was only able to see fuzzy images. Besides that, the room was kept dim for her due to her head injuries.

If she could've clearly seen him, she'd notice that the man was tall and lean. Maybe in his early sixties, his hair was still mostly black, with a hint of gray showing at his temples. She would've seen he wore a nice red dress shirt, cuffs neatly rolled up midway between his wrists and elbows, and that he wore a pair of pressed black slacks. Attached to his belt, she would've seen a badge, and on his hip, a gun. She would've decided he was classy, with a distinguished look about him.

But she could only see more or less the outline of him. Some detail, but her mind wasn't operating at full capacity either. Taking a gamble, she asked, "You're police?"

He had to focus on understanding her words. The poor woman's face was so swollen, his own began to hurt. Earlier when they'd stopped in to check on her, he and his partner had seen her in more lighting. There were so many red, black, and deep purple bruises covering her face, there was hardly any natural coloring to be seen. There were quite a few stitches to go along with her taped nose to complete the picture of having survived a terrible ordeal. Those raw spots would become scabs and would most likely turn into scars, according to Dr. Benson. They'd soon begin to apply cream to lessen the chance and severity, he'd added. They hoped to have straightened out her broken nose.

Having seen her driver's license photo found in her wallet, he was still shocked to realize he never would've said this was the same woman. His partner had agreed as they'd taken her prints and tested for gunshot residue when she was unconscious.

He knew talking had to be difficult for her. Quietly, he responded to her question, "Yes, ma'am. If you're up to it, we have some questions about what happened yesterday morning, but..."

"Yesterday? I've been in here for a whole day?"

It'd now been closer to two days, but the man didn't want to upset her further. "Yes, ma'am. You passed out soon after you arrived here. And later on, you kept drifting in and out. That was to be expected though."

He paused, hating to disturb her but also needing any information she could give him. "We don't want to rush you. But if you're up for a few questions, we'd love to talk with you." He walked a step closer to her bed. "Could you answer some questions for us now? It's okay if not. You tell me straight out, all right?"

Raina wanted to nod but knew better than to move her head. "Maybe for a little while."

"I'm going to grab another officer, if that's okay with you?"

Since he was already walking back toward the door to the hallway, Raina figured it probably didn't matter if she was okay with it or not. He motioned to someone who was apparently waiting outside the door. The two walked in together, closing the door before stopping at the foot of her bed.

The first man spoke again as he pulled a small recorder from his shirt pocket. "We need to record this, all right?" His voice was gentle, coaxing. It was a pleasant voice to listen to.

"Sure. I might pass out on you..."

The men looked at the battered woman, both hating to disturb her. Her speech was slow, and they had to concentrate on what she was saying. The second man spoke up, "That's fine, ma'am. If you do, we'll come back another time. You stop us anytime you need to. Can you raise an arm to signal us to stop, if that's easier for you?" He walked closer to her to pick up her quiet voice.

Before the older man turned on his tape recorder, Raina raised her left arm to signal him to stop. Both men looked at her with questioning eyes. She turned her head to look at the older man, gasping in pain at the too-fast movement. She lay there, willing the pain to recede before she was able to ask, "Do I need a lawyer?"

The older man paused, thinking. "Well, no, but you have every right to have one present. If you want one, we'll simply wait to talk to you. We aren't charging you with anything at all. We just need some answers to understand what happened."

Considering for a moment, she took the chance she'd just be asked questions. If she felt uncomfortable, she could always refuse to say more. "Okay."

As the officers prepared for the interview, she held up her hand again. They both looked at her expectantly.

"You forgot something," she said, forcing out the words through a skin-tight mouth.

"I did?" The older man asked, confused.

"Both of you." She hoped there were only two. She couldn't *wait* to be able to see clearly again.

The two men looked at each other, then back at her.

"I'd like to see your IDs."

The older officer stepped forward, saying, "I'm so sorry! Of course! I'm Detective Lieutenant Ron Kramer." Nodding to the younger officer, he said, "This is Detective Sergeant Channion Scott. We're assigned to your case, Miss Stewart."

They handed their badges to her one at a time, which she dutifully inspected with her one good eye. She handed them back their badges, asking, "Partners?"

Sergeant Scott answered, "Yes, ma'am. We're also related."

She took a moment to look at Detective Scott. She liked his voice too. She judged him to be about five ten, maybe five eleven. If her eyes had been cooperating, she would've been able to appreciate his dark brown hair, cut short and neat, admired his well-built and toned body with the broad shoulders and trim waist she liked to see on men. His soft, yet somehow probing, brown eyes and lightly-tanned skin would've pleased her. Gun and badge also on his hip, he'd have looked solid and reliable. Safe.

Detective Kramer turned on the recorder, speaking into it to record their names and the date. "First, we want to thank you for saving Deputy Mitchell's life. We've talked to the doctors who operated on him. He was in critical condition when you arrived. He's in the ICU now. It was an incredibly courageous thing you did, Miss Stewart!"

She gave a small nod.

"Can you tell us what happened?"

Both were paying attention to the rapid beats on the heart monitor and knew she was getting upset, whether from what she remembered or was trying to. They were warned about her head injury causing possible memory issues.

Detective Scott spoke up with an equally calming voice that steadied her, "Why don't you start at the beginning of your day? What did you do yesterday morning?" Maybe easing her into it would be better, he thought.

Raina tried to focus, tried to think back. Her left hand rubbed the side of her head in a vain effort to relieve the pressure. "I fed my horses and left for..." A sudden thought hit her. "*My horses!*" She looked around the room, the sudden movement sending black waves over her vision and pain slicing into her head. The monitor began beeping frantically in the background.

Hearing the signals through the door, a passing nurse rushed into the room, stopping beside the patient. "Raina, it's okay. *Easy*, Raina... There you go. It's okay. Breathe... and relax." She kept talking to her patient until the beeps began to slow down. The nurse checked the machines and Raina as both men waited, both feeling awful for upsetting her so quickly.

Detective Scott finally spoke up once she was calmer, seeing her panic and concern about her horses. Neither man had a chance to tell her the horses were fine before the nurse rushed inside. "Your horses are being taken care of. We drove out to your place late yesterday afternoon to see if anyone else was maybe there, and we fed them. They're both fine. They were fed again this morning. Your horses are fine, Miss Stewart." His voice was calm and soothing. The monitor's beeping slowed down some more. "Please don't worry about them. We'll be sure they're taken care of, okay?"

The nurse nodded to herself in satisfaction at what she was seeing on the screens and looked at Raina again. "You all right?"

"I'm okay," she whispered to the nurse.

After a bit of hesitation, the nurse finally left after adding notes in the computer, closing the door with a frown and a knowing look tossed at the older detective. Kramer nodded back in acknowledgement before the door closed with a soft click.

Raina tried to relax. It was a wonder she didn't pass out that time. At the moment, she wished she had just to avoid the pain she was in. "How do you know for sure?"

Kramer answered her, "Because he's the one who drove back out there early this morning. He loves horses and wanted to be sure they were properly cared for."

She looked at Detective Scott. "Thank you. I mean it... Thank you."

"You're welcome. It was no trouble at all, ma'am."

"Call me Raina."

Kramer smiled at her. "Okay. After you fed your horses, what happened next?"

She thought back. "I'm a musician now and give lessons sometimes at my house but usually in town. And I sing at a bar, and I sometimes go on the road. I needed to go to the studio... I saw Deputy Mitchell had pulled over a car."

Scott asked, "Can you describe the car?"

Raina looked at him. If her face wasn't so swollen, it would've been full of surprise. "It's *gone?* Both of them?"

"No, all vehicles were there. We simply need verification. *Your* version of what happened. Details, if you have them. Let us know when you need a break, all right?"

"Oh, I understand. I first slowed down because of the curve, and because I just kinda knew there could be a cop nearby—"

Kramer interrupted her, "You 'knew'? How could've you known?"

"It's what I do."

"Meaning?"

"I have a sixth sense about cops and deer. I can sense them somehow before I actually see them."

Both detectives smiled at her. Kramer replied, "I see. We'll try to remember that. Go on, when you're ready."

"He was pulled in behind the other car." She paused, thinking. She also had to pause to let her mouth rest. "It was a four-door car. Tan. The back windows were tinted dark. As I drove by, Deputy Mitchell was in his car, looking down. I assumed he was writing a ticket." She recalled his blonde hair in a flash of memory.

"A few more miles down the road, I saw a car pulled over onto the shoulder. It was heading toward me. I... I think..." She searched her memory, feeling there was something she needed to know but now unable to do so. "It was *just* there, but now I don't... I can't remember..."

Her mind was suddenly blocking her memories, which they were told may happen. If so, they were not to push her for any reason.

The older detective hurried to reassure her, not wanting to upset her or cause her more anxiety or pain. "It's all going to be fine, Miss Stewart. It's okay..." After giving her a moment to gather herself together, he quietly asked, hoping he wasn't pushing her, "In all this time, there were no other cars driving by? Do you remember seeing any other cars?"

"No." Or did she?

Detective Scott looked at her as he summarized what she'd said, "So you were driving toward town, saw a car pulled over by Deputy Mitchell, then another car down the road also pulled over but on its own. But that second one was heading toward you.

"You must've turned around for some reason. Do you know why? Do you remember what happened next?"

Considering her pain level, and that she was in the hospital being questioned by the police, and not being completely sure why, Raina looked up at the ceiling and tried to think. A couple minutes passed in silence as her brain tried to make sense of it all. Her soft response disrupted the quiet in the room when she finally said, "I drove into hell, didn't I?"

Chapter 7

THE NEXT MORNING, RAINA lay there in her hospital bed. Surrounded by the smells, sounds, and that generally mixed feeling of both foreboding and comfort medical facilities gave off, she tried to recall what happened.

Last night, her pain level had shot up so her head was throbbing, and both detectives became instantly concerned for her. Before they could summon a nurse, the monitors connected to the nurse station down the hallway alerted a nurse who was almost immediately at her side. Shooing the policemen out, the nurse took over. It didn't take long for her to pass out.

It wasn't until early this next morning that details began to filter through her mind. Images at first, they began to take shape and form as the hours slowly passed. She tried to relax and let them come at their own pace. Nurse Carter stayed with her as long as she could, doing her best to keep her patient calm as her mind began functioning again.

By late morning, the two detectives were talking with her doctors, anxious at their replies. Sandwiched between her mind possibly blocking out memories as a defensive method to protect itself and the physical condition she was in, Raina Stewart was in a bad way to help them. Urged to let her memories come as they would on their own, the two men nodded.

They went down to check on Deputy Mitchell again and speak with his doctors before they made their way back to their star witness.

DETECTIVES SCOTT AND KRAMER knocked softly and entered Raina's room, smiles on their faces. They were prepared to not get anything of value at all from their witness, but knew they had to try. Both men also wanted to be sure she was okay, and for her to know they were there for her if she needed them.

Seeing the two blurry figures walk in, she tried to focus on their voices as they greeted her. The policemen, she remembered, from the previous night. "I'm glad you came. I think I... have something... to tell you." Her voice was soft, and she spoke slowly through her sore mouth.

Once the recorder was out, Raina slowly recalled how she parked on the side of the road, ran into the trees to see what, if anything, was happening. And when she saw the two cars, and that rifle being pointed at the officer, she ran as fast as she could back to her truck.

"I tried to help him. He was standing there... all alone with three men. He needed a chance..."

Her accelerated heart rate beeped on the monitor. Both men hoped the nurse wouldn't rush back in and kick them out. Trying to calm her before that could happen, Detective Scott coaxed her into relaxing again. Keeping his voice soft and gently taking hold of her left hand, he gave it a reassuring squeeze.

After a couple of minutes, he asked, "When you saw what was happening, why didn't you just call 9-1-1 for help?"

Raina paused, trying to calm herself so those black waves wouldn't take her under. "There was no time... I could only act, help him right now..." Her slurred words were laced with either excitement or anxiety now.

Detective Scott felt her grip tighten on his hand.

She paused before saying as clearly as she could, "I saw them shoot him."

Chapter 8

DETECTIVE SCOTT LOOKED AT the battered woman who'd risked her life to save the life of a total stranger. He greatly admired her. She'd shown instinct, courage, and selflessness. She was a fighter. After being brutally attacked, she still took it upon herself to drive an unconscious law enforcement officer to the nearest hospital. But they still didn't know why she'd turned around in the first place.

Her memory seemed to be fine overall... as far as they knew. What she told them seemed to jive with what they'd pieced together from the scene and evidence. As with most head injuries, though, he was pretty certain she'd actually forgotten more than she knew, but with time even more would come back. That actually concerned him in more ways than one. He and his uncle had spoken with her doctors and were told she was bound to have severe headaches. If so, they could be a sign that her mind was tucking away information. It was yet another concern they had for her.

Detective Kramer was also in admiration of her. He also knew she had head trauma and more would come back to her later. He was more concerned about how she'd handle it. He suspected she'd start having nightmares. He suspected she'd probably need to see a professional shrink to help her get through it all. Family and friends would help her out, too, he was sure. Where *were* they? he wondered.

Raina's head was pounding. She didn't want to do anymore right now. The detectives must've sensed this as she heard the click of the recorder being turned off and the flipping of pages of Sergeant Scott's notepad. She watched them stand up and quietly slide their chairs back against the wall.

Sergeant Scott walked back over to her, wanting to ask a dozen questions more of his own now. He asked only one. It was the one that ran through his mind the most. "I have one last question... Do you regret what you did?" he inquired with quiet respect.

Raina looked at him quickly. In as firm a voice as she could manage, she answered, "No. Not for a minute."

He nodded.

Lieutenant Kramer took her left hand and patted it. "Is there anything we can do for you? Is there anything you need?"

She hated to ask, but she had no choice. "Take care of my horses for me until I get out of here? The neighbor down the road has fed them for me before, so you could ask them.

"And can you please, *please* get me my glasses? They're in my upstairs bathroom. And my organizer? It's on the kitchen counter—I think. I need to call my students and the studio. They must be wondering where I am. I've never been a no-call, no-show before. Being the teacher is even worse!" It took her a while to say all she had to say, and her mouth had a cramp in it now.

Lieutenant Kramer nodded, watching as his nephew made quick notes in his ever-present writing pad. "You bet. Do you give us permission to go into your house to get them?"

"Yes. If you have my truck keys, my house key is on the ring. And there's a spare in the barn's feed room. It's in the cap of the bug spray on the shelf."

Sergeant Scott smiled as he closed his writing pad, slipping it into his pocket. She remembered her spare key was in the lid of a can of bug spray. "We'll take care of it. Don't you worry about anything. Just rest so you can heal. You did great, Miss Stewart. You are truly remarkable, and you've earned the respect and thanks of many people."

He paused before adding, "If you happen to remember anything else at all, you can call one of us, okay? But we'll also be coming here regularly to check in on you." He set a business card on the table beside her, near the phone. He'd already written his uncle's number on it too. "Day or night. No matter how small the detail, all right?"

"Okay. Before you go, can you hand me the TV remote controller thing? It must've fallen because I don't see it." She patted the sheets around her, not feeling the long lump of the remote control and call button combo. "I can't see crap."

Lieutenant Kramer found it by following the thick white cord hanging over the bed and untangling it from her bedsheets. He handed it to her. "Keep it low so you don't disturb the neighbors. We don't want to be called back here for a nuisance call."

Both men smiled when she saluted him.

Sergeant Scott said, "We'll be back tomorrow, maybe even tonight, with your things. Remember to call us if you need or remember anything, okay?"

"You might end up regretting that."

"I guess we'll see, but I don't think so."

He was smiling as he followed his uncle out the door, quietly closing it behind them.

ONCE NEWS GOT OUT that the woman who'd courageously saved a police officer was up and talking, the news crews came calling. The hospital staff had to turn away several ambitious newsmen to keep the place quiet.

The nurses who were caring for Raina were upset that word got leaked. They all swore it wasn't from any of them. They also all knew she wasn't exactly talking like people thought because she was barely able to talk at all. They all knew she needed peace and quiet to recover, so no way was it one of them.

Security had been added and tightened now. All department heads had a mandatory discretionary meeting with their staff, from the doctors to the cleaning crew.

No one was to say a thing to anybody—but all knew someone was bound to. Secrets are rarely ever held after all.

Thankfully, those outside of the hospital didn't know her name. They only knew that the woman was there. Raina Stewart was to be an anonymous person per police orders as they wanted her name kept quiet for as long as possible. The hospital staff could keep out the newshounds fairly easily since they were obvious, but they had to *really* take a stand with a few of the local cops.

No one besides hospital staff, the two detectives assigned to their case, and the deputy's immediate family was allowed in either of their rooms. Or to even know their room numbers. Everyone else had to leave their gifts at the front desk to be delivered.

Those working her case considered it a huge blessing she'd called in on a cellphone instead of using the police officer's car radio. By doing that, she'd prevented everyone with a police scanner in their home from learning her name and too many details they could give to the media hounds that were digging for anything they could get. They knew when the dispatcher had sent out the call to units in the area, but only general details had been given. Another blessing was that the supervisor had also used a phone.

They knew it was bound to get out at some point. And surely those who took lessons from her would wonder if it was their teacher. Since she'd be unavailable for the upcoming weeks, and the incident had occurred near her home, it seemed only logical.

They also were still refusing to release the 9-1-1 tape to those who insisted they had a right to not only listen to it, but to air it. Citing security issues and an ongoing investigation, both of which were completely true, the police kept all the information to themselves. It irritated them that people's insatiable lust for gossip and drama could overpower sensitivity, safety, common sense, and the right to privacy. Not to mention getting justice. The general public only cared about privacy when something happened directly to them.

Raina's room looked a bit like a botanical garden by the end of the next day. There'd been a few cards and balloons brought in while she was still unconscious or sleeping. Now the room was filled with flowers, plants, stuffed animals, and even more of the obligatory helium-filled balloons. Free space was rapidly becoming in short supply.

She slept away the rest of that day, her nurses relieved as she needed the rest. They woke her up to eat dinner since she slept through lunch though. After they helped her to the bathroom and then helped her eat some dinner, Raina went right back to sleep. She didn't even remember doing either.

IT WAS LATER THAT night when Raina received some visitors she'd never forget. She couldn't sleep too deeply without feeling a bad dream was coming, so she was flipping through channels in the hopes of preventing herself from falling asleep again. She knew the nurses thought she'd been sound asleep, but most of the time she actually hadn't been.

She was in pain and so very tired that she *needed* the escape that sleep offered, but there was a part of her that was scared stiff to let herself go to a place she couldn't control. She'd already learned sleep was *not* a peaceful avenue for her anymore.

Although she couldn't watch the shows clearly as the screen was too far away, she could hear them through the TV remote controller device beside her. She marveled at the little speaker in it that was so clear. She'd just switched to a Western movie channel—she could tell by the sound of shooting guns and galloping horses—when an older couple and younger woman walked in. She heard their tentative knock on her door before stepping inside her dimly-lit room.

"Excuse us, Miss Stewart? Can we come in for a moment?" the man inquired.

Raina didn't know what to do. She slowly nodded her head, her finger sliding to rest on the call button for the nurse station down the hall. She couldn't see them clearly in the lighting, but someone wishing her harm wouldn't knock, would they?

Both women took one look at her and began to cry. The man came up to her first and introduced himself in a shaky voice full of emotion, "My name is Conrad Mitchell. This is my wife, Meredith, and our daughter, Bethany. We wanted to meet and personally thank the woman who saved Bryce's life. *Twice*, from what we've been told!" Mr. Mitchell took hold of her left hand and squeezed it, smiling through his own tears.

"We're so happy to finally have the chance to meet you. We were told you needed peace and quiet to rest. We got permission today from Detectives Kramer and Scott and the nurses to visit you to say thank you though." At her blank look, he explained, "Bryce Mitchell is our son."

"I never heard his first name. I only know him as Deputy Mitchell," Raina explained in a low voice. She was trying to hold back her own tears now as crying hurt. "I'm so glad to meet you. How is he?"

Conrad was barely able to understand her. The poor woman's face was swollen so badly she could barely talk. "He's still in the ICU. They've had to keep him sedated. We take turns sitting with him until they kick us out at the end of the day. We hate leaving him alone, but he's safe here.

"There's no way we could *ever* repay you for what you've done, Miss Stewart. No way to cover a debt for what you've done for us, for Bryce. From what we've been told, the only reason he's alive is because of you." His voice cracked.

Meredith Mitchell asked, "Miss Stewart, is there anything at all we can do for you? Is there anything you need that we can get for you? We mean it. We want to help you in any way we can."

Bethany jumped in, saying, "Don't be shy about asking, Miss Stewart. Really. We'll do whatever we can for you!" She smiled at the woman in the hospital bed, trying to not wince at the painful bruising and swelling they could see even in the dim light.

"Well, in *that* case..." She trailed off and heard them chuckle. "Honestly, I couldn't ask anything of you..."

Conrad let go of her hand long enough to give her his business card. "Yes, you can. We *insist*. Here's our number. Wait." He took it back from her. "I'll put it here by the phone on this table, okay? We mean it when we say you need not be hesitant to ask for anything. If we don't answer, be sure to leave a message. Or you can text us, all right? We aren't supposed to have our cellphones on while here in the hospital, you know, but we can get texts."

"If I think of anything, I may take you up on it. So be sure to rescind your offer right now unless you mean it," Raina tried to sound stern. She knew she didn't even have a phone to text with.

They all smiled.

Meredith shook her head, saying, "There'll be no rescinding on you, Miss Stewart. We'll let you rest now before they kick us out. Thank you again. God must've sent you out there that day, so we'll be saying some extra prayers of thanks for watching out for our Bryce." She smiled as she patted Raina's hand, saying, "You take care, dear."

Bethany walked over, took her hand. "Thank you for saving not only my brother, Miss Stewart, but my best friend. We'll never, ever forget what you did for all of us! God or His angels surely sent you to my brother. You were his very own angel, Miss Stewart. Thank you for being there." She gave a trembling, grateful smile. "We'll swing by again if we can to see how you're doing, all right?"

"Okay. Thank you," Raina managed.

They left her alone in the quiet of the night. If only they could quiet her thoughts.

Chapter 9

FLIPPING THROUGH THE CHANNELS on the TV in her room, Raina was wondering how long she was to stay in the hospital. It was going on day four already. She didn't realize they kept patients with cracked ribs for days. Couldn't they send people home the same day now even after some types of surgery?

The swelling in her face was coming down, so she was able to speak almost normally again. But since the nurses wouldn't let her see herself in a mirror, she knew she must still look pretty bad. Assuring her that she'd heal, they said they just didn't want her to fret over it. The anti-scarring cream was put on her body and face daily to help the wounds heal. It didn't escape her notice that they practically covered her entire face with it like a facial and not just a dab here, and a dab there. Not having the strength to fight them, she simply fretted over how bad she imagined she looked. Didn't they keep mirrors from burn patients?

Her only visitors were the doctors and nurses, the two detectives, and the Mitchells, who had stopped by again to say hello and see how she was coming along. They seemed to Raina as a first-class family, and she enjoyed their short visit.

When Lieutenant Kramer dropped off her glasses and her organizer earlier, he'd called all of her students, the studio, Picacho's Bar, and Jason Charles in Kentucky, simply saying she'd had an emergency come up and would be unavailable for a while. That task being done relieved quite a bit of stress from her mental load.

Dr. Benson walked into her room, a warm smile on his face. "Hi there! How are you feeling this morning?"

"Right as rain." At his look, she amended her statement, "Or near enough."

He smiled before he studied her face intently. "Well, your face is healing well, and you're talking much better." Inspecting her nose for a moment, he nodded in satisfaction. "Now, let's take a look here." He shone his penlight in her eyes, hesitating over the one that'd been swollen shut. It was still more of a slit now than fully open, but it was healing. The blood red was fading into a yellow tinge in her open eye. "Any problems with your vision?"

"Of course. I'm nearly as blind as a bat."

He chuckled. "That's why you have your glasses. You're not quite that blind though. And contrary to popular opinion, bats aren't actually blind. It's a common misconception." He studied her eyes thoroughly with another instrument as he spoke.

He made notes in her chart before looking behind him like he was looking for someone. Not seeing them, he turned back to Raina. "I want to stress how important it is for you to be patient. No lifting, bending too much, sudden turns, or twisting... All of which I'm sure you know not to do. I'm also adjusting your pain medication." She nodded as he paused, apparently wanting confirmation she was listening. "Now, your ribs. How do you feel when you move around? Sharp pains? Throbbing? Numbness? Any difficulty with your breathing?"

Nurse Laurel came in, smiling at her. "Good morning, Raina! Sorry I'm late, Doctor. That rascal Mr. Conway spotted me, and I couldn't escape in time. I even kept my mouth shut so he couldn't hear my Canadian accent to remind him of home." The doctor apparently knew who she was referring to and chuckled. She stopped at Raina's side, saying, "You're looking better, eh? Lean forward so Doc here can poke and prod ya, Raina."

Obediently, Raina did as instructed. She'd caught the nurse's accent before and now understood Laurel was a Canadian. She'd figured she was from Minnesota or something. Raina let them prod her ribcage a bit, letting them know where it was tender, which was basically everywhere they touched. They looked over the bruising from her seatbelt and checked her collarbone, neck, and back.

As he inspected her arms, chest, and legs, he asked her questions. Satisfied she was coming along, Dr. Benson nodded. "You're on the road to mending. You need to take it easy still like I mentioned. Your body is going to need time to heal properly. Don't try to rush it because it will only backfire on you." Using his stethoscope, he then listened to her lungs, having her take deep breaths and letting them out. He moved it to her heart next.

"Are you listening to my heart, Doc?"

He nodded before looking up into her eyes.

"That's nice because most men don't."

He laughed as Nurse Laurel grinned at her.

Dr. Benson made notes in her chart on the computer again. "Okay, let's check your head. We'll have another CT scan set up for you shortly. We're backed up a bit on the MRI so we'll do another scan for now. Laurel here will come get you when they're ready. Well, provided Mr. Conway doesn't catch sight of her again!" He smiled at the nurse when she laughed. "Any questions, Raina?"

"How soon until I get to go home? I can recover just as well there as here... and with less cost. And I miss my horses something terrible. Not being with them is harder on me than anything else!" Raina was practically begging the doctor to release her.

He nodded in understanding. "We'll see. Your ribs are still in bad shape, and your breathing is not back to normal capacity yet. And your head took a serious pounding. We need to be sure it's *safe* for you to be released. Now that the swelling has gone down, we can get a better look. We'll go from there. It's still early yet in your recovery. Remember I just told you to not rush it?" He smiled at her again before leaving the room.

Nurse Laurel had her sit forward so she could put the cream on her back. She then tidied up the room while she was there. "Are your headaches going away yet?"

"No. I thought I was expected to have them for a while yet?"

"You are. I was simply reminding you why you're still here. And to mind Doc's advice about taking it slow and easy."

"You think you're pretty smart, don't you?"

"Smart enough to graduate nursing school on my first try! That's smart, eh?"

After helping Raina to the bathroom and back to bed, Nurse Laurel adjusted the pillows. "I'll be back in a while to take you downstairs for the scan. Behave yourself!" She warned with a smile as she left.

Looking over at a sound in the hallway a few minutes later, Raina saw Detective Scott pop his head in. "You decent?" he asked softly, not knowing how sensitive she was to noise yet.

"Depending on what you're comparing me to, sure. Come on in. Did you find someone to feed my horses?" she asked immediately. Her two horses were more like her kids, her best friends. She couldn't help but worry about them. It was killing her not being near them, knowing they were alone back home.

"They're doing fine. I found the peppermints you had in the feed room, so I gave them some. They seemed happy enough when I left there this morning. I let them out in the big pasture again so they can stretch their legs and graze. I also left open their stall doors so they can go in and out on their own. Is that okay with you? I'll put them back in tonight, unless you want them out all the time."

"Detective, I didn't mean for *you* to drive all the way out there yourself! I live pretty far out there, and you must be busy enough. But all the same, thank you. And it's fine leaving their doors open. I only shut them for a little while after it rains. I just don't want them to tear up the ground. It also gives the grass a chance to grow a little taller. And I'll pay you for—"

"No need, Raina," he interrupted her. "I enjoy it. I also brushed them yesterday so they got some personal attention. I don't want you to worry about them, all right? Here, I thought this might interest you." He handed her his phone, tapped the little arrow on the screen for the video to begin.

"*Oh! My kids!*" Raina exclaimed. She got tears in her eyes as she watched the video he'd thoughtfully taken of her horses that morning.

"I took a few. There are three videos total, so swipe to the next screen," he said. He took a chance on the videos, not knowing if they'd help cheer her up or not. But he figured if she could see they were all right, it might help.

Raina's full attention was glued to the screen. She listened and watched as her horses ate their grain, almost being able to smell the molasses. She saw them sniff the phone then him after he gave them some peppermints, apparently looking for more. Raina heard him laugh as he talked to them. She watched the videos again, so homesick she could barely stand it.

After the three videos were done, she handed his phone back to him. "Thank you so much for doing this! It breaks my heart to not be with them, but I can see you're taking care of them. My horses mean the world to me!"

"You're welcome. It was a last-minute thought I had this morning. I'm sorry I didn't think of doing pictures or videos before now."

"Well, you did now, and I'm grateful. It also hadn't occurred to me to ask you to."

He handed her a bag of things from her house he brought for her to do, a new stuffed horse, and some Andes mints.

"How'd you know I love these things?" she asked, holding up the mints.

"I'm a detective." He smiled. He was about to say more when a nurse came in, pushing a wheelchair.

"Hey girl, it's time to go for a ride! Oh... I didn't know you had company, Miss Stewart. I can come back in a minute if you need me to..."

The detective waved her in. "It's okay. We're just chatting. I think she's ready to get out of this bed for a while anyway. Do you need any help?"

Raina spoke first, "No, but thanks for the offer. And don't forget my gown opens in the back so you'd better turn around, mister. I was raised to not moon officers of the law."

With a smile at the grinning nurse, he obediently turned around. He waited for the all-clear to face them again. "How long do you think you'll be gone?" he asked.

Nurse Laurel answered, "Give it about an hour or so, probably less. It's just a head scan. She'll be right back up. Did you want to wait here? Or go with us?"

"I'll be around when she gets back."

As the nurse wheeled Raina down the hallway and into the for-once empty elevator, she didn't say a word. But as soon as the elevator doors closed, Nurse Laurel remarked, "Handsome devil, that one. Dark looks. Killer smile. And he has a real classy look to him, eh?"

Raina smiled. "Once I got my glasses, I noticed that same thing."

The nurse teased, "We could arm wrestle for him."

A little laugh escaped from Raina. "You'd take advantage of a crippled patient?"

"He just might be worth it."

"Mr. Conway just might get jealous!"

Nurse Laurel laughed. "What he doesn't know won't hurt him."

When Nurse Laurel wheeled her back to her room, Detective Scott was still there. Sitting in the chair watching TV, he held a bottle of juice he got from the vending machine. He smiled and turned down the volume when they came in. "Welcome back. Did you pass?"

"I'm sure I nearly aced it, but I have to wait for my test results to come in. I'm ready to go whenever they give me the all clear." Raina smiled. "Now, be a good boy and turn around so I can get out of this chair."

He again turned around as the nurse helped her get situated in the bed.

"All clear," Nurse Laurel called out. "Do you need anything, Raina, before I go?"

Raina shook her head.

"Okey-dokey. You two behave yourselves while I'm gone!" Nurse Laurel joked as she pushed the wheelchair out of the room, closing the door behind her.

Turning back to the detective, Raina asked outright, "Is there something going on that I need to know about, Detective? Why am I still here? I could be at home sitting in my own bed or on my own couch watching my own TV."

It had occurred to her during the CT scan that if the detective on her case brought her things from her own house to keep her occupied, it could only mean she wasn't going home anytime soon. She wanted to know why.

He wondered how to answer her. "Well, Miss Stewart, you still have substantial injuries. I spoke with Dr. Benson. While he's pleased with your progress, he's still worried about some bruising in your head. Now that the swelling has gone down, he said they needed to be sure it's *safe* for you to leave their care, especially since you live alone way out in the boondocks. You don't mess around with head trauma injuries.

"You have a concussion and the effects of one can last for days and even weeks. You still have bad headaches, and now and then ringing in your ears, right?" She nodded. "Still tired?" She again nodded, sighed. He continued, "Well, *that's* why you're still here."

"And...?"

"And what?" he hedged.

"My gut instinct is telling me you're not telling me all of it." She got a worried look on her face. "Did you find out something else happened that I don't recall? Is that it?" She knew she wasn't raped. They'd confirmed that right away and told her once she became aware of things so she wouldn't worry about it. But maybe *she* did something bad?

Channion looked at her before answering. "Raina, you were attacked viciously. I don't think you're able to recall most of it. This is normal, so don't worry about it. But we need to be absolutely sure your head is all right before they can release you. If you're released before you should be and something happened, it could be detrimental to you. Can you understand this? We'd prefer to err on the side of your health and safety first. If something happened to you, what would happen to your horses?"

She sat there, looking into his eyes, reading his facial expression. His concern was apparent, genuine. She nodded slowly, saying, "I can tell you said that because it's the truth and not just a low blow. And I guess I have to trust someone, and you haven't given me any reason to stop trusting you.

"Since Doc Benson and Nurse Laurel told me the same thing this morning, I guess y'all are being truthful, and I have to respect that. If you say I need to stay, I'll stay." She couldn't help herself as she reached out and took hold of his hand to make sure he was paying attention. "Thanks, Detective Scott, for taking care of me but most especially my horses. I mean that."

"Any time, Miss Stewart. Any time."

Chapter 10

TWO DAYS LATER, RAINA was still in the hospital. She knew her facial wounds were slowly scabbing over and worried constantly about what she looked like. Her job was done in front of the public. How could she go back to work with scabs and scars all over her face?

Late at night, when she was sure she was safe from visitors knocking on her door, she cried. She was lonely, and so alone in this situation. Bills at home were soon going to be stacking up, and she couldn't work at all in order to pay them. What about these unexpected medical bills? Her insurance wasn't that great, but she got what she could afford. And those huge deductibles? If she used her savings for those, how long could she not work and burn through the rest of her savings to not be evicted? Or to lose her utilities?

And her horses? Luckily, she recently bought a good supply of hay and grain, so with the grass in the pasture, they'd be at least fed for quite a while. She was more worried about *them* eating than herself. She was fairly sure she had at least six bales of sawdust left in the barn for their stalls. She'd have to ration it out and save as much as she could to make it last longer for them. Not seeing her horses for days on end was breaking her heart and tormenting her soul. They were her family, and her only friends here.

What was she going to do? If she lost her house, where would she be able to afford to put her horses? Her landlord was a sweet, older man, but would he let her stay? Would he understand? Or would he say life is tough, too bad, out you go? And with no recent income, no new landlord anywhere would even rent to her. The only option she could think of was to break into her Roth IRA and withdraw enough funds to at least have a place to live until she got back on her feet. She wondered what the penalties would be. How long would it take to get the money into her bank account to pay bills?

She was overwhelmed with her legitimate fears. With no one to talk to, not being able to play music, or even see her own horses, crying was now her only outlet.

Late at night, before her new crying ritual commenced, Raina was wheeled down to the ICU to visit Bryce. It didn't matter he was sedated and didn't know she was there. She'd already asked one of the new night nurses to help her. The stern nurse had originally said no, but Raina persisted until she gave in. What was the harm? Late at night, there were no visitors allowed, so no one would know she was there. She heard that no one, with no exceptions, was allowed into the officer's room unless they were cleared by the police already, but she reasoned *she* was safe enough.

She wanted to see Bryce Mitchell. She felt a link to him and knowing his family couldn't stay through the night, she instead wanted to take their place. It not only gave her a purpose, but plain and simple, it gave her something to do.

Nurse Ramsey showed up like promised every night and wheeled her down to the ICU. Sometimes the nurses were all too busy with other patients for her to break away when she expected, but Raina understood. When the nurse did wheel Raina down, she left Raina beside the wounded officer and sometimes stayed at the nurse station with the ICU staff. Normally, though, she'd return to her duties upstairs and return to wheel Raina back to her room.

This night it was later than usual before Nurse Ramsey was able to bring her down to the ICU. Raina sat in her wheelchair and again took Bryce's left hand, stroking it as she looked him over. He'd been drifting in and out of consciousness, she was told earlier. They had him on a good dose of painkillers to control the pain, so he most likely still wouldn't know she was there. He'd been awake and semi-coherent a couple of times, but not enough for the doctor's satisfaction. She'd also been told he got an infection that morning and was now fighting that too. As weak as he was, she surmised the medical staff was more worried than they were letting on.

She looked at his machines in the soft lighting and watched the colored lines move in steady rhythms while listening to the soft beeps. "Good evening, Bryce. It's me, Raina, again. I hope you don't mind me calling you Bryce since we've never been formally introduced. It's more personal this way, and I like to think of you as a friend now. They tell me you're fighting an infection on top of everything else now, and that you probably won't know I'm even here. But I'm here anyway. You have to be feeling weak, Bryce, but you have to fight. Don't give up! There are a lot of people here who are pulling for you."

She brushed her hand gently across his brow, feeling the heat. It made her heart ache in anxiety for him. Would he make it? People with infections could die, she knew. With resolve, she made herself focus on something else.

"They aren't telling me a lot about our case. And I don't mind it, to be honest. I have trouble sleeping at night when it's quiet. I always feel there's a nightmare just waiting to pounce on me. It's somewhere just beyond my reach, but it's there. So I'd prefer to not sleep, but inevitably I do. And it makes me wonder about you. Do you have nightmares? What if you did while you were sedated? Who would know?"

As she continued to speak to the unconscious man, Raina heard soft talking behind her, probably at the nurse station. She ignored the voices and listened to the steady beeps on the monitors. She stroked his arm, wondering if the feel of another human could get through the pain medications and let him know he wasn't alone. She finally looked at the clock on the wall. Was it two o'clock already? She needed to get back to her bed and let Nurse Ramsey get back to work! She patted Bryce's hand. "I'd better go. Good night, Bryce. I'll talk to you later, if I can."

She carefully began to back up her wheelchair so she wouldn't bump into anything. She felt someone grab the handlebars of her chair and assumed it was Nurse Ramsey. She whispered, "Sorry, Nurse. I didn't know I was here that long. I guess time got away from me."

The nurse didn't reply until they got to the elevators. As the metal doors opened up, she looked into the warped reflection on the elevator wall, gasping when she saw who was pushing her chair. "What are you doing here, Detective? It's two in the morning!"

"I was in the neighborhood and thought I'd see how you were doing." After the doors closed, he pushed her floor number. "Imagine my surprise when I got to your room and noticed you missing.

"My first thought was something had happened to you, which made me scared. My second was you checked yourself out, which made me mad. When I got to the nurse station, they told me where you were so now I'm just relieved." He patted her shoulder before gently squeezing it. "It's nice of you to spend time with Bryce, even if he doesn't know you're there. He might. You never know."

She tried to look up at him but couldn't. She leaned forward as the elevator came to a stop at her floor, pushing the button to keep the doors closed. She grabbed his hand to pull him around so she could see him. He looked beat. She noticed the fatigue on his face and in his eyes. In the dim elevator light, she asked, "You were scared for me? That was your first emotion?"

He hesitated but spoke truthfully, "Yes."

"Why?"

"Why what?"

"Why were you scared? You were here previously and knew, for the most part, my CT scan was okay, and the MRI they finally took. Obviously if I died, you'd have been notified immediately. So the only other reason you'd be scared is if you knew I was in some sort of danger. It's also the reason why you'd unexpectedly show up at the hospital at this time of day... Or rather, night."

Channion blinked. Her instincts and perception were uncanny. She hit the nail right on the head. And this was at two o'clock in the morning! Most people would be too tired for their brains to work that efficiently. Man, she was something else! He squatted down to be at her level. He was so tired he hoped he'd be able to stand back up on his own power.

She pushed the *close door* button again to keep the doors from opening. "Out with it, Detective Scott."

"As it turns out, there has been a break in the case. It's pretty significant. You could possibly be in danger, but we're not sure of that yet. As a precaution, and since I was driving nearby, I thought I'd stop to check on you and Bryce. I figured I'd sleep easier knowing you were safe and sound... and in bed."

"At two in the morning."

"If that's what time it is, then yes."

"It must be pretty serious."

"Yes, it is."

"*Who* did Bryce pull over, Channion?"

He noticed this was the first time she'd used his first name even though she had permission to use his and his uncle's first names. They wanted her to relax around them and thought it might help if she saw them as friends instead of authority figures and strangers.

Again, her perception was right on. He refused to divulge any information. "Let us work on it a bit more, Raina, then we'll get you updated with what we can. It's an on-going investigation. And you're not only a witness, but a victim."

After standing back up, he wheeled her down the quiet hallway to her room, nodding to the nurse who walked by them. She said she'd be right back in a few minutes. Channion nodded. Waiting for the nurse to help her back into bed, he turned down Raina's suggestion he just stay in the recliner.

"Detective, it's two in the morning! You're beat. What if you fell asleep at the wheel?" she demanded. "If something happened to you while you were working this case, how do you think that'd make me feel?"

He shook his head again. He noticed she went back to his rank instead of his name.

After a long silence, she said softly, "Just take the chair. They won't let anyone else in here with me, so it's safe. Maybe they'll even let you eat breakfast here when you wake up. Plus, it's quiet and probably relatively clean. I promise I don't snore!"

"But I might." He smiled at her as he straightened out the sheets on her bed and moved the pillows as they waited. Running his hand over her hair to move it out of the way, he studied a gash near her forehead that was still stitched. "This is looking better."

When he was done inspecting it, he declined her suggestion again before she could speak. "Thanks for the offer, Raina, but I'd hate to be on the receiving end of the guys at the station when they heard you and I shared a room for the night." He held back his smile, inwardly amazed he even had the strength and energy to joke with anyone at two in the morning, especially after the day he'd had. "I have enough on my plate as it is."

She couldn't help but smile.

Nurse Ramsey came in, smiling at them. "She's pulling an all-nighter, isn't she?" She took one look at the detective and commented, "As are you. You okay, Detective?"

Channion nodded. "Yeah, I'm on my way home. Thanks for taking care of her. Do you need any help?"

Nurse Ramsey could tell the man was nearly wiped out. "No, but thank you. I've got her. You go on home to get some rest yourself. You drive safely, okay? Get yourself some coffee or something. If you want, I can get you some from our lounge..."

"Thank you, but that's all right. I appreciate your offer." Looking at Raina, he smiled. "You get some sleep yourself. Don't make these nurses work more than they already are. Behave yourself while I'm gone."

"If I must, I must." Raina watched as the detective headed out the door, wondering what she'd gotten herself into.

Chapter 11

DESPITE THE OBJECTIONS OF both Detectives Kramer and Scott, Raina was released from the hospital late the following day. They'd tried to talk the doctor into keeping her a while longer for her safety. She wasn't alone in the hospital. But the doctor said he had no grounds to hold her any longer. Besides, there were other patients needing care.

Dr. Benson said unless she got hurt again or had a sudden setback, she was good to leave—as long as she took it easy. He said it'd be better if she wasn't left alone but knowing she didn't know anyone locally, what choice was there? He and Detective Kramer both smiled when Detective Scott asked just how much she had to have happen to her, and how soon, in order for her to stay at the hospital for a while longer?

With a twinkle in his eyes, Dr. Benson asked, "What are you planning on doing to her, Detective?"

"What would work?"

Dr. Benson couldn't help but chuckle, knowing the officer wasn't serious about causing her harm just to get her to stay. "I'm sorry. But if she leaves and has a setback, by all means, we'll let her back through the doors. You can be sure of that."

The two detectives finally relented, saying they'd be there to pick her up themselves late that night when there were less people to see.

Raina was told the news by Nurse Laurel. While Laurel was excited for her, she was also saddened to see her go. "It's so nice to have a fun, cooperative patient. We all hate to see you leave. You've been so sweet to all of us here, and we'll miss your sense of humor. I wish you could stay longer!"

They both laughed.

"Well, you guys are wonderful too. All of you have made me feel safe and well cared for. I'll miss you all. I feel like we've almost become friends." Raina hugged the nurse. "Thank you for taking such good care of me. If you want to, and could, please take some of these plants home, okay? Or pass them around? Wait! How about if you give them to other patients here who don't have anything, or anyone to visit them? And the balloons. If the cards are blank, take them too."

The nurse smiled. "Oh, Raina! That's a wonderful idea! Are you sure?"

"Absolutely." Raina looked over toward the window. "I'll keep those few on the sill. Please, take the rest. There are too many for me to keep up with."

"I'll send someone over to get them. That's terribly sweet of you!" She smiled again at her patient. "Don't you forget if you feel anything is off, you get back in here to get it checked out. You're still to rest like you've been doing here. Walk around if you can for some exercise. But not if you're feeling dizzy. You're not out of the woods yet, Raina. Please don't rush your healing. Let your body do its thing, okay?"

Nurse Laurel sent in a few aides to take away the plants, gifts, and balloons to share with other patients, each one thanking her for her kindness and thoughtfulness. Raina had a small stack of the personalized cards and notes they removed as they carried them out. Her room now felt as empty as it looked.

By eight o'clock that night, she was ready to go home, wearing some of her own clothes Sergeant Scott had thoughtfully brought to her earlier. She wondered what he thought when he went through her underwear drawer. It was kind of creepy to have a male cop go through her personal items, but she figured he was a grown man and had seen it all before. But still.

She smiled to herself when she pictured him blushing as he tossed a pair of her panties and a bra into the duffle bag he'd found in her closet. He'd included both a pair of blue jean Capri pants and shorts, a soft, apricot-colored blouse, and her pair of walking shoes. She assumed her other shoes went into evidence along with her clothes when she came in.

A nurse she didn't know helped her get dressed. Raina chose the shorts as the capris irritated her leg wounds. The nurse gently did her hair with the brush he'd also remembered to bring. Raina had already found out that any quick movements by her raised arms caused her ribs to hurt, including the basic tasks of putting on deodorant and brushing her own hair. They tossed the face cream, lotions, bandages, and whatever else she could take home into her duffle bag. She even tossed in the box of Kleenex.

She was now immensely glad Nurse Laurel had helped her shower and washed her hair earlier. It'd been her first shower since she'd been admitted. It felt heavenly. And as any woman knows, having clean hair after a nice shower makes a world of difference. The clean gown and bed sheets made her last few hours there relaxed until the detectives arrived with her clothes.

The two detectives had moved the few gifts she'd kept to their car as she got dressed and were waiting for her when she came out of her hospital room for the last time. Smiling, she carried her duffle bag as she walked toward them. They smiled back as Channion reached for her bag.

She stopped him. "No, I've got it. But thank you, Channion." She remembered she was to use their first names from now on.

Channion nodded. "It looks like Officer Hicks picked out some nice clothes for you. I wasn't sure what she put together for you, but she said she'd have better judgement than I would."

Raina was surprised, and honestly a little bit relieved, that *he* actually hadn't gone through her underwear drawer after all. "Well, it's easier when you're going through my own clothes and not randomly buying new ones from a store."

Ron said, "The colors suit you, Raina. You look wonderful."

"Thank you, Ron!" His compliment helped boost her confidence as she was still worried about how she looked.

As they made their way to the elevators, she said one more goodbye to the nurses waiting there. She had one more stop to make before leaving. Neither detective objected when they saw her hit the floor for the ICU after Channion had already pushed the *Lobby* button.

When the doors opened on the ICU floor, they stepped out after Ron looked around. He and his nephew waited at the nurse station while she went in to see Bryce Mitchell one more time before she left. Raina was a little surprised she didn't see his family there until she remembered visiting hours were over. She set her bag down by his bed.

Raina felt a little disappointed he was sleeping. She still had yet to actually talk *with* him but always *to* him. Even now, she still had never once heard his voice or seen the color of his eyes. She sighed, reaching for his hand as was her habit with him.

Holding his hand in hers, she said, "Hey, Bryce. It's me, Raina, again. They're letting me out of here. I feel like I'm being released from jail, but I'm sure I'm basically being put on house arrest. I have a feeling I'm going to have a babysitter of some sort for a time, but I'm finally leaving here. I get to go home and see my horses, and I'm beyond excited for that to happen! Your time will come, Bryce. Don't you worry about that.

"I'll be sure they keep me in the loop somehow so I know how you're doing. It would've been nice to hear your voice just once, but it's okay. I will one day. It'll give me something to look forward to, right?" She patted his arm before carefully leaning down. "You take care, Deputy Mitchell," she whispered into his ear.

She was stepping away when he suddenly grabbed her hand.

Chapter 12

"*OH! YOU'RE AWAKE!*" RAINA exclaimed. "Let me call a nurse!" She turned to do just that, but he stopped her.

With a weak tug on her hand, he said hoarsely, "Wait."

Watching her, Channion saw the shocked expression on her face. He walked quickly around the nurse station to Bryce's room with Ron right on his heels. Neither said a word as they watched her lean down to hear what Bryce was saying. He appeared to be whispering in her ear.

Channion whispered, "I don't believe it. He woke up for her!"

Ron turned to get a nurse or a doctor, whoever happened by first.

Out of respect for the both of them, they all stood quietly outside the doorway while the two victims talked. A nurse and both detectives watched as the officer and the woman who saved him spoke to each other for the first time. Channion felt Ron's hand on his shoulder, felt him squeeze it. He nodded in silent acknowledgement of the special moment they were witnessing.

Raina nodded in response to Bryce's whispered question. "Yes, I am... Raina Stewart," she replied, in a strained whisper. She listened again. His voice scratchy and low, he had to talk slowly. It hurt her ribs to lean over that long, but she didn't mind—but then thought better of it. "Let me get a chair, okay? I'm not leaving you... I just can't lean over like that right now." She dragged over a lightweight chair she supposed his family used when there.

He reached for her left hand again as soon as she sat down, and she grasped his. He took note of her right hand still in a splint. He whispered low to her.

She answered, "I was, but it's okay. Really... I'll be fine too." She listened again and said, "I'm glad too. We both did, didn't we?" She smiled at him, misty tears in her eyes.

He squeezed her hand again and kept looking at her like he couldn't look anywhere else. Raina patted his hand with her bandaged right one. "It's okay, Bryce. We'll be fine."

He said something else to her. This time when she answered, she choked back tears. "You bet. How could I not?"

She wiped her tears away, smiled when she heard his next comment. "It's because I'm so happy you're awake, on the mend, and that I finally got to actually talk with you! I'm fairly sure you don't normally make women cry, Bryce. If you do, you need to stop it immediately."

She choked on a laugh since she was also trying not to cry. He gave her a weak smile in return. She saw the tears well up in his eyes. She tenderly wiped away the few tears that slipped over and slid down his cheek.

The officer whispered again to her. Those in the doorway were straining to hear, but his voice was too low. Although they respected their privacy, they were still naturally quite curious.

Raina patted his cheek gently again but said firmly, "Don't you dare apologize, Mitchell. It was *my* decision. Mine alone. You hear me?" He spoke again and she replied softly, "Of course I will. Don't you worry about that at all."

After a moment, she smiled. "Don't sue me, but I'm gonna give you a kiss for good luck, okay?" She leaned over and kissed the officer's cheek. She whispered, "I don't think I've ever kissed a cop before, at least not while he was in bed." She grinned at his short laugh. "I need to let the doctor or whoever in now, Bryce, before they mow down the two detectives holding them back. You rest now so you can get better. You understand me? Your family will be here soon to keep you company again, I'm sure."

He squeezed her hand again, saying once more, "Thank you for saving my life, Raina."

She squeezed it back, whispering through her tears, "You're welcome, Bryce. You're so very welcome."

Chapter 13

RAINA SMILED ALL THE way to the front entrance of the hospital. She was so jubilant at getting to talk to Bryce before she left, she felt like skipping across the entire parking lot. The detectives smiled at her exuberance.

The hospital staff decided to let her walk out the door instead of being wheeled out like regulations dictated, mainly because the officers felt it easier for them to protect her if she wasn't confined to a chair. They also hoped she looked like a visitor and not a patient in case they were being watched. Detective Kramer went and pulled the car around to the doors while Detective Scott and Raina waited inside.

She noticed both men were constantly looking around them as they made their way to the car near the doors. Ron opened the back door for her as Channion got into the front passenger seat. She squeezed in among the few gifts she'd kept from her well-wishers, putting on her seatbelt.

Slipping behind the wheel, Ron fastened his seatbelt before he turned to look at her. "Are you hungry? I bet you're craving some real food."

She smiled. "I am. I think I lost about ten of my unwanted pounds in there. I was trying to get rid of them, so being in there was actually quite convenient. My pants feel a little looser, I have to admit."

Channion looked at her over the seat. "Don't tell me you think you're *fat?*" His voice was incredulous. She had a nice, slim body. Not too skinny, but just right.

She shrugged. "Well, no, not anymore. I just said the hospital took it. I wonder if they'll take that as partial payment? You know, a pound of flesh... Do you know what the going rate for that is?" She grinned at the look on Channion's face.

Ron smiled at her while Channion shook his head and said, "You're not fat, Stewart. Not before and not now. You don't need to watch your weight."

"Well, if I didn't then I would," she reasoned.

Ron was laughing as he pulled out of the parking lot. "She makes a good point."

"Raina, how about if I tell you if you're getting fat or not? I'll watch your weight so you don't have to. If you get too fat, I'll let you know. Deal?" Channion asked, with humor in his voice.

Raina smiled, raised her eyebrow. "Deal. Just be careful how you tell a woman she's getting fat. Frankly, I'm interested in how you'd do such a thing and actually think you're going to live through it."

Both detectives laughed.

"I'll think of something, should the occasion ever arise," Channion replied, smiling. "So, Miss Stewart, it's our treat for dinner. Any place in particular you have a hankering for?"

"A hankering?" She smiled and thought for a moment. "I have a hankering for maybe some Italian. Yes, Italian would suit me. Is there an Olive Garden or a Carrabba's around here? Or someplace else that serves good Italian?

"If not, about anything will do as long as it's not something I have to unwrap or has Jell-O as a main ingredient. And my mouth is still a bit sore, so nothing tough like pizza. Maybe something more along the line of noodles or soup, something soft and squishy like that."

"Hey, I know just the place. Italian it is. Hard to go wrong with that choice." Ron changed lanes to take the exit he needed.

THE RESTAURANT THEY CHOSE was in a nice-sized, brick building with rounded entrance arches, neatly edged with beautiful flowers. Soft Italian music flowed through hidden speakers outside the entrance and the outdoor covered terrace, covered tastefully in what to Raina looked like real vines. Parking near the front door, they motioned for her to lead the way, but Channion still opened the door for her to pass through.

"Thank you," she said as she walked through the door into a spacious lobby.

Without waiting for a hostess to lead them to a table, Ron simply led the way toward the back, away from the other customers. More flowers, probably silk ones that looked real, surrounded their seating area. With a hint of music adding to the atmosphere, it felt intimate, relaxing, and welcoming.

They sat in the corner away from the windows with Raina in the middle, backs to the wall so they could see the entire restaurant. Raina noticed the silent precautions but didn't mention them. They looked over the menu with her, recommending their favorites. They placed their order, got their drinks and their salads—and Raina her soup—in quick time.

"This is a wonderful place for a first date, isn't it?" She blew on her soup to cool it off.

"Are we on a date?" Channion asked, grinning. "Do I really still need a chaperone?"

His eyes twinkling, Ron said, "She meant with *me*, silly. *You're* the chaperone!"

Channion laughed. "Pardon my arrogance."

Raina laughed after she realized what she'd asked. She teased, "Well, you both picked me up, one drove me here, and the other opened doors for me. I'm assuming you're paying and then taking me home—where it ends, by the way. It sure sounds like a date to me!"

Channion joked, "If you need two men on one date, you're high maintenance. I'm out."

Raina deadpanned, "Maybe it just takes two men to equal what one *should* be. Or maybe I'm just making up for lost time." Both men smiled as she continued, "On the other hand, what kind of woman would I be to go on a date with two men at the same time? And with one married, maybe both? Whatever it is, it probably isn't good!"

Both men smiled as they ate their salads.

She finally clarified, "But what I *meant* was, the atmosphere and service here are wonderful. And you guys know it pretty well. Is this like a cop hang-out?" She paused. "Wow, this soup is amazing!"

Ron replied, "You could say it's our hang-out. And yes, that soup is great. It's always a crowd favorite. And this place is a family-owned restaurant."

She sipped more soup. "Most are. Who's family?"

Channion replied, "Ours."

"Oh, I see." She took a sip of her warm tea. She thought for a moment before asking, "How are you two related?"

Channion looked at her. "We didn't tell you that yet?" She shook her head so he explained, "Ron is my uncle. And our extended family owns this restaurant."

"So I can order whatever I want? No limit?"

They saw the sparkle in her eyes. Smiling, Ron said, "To a certain extent. Basically whatever you want to in a reasonable quantity. We're flexible."

"Your turn to buy tonight, isn't it?" Channion questioned with a grin, pointing his fork at his uncle.

"Depends on how much she orders," Ron replied, smiling. "Raina, order whatever you want to. It's our treat, so don't feel shy. We can also write it off as an expense!"

Ron got a text to call in as their meals were being served by a personable brunette; Cousin Danielle, according to Channion. Ron stood up to take the call where it was more private, leaving Channion and Raina together.

Channion studied her for a second before asking, "Are you going to be comfortable being at your place alone, Raina?"

She hadn't considered that possibility at all. After some hesitation, she replied, "I guess so. I've been on my own for a good part of my life, so it never occurred to me that I wouldn't. Are you worried about me being alone due to impending danger, health issues, loneliness, or because of possible nightmares?"

Channion chewed and swallowed before answering her. "All the above, I suppose, and pretty much in that order. If you want someone to stay with you until this is over, we could find someone for you. We have a few female officers to make you more comfortable. It'd be best for you to not be alone, especially since you're still healing."

Truth was, neither he, his uncle nor their fellow officers felt she should be without protection if what their leads were telling them were true. Bryce was already being watched over. Only those working the case knew this though. Channion was actually only asking to feel her out since they were planning on setting her up somewhere safe right away.

If she elected to stay home alone tonight, they'd have her place under constant surveillance. They needed to move her and her horses out as soon as possible. But they figured to allow her to go home for at least a night or two to help her transition into leaving and to pack anything she needed. They were already making plans for her horses to be moved.

Raina admitted, "I really wouldn't want a stranger staying with me. I don't want someone there I'd have to feel obligated to entertain or talk to. I prefer to be on my own. And I don't want to put anyone in danger by being around me, if you think that's an actual issue."

"Raina, we really think it best for you to have someone there who can protect you and help you while you heal. With your injuries, you're going to need some help. If you're in danger, we're duty-bound to protect you until we feel it's safe."

She sat there, thinking about what he said. She didn't want to make anyone's job harder, but she was telling the truth about having a stranger around her. "I see." She paused, wondering about the implications for a moment before blurting out, "How about you? Could you be like my bodyguard or whatever?"

"I don't think that'd be a good idea."

"Why not? You're already on the case. And I feel safe with you. I trust you," she stated. "Plus, you can feed my horses for me if I want to sleep in." She smiled at him before taking another bite of truly excellent spaghetti.

When Ron came back to their table, his expression was contained when he sat down. As he cut into his fettuccine, he asked, "So, what'd I miss?"

Since neither answered right away, he looked up, glancing from one to the other. Raina finally replied, "Well, Sarge here was asking if I'd be comfortable alone at my house, and I said I think so. He offered to have a female officer over, but I'd prefer him. Or you, even."

Ron continued chewing while he thought it through. "That's not a bad idea, Channion. You could—"

"Wait... Me?"

"Sure. You're already on this case, so there's no need to read you in, and you could protect her if needed. If she should remember something, she wouldn't have to call you or me because you'd already be there. I think she'd be more comfortable with one of us, and since I have your aunt to take care of, well, that leaves you.

"Just for a while to make sure she adjusts to being home alone again. Besides that, she's still healing and shouldn't be alone. Dr. Benson even said she shouldn't be alone as she'll need help with some things. What if she had a setback of some sort? Let's be sure she's safe for a few days, and we'll all go from there."

He was hoping his nephew would take the hint that he needed to take her offer. It'd probably make it far easier to explain to her later on when they wanted to move her somewhere safer, or at least have a protection detail. Hopefully, easing her into it now would be less stressful and more comfortable for her since she seemed open to the idea.

Channion hesitated. A female officer would be a far more professional and wiser option. They hardly knew Miss Stewart after all. What if she wasn't what she appeared to be? Would she set him up for a sexual harassment case? Policies were set up to avoid these situations for a reason.

On the other hand, what if she needed security protection and no one knew it yet? It'd probably only be for a couple days or so, anyway, until they moved her somewhere safer. They could still have a female officer with them too.

Seeing his hesitation, Raina offered a compromise. "How about this? I stay alone to see how it goes. If I feel uncomfortable or even scared, I'll call you. Then you can come over and stay with me. Or a female officer. Maybe both. Fair enough?"

Ron was thinking about his recent phone call. "No, not really. We also can't leave you alone out there as you have no transportation now. And you're too far out for a quick rescue. You can't leave due to your horses unless you found a neighbor or someone else to take over.

"But we don't want *anyone* on your property except us, Raina. We don't even want people to know *where* you are. Frankly, it makes more sense to have him there from the get-go. We can get a female officer out there as well if that'd make you both more comfortable."

Ron looked at them both before turning his gaze on his partner, both officers knowing this smoothly took care of their dilemma of not leaving her alone. His nephew had caught on to the hints and knew something was in the wind.

Raina had to admit she forgot about not having a truck. She didn't even have her phone! "Okay. I understand what you're saying. And I'm okay with it being just us. As long as he's trustworthy, and I don't have to worry about him."

"He's extremely trustworthy, Raina. Are you?"

"Yes."

Turning to his nephew, Ron said, "You can stop by your place to get your things and drive her on over, or even just stay at your place tonight if you're too tired. Her horses are outside, right? So they'd be okay until morning?

"If we feel the need to keep her under constant watch, we can look into getting a female officer to do it. We both know a couple personality-wise who'd be a nice fit, especially if we had to go long term."

He casually dropped this last line simply to plant the seed in her mind that this was a likely scenario. His nephew knew what he was doing, so he agreed.

"We should take care of her horses, so it'd be her place over mine. I'm sure she's more than ready to see them again! But I'll need to go get some things from home first."

His uncle nodded. "That sounds like a plan. Get enough for two or three days to save the trips. Just check in with me so I know where you are."

"Of course."

With the soft music playing in the background, Raina ate her spaghetti while she listened to them talking almost as if she wasn't even there now, making plans that inevitably were going to change her life.

WHEN THEY FINISHED THEIR dinner, Ron drove back to the police station so Channion could get the police car he normally drove. They transferred all of her things to Channion's car while she stood there, quietly watching. She held the take-out bag they gave her from the restaurant since she probably wouldn't have much at home to eat until they could get to the store.

Feeling a bit like a charity case, she'd shyly requested some more of the soup and spaghetti to take home, and they had readily agreed. They'd added some more options in themselves. They simply waited at the restaurant while it all got cooked and Danielle bagged it. The large bag in her arms smelled heavenly. It was tempting to eat more right then and there, but her stomach had let her know earlier that her limit had been met.

When his uncle said goodnight to them, he reminded them to stay sharp and to drive safely.

Chapter 14

AFTER STOPPING AT HIS house for him to get what he needed, they drove back through town, heading west toward the open countryside where she lived. She began to fidget.

Channion finally asked her what was wrong. "Are you nervous about going home? Or because I'll be there with you?"

Raina sighed. "Not yet. I'm just not used to being in the passenger's seat. It's an uncomfortable feeling. I can't even remember the last time I was in a car and not behind the wheel. Besides tonight, I mean, going to the restaurant. It still felt odd, but the back seat feels differently than the front one."

"Want to crawl into the back seat?" he asked with a playful smile, trying to help her relax.

"Is that an invitation?" She smiled back at him and playfully batted her eyes.

He laughed. "No. Geez, Raina. We're going to be professional here. You're not going to be difficult on this issue, are you?"

"Well, I will *try* not to be. You just want to keep me up here right by your side instead?"

He grinned, shook his head. "That'd be fine." He looked at her profile, partially lit up by the dashboard lights. He could tell she was smiling. He turned back to the road. As he drove, he distracted her by asking about her work, learning she'd been in office management before making music her new career.

Glancing at the detective, she asked, "What about you? Would you find office work soulless, boring? Does being a cop ever feel like a dead-end job?"

Channion thought for a moment. "Well, I do some of that office work now. But when I'm on the street patrolling, or working a case like now, there's a real purpose to what I do. A fair amount of working a case *is* actually done at my desk, but there's still quite a bit done on the streets, chasing down leads.

"But for sure, my career choice has a purpose. There's a real meaning to it. And I hope to God it isn't a dead end for me!"

Raina gasped, slapping her hand over her mouth. "Oh! I totally didn't mean to say it like that. That was an unforgivably poor choice of words. I'm *so* sorry!" She felt mortified at the implication she'd inadvertently made that he could be killed on the job, especially with her and Bryce's current situation.

"Don't worry about it. I was teasing you." He put on the turn signal and applied the brakes to take a turn. "I know it's just a turn of phrase, and most people don't think about what it could mean literally. We all do it. Like a wife telling her husband she 'could kill him for that,' and all he did was leave the toilet seat up again causing her to fall in. It's just something most of us say and do so casually, it doesn't hold any real meaning."

She shook her head. "Well, I don't know if I could joke about it like you do."

He explained, "Cops have different ways of coping. We never truly joke about dying, of course. But if we take everything literally, we'd all snap in no time at all. Humor has its dark side, I guess. And we don't always dwell on the literal side of things—at least, we try not to. Obviously, any cadet or veteran would know something *could* go wrong on the job, and they'd never make it home.

"But this is also true for everyone else, no matter where they work. Some positions like law enforcement and the military just have a higher risk value.

"Working in this field, we see everything man has to offer. Violence, greed, liars, thieves, drugs, alcohol, sordid histories. And that's probably in just one so-called normal family. It's fair to say there's a felon in every family out there. Sometimes it seems like every case is the same as the one before, just with different names, and a slight variation of the crime."

She understood. "Same book, different cover?"

"Exactly."

Quietly, she asked, "What about my book?"

He looked over at her before answering. "Yours has a few extra chapters."

They talked as he drove down the dark roads. She enjoyed his company, so she felt comfortable with him. He could make her laugh, which is something she loved to do—it just hurt right now if she did. He laughed, too, and she thought his was a good, hearty one.

Her heart began to thud as they came upon the curves that'd lead them to the crime scene. She wiped her left hand on her shorts as it got clammy suddenly. Channion noticed even in the dark. In support, he reached over and briefly held it with his right one.

He figured this would happen. Going back the first time would be the hardest. At night, she wouldn't be able to see as much, but it was the fact she knew where she was.

And what had happened here would be fresh in her mind—depending on how much she remembered.

They passed the area where the cars had been. She barely looked over and tried to keep her eyes straight ahead. She knew her truck had been towed back with the other two cars as evidence. She'd been told the insurance company would count it as a total loss, probably because the airbags deployed. She was also told that was probably how her wrist got hurt. Airbags may save lives, but they were also known to seriously injure people. She figured she was all-around lucky that day.

He turned onto her road, slowing as he neared her driveway. He turned into it and stopped by her front porch, parking the car facing out toward the road. He turned off the engine and lights.

When he handed her the spare key, she said, "It's more than a little disturbing to have a man I barely even know hand me my own house key that he has in his own car. Do you want to know how creepy this feels to me?"

He admitted to himself it *would* be odd, if not creepy. Moreso to a lone woman in the dark. Trying to keep it light, he offered, "Well, I could call the police for you, but I'm already here!"

She actually laughed, then groaned as it hurt to do that.

He grabbed his bags while she took the food and her hospital bag and walked to her front door. Raina unlocked it with the creepy key while he looked around for her safety.

She flipped on the living room light switch and looked around. Nothing seemed out of place, but yet it felt differently to her. She slowly looked around again. After simply standing there a moment, absorbing the feeling of being home again, she turned to face him. She adjusted her grip on the carry-out bag she held as she let it sink in a moment why she had a man—this one in particular—in her living room.

He still stood by the door, his own bags in his hand and slung over his shoulder, allowing her the space he felt she needed. He didn't say a word as his own eyes roamed the room. It was quiet as a tomb.

Raina finally spoke up to break the silence and the tension she felt. "I have a spare room upstairs. Let's see what condition it's in. But let me take care of this first, okay?"

She set her hospital bag down on the couch, then put the restaurant food in the refrigerator, moving around items to make room. She figured she'd need to go through it and toss out old food tomorrow.

She led the way up the stairs and down the hall. "Bathroom is here. There's another one downstairs in case we need it at the same time. Each one has towels, soap, whatever. Use anything you need. And here is your room." She flipped on the light. "You're my first guest here, so I've never used it for anyone before now. I hope it works for you." Her voice sounded a bit anxious as she stepped back to let him enter.

Channion surveyed the room with a quick glance. It had a desk with drawers, a lamp, and a fan. Even a bookcase. But no bed. He looked at her.

She smiled. "Can you handle an air mattress on a frame? It'll take about fifteen minutes to set it all up. I have sheets that fit it. I've used it myself, and it was pretty comfortable. If you don't want to use it, or you just don't like it, you can use the couch or even my bed."

He raised an eyebrow at her, looked at her with a grin. "I thought we agreed to keep this strictly professional, Miss Stewart."

She grinned back as she walked to the closet, teasing him when she said, "Your choice, Detective Scott. But I *meant* we could switch rooms while you're here. Or you can take the couch, like I said. Also your choice."

He set down his bags in the hallway and helped her set up the portable bed frame she had stored in the closet. It was far too heavy for her in her condition, so he set it up himself. As he filled up the air mattress with the use of a little electric pump, she went down the hall to her little linen closet and got clean sheets for him. She grabbed fresh towels for the bathroom too.

The noise from the pump made her head ache so she stalled for time until the mattress was full of air. She put the fresh towels in the bathroom, gave it a quick clean to ease her conscience, and stocked it before she stopped in her room to get a couple of pillows from her own closet that he could use. She slipped the clean pillowcases on them and sat on her bed to wait.

Once she heard him turn off the pump, she returned to the spare room. Her ribs hurt from cleaning the bathroom, but she wouldn't complain. She helped him put on the sheets, and then tossed the pillows on top.

Looking at it, he said, "I should be fine here. I'll need to add some more air to it once the material stretches out some more. Are your ribs sore?" He noticed she had flinched more than a couple of times. He was also catching on to her breathing pattern. When it hitched, he knew she had just done something that hurt.

"It'll pass. We need to go feed my kids now. Let's go!" She smiled at the thought of seeing her horses. With any luck, they'd distract her from the headache she felt building.

Channion stopped her by putting his hand on her shoulder when they got to the back door. "New house rule. Any time you need to go outside, I go too. And more importantly, I go first."

His look was serious, bringing home to her the fact that she was possibly in actual danger. He still wore his gun in his holster. How did she forget that?

She nodded. "Understood. Lead the way, and walk fast! Trust me, I'll keep up."

He wasn't sure if he preferred her house not having automatic flood lights like his did or not. He led the way to the barn, noting there was a light pole outside of it, but no light was coming from it either.

She flipped on the aisle lights once they reached the barn. Her two horses had their heads over the half doors, ears pricked forward. Their eyes blinked as the lights came on. As she spoke to them, they nickered and tossed their heads.

Channion smiled. "See? I told you they missed you! They're happy to see you back home!"

He watched as she lovingly spoke to both of them, rubbing their foreheads and smoothing their forelocks. She blew on their noses and kissed them as she spoke to them. She wrapped her arms around their necks, breathing in the sweet smell that belonged only to horses. Her eyes filled with tears of relief and happiness because she was finally back with them. She was even happier because her kids seemed happy to see her too.

He couldn't help but smile at her. She obviously missed her horses more than even he realized. It made him happy to see her looking so carefree, despite what she looked like and was going through. He had an awful gut feeling her life was only beginning to be disrupted and didn't know how to warn her. Giving her some moments of peace right now was the least he could do.

She leaned against the palomino's neck as she looked at the detective. Her eyes were still misty with happy tears. "I suppose I could introduce you formally to my kids, huh?" Patting the golden neck, she said, "This beauty is Aspen Glow, or just Aspen. He was born in Colorado in the autumn with the sun shining through the golden aspen leaves."

She breathed in the sweet scent of her horse. Oh! The sweet, familiar scent of her horses! she thought as she hugged him again. She didn't want to let him go.

Channion grinned as he came over to pet Aspen. The tall gelding raised his nose, blowing gently on Channion's face. His velvety lips nibbled at Channion's hair.

Letting go of her horse, Raina smiled. "Hey! Aspen likes you! I guess that means I can trust you since my horses do." She saw the detective's grin. "Let's see about this guy over here."

Reaching out to scratch behind the sorrel's ears before hugging him, too, she said, "This is Royal Rodeo. It's spelled like rodeo but pronounced row-day-oh, like Rodeo Drive. I call him Rodeo."

Channion waited to see what Rodeo would do and smiled when the horse sniffed his pockets, looking for a treat. "He did this to me when you were gone. You must carry treats in your pockets."

Raina shook her head. "Nope." She grinned. "He's *frisking* you!"

Channion laughed as he slid his hand down the long reddish-brown neck. Holding the horse's head in his hands, he looked into the horse's large brown eyes. "There's such gentleness and intelligence in a horse's eyes, don't you think?" he asked. "Rodeo here has exceptional eyes. Don't ya, boy?" He looked into the dark brown eyes again for a moment. "His eyes see more than most, don't they?"

Pleased with his observation, Raina nodded. "Yes! I've always thought so. Funny you caught that too."

Intrigued now, Raina studied the man and the horse in silence for a moment. It seemed the man saw more than most too. No other person had ever commented on Rodeo's eyes before. There was just something special about them. It was like he could look inside of you and see your secrets, your fears. And then he'd help you conquer them.

Raina looked over at Channion as she went and stood by Aspen again so she could give him some more attention. "Yes, horses are the best. I've had them for years now and hate to think of my life without them. They're an anchor for me, you know?"

They spent about thirty minutes in the barn, listening to the horses eat while petting them. They also checked the automatic waterers. She would've been happy to stay out there longer, but she knew Channion was probably as tired as she was.

She ran her hand down the white stripe on Rodeo's face. "I'd be thrilled to simply stay out here with them. I could just camp out in the barn, but it's probably best we go back to the house. I hate to leave them though."

He nodded. "I understand. But morning will be here soon enough, and you'll be right back down here. We can spend more time with them tomorrow, probably as long as you'd like."

Nodding, Raina was already excited at the prospect of coming back down. Satisfied her kids were taken care of for the night and beyond happy she finally got home to see them again, she gave them another goodnight kiss. She turned off the lights before they made their way back to her house.

"Make yourself at home, I guess," she said as he locked the back door once they were inside.

He did. The first thing he did was to go through the entire house to make sure all the windows and doors were securely locked. They finally went upstairs and got ready to crash into their beds. Raina took a glass of water up with her, knowing her head would be hurting worse soon, and she'd need to take the Tylenol they gave her at the hospital. She was thankful she'd been able to shower before coming home.

Outside of his room, Raina paused before saying, "Thank you for being here, Channion. I'm sure you'd prefer your own bed at home, but I do appreciate you being here all the same. At least you don't have to worry about driving all the way out here just to feed my horses now." She smiled at him.

"Well, yes. There is that." He grinned back. "But as I mentioned before, I enjoyed doing it."

Looking at her closely, he could tell she was wiped out. Nervous and excited to be home, he was still betting she'd fall asleep as soon as her head hit the pillow. He mentioned, "I'm usually up and around by six or seven. You don't need to get up when I do because you need to sleep in. Doctor's orders are for you to rest.

"And I brought along some of my papers so I can work from here for a while. We're not on a strict schedule at the moment. Remember, the first order of business is for you to rest and heal. You sleep as long as you need to. And don't worry about having to entertain me."

They both smiled, remembering their earlier conversation.

He reminded her, "Always remember, we're the other's shadow. I leave, you leave. You stay, I stay. I don't leave you here alone now. We'll figure it all out in the morning. Your horses were fed late tonight, so they'll be fine in the morning if you sleep in."

She nodded. "True enough. Well, if I'm not up when you are, make yourself at home. Do whatever you want to in the kitchen, using the bathroom, watching TV. I put fresh towels in the bathroom while you were setting it up in here so feel free to shower. But if you make a mess anywhere, you'd better clean it up!" He grinned at her firm tone. "Well, I guess that's it. Good night, Detective Scott."

"Goodnight, Miss Stewart," he replied as she headed toward her room. He called out, "Raina?"

She stopped and turned around.

"Welcome back home."

She smiled in response to his soft tone and his thoughtfulness. Both melted her heart. She replied in kind, "Thank you."

Before she closed her door, she paused. He was still watching her. As seriously as she could muster, she asked one question. "So what exactly are you going to say to the guys down at the station when they hear you slept over at my house?"

He heard her laughing, then her immediate groan of pain as her door clicked shut. Chuckling to himself, he only partially shut his door as he needed to be able to hear anything outside of it.

He slipped into his sweatpants and a comfy t-shirt. Testing the air mattress, he plugged the little air compressor back in and added some air until he felt it was firm enough for him. He plugged in his phone and set the alarm, turning down the volume in case she was a light sleeper. He checked his gun before he placed it underneath the spare pillow and turned off his light. Exhausted himself, he fell asleep almost immediately.

Chapter 15

To HER DISMAY, HER headache came on with a vengeance less than an hour later. She'd downed the Tylenol and waited for it to kick in. Lying in her bed, she tried to relax. She took deep breaths like one of her nurses told her to do. She'd even propped up her pillows like in the hospital.

She finally got up, used the bathroom, splashing cool water on her face, hoping that might help. Back in her bed, a familiar place she'd practically dreamed of lately, she hoped it'd help her relax and sleep finally. By the time she felt the little drug beginning to work, her head hurt so badly she was miserable. She turned her bedside lamp on low and sat up on the side of her bed. Her toes curled into the carpet, she tried to think of anything but her aching head, but nothing worked. Maybe she was trying too hard.

Another half hour passed. By now, she was so exhausted and achy she couldn't stop the tears from rolling down her cheeks. She drank more of the water and blew her nose. She slowly stood up, making certain she had her balance before turning off her lamp and quietly opening her door. She crept by Channion's room since she noticed his door was partially open. Making her way down the stairs, she used both the wall and the railing to keep her balance.

She sat down on her couch in the dark living room, wrapping herself in her fuzzy throw for comfort. She reached over and grabbed the little stuffed horse from the hospital bag. Hugging it tightly, she looked out the window into the night and prayed her head would stop hurting soon.

———————

UPSTAIRS, CHANNION AWOKE TO the sound of her door opening again. Being in a strange place, he slept even lighter than he normally did, besides the fact he was there for her protection. He stayed where he was, thinking she had to use the bathroom again.

When she crept by his room, he looked at his watch. It was almost two o'clock. What was she doing up?

Out of pure curiosity, he got out of his bed and walked to the door. He was thankful for the nightlights she had in there so he wouldn't stub his toe in the unfamiliar and dark room. He opened his door the rest of the way, sticking his head out, just listening.

When the air conditioner clicked off, he heard her crying downstairs. Concerned, he walked to the top of the stairs. Maybe she wanted privacy. She'd been through a horrible ordeal, and it was probably catching up with her now that she was home. He listened to her for a while longer before deciding he should check on her. Quietly, he walked halfway down the stairs, just far enough where he could see her. He saw her in the moonlight, sitting on the couch, rocking with her head in her hands.

He ran down the rest of the stairs to her. "Raina? Sweetheart, are you okay? What's wrong?" He gently removed her hands from her head, looking at her closely in the moonlight.

She was now embarrassed he caught her crying in the middle of the night. "I'm sorry to have woken you." She spoke in-between her tearful sobs. She blew her nose again, tossing the Kleenex into the little trash can beside the end table. "I tried to be quiet so I wouldn't disturb you. I even came downstairs so I wouldn't. You weren't supposed to follow me." She sounded pitiful.

"It's all right." He considered leaving her alone. But then figured he was already here, so he might as well stay and try to help her. "What's the matter?"

His concern made her cry more. It was so nice to have someone around who cared for her, someone she could lean on if she needed to. "It's my head. Dr. Benson told me the headaches would go away, but he said it might be a while." She held her head in her hands again, rocking back and forth. "Oh! It hurts!"

"Didn't they give you anything for them?"

"I already took the Tylenol."

"Take some more," he advised.

Such a simple solution, she wished she'd thought of it. Oh, wait. She had. Her fear was her body would build a tolerance to it, and she'd have to take more and more. Too many would probably be bad for her stomach, so then she wouldn't be able to take any. *Then* what would she do?

"Sweetheart, where's the Tylenol?"

"Upstairs in my room." She blew her nose again, careful not to hit it as it was still sore from being broken.

"Did you want to return to your room, or stay down here?"

"Here, I guess." She lifted up her glasses to wipe her eyes.

"Okay."

He ran upstairs, grabbed the bottle, and returned downstairs to the kitchen. Running a clean dish cloth under the faucet, he wrung it out in the sink. Taking it and a glass of water to her, he made her take three more pills and set the glass aside. He gently wiped her face and set the damp cloth on the glass.

Hesitating a moment, he went upstairs, stopped in the bathroom and returned to his room. A moment later, he came back downstairs with his phone, gun, and pillows, which he tossed on the end of the couch. He placed his gun on the floor but within easy reach. Putting his phone on silent mode and turning off the alarm, he placed it on the arm of the couch.

What he did next so surprised her, she couldn't even react. He gently picked her up in his arms, sat back down on the couch, cradling her, and using his pillows to help support her. He told her to stretch out her legs. He smiled when he saw the stuffed horse and handed it back to her before he tucked the throw blanket around her. He removed her glasses and placed them on the coffee table.

He grabbed his gun, slid it beside him between the seat cushion and the couch. He then settled back in place, propping his legs on a throw pillow he took to cushion them on her coffee table. Being mindful of her cracked ribs, he held her and patiently waited for the drugs to kick in, gently stroking her arm until she finally quieted.

Held safely in his arms, comfortable and tucked in, she drifted off to sleep.

Oddly content, an exhausted Channion did the same.

Chapter 16

CHANNION AWOKE JUST AFTER seven o'clock, still cradling a sleeping Raina in his arms. In the sunlight shining through her windows, he could see the dried tear stains still on her cheeks. She looked dead to the world. He'd felt her body twitch throughout the night, probably from bad dreams.

Exhausted, he wanted to stay there, but he knew he had work to do. It was time to get up and start his day. He dozed off instead.

When he awoke again, he checked his watch. It was almost ten. He rarely slept in this late! He immediately checked his phone for missed messages and was relieved at not seeing any. He sent his uncle a text to check in.

Glancing at the woman still sound asleep in his arms, he sighed. He hated to wake her up and if he moved, she most likely would. As carefully as he could, Channion slid out from under her, adjusting her head and shoulders on the pillows before he stood up. She barely stirred. He rubbed his stiff back and stretched a bit. Grabbing his gun and phone, he went upstairs. Making his way to the bathroom to get ready for the day, he let the hot water in the shower ease his tired muscles. He felt more alive when he got out.

When he came back downstairs, Raina was still sleeping soundly on the couch. He tried to keep quiet in the kitchen while he searched her refrigerator for something to eat. He decided to eat some of the lasagna from the restaurant as it just needed heated up. The microwave beep and the door closing didn't seem to bother her, he noticed. He sat at her little table beside the window, wondering while he ate if he should feed the horses for her. He decided against it, knowing she'd enjoy the task herself.

With the smell of food in the air, Raina woke up. Feeling disoriented, she had to think about where she was. When she realized she was home and on her couch, she stayed where she was and relished the feeling. When she heard movement nearby, her heart skipped a beat before it thudded hard in her chest. She wasn't alone. Cautiously looking over toward the noise, she saw Detective Scott walk back into the kitchen and heard water running in the sink.

Good grief! How did she forget he was staying with her? Now she felt stupid as the thought came to her that she awoke to the smell of cooking food. And food didn't cook itself.

She quickly looked to see what she was wearing as she normally didn't wear much when sleeping. She gave a quiet sigh of relief at seeing her longer nightshirt on. Last night, at least, she knew he was there, she thought wryly to herself. But nightgowns were hardly made of thick material, and now she worried about not having on a bra. He was still a complete stranger to her, and a male one at that.

Sitting up, she put on her glasses and just sat there. She pulled the throw over her bare legs as she tried to remember why she was on the couch and not in her own bed. It took her foggy brain a moment to recall the night before. When it all came back to her, she was mortified. How was she to face the detective now?

Channion was walking back to the little dining area when he saw Raina sitting up on the couch. He tried not to smile at her bed hair and ignored the smooth shoulder where her nightshirt had exposed it. But he did smile when he saw her absentmindedly petting the stuffed horse on her lap.

Walking over to her, he could see she was embarrassed. "Good morning. I figured you'd want to feed the kids so I didn't. How're you feeling?"

Raina felt like dirt and probably looked like it. Ignoring his question, she looked up at him and asked one of her own. "Did you make me eat more pills last night?"

"Yes. I had to hold you down and shove them in." At her surprised look, he shook his head. "I'm kidding."

"Oh."

"But I did have you take more. Just a few. You needed them."

"Did you sleep here on the couch with me?"

"You wouldn't let me leave. What was I supposed to do?" he asked, grinning.

"I didn't order you to sleep with me." After a split second, she asked, "Did I?" She sounded appalled.

Channion laughed. "No. But you did need some comfort. Since I was here, I was more than happy to be there for you." He turned serious as he studied her. "How're you feeling now?"

"Better. Thank you."

"Do your headaches come on hard like that all the time? You were in some pain. Do your doctors know?"

"Three yeses there. But last night's was a doozy all right. It must've been worse than usual because of being home or something. Stress of not working, having bills needing paid, missing road trips and singing gigs, being in possible danger, and having a cop sleeping in the next room for possible protection. There are so many things to choose from right now." She ran her hands through her hair.

"So you just take Tylenol? That's it?"

"Yep. There's not much else they could give me. Thankfully, I'm not drugged up on something addictive." She needed to use the bathroom, but she didn't want to stand up in front of him in her nightgown. She couldn't believe she was feeling shy in her own home.

Channion looked out the window. The sun was up, and he could see the sparkling dew on her grass that was still in partial shade. It needed to be mowed. They'd get to that, he supposed. Thankfully, he'd done his own grass a few days earlier.

Looking back at her, he said, "Well, I'm going to work on some things I brought with me. If you need anything, I'll be at your table... If that's okay?"

She nodded and stood up as soon as he walked away. She headed upstairs, using the railing for balance. Once she was dressed, she was feeling more confident and relaxed. She ate some eggs and toast and drank some water to wash down the Tylenol. Excited she was home and back with her kids, she headed out to the barn with an armed Channion. She fed them, happily talking to them as she did. After a bit, she asked if she had time to brush them.

Channion nodded, letting her do everything he sensed she needed to do. "Do whatever you want. I'm sure they'd love your attention. I can tell by how sweet they are that you spend time with them. Enjoy being home. There's no rush."

Horses were excellent therapists, he thought. Being with them was the absolute best thing for her right now.

He sat on the lone plastic lawn chair in the aisle, his legs stretched out. He rested his head against the Mexican blanket she had hanging on the wall and closed his eyes. He adjusted his gun and holster, linked his hands over his flat belly and got comfortable. He heard the radio playing in the background, and her quiet voice talking as she brushed her horses. He heard the horses blow through their noses as they ate their hay, and the water running in their automatic waterers when they drank.

Content, he sighed.

Raina smoothed every little hair she could find to brush on her horses. Being physically impaired, it took longer but neither she nor her kids cared at all. She ran her hands over their glossy coats with pleasure. She took her time combing their manes and tails while they munched their way through their piles of hay, occasionally turning their heads to look back at her as if to make sure it was really her.

She glanced at the detective again as he rested in the chair. He'd gotten up and looked around a few times, searching for anything that seemed off. While she appreciated him doing that, it also unnerved her.

Preparing to clean Rodeo's hoof, she gently tapped his leg with her fingers. The sorrel gelding obediently lifted his leg for her as he chewed a mouthful of hay. Neither her head nor her ribs liked being in that bent position, so she decided no more hooves were to be cleaned until she healed more. Tossing the hoof pick into her grooming caddy, she glanced again at her bodyguard.

"You awake?"

He immediately opened his eyes. "Yeah. Just resting."

"Can you help me clean their stalls? I think I can do it, but I'm not supposed to."

"Of course." Channion got up to get the wheelbarrow and manure fork.

She could tell he'd been keeping up with them as it only took one wheelbarrow load for both stalls. Since the doors were open to the pasture, the horses spent most of their time outside anyway. He took a bale of sawdust, splitting it between the two stalls. She was grateful for that as she needed to conserve it.

"I'll need to get more sawdust soon. But it might have to wait since I'm not working. And I'll need to pay for delivery now since I don't have my truck." That thought, another financial worry, had just come to her.

"Don't worry about that right now." He knew they needed to tell her about moving them all out soon. He wondered if he should just tell her now. He decided against it so she could enjoy the moment.

"Thanks for helping out," she said as Aspen blew on her cheek. She ran her hand down his warm, sleek neck. Clean stalls and happy horses made her sigh in simple happiness.

"You're welcome." He watched as her horse blew on her cheek and saw her smile.

She got some peppermints and walked back over to her horses. Grinning, she placed one of the wrapped candies in the detective's hand as she passed by him. "For a job well done."

Channion unwrapped it. "There were *two* stalls..."

"That mint has *two* colors..." But she handed him another mint with a smile when he laughed.

Answering his ringing phone, Channion watched her as he talked.

Feeding Aspen first since he was closer, she held her hand flat and felt the gelding gently take the mint from her hand with his velvety lips. She listened to the mint being crunched in his teeth before doing the same to Rodeo, who at the sound of the crinkling wrapper had quickly left his hay and stretched out his neck to her, impatiently waiting his turn.

Aspen nickered at Channion, then looked back at Raina, his eyes beseeching her for more. His long neck reached out toward her, clearly wanting more of the sticky candy. He nickered again, demanding another treat. Popping one in her own mouth, she grinned at the fact everyone in the barn was now eating candy.

Obligingly, she repeated the process again with her kids. She smiled as the two horses crunched loudly. She let Rodeo lick her hand, knowing he was looking for every last taste of peppermint he could get. Aspen nickered at her, so she walked over to him to let him lick her other hand. That was the only way she knew to convince her kids that the candy was all gone. "Blackjack dealer's hands," she'd tell people. Once they saw her empty hands, they accepted it and went along their merry way.

"Was that your uncle?" she asked when he hung up.

"Yeah. He wants to talk to you at the station whenever we're ready. We don't even have to go in today since your rest is most important."

He watched her pet her horses on their necks as they blew their now-minty breath in her face. He watched her smile and blow back into their noses. She ran their silky forelocks through her one good hand a few times. Both horses seemed to be truly enjoying all of the attention.

Looking his way, she replied, "Okay. Well, let me get cleaned up. I'll make my shower a quick one... or try to. I'm moving a bit slower right now." She pet her horses on their necks again, telling them goodbye and kissing them on their muzzles. "I'll need to change my bandage on my hand too. I've gotten it pretty dirty."

He pet the horses himself. "There's no need to rush. Take as long of a shower as you want. You're supposed to be resting anyway, so take your time." He didn't add he could tell she was hurting and the shower might do her good.

As he walked with her back to the house, his eyes looked in every direction for anything suspicious.

After she carefully took a long shower, brushed her teeth, put the cream on her sores, brushed her hair and got dressed again, she was in pain. They ate some of the restaurant food in her little dining room for a small lunch. He had cake for dessert. She had four Tylenol.

Debating, she finally said, "I can't put the cream on my back sores... Can you? I guess a female officer would be better for it, but..."

He hesitated for a split second. "I suppose I'm a professional and can handle it."

They went upstairs to the bathroom. She handed him the anti-scarring cream and turned around. "They're mainly near my shoulders, I think. You can probably just pull down my tank top to reach them... It's loose... Or lift it up... I guess I have to trust you..." She knew she was blushing.

Channion nodded. "You can." He tugged down her top and immediately noticed the bruises. "Do they hurt?" he asked as he smeared the cream on the sores. He noticed she got goosebumps when the cold cream touched her skin.

"Not as much now. They're tender but not painful."

"I think I see some that are lower... I'll need to lift up the bottom to reach them." She nodded.

When he was finished, he placed the tube on the counter. "You're all set."

"Thank you."

"You're welcome. I'll put it on your tab and bill you later."

She smiled at him when she turned around. He washed his hands as she walked out.

He'd unloaded the plants and the balloons she'd kept from the hospital as she showered. Ready now, they locked up the house and headed into town. Although Channion told her they could wait, she felt it was better to get it over with.

She kept her eyes closed as they made their way toward the crime scene. She just wasn't up to seeing it in daylight yet. It'd happen sooner or later, but at the moment, she preferred later. Channion understood and made small talk as he drove. She knew when they were there because his talking slowed down as he surveyed the site. She equally knew when they were past it because his talking resumed to normal. He got another phone call. She listened to the one-sided conversation as they sped along.

After he hung up, he said, "We want to go over a few things with you and give you a rundown on what's what. We want to keep it all official, so we prefer to do it at the station. We'll try to keep you from getting too much attention there, but the fact is, there are some who will want to thank you." He glanced at her. She was looking out the windshield. "Are you comfortable with people coming up to you?"

"I guess. I'd prefer to not be the center of attention... Do I look okay? I mean... These scabs all over me—"

"Are temporary," Channion interrupted. "They're marks of your courage and bravery. Be proud of them, not embarrassed."

She nodded as she tucked her hair behind her ear. She adjusted the air vent blowing on her. "Now that I can think a bit more, I'm scared it's all going to come crashing down on me and I'm..."

"You're what?"

She built up her courage to voice her fears and concerns. She could trust Detectives Scott and Kramer, she knew that, but voicing them would take her one step closer to accepting that all that'd happened actually *did* happen. And worse, she knew she didn't even remember all of it because she had gaps in her memory.

"I'm beyond scared. I'm scared of that moment when it all comes back to me, and I'm faced with the horror of it. Dr. Benson told me as my mind healed there's a chance I'll remember a lot more than I have so far.

"I'm scared to realize that there was a really good reason why I was in the hospital. And in such bad shape I still don't know what I looked like when I arrived there. Now that I've seen my face and back over the past couple of days, I can't imagine what I looked like before, or how I got that way.

"I'm scared one day I'll be alone and have a panic attack. I've heard about people having something like that happening to them. Or what if it happens in public? What if I'm sleeping and have nightmares? What if I start jumping at shadows?" Her voice cracked, and she turned to look out the side window.

Channion didn't say a word. He knew she needed someone to just listen. He waited for her to get her composure back.

She spoke softly, "I'm scared my life as I knew it is over, and I'll be forever changed in ways I don't even know yet. I'm even scared that people may put me up on some sort of a pedestal so high that I'll become paranoid about falling off, disappointing everyone who finds out I'm just a person. That I'm just me. That I'm not a superhero but just a regular human trying to make a living. And that I'm not perfect."

She was quiet for a moment before she felt she could speak again. "And I don't want people to think I'm all sorts of brave because I saved Bryce. It's not like I drew up a plan and was brave enough to execute it. I have a feeling that what I did, it was purely a spur-of-the-moment, once-in-a-lifetime thing. That doesn't make me brave, especially because I survived it. It makes me lucky."

She wiped her hands on her shorts. She summed up her worries when she whispered, "I'm scared of not knowing what else to be scared of."

Channion understood. Seeing a spot ahead to pull over, he slowed down and brought the car to a smooth stop. He put it in *park* and turned to look at her. He gently turned her face to look at his. She was so vulnerable at that moment. He could see it in her eyes, and how she was withdrawing into herself right in front of him. That worried him as he knew it was probably the worst thing she could possibly do. She needed to stay open to others and life, but he understood she was scared of the unknown and having to bare her soul to a virtual stranger.

He looked into her eyes while he spoke, "Raina, what you did *was* spectacularly amazing. Don't you ever forget that you alone are responsible for saving another person's life. That *was* brave! You obviously had it inside of you to do because you did it... And with no thought about yourself. Maybe it *was* the only time in your life that you'll do it, but the fact is, Raina, you *did* do it!

"Bryce Mitchell is a beloved son and brother, a nephew, a grandson, a friend, a brother-in-arms to me. A human. *You* were there when he needed someone more than he needed anyone at *any* other time in his life. Was it coincidence? Was it God putting you there specifically at that moment? Who can say?

"If people put you on a pedestal, it's because you already earned your spot on it. But I understand your fears of people wanting, or expecting, you to be the perfect human being. With time, the craze will lessen when people find something else to latch onto. And there's *always* something new for people to latch onto.

"But I also think worrying about what others think of you is a waste of time because, truth be told, they seldom are. *They're* already worrying about what others are thinking of *them*. That's how it all balances out in some respects.

"There are a whole lot of us who will never forget what you did. To know that out among all the criminals, all the crazies, all the ungrateful, judgmental people we deal with on a daily basis, the slanted, relentless media, the politics... To know there's still at least one true, honest person for us to fight for is beyond great. You're the kind of person that made me want to join the force to protect." He rubbed her chin with his thumb. Her tears fell down her cheeks and landed on his hand.

"I won't lie and say you won't have some difficult times still coming your way. You will. Accept that as fact now. I won't ever lie to you if I can help it. But you must remember you're not alone.

"Raina, don't ever forget you have lots of support to draw on, to lean on. I want you to know you can *always* come to me or my uncle when you need someone to talk to, for someone to just listen to you, to help you when it's needed.

"Don't be afraid, or too proud, to ask for that help when you need it. *Don't* try to do this alone. I know you'd prefer a close friend or family member to talk to, but this is an ongoing case, so we need you to not talk to others about it at all, you understand? We can find you a professional to speak with, if you prefer. We can set that up. And honestly, we probably should for your mental and emotional health. That's your decision though.

"*If* you have nightmares or panic attacks, we can deal with those. They'll most likely pass on their own with time. But being prepared, knowing that they *can* happen makes you stronger already to deal with them. Okay?"

At her nod, he continued, "And if you disappoint people, don't worry about it. We all do, sooner or later, because not even one among us is perfect. Even when we try our absolute hardest, we're bound to disappoint someone. Sometimes even ourselves. It's just a fact of life." He patted her knee.

"You'll be fine, Raina, but it *will* take some time. No one knows how much, but it will. I suspect you're going to feel like you're on a rollercoaster. But remember, you're already tough, resilient, and intelligent. You're more courageous than anyone I've ever known, but you are *still* a human like the rest of us."

She nodded. "Thank you. I just don't want to disappoint anyone. To know there is someone I can talk to, who understands maybe what I'm going through, is a relief. And I'd appreciate it more if they aren't a professional shrink who will charge me an arm and a leg just to talk to them. They'd probably just twist everything I say into something else anyway and have me committed."

She looked at him and said in a quivering voice, "But I'm still afraid of the unknown. I don't think there's anything to help me with that."

"Who *isn't* afraid of the unknown? To some extent, everyone is. Embrace it as a challenge to overcome, not an obstacle that will stop you, beat you down. What's that saying, something about the only thing to fear is fear itself? We can face it together, and then step outside of that fear to work it out to get to a point where you can move on.

"I'd be lying if I said your life will go back to being the same. It won't. You're probably going to have more awareness of things now. You may have the jitters, but you may not. No one stays the same throughout the entirety of life because all lives change at some point from, or for, an infinite number of causes. You're still in the same boat as me and everyone else. Don't be thinking you're all *that* special because you're not. Okay?"

Raina nodded, a small smile on her face at his last comment. She understood what he was saying. And she truly appreciated his slice of humor to help her cope.

Channion patted her knee again. Putting his car back into *drive*, he checked the road and drove forward. "You'll be fine. Remember you're not alone. Not anymore."

Chapter 17

SHE GOT MOBBED AT the police station. They stopped at the front desk to get her a Visitor's Badge, and that's all it took. She had her good hand shook, shoulders patted, and told so many times of the other officers' appreciation, she could only smile and nod. She accepted and was honored at their appreciation. She was also overwhelmed.

Channion finally steered her toward the elevator and once the doors closed, he studied her closely. She looked a little shell-shocked, but otherwise, she was holding up.

With an unexpected smile, she asked, "They don't think I'm going to remember their names, do they?"

He smiled and shook his head. "If they're in uniform, it's on their name badge so that'll help you. But I doubt any of them expect you to recall their names from just one, brief meeting."

She asked to go to the ladies' room before meeting with Ron, so he showed her where the restrooms were located. She needed a moment to prepare herself too. Walking back out, she followed him through a maze of desks and walled offices. It took a while because she kept getting stopped by more officers. She was relieved when she spotted Ron at his desk. He smiled and stood up when he spotted her and his nephew walking toward him.

"Miss Stewart, you look ravishing, as usual." He offered her a chair.

"And I always had this image in my head of LEOs being the truthful sort," she said, straight-faced. She sat down, putting her spare purse from her closet in her lap.

"We have our moments," he said with a smile and a twinkle in his eyes. He spotted another detective coming over and glanced at Raina. When the man stopped and stared down at her, Ron made the introductions. "Raina Stewart, this is Detective Luke Reinhold."

Luke couldn't help but be impressed. He'd had no idea of what the woman who saved Bryce looked like, but he certainly wasn't expecting what he was seeing. She was certainly attractive even with the scabs and bruises on her face. He guessed she'd be a knockout once she was healed.

"I know you've been through a lot, and you're here today for a reason, Miss Stewart, but I wanted to stop by and meet you in person. And to thank you for what you did for Bryce.

"I've heard so much about you that I just had to meet you myself. I'm glad I did. It's not often we get to meet a hero who's a civilian. Especially one who's as attractive as you are."

If he was expecting her to give him permission to use her first name or thank him for his comments, Raina didn't care. His eyes roamed over her from head to toe for the second time, immediately making her bristle inside.

She instantly pegged him as a flirt and a womanizer. And a disrespectful creep. Besides his sharp style of dress, he had this air about him that made him come across as a ladies' man. She didn't mind them usually—but that didn't mean she could stand them either.

Besides, to her way of thinking, her being attractive shouldn't weigh in at all on saving another human's life. Not to mention she was anything *but* attractive in her present condition. But what set her off was his flagrant manner of looking her up and down, not even bothering to disguise what his thoughts most likely were.

Now quite annoyed, she was trying to tamp down her feelings. Not feeling well made her feel even more irritable... and far more quickly. Before she could stop her own mouth, she heard herself say in a voice filled with annoyance, "You just remarked you think I'm attractive. What if I was an ugly civilian hero? Would you still think the same of me for saving Bryce? Do you think he'd even care?"

Both irritated at his manner, Ron and Channion waited to see how Luke would respond. He was certainly thrown off balance since using his smile and giving smooth compliments usually won over women fairly easily. A handsome man in uniform, or dressed in the expensive shirts and slacks as he normally was, tended to make favorable impressions on women. And Luke used this to his advantage. Often.

While irritated, Channion was also fascinated at her reaction to Luke. She looked like a cautious cat, ready to hiss and strike, hair standing up on end. He leaned back in his chair and simply watched to see what would happen next.

Luke sent her his broad smile—one that looked patronizing to her—and replied, "Well, of course I would still think the same of you. It's just a bonus, that's all." He even placed his hand on her shoulder.

Instinctively, she leaned to the side, away from his hand. He immediately removed it, sensing she wasn't comfortable being touched. He should've known better than to touch her without permission, but he did it anyway. It was partially just a natural action. Partially.

Coolly, Raina replied, "Personally, I don't see what difference it'd make at all."

"I guess it doesn't. Not really."

"Then why bring it up in the first place?" Raina snapped, not backing down at all. She obviously wasn't intimidated by a police officer, as many were. "When I met the Mitchell family, incredibly not a single one mentioned my looks. They seemed far more genuinely concerned about my health, and if I'd live."

Luke had the distinct impression Miss Stewart wasn't the average woman who liked being complimented on her looks. If anything, she seemed to *dislike* it. Maybe she was self-conscious due to her scabs and bruising, he thought.

"Our families go way back, so I can say they're certainly a genuine family. And I'm sure they're concerned for you as much as Bryce." Luke looked at Ron and Channion, who were simply watching. "I know you have work to do, so I'll leave you alone now. It was nice to meet you, Miss Stewart."

They watched him as he walked away. He stopped, turned, and said to Raina, almost as an afterthought, "By the way, I'm sure if you asked Bryce, he'd approve of the bonus too." Luke grinned back at her as he walked away again.

"Very well done, Raina," Ron said with approval. "Luke *was* patronizing you, and you stomped him. You let him know you weren't impressed. He's a talented detective, and he can be a good friend. But as a heads-up, he does enjoy the ladies if you know what I mean. You don't seem the type who'd fall for his charm, but I feel obligated to warn you."

She nodded. "Yeah, I picked up on that immediately. He's probably not a bad sort but is a major flirt in general. But he's also in a professional position, and he should know he can't ogle women with those lustful eyes of his. It's beyond disrespectful, degrading, and unflattering.

"If he's going to go around eyeing women like pieces of meat, he needs to carry around inspector stickers so we know if we passed his inspection or not. I'd rather shove them up his..." Raina caught herself and shut up.

Both detectives smiled at her angry jab at their co-worker. She had a temper, Channion thought, surprisingly pleased. She wasn't weak and had spirit. She'd need it, he decided.

She felt her blood still simmering as she added, "Those types of men are usually looking for one thing from a woman, and I don't happen to be one of them. You can tell him that the next time you all meet in the locker room. I resent being looked upon like a piece of fresh meat.

"For the record, if *he* were assigned to my case, I'd absolutely have demanded a female officer on my protection detail. Probably more than one."

Both men appreciated her honesty and smiled genuinely. Neither could fault her feelings, truth be told. Frankly, they agreed with her.

Ron got serious. "Okay, this is the way I'm seeing this play out. I feel you need to know what's happening, and we can do so to some extent. I also see that with all the looks still being shot our way, we're going to be less than comfortable and private out here. Son," he said to Channion, "let's go to the conference room for some privacy." He grabbed some files and stood up.

The three of them walked through the maze of desks, down a hallway that'd been re-tiled fairly recently and into a small conference room. Raina's hands began to sweat as she waited for the two officers to get settled in across from her.

Ron said, "This is all confidential. We both feel we can trust you in this matter. Are we misplacing our faith in you, Raina? Or can we trust you with what we're about to tell you?"

"Yes, absolutely. You can trust me. And I'll help you in any way I can, if you need me to."

He nodded. "Okay. What we have here is a huge can of worms. As it turns out, Deputy Mitchell ended up pulling over a man who has links to weapons smuggling and sales, both domestically and internationally. Now, we never had a whole lot that was concrete on him so we never arrested him. Or rather, never got him indicted.

"When Deputy Mitchell ran this guy when he pulled over his car, my guess is all of the information wasn't relayed to him. From what we've recently gathered, dispatch simply didn't have verified information to pass on to Bryce to warn him of who he'd pulled over. He also had more than one alias.

"In reality, it wouldn't have mattered since the guy apparently had some friends just down the road, of all things. Obviously, there's no way any of us could've known that. For what reason they were there, at that particular time, we don't know yet for certain. Only guesses at this point.

"The man who was killed that day was a small fish, maybe medium-sized. We want the *big* fish that thinks the world is his personal ocean. What you—"

"I killed a man, didn't I?" Raina interrupted, softly. She was stunned that it hadn't really occurred to her before this moment. Being in the hospital herself was enough of a distraction, and her memory was only beginning to come back. But she did recall that. "I mean... not on purpose. Not really... He could've gotten out of the way, but it *was* my truck... Would it be smart of me to get a lawyer? I think I should get one. But I can't afford one..."

Panic began to well up inside her, and it showed on her face. "Am I going to get sued by... by his family? Am I going to prison? I was only trying to save Bryce's life... To just give him a fighting chance to protect himself... I didn't know I'd..."

Ron quickly stopped her rising panic by laying his hand firmly on hers. With his other hand, he grabbed her chin and made her look directly at him. Tears were welling up in her panic-stricken eyes.

He said firmly, "Breathe... Let it out slowly. Take a deep breath. Again." When she did, he went on, "Raina, we aren't planning on sending you to prison. No one is."

"But—"

"No. If you want a lawyer, you can always get one. But there's no need at this point. What we're talking about right now, it's just between us. It's okay. We aren't looking to file charges against the woman who saved an officer's life from three would-be, cold-blooded murderers, and who almost died herself in doing so."

Long minutes passed. Both men gave her time to get her emotions back under control to be able to think clearly. She finally nodded, letting them know they could continue.

Ron resumed where he'd left off. "As I was saying, the man who was killed was a link to another, bigger man. That's our theory, anyway, but we have a good foundation for it being true—"

"I'm sorry," Raina quietly interrupted again.

"For what?" Ron asked.

"For killing someone you needed to find the big fish. I mean, it wouldn't have mattered, I still would've..." *rammed him with my truck?* "... done what I did to save Bryce. I'm just sorry I screwed up your chances to get the one you really want."

She now looked so forlorn and apologetic, they didn't know what to say to her.

Channion said, "In the end, you probably helped us eliminate a bad guy. And, more than likely, saved a whole lot of lives down the road. Ones that we'd maybe never know about. Quite possibly, even more law enforcement officers were saved by what you did. Think of it that way."

Ron agreed. "Yes, Raina. That's an excellent way to look at it. We still have more to go on, and the fact is, we got both of their cars thanks to your spontaneous actions!"

"What was so special about their cars? Were they stolen?"

Ron smiled. "The cars themselves? Nothing. It was what these guys had *in* the cars that has us all excited and working around the clock!"

Channion took over. "When you disabled both of their cars, you inadvertently gave us a whopping amount of evidence and leads to go on." Smiling, he added, "We can't thank you enough."

Chapter 18

SHE SAT THERE, DUMBFOUNDED. "Are you saying those cars were full of what? Guns? Ammo? Stuff like that?" They both nodded their heads in unison. She was momentarily speechless. "*I* did that?"

The detectives laughed. Ron replied, "You sure did. Lots of what was recovered we've been tracing from different sources and areas. Some of it we've been looking for... well, for quite a while. And you come along and hand it to us."

"I'd say you owe me another nice dinner."

Ron agreed, saying, "I think we can do that." He got somber again. "We've been able to trace some of this evidence. We've been in contact with other police stations and agencies scattered just about everywhere. The ATF agents are working with us to—"

"ATF?" She couldn't believe it. "This really *is* serious, isn't it?"

Channion nodded his head solemnly. "Quite serious. They have more resources than we do, so we're handing over most of what we've got. Since many of the weapons we traced cross state lines, that makes it their jurisdiction more than ours. Theirs and the FBI. But *we're* mainly coordinating with just the ATF office, and *they're* partnering with the FBI on their end.

"However, because of this particular situation, Bryce being an officer we know who got shot, and you being there, well, they're asking us to continue to assist them in any way we can. They want us to hand over everything we have. There's a little issue with this as the one thing we refuse to hand over to them is you. We'll simply pass on anything you give us. It's a joint operation that as of now is running along smoothly."

He paused, looking at her and gauging her mood before saying, "And we're hoping we can get some more information from you. Is there anything else you've remembered that you can tell us, Raina? Anything that you thought maybe wasn't important so you dismissed it?"

She shook her head. "No. I swear if I think of anything, I will for sure tell you. Dr. Benson said some things may come back to me as my head heals, so maybe later…" She trailed off, thinking. "But he also told me in many cases, with a concussion as bad as I got, the person simply can't remember what gave it to them. Pieces here and there, maybe?"

Ron nodded. "We in no way want to risk your life, or your health, in asking for any help you can give us, Raina. Our main concern, besides your healing, is your safety. We don't know for sure if this man will want to tie up any and all loose ends."

She immediately understood what he wasn't saying. "By that you mean, *kill* me? I'm a witness now. As well as being a woman who not only killed one of his men but handed the police department, ATF, *and* FBI carloads of his weapons and ammo…" Her voice understandingly shook. "*Of course* he'll want to kill me! I would if I were in his shoes. Wouldn't *you?*"

Raina had a million thoughts racing through her mind. A new thought jumped in, stopping all the rest. "*Bryce!* They'd for sure go for the officer who started this whole thing, wouldn't they? What about him? If this is as big as you're telling me, wouldn't they want to get him too?"

They respected her even more in that instant. It was apparent she was coming to grips with the fact she was now possibly in serious danger, and the first thing she asked about was the safety of the injured and helpless officer.

Channion said, "We already have a protection detail with him. We need to keep this all confidential, Raina. For the safety of everyone, we all need to keep our mouths shut, and our eyes and ears open. Can you do that?"

She nodded. *What* had she gotten herself into?

Channion said, "Normally we wouldn't tell a victim or a witness too much about a case they're involved in. However, we have permission with you. The main reason for that is because it's your safety, your life, at risk. We feel it's better for a person to know what the situation is rather than shielding them from the truth. You seem to have natural instincts, so knowing something could still happen can help keep you more aware."

Trying to come to terms with what she was hearing, she said, "I appreciate that. I'd like to think I'd react more quickly under some sort of an attack if I knew I should, you know?"

Both detectives nodded before looking at each other.

Channion said, "The biggest thing on our minds right now besides your recovery is your safety. We don't know whether or not the head of this thing knows about you, your name, or where you live. We don't know his... But that doesn't mean he doesn't know yours. We need to take extra precautions. As such, we have a number of options."

When he paused, Raina said, "I probably won't like where this is going, so just tell me what they are."

"One, you can go into protective custody with a full detail and be moved from the area for an indefinite time while we work the case. Two, you can move to a new location, meaning another state, that no one knows about. Basically, starting over elsewhere. This isn't foolproof as your name would remain the same."

He paused. She waited.

"And...?" she finally prodded.

"Three, you can stay here and basically become part of both Ron and I. We've already received the official approval to do this. It got cleared earlier today, as a matter of fact. In essence, we become each other's shadows. Anywhere you go, one or both of us go, and vice versa. It's safer to have two guards minimum, but we can go down to one at times to draw less attention, depending on other options we'll get to in a minute."

She looked out the window while she thought it through. "But that means I can't work until this is solved, right? Or are you thinking I still can? Surely you two can't simply take off every time I need to give a lesson, or go to work at the bar, or go on the road to perform. I *have* to work!

"Sure, I have savings but not *that* much! And I'll have all of those insurance deductibles to pay. And I'll need another truck as soon as the insurance check comes in. Plus, I have normal, everyday bills, and my kids to feed.

"Option one is only good if you actually solve the case—and quickly. Based on what Ron said, you guys haven't been able to get enough to even indict anyone... The implication being years! So I don't see that option even being one.

"Option two... If the big fish guy *does* know who I am and my information, moving is just geography. I'm sure he'd just send someone to finish me off. Unless I went into Witness Protection and everything is new for me, this isn't a solid option. And what about Bryce? What will *he* have to do?

"Option three is I stay here. I still work, with you guys tagging along... *How* exactly do you expect any one of these options to work?" She was feeling overwhelmed, and she fought to keep the tears from her eyes as she felt the stress hit her in her gut.

They couldn't sugarcoat the situation, so Channion simply agreed. "I didn't say it was going to be easy. We'll have to work out schedules the three of us can live with and work around. With the ATF handling a lot of the load now, it actually frees up Ron and I to protect you.

"The biggest issue we have to deal with soon are your horses. We know of some people who can take them indefinitely. They're extremely trustworthy and love animals. They live out in the country a couple of hours from here. They have a nice barn and fenced pastures already because they sometimes have cattle. Two horses wouldn't be a bother for them. Aspen and Rodeo will be safe there. They also won't charge you for board—just for their feed and care, like for a blacksmith."

She nodded. Her heart broke at the thought of sending her horses to a stranger just so she could leave the house. Not only did *she* need a babysitter now, but so did her *horses!*

He was relieved she agreed so readily. He didn't think she'd chance her horses' safety over her pride, but he knew she hated being away from them too. "Consider it done. We'll set it up to move them within the next couple days so you can spend some time with them first, all right? They have a truck, but is it okay to use your horse trailer so it's not there either? You can take all of your tack over there too."

She nodded again, tears glistening in her eyes.

Leaning forward, Channion covered her hand with his in comfort for a moment. Quietly, he said, "It's safer if they aren't there. I know you love them and look forward to seeing them every day, but it's a routine going back and forth to the barn twice or more daily. If you're being watched, it'd give them a perfect opportunity for a shot. There's no cover between the house and the barn. And cleaning the stalls? Pushing a wheelbarrow repeatedly back and forth outside? We *need* to move them, Raina. And we need to move you, too, as soon as possible."

Her heart skipped a beat just thinking about it. "But what if I'm *not* being watched? We could go through all of this hassle for no reason at all. And for how long?"

"I can't answer that. It could be for nothing, or it could be for everything. It's better to play it safe. We also think it's better for you to leave your place for a few other reasons." He waited for her to object, but she didn't make a sound as she looked at him.

"One, you're so far out. If something were to happen, help is far away... As you've already experienced. We'd be cut off. Secondly, you have no alarm system for protection... especially at night when sleeping. Even having a guard on, that's not always enough. Staying there, we'd need two or three guards for round-the-clock security so the others can sleep. Thirdly, finding where you live would be a piece of cake if they get your name. A layman could do it—and these are professionals.

"And if they find out your name, you have your website for them to go to. And that has your personal information, and I assume, some photos on it?"

"Yes, but my personal address isn't listed. I got a box for business mail. I've never used my home address for business as I was taught that was unsafe. My website is an effective tool to have, but there's limited personal information on it. Many of my students here are from word-of-mouth, but I need my website too. Everyone checks for websites nowadays!"

Raina felt her insides tense up as it all began sinking in, as realization struck home. She looked from Ron, who hadn't added anything yet to this conversation, back to Channion. "In essence, what you're telling me is that the decision has already *been* made. But you're trying to let me feel like *I'm* the person making one of those three choices the correct one, probably to let me feel in some control of my own life?"

She was quick, they had to give her that.

Channion nodded, leaned forward, his elbows on the table. "I'm sorry, Raina. But this is a serious situation. These are professional criminals. What you did was lead us right to them—at the very least a lot closer. We doubt they're going to just let it go. While they seemed to have made some critical errors that day, that doesn't mean they're sloppy the rest of the time.

"If what our leads are telling us is true, this organization has been around for a long, long time. That means it's been run professionally. We don't know what made these guys do what they did that day. To us, it seems completely out of character.

"None of us want to make you move, even temporarily, but we'd prefer to be safe than sorry. I'd rather play it safe because if that 'sorry' part came, there may be no coming back from it." He added softly, "I don't know how I could live with that. Especially if it'd been in my power, even in the smallest way, to prevent it."

She understood immediately what he was saying. If indeed she was in danger, she was easy pickings for professional criminals. She wouldn't be given a chance of living through another attack. She'd be snuffed out like the flame on a candle. And there'd be no coming back from that.

With Detectives Kramer or Scott with her, they'd be in danger too. How could she live with herself knowing they got injured, or even killed, just because she didn't want to move from her house?

She realized her best bet to protect these two officers was to pick any option *except* number three. If she were put in Witness Protection, could she handle giving up her entire life? Her friends? Would she be able to keep her horses? Although it wasn't said as an option, she was positive it was on the table. Maybe as a last resort.

Slowly, she nodded that she understood. "But what about the lessons I give?"

"If you choose option three and stay, you can still give the lessons—but only at the studio. No more home lessons, mainly because you won't be there. We can have help from ATF for surveillance and undercover security pretty much anywhere we go with you. We want only a limited amount of trusted people in our circle to help prevent leaks. If we learn something new as we go along and need to stop the lessons? Trust me, we will."

"And singing on the weekends at Picacho's? And rehearsing with the band I sing with?"

"The same. You'll be guarded, but no one will be the wiser. We'll figure out a cover story." He answered her before she could ask the next question, saying, "Same when you need to go on the road.

"Frankly, going on the road may be the safest bet. There's less routine to it, dates are mixed up, locations, venues. It's harder to plan an attack that way. You need to remove any information in regards to upcoming trips from your website until we get this cleared up. You'll just need to market yourself in the area you're going to."

He knew this was risky business for her. This was how she made her living, and it all had to be curtailed for her safety. Could it work? What if they already knew her, had already checked her website? They could already know her schedule. They could also just Google her name and upcoming events would probably pop up.

This not knowing what the criminals could already know was the hardest—and most dangerous—aspect of his job.

Ron finally spoke. "Speaking of work, how soon do you think you're going to be able to begin working again? I think you still need to rest, but this is your decision."

She counted the days in her head. "It's been nine or ten days now, right? Let me try to schedule a few lessons for the next couple of days to test out my condition. I'm off this weekend from the bar. I do have scheduled performances fairly regularly over the next few months. I normally list them on my website, but I agree with you that I need to remove them."

Both detectives nodded in agreement.

Ron led her out of the room to an empty desk, showing her how to use the phones after she said she needed to at least *try* to work. She pulled her organizer from her purse before she called the studio to check in. Lorenzo Walsh, the owner, was relieved to hear from her and happy to have her coming back. They worked out the details with minimal fuss of her needing a full-time room.

Within a couple of hours, she had the next three days of work laid out. She set up just a few each day as tests. She made a copy of her schedule for the detectives. Walking over to their desks, she looked around for them. She'd seen them there earlier, but she didn't notice when they left.

She went to the restroom before returning to their desks to wait for them, wondering if she was going to make it out of this alive.

Chapter 19

RAINA'S HEAD WAS GOING to either explode or implode. She just wasn't sure which. At the moment, she didn't care since either one would theoretically end her suffering. She took three pills and washed them down with a cup of water she got at the water cooler. She wanted to take more but feared they'd make her sick with no food to take with them.

Sitting there trying to ignore her headache was useless. She blamed it on not getting much quality sleep, a messed up sleeping schedule for the past week or so, being in a wreck she'd deliberately caused, worrying about her horses, and the stress of being a witness to a criminal organization. And it simply could just be PMS too. A girl could only take so much.

When Ron and Channion returned, they looked pleased until they took a good look at her. Ron knew at once she was off. "Are you all right, Raina? You don't look to be feeling well."

Channion recognized the look on her face. He quickly squatted down to her level, asking quietly, "Scale one to ten...?"

She felt so miserable she couldn't even fake a reassuring smile for him. "Working its way toward nine."

"How many?"

"Three. I didn't want to risk throwing up..."

Standing up, he said, "Ron, I'll take her back to her place for tonight. She needs to rest where she feels comfortable. I'll call you later to check in."

Ron nodded. He helped Raina stand up, handing her the purse she'd placed on the floor. "You go on home now and rest. Doctor's orders."

"I gave you both a copy of my schedule." She pointed to the piece of paper on Ron's desk. "I left another copy on yours," she said to Channion.

Seeing it, he folded it up and slipped it into his pocket. "Let's get you home."

In the parking garage, he led her to a police truck instead of the car. At her questioning glance, he answered, "I think a truck will be much easier for you to get in and out of. The car's too low for you with your injuries, so I asked them to switch me over to the truck. There weren't any available SUVs, otherwise we would've gotten one of those. You were just the excuse I needed to put in the request with a reasonable hope it'd go through quickly."

Despite her raging headache, Raina was deeply touched that the detective was that thoughtful. He was correct. The car *was* difficult and painful for her to manage. He'd obviously noticed and immediately did something about it. "Thank you. This *will* be much easier."

Opening her door, he helped her in.

BY THE TIME THEY got to her house, Raina had dozed off. When he pulled to a stop in her driveway, once again facing out, he lightly shook her shoulder to rouse her. "Raina? We're home."

It took her a moment to get her bearings. He walked around to her door to help her out. She leaned against his truck for a moment, her balance being shaky due to her headache and fatigue. "Are you okay?" he asked.

"No balance yet, and I feel a bit nauseous. Gimme a sec..." She closed her eyes again, leaning her head back against the truck window.

Not sure what to do with her, he asked, "Can you make it into the house on your own, or do you want me to carry you?"

With her eyes still closed, she replied, "Carrying a woman into a house is usually a romantic thing. I'll walk and keep it professional."

He couldn't help but smile. She had grit. Grit and a sense of humor. He completely appreciated both.

Walking to the front door, his arm went around her waist when she leaned into him for support. He tightened his hold as she wasn't looking too good to him, loosening it only long enough to unlock her door and get them inside. He locked it after them, looking with a cop's glance to make sure nothing was out of place. He helped her up the stairs, worried she'd fall down them in her condition.

Channion returned to his truck to get his workload and set it up on her little dining room table. Concerned, he went upstairs to check on her. He found her flat on her back on her bed, her head turned toward the wall. There was a folded washcloth covering her forehead about to slide off. She hadn't even taken off her shoes.

He walked over to her, removed the damp washcloth, untied and removed her shoes, lining them up against the wall out of the way. He covered her with a blanket and wondered if she should be propped up more with the pillows. He decided to leave her be.

Taking the washcloth to the bathroom, he ran cold water over it, wrung it out, and headed back to her room. He placed it across her forehead again. He stood there and simply looked at her. She was out cold. He brushed his knuckles over her skin to wipe away drops of water that dripped from the washcloth, and then gently ran them over her cheek for himself.

Satisfied, he went back downstairs. He went out to her mailbox and gathered all her mail, placing it on her kitchen counter. Looking around her house, he tried to imagine where anyone could hide and lie in wait for either one of them. He made his way to the barn, giving some attention and mints to Aspen and Rodeo when they saw him and trotted over. He scouted the area from there. After he walked around her house, looking for any shoe prints or anything out of the ordinary, he went back inside.

He checked on her again, removing the cloth from her forehead. She hadn't moved a muscle. As an afterthought, he turned on the bathroom light in case she woke up when it was dark so she could see better.

Using her microwave to heat up some of the leftovers from their dinner the night before, he ate as he read reports. After he washed his dishes, he sat down at the table and got back to work.

IT WAS ALMOST TEN that night when Raina finally stirred. She opened her eyes, groggy and disoriented. She could see the light from the bathroom spilling into the hallway and slightly into her room. She rolled slowly to her side, saw the illuminated clock and looked again. She had slept for over five hours!

Gingerly getting up, she made her way to the bathroom. She vaguely wondered if he left the light on deliberately for her, or was he just one of those people who left lights on for no reason? Or did she forget to turn it off?

When she got downstairs, it was quiet and dark. Turning on a couple of lights, she saw the detective's folders on her table. She looked around for the detective but didn't see him. It wasn't until she walked around the couch that she found him.

Her heart turned over when she saw him stretched out on it, sound asleep. Gun still in his holster, his head was resting against a throw pillow. She saw the little stuffed horse was tucked beside him. She smiled and wondered if he did that on purpose. Or was it just still there from earlier, and he didn't care to move it?

Quietly, she sat in the chair, looking at him while she absorbed her new situation. Knowing she was leaving soon made her melancholy. How she loved this place! But she knew it wasn't worth the risk, not if what she was being told by professional policemen was true.

Channion had heard her come downstairs and could sense her presence in the room. He finally opened his eyes. "I already fed the kids."

When he started to get up, she shook her head. "Get some more sleep, Channion. It's okay. It's all quiet. If I hear or see anything, I'll come get you."

"You sure?"

"Yeah."

"Are you feeling better?"

"Yeah." She was touched he thought to ask her. "Go back to sleep."

He nodded and got comfortable again. He closed his eyes.

She got up and laid the throw over him. Knowing he had to be tired and needed to be sharp, she let him rest. She decided it was her turn to be the bodyguard.

Chapter 20

WORKING AGAIN AT LORENZO'S Music Studio was a blessing and a curse. The blessing was that she was relieved to be working again, assuming the music didn't cause her head to explode. The curse was when she walked in the door, everyone exclaimed in concern about her bruised and still-battered face.

She figured she'd have to explain her cover story every time a student came to her too. She'd been careful with her make-up, but it couldn't cover up everything. Thankfully, she had Channion there to help be a buffer to the endless questions.

Channion didn't want to be obviously guarding her as their general cover story was he was a friend just helping her out. He'd removed his side holster and strapped his guns to his ankles so his pants would cover them.

He sat at a desk in the adjoining room where he could see her through the shared door but also wouldn't be readily noticed. He was thankful it was an interior room with no windows to the outside. Once in a while, he'd put down his phone from reading the news to simply observe her.

Raina's first music lesson since she landed herself in the hospital, and then with a bodyguard, went well. Her student was a sweet one and easy to teach. She'd deliberately chosen her to be the test lesson. A little girl with a single parent dad, she was excited to learn how to play the piano. From the look on her face, she idolized Raina.

The second lesson went smoothly as well. This was a vocal lesson for a teenage girl who wanted to enter an annual school talent contest. Her mother had heard about Raina from a friend who heard her singing at the local country bar and suggested she contact the singer and see if she had any advice. Raina had told her to bring her daughter to the studio, and she'd see what she could do to help her out. The girl had a nice voice, but her lack of self-confidence was ruining it.

She'd been getting better every lesson though. Raina enjoyed working with her and hoped that after the talent show that'd happen in a few more days, she might keep coming in for lessons. It was helping the girl's self-confidence, and both her mom and Raina wanted to see that continue. Besides that, Raina seriously needed the income.

The first time Channion heard Raina sing he was in awe. Her voice had such a unique sound to it. He'd completely forgotten what he was reading on his phone the second she'd joined the teenager on a tough part of the song to help her get the rhythm correct. He just listened for the rest of the vocal lesson.

After the teenager left, Raina walked in and sat in the chair across from him. She set a bottle of cold water on the desk, careful to keep it away from his phone in case it spilled. Feeling a headache coming on, she took three pills.

"What're you doing here, Raina?"

She didn't know what he was referring to, and the confused look on her face told him so. "I told you. I need to work..."

He explained, "No. What are you doing *here*? Why aren't you out there with a recording contract making millions of dollars a show? Your talent is being wasted here!"

She looked sincerely surprised... and pleased. "Really? You think I have what it takes to be a superstar?"

He could tell she was genuinely asking and not fishing for compliments. "Are you serious? Raina, leave this place, and go conquer the world!"

She smiled broadly. "Thank you. That means a lot to me. As to why I'm here, well... I guess I figured I was too old to try it in Nashville, New York, and LA. They like them young, manageable, and sexy. And that's not my cup of tea.

"You also have to basically stick to one genre of music. Here, I can sing whatever I want. I'm free here, not being told what to do, when, or how to do it. I'm my own boss and, within reason, can take off when I want to.

"And honestly, who really makes it? There are thousands upon thousands out there looking to make it big. I'd just be lost in the masses until I got my lucky break, *if* it ever came along." She took a drink of her water before saying glibly, "However, I would *love* to make the amount of money they do!"

"Scared to try it?"

"Of course I'd be scared to try it! I mean, when you sing, dance, write, or act, they're judging you and your talent. It'd be extremely personal. They're more likely to crucify you than love you. I have thick skin, but I don't know how long that thickness would last being constantly browbeaten by rude critics.

"The general public can often be horrible, judgmental, and filled with armchair experts with nothing more to do than tear someone down to build themselves up. Ninety percent of them judge people for something they can't even do themselves, let alone even tried! They all just need to shut up and mind their own business. But I digress."

Channion smiled, completely agreeing with her about the general public. As a cop, he dealt with it on a daily basis in one way or another, if not in more than one way.

Raina was riled up now and continued, "This industry? Music is a difficult business... even as it seems like it'd be the easiest. I mean, it's *music*. It's supposed to make people happy and want to dance, sing along, make memories, or whatever. Can you imagine a world with no beautiful music?

"If you're one of the dedicated, and lucky, ones who *do* make it big, your life is no longer your own. Every little thing you say and do is seen, taped, rumored about... I couldn't take that for too long, no matter how much they paid me! No way would that life be for me. I like living on the down-low. It keeps one free and humble." With a rueful smile, she added, "And poorer."

He smiled, finding her to be an interesting person. He didn't get to meet too many interesting people outside of arresting them.

About an hour later, she began her last lesson of the day. It was thankfully a quiet one. A newer student, there was little music actually played. Raina was just beginning to teach the young boy the notes and how to read them. His patient mom sat in with them so she could help him out when he practiced at home. Raina didn't seem to mind she was giving two lessons for the price of one.

After the lesson was over and they left, Channion mentioned it to her.

Smiling, Raina agreed as she wiped down the desk and chairs to be ready for the next day. "Well, I actually suggested it to Rosemary. See, Kenny was adopted by Rosemary and her husband, Carl.

"She stopped by here one day asking about music lessons for their newly-adopted son. She's sincerely trying to find out what Kenny likes to do to build up his confidence. I noticed the first time I saw them together there was a slight gap between them. It wasn't so much a rift, but they also weren't quite a unit, I guess.

"So the next time they came in, I asked Rosemary to assist me. Since *she's* also learning, that puts them both on the same playing field so there's no adult/child gap. They're just two students learning about music together. With any luck, it'll make good memories for them to share. *And* hopefully rid them of the slight tension that exists between them. It must be quite an adjustment for them all to start a family like that."

Channion headed toward the front doors with her to leave. He was thoughtful when he quietly told her, "You have a good heart, Miss Stewart. A very good heart."

THEY HAD PLANS TO eat at his aunt and uncle's house later that night. Not having anywhere else to go, they decided to go early. Channion pulled up at their house, parking far to the side so his uncle could get into the garage when he arrived later.

He rang the doorbell to warn his aunt they were there early in case she didn't get his text, unlocked the door with his key and led Raina into the living room.

"Aunt Janet! It's me, Channion! Where are ya?" he called out cheerfully. Turning to Raina, he said, "Doesn't that smell great? She's an amazing cook!"

They heard feet coming down the stairs before they saw the older woman who belonged to them. "Channion! Give me a hug, you!" She all but flew into her nephew's outstretched arms to get a bear hug from him. Stepping back, she surveyed him. "You're..." Her voice trailed off when she noticed Raina.

"My lands! You must be Miss Stewart! I'm sorry I didn't see you there. All I saw was Channion here!" Mrs. Kramer took Raina's hands and gently squeezed them. "Ronnie talks highly of you, Miss Stewart. It was so wonderful what you did for Bryce! I still can't believe it happened. And look at you. You're the one who done it. I'm so honored to meet you!"

Janet Kramer was a lovely woman. Time had been a little hard on her, but she still had such spirit and a natural friendliness. Raina noticed her nice cheekbones, deep eyes, straight nose, full lips, and rich, mostly-gray hair. She could see some black hair beneath the pretty gray. Raina suspected the only reason she looked a bit aged was being in love and married to a cop for probably most of her adult life. It had to be stressful at times, the not knowing each day. Her voice was on the deeper side.

"Mrs. Kramer, it's so nice of you to invite me over to your home for dinner. It smells wonderful!" Raina smiled. "Channion here was practically drooling the second he opened the door."

Mrs. Kramer laughed heartily. "You keep an eye on him, young lady. At the table, there won't be anything left between him and my Ronnie. If you want something, you just jump on that table and grab it before they do!" She looped her arm through Raina's as she led them all toward the kitchen. "We don't judge anyone for jumping on the table, but we *do* judge them on their landing when they fall off it!"

Raina laughed.

Grinning, Janet said, "Channion, there's some sweet tea in the fridge. Would you like some tea, Miss Stewart?"

"Just call me Raina. It's less of a mouthful. And sure, I'll take some tea."

Janet patted Raina's hand. "And you must call me Janet. My Ronnie tells me you've been through hell in a handbasket, and that he and Channion are here to fix it all up for you. Don't you fret any, Raina. My boys will take fine care of you, fine care!

"Now you just straight up tell me, is pot roast okay? If not, I can whip up something else. It's in the crock pot, so it'll be really tender and juicy. And I made up some of my special mashed potatoes, and I got green beans from my garden. Or I can do tomato soup, cheese toasties..."

Raina was touched her hostess thought of asking her. She wondered if her husband had mentioned some things were still a little harder for her to eat. "If it tastes as great as it smells, I'll be in heaven. I'm sure it'll be more than fine. That's nice of you to ask me... Thank you."

Janet smiled.

Raina had to ask, "But a cheese toastie? That's a grilled cheese sandwich, right?"

"Yes. Do you prefer that? It's not a problem at all for me to—"

Raina interrupted to reassure her, "Oh, no, no. The roast sounds perfect. It's just that no one else I know calls a grilled cheese a 'cheese toastie'! I've only ever heard that in my own family."

"Really?" Janet inquired. "Well, maybe that's a sign you're supposed to be here then!"

Channion said, "That is interesting though. To me, it's a cheese toastie. Of course, it's a family thing for me too. Seriously, who actually *grills* it? Why is it even called a 'grilled cheese sandwich' if it's not even grilled but toasted?"

Raina shrugged. "Beats me. *You're* the detective!"

Janet laughed before saying, "I might hazard a guess and say it's a Midwestern thing. Maybe not, but it seems like other people I know who say cheese toastie are from the Midwest. Maybe it's more of a regional thing... Or just goes by family like ours."

Raina joked, "Maybe we're distantly related and just don't know it!"

Janet smiled. "Wouldn't *that* be something?"

Channion smiled at Raina as he handed her a glass of sweet tea. Warning her, he said, "Now, Aunt Janet loves the 'sweet' in sweet tea. Her grandma was the one who started her on Southern sweet tea many, many, many years ago. I can water it down for you. Don't be shy if it's too sweet for your taste."

Janet eyed her nephew. "That was a couple too many 'many's, young man. I'm not *that* old!" Channion smiled at his aunt as she turned her attention to her houseguest. "One piece of advice, Raina. Take what my nephew says with a grain of salt. Have a taste of my tea now and tell me what you think!"

With two sets of eyes focused on her, Raina felt silly sipping her tea. Once the sugar hit her tongue, she quickly pulled back. "Holy Moses, Janet! Did you think to add any water to your sugar?"

Janet and Channion burst into laughter. Gently hugging Raina, Janet then wiped the tears from her eyes. "Ronnie said you were direct and had a wonderful sense of humor. He said I'd like you. He was wrong though." Cradling Raina's face in her callused hands, she declared, "I *love* you!"

His AUNT HAD REFUSED their offers of help and told them to sit. Obediently, Raina took a seat at the kitchen bar next to Channion, both drinking their watered-down sweet teas. Raina listened to how Ron and Janet met at a dance a local church had put on over four decades earlier.

Her Ronnie, as Janet called her husband of thirty-nine years, was the love of her life. Janet was stirring some cake batter as she talked. "Lord! He was a handsome chap! The first time I laid my eyes on him, I just knew he was for me." She poured the batter into the floured baking dish. Wiping her fingers on a washcloth, she paused, reminiscing.

"He was a confident young man when it came to everything but the ladies." She wiggled her eyebrows, making both Channion and Raina burst out laughing. "I thought he'd never ask me to dance with him. As a matter of fact, *I* had to ask him."

She put the empty bowl into the sink, turning on the water to let it soak. "See, there was this other girl. I won't mention her name, but Gladys," she said with a wink, "was fixin' to steal him away from me. She was a cantankerous and nasty-spirited woman—but only to us girls. She might've been blessed by the gods with the perfect body, but that was it. Everything else about her was pure poison. To the men, why, she was as sweet as my tea.

"Now I didn't like the notion of her swooping him out from under my nose, so I jumped up from my chair and made a beeline for Ronnie before she got to him. I got there just in time to save him from certain ruin!"

Raina laughed in delight. "Wish I was there to see it! How long did you date before he asked you to marry him? Or did you ask him that too?"

The older woman grinned. "If you're asking in terms of years, it was a year too long. The man moved so much slower back then. I thought he'd never get around to it. I wore my ma out complaining to her about him not asking me fast enough. She finally got to leaving the room anytime I mentioned his name."

She smiled with the memories of decades past. "Poor ma, I just wanted that man so much it's a wonder I didn't scare him away for good. She had to listen to me wonder what was taking him so blasted long. Bless her heart! One time, she said he probably would've already asked me if I could just keep my mouth shut long enough for him to get the words out!"

Channion and Raina laughed.

"My daddy, well, he got a kick out of it. To him it was just a game of sorts. While he was pleased with my choice of Ronnie, he also wasn't quite ready to let his little girl go either. I know that's pure truth because he told me.

"My daddy was one of my best friends. He taught me and my dear brother how a man should treat a woman by how he loved and cherished my ma. I miss them still today. They were such wonderful parents. Oh! Now I'm starting another story there, aren't I? Let me finish our story first."

Janet put a small plate of soft fruit in front of them, signally them to eat. Raina was now certain either Ron or Channion had told Janet to offer only soft foods for her. She chose some kiwi, sliced banana, and watermelon.

Washing her hands, Janet continued, "So it was a couple of years, or thereabouts, and he picks me up in his light blue car that he swore he'd keep forever. We go out to this romantic picnic area, and well, I just *knew* he was going to ask. I said yes before he ever actually got the question out of his mouth, but he finally got around to it!"

"You always were impatient," Ron called out as he came down the hallway, having entered from the garage door entrance. "Hey, Raina, Channion." He kissed his wife when he walked into the kitchen. With his arm around her waist, he smiled. "She's telling on me again, huh?"

"Only the good stuff." Raina smiled. "She was just getting to the juicy stuff when you came in. I think we're almost to the honeymoon now."

He laughed. "Channion, you're watching my back, right? Don't let my girl spill too much about me!"

Channion grinned and nodded as Ron took a glass from the cabinet and poured himself some tea. Raina smiled when she noticed he filled it only about half-full and topped it off with water. Ron drank some before he said, "Well, I'm gonna go get cleaned up. How soon, dear?"

His wife answered, "Whenever you're ready. The roast is done and is simmering in the crock pot. The cake will be done in about half an hour. Take your time. We're all good down here." She kissed his cheek and sent him on his way. "Now, back to us..." She happily chatted on about her husband as she wiped down the counter.

HAVING DINNER WITH SUCH an open, welcoming family was a new experience for Raina. She didn't know if she'd ever been sucked into a family as easily and as quickly as with the Kramers. She was an unknown, a complete stranger, but they were so down-to-earth with her, it was hard to *not* relax.

Their own two daughters, Stephanie and Sabrina, were grown and lived elsewhere, but their nephew Channion had stuck around, she learned. He was more like their own son than their nephew, and he seemed to treat them as more than just his aunt and uncle. Raina was fascinated by the family dynamics and enjoyed listening to their stories after dinner.

Relaxing on the couch, Channion said, "Next week at our family reunion, you'll meet my cousin Ty. He lives in Arizona and works at a huge horse place out there, so you'll have something in common to talk about. He also has a palomino—Monte."

Raina felt a moment's hesitation. "You have a family reunion next week? Won't I be in the way? I can stay with someone else so you two can be free from work for a while. I don't want to intrude on something like that."

Janet spoke before anyone else could. "Of course you're coming! We wouldn't have it any other way. You won't be intruding, so don't you worry any. Channion," she looked right at her nephew and steamrolled right on, "You be sure she's there, or you'll answer to me." She gave the look only a mother, or a respected aunt, could give and be obeyed without another word being spoken.

"Yes, ma'am. She'll be there. If not, neither will I!"

Ron exclaimed, "Sure, Raina! You'll fit in with no problem. And Ty is a great kid." At his nephew's perturbed look, he corrected his description. "Man."

Channion nodded.

Wondering about something, Ron probed by casually stating, "He's single. He's also loyal, works hard, loves animals, and treats ladies with respect. It's hard to find a guy like that nowadays, don't you think?"

Although the question was directed to Raina, his eyes were watching his nephew.

He didn't notice any difference in his nephew's body language so he continued nonchalantly, "Yep. Ty is a nice, upstanding man. A man's man, if you will. Well-traveled, very smart, kind, and his sense of humor will match nicely with yours, Raina. I have no doubt about that!"

When his nephew looked over at him, eyeing him speculatively, Ron casually asked, "Are you dating anyone, Raina?"

The question came completely out of left field. Raina was speechless for a moment, but she knew a matchmaking set-up when she heard one. Instead of answering Ron directly, Raina smiled at him and said, "Not anymore, since I'm apparently supposed to get with Ty. I'll need to check my schedule, though, to make sure I can work him in."

They all laughed, but Ron didn't let it go. He tried to use humor to find out for sure. "Well, he won't ask you out if you're dating someone else. He'd never poach. So he'll need to know, preferably in advance."

Looking now at Channion, she quizzed, "Isn't that in my file? Somewhere between the information you'd find on my driver's license and the fact that I love mint and chocolate?"

Channion chuckled. "Ronnie," he teased his uncle, "must've missed that part. Maybe you should refresh his memory as he *is* getting up there in years."

Fact was, he honestly didn't know himself. Surely she would've said something by now if she was dating someone, right? Wouldn't he have visited her in the hospital... if he'd known?

Raina knew a fishing expedition was in the making, so she answered with a noncommittal shrug, saying blandly, "Well, be sure he's read in before Ty gets here. What day is he arriving?"

She had neatly avoided answering their questions. Ron noticed, as did Channion. Janet grinned at their guest as she knew both men were now intrigued.

"One day." With a straight face, Channion replied with a deliberately vague answer himself before he looked at his watch, then stretched his arms. "Well, I hate to break up this little party, but we need to get going. It's a long drive, and we've got the kids to feed. Besides that, Raina's supposed to sleep more than she's up and moving, so we need to go. It's gonna be past your bedtime soon, young lady."

Janet gasped. "Raina, you have kids? Why didn't you bring them with you tonight?"

Raina laughed. "Oh! That's as rich as your sweet tea, Janet!" This caused everyone to laugh. "My 'kids' are actually my horses. That's what I call them, so Channion is just using my lingo. I don't have any human kids, so don't worry. I didn't leave them locked up in the basement or anything like that. I don't even have a basement. Or kids. You might need to pass that information along to Ty."

Janet chuckled at her humor. "Oh, I see! That's so true how our pets become like our children. We lost our Shepherd just a few months ago, so we fully understand that feeling of how they become family. We miss Sheba too much to think about replacing her yet."

Raina nodded in understanding, and her heart felt sorrow. "I'm so sorry to hear that. You can never replace them but just give another a loving home. It's a difficult time when you lose a beloved pet, isn't it? The grief sometimes feels worse than losing a human family member."

"Yes, you understand. Thank you," Janet said, pushing past the sadness in her heart at the thought of their pet. "Well, you go on home and feed your kids their dinner. Give them extra hugs and kisses."

After hugging his aunt goodnight, Channion watched as she enveloped Raina in a big hug while being mindful of her sore and battered body.

Janet told Raina, "Don't drag your feet coming back here. And I mean it when I say you're more than welcome to our family get-together! The more the merrier, I say."

Chapter 21

ON THE WAY BACK to her place, Raina commented, "You have a wonderful family living in that house. It's a nice thing to see nowadays. You three are obviously quite close. What about your parents? Are you close to them like that?"

Channion was quiet for a moment. He stopped for a red light, waited a beat. "My parents are gone. Dad was a policeman. He was killed in the line of duty when I was a teenager. Mom passed away from cancer about four years ago. I miss both of them every day."

"I'm even more sorry now for my dead-end job comment the other night... I'm so sorry. I didn't know..." Raina's heart went out to him. She felt like the worst excuse for a human.

"I appreciate that. How could've you known? And I don't dwell on it..."

"I'm still so sorry. I bet losing your parents like that was unbearably hard to deal with. One taken so quickly with no warning, and the other suffering, wondering if it would ever end." Her eyes watered up with tears just thinking about it. "Either way is awful. I'm sorry you all had to go through that."

He nodded. He could still get a lump in his throat when he remembered those two life-changing events. The light turned green and, after looking for red light runners, he drove forward. "It was exactly as you said. One you couldn't truly prepare for, so it was definitely a time of great shock and disbelief. And the other, I wanted her suffering to end, yet I didn't want to lose her. And losing Mom was the only way for that to happen.

"Losing Dad about destroyed Mom. I remember Janet once told me if it wasn't for me, she wasn't sure Mom would've survived losing him. Janet said she just crumbled and went to a dark place for a while.

"In my own shattered world, I guess I didn't notice because she was still somehow always there for me. And I tried to be for her, but I guess I never really understood the depth of my mom's anguish. But she pulled through. We both did, for that matter.

"Janet and Dad were brother and sister, so she was hurting from losing her brother. With Ron being a cop as well, it probably made him think of his own fears of mortality. It couldn't have been easy for him as a fellow officer or as a family member, but they were still there for Mom and I. We were all there for each other, I suppose. Much of my family is in law enforcement, so we had a ton of support. But all the support in the world doesn't replace the one who's now missing forever."

Raina thought about it for a moment before asking, "What were their names?"

He was mildly surprised she thought to ask that question. Knowing their names made them more personal and real, not just a sad family story. He was also a bit surprised that he opened up to a stranger about his family like that. "Jason and Nicole. They sometimes went by Jay and Nikki."

She repeated their names. "Jason and Nicole Scott. Those names go quite well together. They're solid."

He turned onto the highway that would take them back to Raina's. "I never thought of it like that. But they do sound solid, don't they?" He paused for a moment. "When Mom got sick, she beat it the first round. We had hope, but she got sick again. She was a fighter, but some things just can't be beat.

"Again, Ron and Janet were there. And Ty, of course, even though he lived far from here. He came here shortly before she passed, so he was here for the funeral. He also stayed with me to help me cope. I suppose I helped him too. He and my mom were close, seeing as how we're like brothers ourselves. It tore him up some, too, when Mom died."

Raina nodded that she understood. "What about your cousin Ty? Since I assume I'm going to meet him soon, tell me about him."

Channion smiled. "Fair enough. Ty and I saw each other every summer growing up, sometimes on winter breaks for the holidays and stuff like that. We were like separated brothers instead of cousins. We always seemed to click and had this bond. We both went into law enforcement—following our dads' footsteps there. He finally got out of it, decided to move to Arizona and got a job at the horse facility he's at now. He loves it out there."

"You ever go visit him?"

"Yeah, I've been out there a few times. He works at a place called Harmony Hills Equestrian Center. The woman who owns it is a knockout, and I never got why she and Ty don't get together. They have a great chemistry. I guess they don't want to try it and have it go south, but I don't know. Dating someone you work with *and* for can be mighty tricky.

"Both are very private people, and I totally respect that. Morgan's always been terrific about letting Ty off to visit family when he asks. I'd have to say he's her best friend, or at least one of them. And I'd have to say she's one of his too. He's happy out there."

Raina looked out the window for a minute as she thought it through. She'd had male friends who were just that. Friends. As great as they were, they were still just friends. Chemistry was there, but there wasn't that spark to light a fire or even much of an ember in the romance department. It didn't seem all that odd now that she thought about it.

She said, "Well, some of us prefer being single. The freedom to be ourselves, run our own lives. Do what we want, when we want. But not every woman is like that. Some want a bit more."

"So why aren't you hooked up with anyone?" He took a chance that she wasn't, but he wanted confirmation.

She shrugged. "I haven't found what I was looking for in anyone I've met. It's as simple as that, I guess. And I'm new to this area and, in all honesty, this hasn't been on my list of things to get done."

"Do you want to get married someday?"

She grinned. "Is that a proposal, Detective?"

He laughed. "I'm just wondering, that's all. Even independent women can be good at the married life."

"True, but I want to be sure it's the right guy for me. I'd much rather be single and happy than to be with someone just for the sake of being a couple and being miserable. Nowadays, it's so extremely hard to meet someone and to know if they're for real. On the other hand, it's probably the oldest story in the world.

"There are so many con men and crazies out there! Sometimes it's really scary to think about dating a complete stranger without having an armed escort to be sure it's safe. Or checking in with a friend every five minutes for safety.

"And I'm not into that whole married, get separated, get back together, divorce drama. It may be old-fashioned, but I want to stay married. Well... unless there was a case of abuse or something like that, of course. And I'll never be someone's doormat.

"It's hard to say what I want, but I know what I *don't* want. And it seems all I ever find are the don't-wants. I need that chemistry and that spark, but it's way more than that."

Raina searched for what she wanted to explain in words a guy might understand. "I want us to be *friends*. I want him to be someone I *want* to hang out with. Someone I *know* I can depend on. Like if he says he'll do something, I just want to know it'll *get* done. Y'know, most women aren't naturally nags. Men turn us into them. But more importantly, it shows that he respects me and our marriage. And I'd do the same for him because it's a two-way street.

"And be so comfortable with each other, we could stay at home and, I don't know, sit around and talk, watch TV, read books, or play board games. And be completely fine with it. I don't want to stay home *all* of the time, but I don't want to be *out* all the time either. Just a happy balance. I'm probably asking for too much. Apparently I am.

"Someone who's not high-maintenance. Someone who can offer comfort—and not expect sex for it like it's a payment of some sort. He needs to have a fun side as well as a mature, responsible side. And smart with finances, and who honestly respects women. It's insane to hear men say they do, but their actions say something else entirely. Worse, they don't even know they're doing it because it's always been that way! Worse yet is if they *do* know and don't care. If we try to inform them it's wrong, then they think we're a bitch. Women can't win.

"It didn't seem to be this hard decades ago. I'm sure it was, but it just seems impossible now!" She paused. "But for now, I'm actually content being single. It seems to suit me."

Channion thought about what she said. "I understand. It's kind of the same with me. And being in the career field I've chosen makes it that much harder. Some of my past girlfriends couldn't take the pressure of dating a cop. The long and random hours I sometimes have to work often created havoc for dates.

"Sometimes it was simply a lack of chemistry or finding out later on there were deal breakers. And no matter how hard I tried, to me the job is who and what I am. You know, a cop is always working—he's just off duty sometimes. Our training is ingrained in us because it needs to be. That's just the way it is."

Raina could believe it. "Well, at least they fizzled out *before* you got married or started a life together. It's better to know at the beginning if they can't handle what you do for a living. Adding kids in the mix makes for a mess." She waited a beat before asking, "What about you? Do you want to get married someday?"

He grinned. "Sure! But since we just met a couple of weeks ago, maybe we should give it a little more time first."

"Ya think?" She was laughing as he turned into her driveway.

Chapter 22

She heard screaming and yelling. Her head hit the hard pavement, and she felt hands grabbing her hair. She tried to scream, but nothing seemed to come out. She grabbed onto the hands, trying to get loose. She twisted and squirmed, feeling the weight on top of her. Every time she moved, she felt searing pain throughout her body. Now she could barely move. Her feet couldn't get a grip on the ground to try to roll the weight off. She saw bright lights, flashes. She felt herself getting weaker but still fought with everything she could muster. That's when she heard gun shots, and her body went numb. She'd been shot.

She sat up with a scream of pain and terror ripping from her throat, sitting up so quickly her ribs sent sharp spears of pain throughout her whole body. She cried out in real pain then. She was shot! She threw off her covers, looking for bullet holes and blood.

She felt strong hands grab her again and began to fight like a wildcat. Every twisting move she made sent shock waves of pain throughout her body, making her scream in fresh pain and terror.

"Raina! *Stop!* You're hurting yourself! *Raina, wake up!*" Channion held onto her, trying to shake her out of the nightmare she was trapped in. She was fighting him like he was attacking her. "*Wake up!* Raina, it's me, Channion! You're safe!"

He finally grabbed her bodily and pushed her down with all his weight onto the bed to keep her from thrashing around. Man, her ribs were still cracked and not fully healed! He held her down while she struggled, kept calling out to her to wake up. He was amazed at her incredible strength. She was slim in body type, but she packed a whale of a punch even still physically impaired.

His voice finally began to penetrate the black shadow world she was in, and then through the gray haze. She stopped squirming and bucking, stopped screaming. He could feel her great heaves while gasping for air, and her crying out at each great gulp she took. He knew his weight was probably causing her pain, too, but he refused to get off her until he knew she was awake and in control again. He could feel the cold sweat on her skin.

"Raina? Are you awake? Raina, you awake now?" he asked, his voice full of concern. He leaned up on his elbows, looking down at her face in the dark room. In the glow of her nightlights, he couldn't see much. She seemed to be coming out of the terror as tears ran down her cheeks. He rested his cheek against her hair, giving her time to surface.

A couple of minutes later, he slowly and carefully rolled off her, hoping he hadn't caused her any more damage. She covered her eyes with her left hand, trying to break free of the memories. Her breathing was still fast and hard, each breath reminding her she had a rib cage that didn't much like her at that moment. She was shaking almost violently.

"Raina... You okay?"

He reached over, turned her lamp on low. He looked to see where he'd dropped his gun when he realized she wasn't being attacked in her own bed. He'd quickly placed it on the floor before grabbing her, fearing in the struggle to wake her up it could've gone off. He spotted the gun near his feet, reached down and carefully set it on the nightstand, facing the barrel away from them after making sure the safety was still on.

He removed her hand that was covering her eyes and gently cupped her battered face to look at her closely. He noticed her whole body was shaking and ran his hands up and down her arms in a bid to warm her cold, sweaty skin, hoping the human contact would also help calm her.

His voice was soothing as he said, "It's okay, Raina. You're safe at home. I'm here. No one else. Just us. You had a nightmare. You're okay. You're okay."

He kept talking to her until she got herself under control. Sitting on the side of her bed in the dim light, he comforted her. He pulled up her sheet, hoping to warm her body from the chills. He continued to rub her arms until she finally nodded. He went to the bathroom to get a washcloth, wet it and wrung it out. He grabbed some toilet paper for tissues and hurried back to her.

Blowing her nose hurt like the devil, but she had to. Channion gently wiped the sweat and tears from her face and neck. When she tried to sit up, she gasped and grabbed her ribcage.

Channion was truly concerned she'd hurt herself in her fight with the demons. He wouldn't let her sit up, tossing the washcloth on the bed so his hands were free. "Raina, do I need to get you to the hospital? Tell me exactly what you're feeling so I know. *Don't* sugarcoat it." His voice was firm.

"It just hurts. A lot. Like when I first woke up in the hospital." She took a small breath as she lay beside him. She kept her arm around her middle. "But I think I'm okay. I just..."

"Let me look."

"What? No! Channion, I'm okay. Really. You can't do anything anyway..."

"Don't argue with me, Stewart. I need to be sure. Let me check your ribcage. I'm a policeman, so don't worry about feeling shy. This is purely professional. I need a visual to be sure..."

He lowered the sheet to her waist and was already shoving her nightshirt up toward her breasts. She knew she couldn't fight him and not seriously be in danger of causing more damage. Swallowing her pride and dignity, she allowed him to push her nightshirt up to the bottom of her breasts. He was being decent and only wanted to see her mid-section, so she tried to relax.

He gently pushed on her bare midsection, her ribs. He could see in the low light how discolored her entire torso still was from the beating she'd taken the day of the attack.

"Tell me what you're feeling," he instructed as he made his way up her torso. Thankfully, he didn't see any bones protruding her skin, which was his first fear. He was still scared he'd feel a bone tip as he carefully ran his fingers over her skin.

"Hurts. Hurts. Yeah, tender there. And there. Ouch! Channion, stop. Stop!" She had fresh tears in her eyes.

"I think we should be safe and get you to a doctor right away."

"The ER? Now? If it's cracked ribs, they'll just say have some Tylenol. I have that here. I want to stay home, Channion. I don't want to go back to the hospital. I want to stay home." She pleaded with him with her eyes as well as her voice. "*Please?*"

"Honey, I don't think you realize how hard you were thrashing around. What if you broke a rib? You could puncture an internal organ and bleed to death on me." Making his decision, he carefully pulled down her nightshirt to her waist again and stood up, careful to not jar her.

Looking at her with a firm face, and with an even firmer voice, he said, "Let's go, Stewart. Come as you are... You're decent. Otherwise, I'm calling for an ambulance. That's probably a smarter choice since you'd be on a stretcher. It'll just take a while for them to get here. Your choice, so pick one. Now."

His voice was hard, unyielding. He hated to browbeat her, he really did. But he was scared she'd hurt herself, and even now could be in danger from internal bleeding, or... Well, he didn't know. All he knew was he wanted her under the care of a doctor as quickly as possible.

"I'm not going in my pjs, Channion!" Since his firm look stayed steady, she relented. "At least let me put on some clothes I can wear in public. The bottoms look like shorts, so I'm fine there. Please help me up..."

It was he who relented this time. After all, he was getting what he wanted. He had no plans on telling her how much she'd scared him, and his worry for her was great. Easing her carefully off the bed, he stepped back. When he was sure she could stand on her own, he grabbed his gun and quickly walked out while she changed her clothes.

He changed into another shirt, a pair of jeans and slipped on his socks, shoes, and his holster in record time. He grabbed his keys, wallet, and his phone as he made his way out of the room. He quickly used the bathroom and splashed cold water on his face, running his wet hands through his hair. Drying his hands and face, he expected her to be ready for him when he was finished.

He waited outside her door, but he didn't hear any sounds from within. Worried, he knocked before he slowly swung the door all the way open. She was sitting on the bed. She didn't even bother to wipe away the tears rolling down her cheeks. They simply dripped down from her chin and jawline to her lap.

Insanely, that tiny detail scared him the most. Any normal person would wipe them away as a reflexive action. But not her. She just sat there, not moving a muscle.

"It hurts too much when I move for me to change clothes," she whimpered. "I'll go as I am, but I need some shoes. And my glasses..."

He gently wiped her face with the washcloth again before sliding on her glasses. He put her phone in his other back pocket in case it was needed. He went to her drawer and got some socks, slipping them onto her feet.

"Your shoes are downstairs, honey." Helping her stand up again, he guided her with his hand on her back as they made their way slowly toward the hallway.

"Wait. Let me use the bathroom first." Raina was embarrassed, but hey, she needed to go.

He waited in the hallway, wondering if she needed help. Would she be too proud to ask for it? When she finally came out, he helped her down the stairs.

"Stay here while I get your shoes." Getting them, he knelt down. She placed her hand on his shoulder as he slipped them on and tied the laces. He heard her ragged breathing and tried to hurry.

Channion led her to the truck and painstakingly helped her get in. He put their phones on the console before he strapped the seatbelt around her, gently closing the door before rushing around to the driver's side. He wondered if maybe the back seat would be safer, but he didn't want to waste the time to move her or take the chance of hurting her more.

As he was getting in behind the wheel, he stopped, briefly debated. Not willing to take the chance, he ran back inside her house, grabbed the case files from the table, and his phone charger from upstairs, and ran back out, locking and slamming the door again behind him.

HER BREATHING WAS WORSE by the time they reached the hospital. He drove straight to the ER doors, stopping as gently as he could to avoid jarring her and turned off the emergency lights he'd turned on to get there quicker. Carefully, he helped her out of the truck. He took her straight to the admitting desk, grateful at seeing a nurse behind the plexiglass window.

He flipped his badge to the nurse, who quickly came around to assist Raina into a wheelchair as he held the chair still. An ER nurse wheeled Raina into a curtained room as Channion followed, refusing to leave her side. Taking her vitals as Channion explained what happened, the nurse nodded. Concerned, she prepped her for X-rays and off they went. Channion filled out the paperwork as they took the X-rays, making note of Dr. Benson as her original doctor.

When they wheeled her back out, Raina's face was pale. She smiled weakly at the concerned detective, grabbing his hand to get his attention when the nurse wheeled her to his side, whispering, "Don't worry, Channion. I'll be fine. In fact, I *am* fine."

"I'll just wait to hear that from the hospital staff, if you don't mind." He held onto her hand for a moment, noticing how clammy it was. He also felt it shaking.

She was wheeled back to her curtained room and helped into the bed where they had to wait for the results. The doctor finally came in, hung up the X-rays and flipped on the light. He explained what they were seeing from her ribs and her wrist since she'd mentioned that hurt too.

He pulled out his pen light, checked her eyes. After placing his stethoscope around her front and back, he listened to her heart and lungs before he began probing her head, neck, and shoulders. He slowly moved down to her ribcage, then checked her arms and legs. As he worked on her, he'd ask questions about her pain.

Nodding at her answers, the doctor asked one more, "Now, *your* overall personal description of yourself, Miss Stewart, would be what?"

"I have a throbbing body, an aching hand, a head that's ready to explode at any moment, and I'm cold."

Channion broke in at that. "I thought you just told me you were 'fine'?"

"Don't start with me." Her voice was low, a mixture of humor and pain in it.

He and the doctor smiled despite themselves.

"Don't ever lie to me again, Stewart," Channion ordered.

When she didn't answer immediately, he leaned down in front of her face and stared at her. Giving in, she whispered, "I won't."

The doctor made more notes in her file on the computer. Turning to the detective, he stated, "You were smart to bring her in right away. I could rely on just the X-rays, but I'd rather be safe. I'm sending her up for the scans first thing in the morning."

Looking at his watch, he added, "Considering it's about three-thirty now, it won't be too much longer. I'll put you up in a room until then. The admitting specialist will be here in a few minutes so hang out here. Do you need anything else?"

They both shook their heads.

Raina almost hated they were now alone. The doctor and nurse were her buffers. "Go ahead and just say it to get it over with." Raina prepared herself for his scolding as she tried to manage her pain. At his questioning look, she replied, "I told you so? See, this is why you should listen to me without arguing? Something along those lines?"

Channion smiled down at her. "Since you know what I'm going to say, no use wasting my breath."

"That's *it?*" Raina could only look at him.

"I don't believe in kicking a person when they're already down." He laid his hand on her shoulder, gave it a gentle squeeze.

A different nurse walked into the room, telling Channion to wait outside the curtain while she worked on Raina. She cut off her nightshirt so Raina wouldn't have to lift her arms to remove it. After wrapping her ribs, she carefully slipped the light blue unisex hospital gown on her. She put a new splint on her right arm and wrist after bandaging it. The sympathetic nurse tried to work fast as she knew Raina was in a lot of pain. The nurse put her clothes and shoes in a plastic bag and set it at her feet.

Once she was done, the nurse drew back the curtain so she and another nurse could steer her bed out. Once alone in the deserted hallway, the nurse motioned to Channion, saying, "You want to push her around, don't you? Here's your chance!"

With a smile at her humor, and Raina's groan when she tried to not laugh, he helped wheel Raina's bed down the hallway to her room.

TEARS SPRUNG TO HER eyes as she was transferred from the rolling bed to the stationary one in her new room, but she didn't say a word. Nurse Ramsey raised the bed, then adjusted everything for Raina until she was more comfortable. The nurse gently wiped away the tears with tissues she grabbed from the nightstand before hooking her up to the monitors. "Hey, Raina. Remember me?"

Gamely, Raina tried to make the best of the situation. "Of course. You were my midnight chauffer, Nurse Ramsey. I guess I missed you the most because I came back on your shift."

Grinning, Channion shook his head while the nurse laughed. The nurse offered to put her glasses on the little nightstand beside the bed, but Raina said she'd leave them on.

When she was done putting the notes in the computer, Nurse Ramsey said, "Well, I'll leave you two alone now. The scans will be around nine, maybe before, so you have time to catch up on some sleep. There's a pillow and pillowcases in the corner closet there if you need one to sleep in the chair, Detective Scott.

"We'll try not to disturb you when we do our checks. If you need anything, let us know. The monitors will let us know if anything else happens... which we aren't expecting." The nurse added the last when she saw the questioning glance from the man beside her.

Channion nodded. "Thank you. We appreciate it. Would you be able to stay with her until I return? Make sure no one enters this room? It won't take me more than fifteen minutes. I'm sure you're busy, but I can't leave her alone."

"Absolutely, unless it's an emergency call."

"Of course." Channion said to Raina, "I just need to move the truck out of the way. I'll be right back."

She stared at the ceiling, tears brimming over, while she waited for Channion to return. Nurse Ramsey noticed the tears and gently wiped them away.

RAINA WOKE UP A while later. Feeling beyond groggy, she could barely open her eyes. When she finally was able to keep them open, she had no clue where she was. Her heart pounded in her chest as she tried to recall how she got to wherever it was she was. There was a little light coming through the closed blinds, and a little overhead light placed slightly behind her.

When she realized she was once again in the hospital, she wanted to cry. She was crazy homesick. She wanted her own little house, her own bed. She wanted to walk down to her barn and be with her kids. They were all she had to hold and hug. They also represented normalcy for her, making this nightmare she was living seem like it was just an insanely bad dream.

How long would she be here *this* time? she wondered.

Something else was off, but it took her foggy brain a moment longer to figure out what it was. It occurred to her that she *felt* someone else in the room, and her hand felt weighted down. Instinctively, she stiffened. She slowly turned her head to see Channion's nearly beside hers.

He'd moved the recliner to be as close as he could be, short of climbing in bed with her. The weight on her left hand was his right hand covering it.

Why was he holding her hand? The only conclusion she thought made any sense was he was scared she'd have another nightmare and hurt herself before he could get to her, even from a few feet away.

That being said, she *was* scared to go back to sleep. Raina didn't even remember falling asleep before. Had they drugged her? If so, she was all for the drugs, just not the sleeping part.

Listening to his steady breathing calmed her. Her brain soon began shutting down, and she felt a black curtain coming over her. Taking comfort in his nearness, she drifted back to sleep.

Chapter 23

THE NEXT TIME RAINA woke up, she heard voices speaking quietly in the room. She opened her eyes to see Channion and his uncle talking in the corner.

"Don't you know it's rude to whisper in a lady's presence?" she asked, her voice hoarse.

They both turned to look at her, their serious expressions turning to smiles almost instantly.

"Good morning, sunshine," Ron said as he walked over. "I heard you scared thirty years off my partner here. That's not something a lady should do, you know." He studied their witness as he spoke, looking for signs of her breaking down, mentally or emotionally.

She looked at Channion, who walked over to the other side of the bed. "I know, and I'm so ashamed about that." She tried to sound lighthearted like Ron, but she gave it up. Looking somber, she said, "Seriously, I'm sorry I scared you. How are you?"

Channion looked at her, studying her much like his uncle did as he answered, "I'll live. How about you?"

"Same, I guess. What time is it?"

"Nine-thirty or so. We decided it was better to let you rest as long as you were able to do so comfortably. I was filling in my uncle with what happened, but I'll let them know you're awake now so they can scan you."

He pushed the red call button on the TV remote controller to connect to the nurse station down the hallway. When a nurse answered, he told them Raina was awake now and may need them. He set the controller back down on the bed when she replied they'd be down in a minute or two.

As they waited for a nurse to come, Channion inquired softly, "Do you remember what your nightmare was about? You screamed, and I thought someone was in the house attacking you. When I got to your room, you were rubbing your hands all over yourself like you were looking for something.

"You weren't awake, though, but I didn't realize that at the time. When I touched you, you went absolutely ballistic. I'd swear on a stack of bibles, Raina, I wasn't sure if you were going to kill me... or yourself."

"I'm sorry. I'm so sorry," she said quietly, looking into his soft brown eyes.

"For what? You were trapped in a horrific nightmare. You weren't even awake. Can you tell us what it was about? Why were you rubbing your hands over yourself?" Channion's voice was calm, soothing as he coaxed her to talk. "Do you remember?" he asked when she didn't immediately reply.

"I was looking for bullet holes," she whispered.

Surprised, Ron asked, "Bullet holes?"

"I remember screaming and hearing yelling. I saw lights or flashes—I don't know which. And then I think I heard gunfire, and I thought I'd been shot. So I was looking for bullet holes." Her voice was shaking by the time she finished.

Channion and his uncle looked at each other silently. Her memory seemed to be coming back. While they were expecting it would, *hoping* it would, they also knew those memories weren't going to be happy ones.

Her eyes glistened with tears, but she tried to hold them back. "Did that happen to me? Was that a memory returning? Or something else? What about the gun shots? Were those real?" She looked back and forth between the two detectives.

Ron nodded and reached for her hand, held it firmly. "You were attacked in a pretty terrible way, Raina. These are apparently memories that are trying to break free. As frightening as they are, it's actually better for it to happen. You don't want repressed memories in your mind for the rest of your life."

"You're so young with so much time in front of you. It's healthier to get them out and dealt with as they come." He paused before saying, "You obviously never got shot though."

"What then? Maybe they weren't even gunshots? Maybe like a car backfiring?"

Ron shook his head. "Those *were* gunshots you heard, but you weren't the target."

"So... Whoever was attacking me... *They* got shot?"

"We don't know how badly, but yes, we think he got hit," Ron answered.

She was quiet while she tried to think it over again. The detectives couldn't lead her to any conclusions, so they remained quiet. Both were praying she was in the process of remembering something else and waited for her to relay it to them.

"He was shot by one of his own people? No, that can't be."

She closed her eyes, replaying what she knew, or thought she knew, carefully in her mind. According to her talks with the detectives while she was in the hospital before, she had a general idea now of where the vehicles had been. As her mind healed, a new piece of memory would get added. Last night's images flashed in her mind as she tried to concentrate.

To the best of her knowledge, her truck and the wrecked cars were to her right, if she were on her back on the ground. But the sounds of gunfire came from her left. Her eyes still closed, her head turned in the direction her mind was replaying.

But was she really on her back? Or was that just as she saw it in her mind, like she was seeing it all happen from high above?

As far as she was aware, there was only one other person at the scene who had a gun. And who was on her left. She was trying to run toward him when she was shoved to the ground.

Eyes still closed, she felt warm tears spilling over. She slowly opened them, turned to look first at Channion, then his uncle. "It was Bryce. Bryce saved my life, didn't he?"

Chapter 24

ONCE THE SCANS WERE done and reviewed with them, they released Raina from the hospital that afternoon with stern warnings and instructions to take it easy. Bed rest was mandatory. When he came on shift, Dr. Benson heard she'd been re-admitted and personally took over her care.

As the doctor was checking her over himself, he directed his comments at Channion, a twinkle in his eyes. "You sure didn't waste any time getting her back here, Detective."

Ron grinned.

Channion defended himself. "I didn't do anything, Doc. It wasn't me. It was all her. I swear!"

Ron and the doctor smiled while Raina wondered what they were talking about. It was apparently something only the three men knew about.

Nurse Laurel kicked the detectives out of the room and again helped Raina take a shower and washed her hair for her. Her Canadian accent entertained Raina. "You don't need to be doing this at home right now. Let's take advantage of you being here, all right?"

Raina was all for it. Laurel helped Raina back into her clothes from the plastic bag and the shirt Ron bought for her in the gift shop since she didn't have any more clothes with her to wear. Laurel dabbed the healing cream on her wounds, which she thought were healing nicely.

"Take this tube home with you too." She handed it to her patient.

Although Raina wanted to see Bryce while she was there, both detectives refused her, almost in unison. She figured they had good reasons.

After leaving the hospital, Channion told her he'd called Lorenzo and cancelled her lessons for the day. She was thankful she didn't have to call them herself. Her concern was more for her horses because they hadn't been fed yet, but at least they were able to go outside to the grass.

As they neared her home, Channion broached a subject he knew would be upsetting to her. "I think we need to move you now, Raina. We need to call my friends and move your horses out today and get you somewhere else. My gut is telling me we need to do this. It's for your safety, Raina, and theirs."

She nodded. "I trust you and your instincts. You're a professional and know your stuff. I'm an amateur musician. I'd much rather err on the side of safety. If you end up being wrong, it's worth it to me for my peace of mind."

"I know you'll miss it," Channion offered her some sympathy. "But you'll be able to come back." Probably, he added to himself.

"Yeah, I will miss it. I love it out here." Her eyes got a little misty at the thought of leaving her humble little house in the country with the cute little barn, and the pasture lined with tall, old pine trees. She'd known it was for her the first time she saw it.

When she'd seen the ad for it, she'd immediately called the number. Within two hours, the landlord had come out to show it to her. An elderly widowed man, Mr. Farley said he used to live there but had to move into town due to his own health issues. But to him it was home, so he couldn't bear to sell it. After some time, he thought he'd rent it out if he could find the right person.

Within an hour of being in Raina's company, he decided she was the one. He loved the fact she had horses as he'd built the little barn for his wife's horses before she passed away a few years earlier. As they'd toured the barn and the pasture, Raina learned his son in Missouri had the horses now so his grandbabies could ride and spoil them. To her surprise, instead of raising the rent because of the horses, he actually lowered it.

Raina figured he was a sweet, sentimental man. She promised to take great care of his home. It didn't take long before Raina began to think of it as her very own.

And now she was being told she had to leave it. What about her kind landlord? What about him?

"I'll call my friends and help you pack while we wait for them to get here. If we feel it's safe, we'll let you visit your horses now and then, all right?"

Raina nodded.

When they pulled into her driveway, she wondered if it'd be the last time she'd see it as her home. Feeling sad and melancholy now on top of her pain, she walked to the front door, unlocking it with a sigh as she wondered if this was the last time she'd unlock her very own door.

Where would the cops put her? Raina wondered as she pulled out the key.

Channion reached around her, swung open the door, took one look inside, and instinctively slammed her to the wall.

She was too startled to even yelp as she hit the wall with her back. She barely registered the instant pain she felt when she saw that Channion had his gun out, putting himself between her and the room.

It was destroyed.

She could barely see around his broad shoulders and back. Peeking around him, she saw the furniture was torn apart, framed pictures were smashed, broken lamps were on the floor along with the plants and gifts from the hospital, the potted dirt spread all over the carpet. She saw one balloon reading *Get Well Soon!* still floating, but barely higher than the wooden bookshelf that was tilted over on its side.

Now she was being *robbed?* She couldn't believe it.

Channion pulled out his phone and quickly called dispatch for backup and CSIs. He hung up, his eyes still searching for danger.

Her body was screaming in pain, and it took all she had to keep her cries inside, her tears banked. She felt the adrenaline rushing through her veins as she stayed right with the man intent on protecting her, who was willing to die for her.

She'd already put two and two together. It *wasn't* a random robbery.

They'd found her.

Raina had an insane urge to run out the front door, screaming as loud as she could, to just run and run until she couldn't run another step. But she didn't. Couldn't.

Instead, she followed Channion as he led her to the hall closet, told her in a whisper to stay there while he checked the house. He closed the door quietly... Her pale face the last thing he saw before it clicked shut.

She thought he'd never return. Standing in the dark space, straining to hear anything made her hear things that weren't even there. Her heartbeat sounded abnormally loud in the enclosed, dark space. It was hot in there. She felt sweat run down her back. It was hard to breathe in the small space, and she wondered if she was getting claustrophobic.

For now, her physical body pain was almost forgotten in her effort to use her other senses to feel any possible danger coming her way, but the throbbing and sharp pains from her ribs brought tears to her eyes in her bid to keep silent.

When Channion let her know it was safe before opening the door, she felt such relief.

"What about my kids?" she asked, her voice full of worry.

He immediately closed the door again, this time leaving a crack for air, with the same instructions to stay there. She nodded, scared to her bones.

When he got to the barn, his gut instincts kicked in hard. It may have been the uneasy, eerie silence. It may have been the negative aura permeating the air. As soon as he walked through the wide doorway, he felt sick.

Holding his gun out, he slowly walked down the aisle, looking for danger. He quickly checked the rest of the barn, careful to avoid contaminating the scene as best he could.

They'd been there too. He saw both Aspen and Rodeo in their stalls, shot in their heads. They never had a chance, but they wouldn't have thought they needed one in the first place. They were beautiful, innocent, trusting animals. There was no cause to kill them. He felt pure rage bubbling up inside him and fought to get it under control.

They were her kids. She would never, *ever* forgive herself for this, he thought.

He didn't know what to do to help her through this devastating turn of events. The only solace he could take was it was quick and surprisingly humane. They could've tortured the horses as a warning to her, but they didn't. Why didn't they?

Why destroy her house, ripping it apart and smashing everything to pieces, but then come all the way to the barn to humanely kill her horses? Were they simply depending on the death of her animals to be warning and threat enough? Or a warning that all it took was one head shot... And that was what she should expect herself? It just wasn't adding up.

He stood in the barn aisle for a moment, trying to move past the shock of what was happening to her. How much could she take before she just couldn't take anymore? How would she react to this news? How strong was Raina Stewart?

As he jogged back to the house, he realized they could've been watching and waiting for him to leave the house so they could snatch her. He broke into a run and took the three back steps in one of his, rushing through the back door, gun still drawn.

Channion called out to her before he opened the closet door. He hugged her when he saw her standing there, fear on her face. He couldn't seem to let her go as he felt her strong arms come around him. Mindful of her ribs, he just held on.

Because he didn't immediately tell her that her kids were fine, she knew instinctively they weren't. And when he didn't let her go, her heart shattered into millions of tiny pieces.

"No, no, no, no..." she whispered in his ear. "No, don't tell me my kids are..."

He cradled her head against his shoulder and just held her. She heard his whispered, tortured reply like it was coming from a thousand miles away. "Raina, I'm so, *so* sorry. Honey, I..."

She screamed out in tormented pain at the loss of her horses. He couldn't hold her up in the little closet as her knees gave out, and she slid to the floor, crying in heart-wrenching sobs. In the condition her body was in after the night before, she was in as much physical pain as the emotional now. She pushed him away when he tried to hold her. She was simply inconsolable. Her screams and cries tore at his soul.

He sat on the floor in front of the closet, his gun in his lap, trying like hell to not cry right alongside her, guilt weighing heavily in his heart. He needed to get her back to the station for safety, but how could he get her out of the closet without injuring her? He had tears in his own eyes, which he quickly blinked away when he saw his fellow officers arriving for backup.

He pulled himself together as he stood up. Trying to remain stoic, he reached out his hand for her. "Honey, we need to go..."

She didn't want to go anywhere. Her heart hurt so much, she couldn't even think straight. She slapped his hands away, kicked at him as she burrowed back into the closet, sobbing uncontrollably.

He decided to leave her alone and walked through the once-happy home she'd made to meet the officers outside. He had his badge out for identification as they were exiting their cars, guns drawn. He summed up the situation quickly, told them to give him a moment to get her out.

He reminded them to not use the radios to prevent the police scanner owners from listening in. They nodded. One got on his phone and informed dispatch they were there, and what was going on. The other did another perimeter check, mindful of disturbing any potential evidence. Another squad car sped up the road toward them, siren off but its lights still brightly flashing.

Channion walked back to the front porch, sitting down on the top step. He pulled out his phone and called his uncle. It hadn't even occurred to him to call his partner before now.

Ron answered on the second ring. "Hey! I'm pulling into the station. You'll never believe what the ATF guys got for us! They said they think they found... Channion, are you all right?"

"No." He pinched his nose, squeezed his eyes shut, fighting like hell to keep his emotions in check.

Ron's concerned voice came over, trying not to panic, "Are you hurt? Is Raina? What's wrong?"

"No, we're not hurt. We got back to her place and... They've been here, Ron. They tore the place to pieces." He paused, hearing her still sobbing in the background behind him through the open front door. Quietly he said, "They killed her horses, Ron. The bastards killed her kids."

RON RACED TO RAINA'S house as fast as he could get there without having an accident. His heart was breaking apart for their witness. He knew she was going to blame herself for this.

Ron was taken aback when he looked inside the front door. He'd been there only once before when Raina was in the hospital. He'd come out to get her organizer and eyeglasses. It'd been clean and homey.

Now it was just another crime scene.

He saw CSI Madison Jewell dusting for prints. She told him they were out back. Deciding to look over the scene first, he slipped on the shoe booties and the disposable gloves another CSI handed him. He walked throughout the house, his experienced eye taking in the details. He made his way back out the door, removed the gloves and booties, and jogged around to the back of the house.

Ron saw them a few yards away in the grass by an oak tree. Raina was lying on her back with Channion sitting beside her, his back against the tree. Two other officers were nearby keeping an eye out, just in case.

Ron felt the warm summer breeze as he walked in the tall grass toward them. His glance moved down to the barn, then back to his nephew. His gun was in his lap, Ron noted. He was keeping his guard up. They must've cleared and secured the area, otherwise he wouldn't have allowed her outside at all. A part of him thought he should've rushed her back to the station for protection, but he trusted his nephew's judgment.

He approached them and when Channion looked over at him, neither said a word. Ron sat down beside Raina, saying softly, "I'm sorry, Raina... I'm so sorry this happened. I can't tell you how sorry I am about all of this. Your horses... I know there are no words, Raina, none at all to help."

"I should've left earlier. I should've moved them earlier like you guys told me I should do," she whispered. She turned her head to look at Ron through pain-filled eyes, red and swollen from crying. "It's my fault, isn't it? If I'd moved them..." Her voice broke.

Looking at her, Ron concluded she was in a state of shock and decided to be firm with her. He took hold of her hand, finding it cold to his touch.

"It's no one's fault. Certainly *not* yours, Raina. You stop blaming yourself right this instant. The only ones at fault here are the ones who actually did it. There was no call whatsoever for them to have at your horses. Those horses of yours were innocent, sweet-natured and wouldn't hurt anybody.

"And you didn't delay moving them. None of us did. We were moving them out today. We just wanted to give you some time together first.

"It was simply a message, Raina. There's no blame to be put on any of our shoulders. We had no way of knowing they even knew your name, let alone where you lived. We wanted to be one step ahead, and we weren't.

"This is *not* your fault, and it's *not* Channion's. I know he's sitting here right beside you blaming himself. I can see it in his face. *Neither* of you are at fault."

She heard the words, knew somewhere in her mind they were true, but she still blamed herself. She'd made Channion tell her how they'd died, and he'd been honest. She'd also made him take her down to them to say a final goodbye once the CSIs arrived.

He owed her that much, she'd said. He didn't argue.

When she was done saying her goodbyes and tearfully apologizing to Rodeo and Aspen for not being there to protect them, Channion had had to practically carry her away. Her sobs had rendered her almost incapacitated. He'd led her to the oak tree, making her lie down so she'd be less of a target in case they were being watched. She was also in less pain lying down. She'd refused to go back into the house which had to be taped off anyway, and she couldn't stay in the barn.

Channion's first instinct was to get her to the station for protection—and would have if the other officers hadn't shown up as quickly as they did. He was actually surprised at how fast they'd arrived. It must've taken him longer to clear the house and barn than he realized.

Since he had backup, he decided to give her a short time for closure, to maybe even be able to tell them if anything was missing, anything off that she could see through the destruction. But mainly it was for her to adjust to one more gut punch or rather, two. He thought about putting her in the truck, but in the end, he picked the tree and high grass for cover while the others began their work and helped keep an eye out while he waited for Ron.

Lying in the grass, she knew once she left there in a short while, she'd never come back.

It was over. All of it. Her effort at building a new life in a new place had completely backfired in less than one year. She didn't know what to do or where to go. She didn't know what came next.

And she didn't even care.

She felt Ron's hand on hers, and she grabbed it as she forced herself through the shock, the pain. She forced herself to think, to begin dealing with what she'd been dealt.

"I need to call someone to bury them," she began, her voice tortured. "Can I even bury them here? They deserve respect. I don't know who..." Tears began streaming down her face again. She used her other hand to wipe at them. "And I think Mr. Farley needs to be called..."

Ron said gently, "We'll take care of it, Raina. Don't you worry. And I promise we'll take excellent care of them. We'll take care of everything."

Having recently lost their own dog, he knew exactly how she felt. Pets weren't just animals to them. They were family and deserved a burial befitting their stature. Animals gave unconditional love and support, far more than most humans. Some may scoff at that thinking, but one who truly loved animals didn't think any other way. Animals had souls behind their eyes. Beautiful souls that were purer than most any human.

Ron and Channion turned as Madison walked over. She said, "We're getting it organized and bagged now. If there's anything you want or need to get, let's get it now so we can clear it. Mike is ready whenever you are.

"We swept the house for bugs, and it's clean. We also checked your truck, Channion, and it's clean too." She paused. "All the lookouts are saying it's quiet. No sign of anyone around here, watching. And the ATF guys Ron called just called us to say they're on their way."

Nodding, Channion said, "Thanks, Madison. We'll be up in a minute."

Madison hesitated, her own heart aching at what the woman lying in the grass was going through. Crouching down beside Raina and taking her hand, she said, "I'm terribly sorry you're going through all of this, Miss Stewart. If you need anything, anything at all, please let me know."

Raina looked at the other woman and gave an imperceptible nod. It was all she could muster at that moment.

Standing back up, Madison walked toward the house, knowing the three would follow when they were ready.

After a few moments, Channion helped Raina to her feet. When her knees buckled on her, he wrapped his arm around her waist and let her lean on him. Ron rubbed her shoulder in support, worry in his eyes.

With heavy hearts and spirits, the three walked back toward her house.

As they walked, the two detectives pondered over the one glaring question: *How did they find her?*

Chapter 25

UNSURPRISINGLY, SHE WAS MOVED to a secure location. What *was* surprising was where they chose.

Later that evening, Channion followed her into his house, carrying bags of groceries they had another person buy for them before they left the station. Meeting in the safety of the parking garage, they transferred the groceries into his back seat, cramming in the bags over her things that weren't in the covered truck bed. They wanted her kept out of the public eye until they got a grasp of what was going on. To be prepared, they bought enough to last quite a while in case they had to hole up.

Parking the truck in his garage, he waited for the garage door to close before they got out. He immediately reset his alarm.

As they unloaded the groceries in the kitchen, he told her, "Whatever you do, don't open any exterior door or even a window because they're all wired to the alarm system... which is connected to emergency services. This door here to the garage is okay but not the actual garage door. While you're here, that alarm is to be on at all times. Understand?"

She nodded. She hadn't said a word since they'd left the station. He took some of the frozen food to the deep freezer in the garage. She was gathering up the plastic bags, shoving them into one when he walked back in.

"I'm going to give you a tour of my place so you know where everything is, just in case. I'd rather be prepared, okay? I'll unload your things from the truck later while you rest. Let's start downstairs..."

Even with the distraction of learning his house, he noticed her demeanor was still far from her normal self. She looked defeated. The light in her eyes had been extinguished. Could he help her with that, or was it just going to take time to work through the shock?

He flipped on the lights as he led her into his basement.

She was surprised to see a Total Gym, treadmill, rowing machine, and a stationary bike. She saw what was probably a chin-up bar bolted securely to the wall. He even had a TV mounted to a wall near an old, full-sized refrigerator, and a microwave on a little desk. An old, beat-up radio that had seen better days was on a small table underneath the TV.

"You have your own little gym?"

Channion was relieved she'd finally spoken. "I don't like public gyms. When I'm working out, I don't want to wait to use a machine. I also don't want to worry about someone else's sweat and who knows what else on it. Here, I can work out whenever I want to depending on my schedule and motivation level. Working out also helps me think. Here, I don't have any distractions."

"I guess this is your man-cave?"

He was glad she was making the effort to re-connect with him. He knew it couldn't be easy for her. "Yeah, I guess it is. But since I live alone, that term could actually apply to the whole house."

Back upstairs, he turned off the alarm and looked outside before leading her out. "To be on the safe side, you should know the lay of the land. Come with me."

As she followed him in the late evening dusk, she still couldn't accept or believe that her horses were gone. Her home was gone... and even her truck. Everything she had was *gone*. Was this real, or was she in a nightmare that *seemed* real? Her sense of security was shattered. And on top of that, her body was constantly aching.

Only half-listening to him as he showed her places to hide in or run to in an emergency, she followed him around a little shed and looked up. She stopped and gasped. "Oh! That's gorgeous!"

She found herself looking at a beautiful pond surrounded by an old, wooden fence with flowers popping up around it, some in bloom. They were on top of a small hill, so she figured he never worried about flooding. She saw a small boat on a boat lift under a metal canopy near a well-maintained little dock that had a small building beside it. There was even a nice-sized sandy beach. She saw a couple of all-weather chairs and a beach umbrella in a metal stand that was currently folded down, apparently a permanent fixture. "This is yours?"

He was pleased at her reaction simply because she had one. He'd felt her slipping deeper inside herself just moments before.

"Yep. It's one of the places I spent a lot of my time at as a boy. See over there?" Her gaze followed his arm to where he was pointing. "We had a rope tied to that tall tree. Of course, we had to see who could swing out the farthest." Pointing to the other side, he said, "That spot over there is one of the best fishing holes in the pond. Ty and I spent a lot of time out here when we were kids."

"So this place was your home growing up? Your mom and dad lived here?"

"Yeah. I've added onto it a bit over the years. Our land was part of a larger tract owned by the family. It was deeded to my parents as a wedding gift. Dad, Uncle Jack, Ron, and I built that little beach when I was about ten or so. I've added sand to it over the years obviously. Mom did all of the landscaping, so I try to keep it all going.

"The two chairs are weighed down so the wind hopefully doesn't blow them away. I got tired of hauling them back and forth from the shed every single time I wanted to sit out here." He slipped his hands into his back pockets and looked around before he said, "And Ty was on hand to help me set in that umbrella. There was some drinking involved that summer, so we're both pleasantly surprised it's actually still there."

She smiled before asking, "What's that little building?"

"Well, it's a small boat house. There's a little bathroom, a small kitchen area with a little fridge and a sink, a chair or two, and a tiny table. There's a lean-to on the other side to store stuff. When family is here, some will camp out down there. Ty and I clean our fish down there too." At her look of disgust, he laughed. "Not a fisherman, Stewart?"

"I can't stand seafood or fish. I can do tuna, but that's about it. I liked to fish as a girl but honestly preferred to row the canoe we had. I've caught a few, but it just bored me to sit there. And I felt bad for the fish. I could bait the hooks, knew my bobbles and lures, but it was too boring."

"It's relaxing."

"*Boring.*" She smiled as he playfully poked her arm with his finger. "So I would row the boat, and my brother would troll along behind."

Channion realized that was the first time she'd ever mentioned her family since they'd met. "Are you close?"

"Not anymore. As kids, we were almost inseparable. Now we go years with little to no contact, and he doesn't seem to care at all. I finally gave up after years of trying to stay a part of his life. When he got married, he joined her family like he joined the Marines. *They* all became his family, and he immediately acted like we didn't even exist. To this day, he's even worse.

"I don't even know how many kids he has, but it was I think five the last I heard. He never even let us know after the first three they had any more! I found out about the last two by sheer accident. Who knows how many he has now?"

Channion nodded. "It happens to a lot of families. It's such a shame because it doesn't make any sense. In my experience, it's generally caused by religious or political differences. Or sometimes drugs. But *how* can you be so close to someone growing up to just later forget them or act like they no longer exist?" He paused. "What about your parents?"

"They divorced when I was little, in grade school. He and I became estranged, we'll say. So it was just basically me and my mama taking on the world together. She passed away when I was in high school."

"Accident or sickness?" he asked quietly.

"I guess you could say both." She looked around the pond before quietly elaborating for him. "Drunk driver. His sickness over alcohol caused the accident that killed her. One of the reasons you'll rarely see me drink more than one or two at a time. I do drink socially but never get past the buzzed stage.

"I can't stand drunks at all. The fact I sing in bars now is a bit ironic, but the bartenders and the owner are good about keeping the drunks either out or under control. And I refuse to be around anyone who enjoys drinking too much." Looking at him, she added, "One of those things I don't want but find nonetheless."

He understood she was talking about men she'd met over the years. "Being in law enforcement, I rarely drink either even though it's a job that seems to call for it. The stress can sometimes feel overwhelming and having to deal with the public in general can often be frustrating.

"We're really here to help, to protect, but many simply don't see us that way. They treat us police worse than ever, not owning up to the fact *they* are the reason there are so many issues for us to deal with in the first place.

"There are far more criminals and everyday citizens than cops out there. Look at the ratios. It's plain common sense. A small city of say, three hundred thousand may have only three hundred cops. And those not all at once because we're obviously on different shifts.

"We can only do so much, but everyone thinks we can be everywhere instantly. And their case or call is more important than any others. Now that being said, not all three hundred thousand are acting up at once. But you know what I mean.

"If those who are complaining about and mocking us, trying to tear us down, sending the media and overpriced lawyers on us... If those people decided to actually *assist* us, turn in known criminals, help us follow leads, not break driving laws, and simply obey the laws that apply to everybody, everything would drastically change. Or how about *they* go through the Police Academy so *they* can now be a part of the solution instead of the problem?

"You know, the majority of police are good. But the bad ones instantly erase all the positives we've done. We're hopelessly outnumbered in the scheme of things. We just have to rely on some public people to be honest citizens to help balance it all out. People like you."

Raina could see this subject was a deep and sensitive one to him. Empathizing with him, she offered, "You sound like you need a drink."

He laughed, surprised at her dry humor at a time like this, then sighed deeply, shaking his head. "But with all I deal with on a daily basis, amazingly enough, I've never been drunk. Even when Ty, me, and our other cousins hung out here on the beach, camping overnight, we never got drunk. Of course, if we had when younger, Mom or Dad would've known soon enough and tanned our hides. Then Dad was gone, and I guess we just never had the urge to try it and see what it was like.

"Maybe I should say I'm speaking for myself. It wouldn't surprise me to hear about a couple of my cousins having some rip-roaring times when not here. Actually, I know some have, but it's never been my thing. Or Ty's that I've ever known about. It's probably one of the many reasons he stays with me when he visits."

"Except for that umbrella summer?" she teased. "What was that all about? Or can I guess?"

He gifted her with a broad smile, his eyes shining with humor. "You'd probably be right. Dang women breaking our honest hearts to pieces."

She had to smile back.

They made their way back up to the house. She paid more attention now to what he was showing and telling her. She appreciated him trying to think ahead so if the worst happened, she'd have a fighting chance of escaping, surviving. Although right now, she didn't even care. Why bother?

Back inside, he unloaded her suitcases and bags and took them to her new room. She took a long shower. As the water fell, so did her tears. She figured he couldn't hear her sobs over her horses in the shower.

She couldn't bear the thought she was now alone in the world even more than before. They were all she had. Because she was crying, her physical pain got worse and caused her to cry more.

She just couldn't catch a break, she thought. She was miserable. When she felt she could face the detective relatively soon, she turned off the water and grabbed a fluffy towel.

In her new room, she had to go through a couple of suitcases before she found her underwear and pjs. Once she was dressed, she just sat on the bed, staring at the wall. Her mind was blank. She wasn't even sure how long she sat there before she forced herself to sort through some of her things.

Her clothes had been scattered everywhere in her old room, but they weren't all torn up. CSI Madison shoved them into bags so she could wash them later whenever she landed somewhere. Raina had watched from the door as Madison got out her suitcases and duffle bags, packing up her things so Raina wouldn't cause herself any more pain.

In a daze and feeling numb, Raina had watched as her life was shoved into bags and zippered boxes on little plastic wheels. She'd made sure she got the framed photos of her and her mama, and the ones of her horses from the shelf. They'd packed all of her bathroom supplies in another suitcase. Madison had even tossed in some toilet paper for cushioning.

Ron and Channion carried out her suitcases and bags while she and Madison went to her little office. Raina wanted to get her instruments and music for when she was on the road. She also wanted her lesson and music books. She'd been dismayed when they'd walked through the doorway. Whoever had come out to kill her had ripped up most of her music books and smashed her autoharp and keyboard to pieces.

Raina thought it rather symbolic they'd also killed her music.

WHEN SHE FELT SEMI-SOCIABLE, she headed downstairs. She wore her longer pair of pj bottoms since they'd still been in a drawer. And to her, that meant clean and untouched by evil hands.

She smelled the food before she made it halfway down his stairs. She stopped in the kitchen doorway and watched him at the stove. She saw the Hamburger Helper box and the fresh salad he'd put together on the counter.

When Channion turned and saw her standing in his own kitchen, all freshly cleaned and in cozy pajamas, his heart skipped a beat. It was hard to picture her as the same woman he'd first met in the hospital room.

Look at her now, he thought to himself. Even looking incredibly sad and worn down, she still had enough fight in her to keep plugging along. But for how much longer? he wondered.

He could tell she'd been crying, probably while she'd showered. Crying was a part of grief, so he was glad to know she wasn't trying to bottle it all inside. But tears could only heal so much. He had an insane urge to give her a hug, wondering if that would be professional. Would she misread it as something else?

"Come here," he said before he could stop himself.

She silently walked over to him.

"Don't misread this, all right?"

"What?"

"This." He pulled her closer and gently hugged her.

As they sat down to eat, she asked about the next day's plans.

He looked at her for a moment. "You have those lessons still if you're feeling up to them. If not, Raina, it's perfectly okay to take the day off. You *need* to grieve. It might hit you again later on once the shock wears off some more. You don't have to do anything you don't want to do, or that you're not ready for. Besides, you're supposed to be resting.

"It's also safer for you to not be out and about. They're bound to know where you work. Or they'll figure it out if they don't. But for now, we'll add security detail if you want to continue to work."

She said firmly, "I *need* to work as much as I reasonably and safely can. If I stop, I'll lose any momentum I even have. I'll be stuck in a perpetual re-start mode if I don't keep going, Channion. Even though, no, I *don't* want to go to work, I need to.

"I *know* I need to rest, to stay hidden. And in all fairness, that's all I *want* to do. But if I stop, if I give in and hole up, I'm terrified I'll never come out again. I can't let them break me, Channion. I don't know if I'll have the strength to pull myself out again. Right now, I'm hanging on by a very thin thread.

"But equally important to me, I don't want to put you or anyone else in danger. Definitely not for what could be seen as stubbornness or an attitude of being invincible. Neither of those are the truth."

He nodded, admiring her grit and attitude. But he was also fearful she was going to push herself too far, too fast.

"And I need to call my landlord and let him know..."

He was shaking his head. "We already took care of that for you. Ron went out and talked to him in person after we left the station. Ron called me while you were in the shower. Mr. Farley is sympathetic and extremely concerned about you.

"He knows this isn't your fault. He said to tell you that you're more than welcome to stay on, if you decide to go back. Either way, you're not to worry about the house in the meantime. Mr. Farley also sent his sincerest condolences about Aspen and Rodeo."

"Please tell Ron thank you for doing that."

He nodded. "We'll need to forward your house mail too. You said you have a post office box, right?"

She nodded. "But I never got my truck keys back, and my post office box key is on the ring. It's probably overflowing by now. My other key... is at the house." She sighed as she looked at him. "It's probably safe there for now. I'll need to go back to get it sometime. It's in my filing cabinet."

"I'll see about getting your key ring back. That shouldn't be a problem."

AFTER THEY ATE, THEY sat in the living room and further discussed the next day's schedule. He wanted her to stay home while she insisted she needed to work. They compromised: She'd work, and they'd see how it went.

They finally went upstairs together. She had to ask him to put the cream on her back again. They both figured this was a new, temporary routine. Facing away from the mirror, she carefully lifted up her top while he applied the cream to her wounds. Neither mentioned it when she shivered when the cold cream touched her skin.

When he was finished, he washed his hands as she lowered her top. After he walked her to her room, he made sure she had everything she needed. He walked to the bathroom and returned, handing her a roll of toilet paper because he didn't have any tissues. His thoughtful gesture made tears well up in her eyes.

When he went to bed himself, he kept his door open in case she had another nightmare.

Chapter 26

RAINA LAY ON HER back in yet another bed that wasn't her own, her upper body slightly propped up to ease the pressure in her torso. She pulled the lightweight sheets and the soft blanket up to her chest before crossing her hands over her stomach, staring at the dark ceiling while she listened to the wind blowing outside the windows. They'd called for a thunderstorm, and it sounded like it was finally blowing in.

It was a mistake to let her mind relax as the events ranging from last night's horrible nightmare, the dash to the hospital, finding her home destroyed, her beloved horses killed, and her having to move out and go into what was basically a safe house all caught up with her. All of that had happened in less than twenty-four hours, she realized.

Now that it was quiet, and she was alone, the enormity of her situation hit home. She felt the sobs coming from deep inside and covered her mouth so Channion wouldn't hear as hot tears rolled continuously down her face. She tried so hard to not cry, she choked.

She simply kept seeing her horses in her mind's eye, being shot and falling to the ground. Did they wonder where she was? Did they wonder why she wasn't there to protect them? Why did they have to die alone, without her there to comfort them in their last moments? To say their goodbyes? For her to say her own?

It hurt her ribs to cry but the more she tried to hold it in, the worse it got. She simply had to let it out. Her life was in complete and utter shambles. She didn't know what to do anymore. Not even her own friends could help her out of this because they couldn't even know.

She cried for her kids being taken away so ruthlessly from her, her loneliness, that sense of being completely unanchored, and feeling more scared than she wanted the two detectives protecting her to ever know. She was, quite simply, terrified of what else could happen. Would she make it out of this alive? How lucky could any person be? Would either of the men guarding her get killed because of her?

She tried to be quiet as she let her emotions out but to her hyped-up senses, she figured she wasn't nearly as quiet as she hoped to be. And that thought just made her cry more. She couldn't even cry quietly. How pathetic was that?

She blew her nose again and again using the toilet paper from the nightstand, wiping the tears from her face. Her skin soon felt raw.

Thoughts were now racing through her head, so many she couldn't hold onto any of them. She was going to drive herself mad. The one thought she *could* hold onto was that she didn't want to be alone anymore.

She knew she should stay where she was. She was an adult. A grown woman who'd dealt with the curveballs that life had already thrown at her all by herself. But she couldn't deal with this barrage of curveballs alone.

Her limit had finally been reached.

Before she could talk herself out of it, she put on her glasses and slid slowly out of the bed, having the presence of mind to be sure she had her balance before moving away from it. She made her way out the open door and walked down the hallway to Channion's room, her feet moving silently on the carpet.

"Channion?" she called out in a timid voice. Did he sleep with his gun under his pillow?

He'd heard her in the other room but decided to leave her alone to deal with it as she saw fit. He didn't want to embarrass her by going to her, so he just laid there, listening to her crying. It tore him up inside, knowing her life had been completely shattered—and in such a short amount of time.

He barely saw her as she walked into his darkened doorway, but he made out her silhouette from the small nightlight in the hallway. Lightning flashes lit up the room through his window with blinding brightness.

"Raina? What do you need?" He didn't know what else to say to her. He knew he couldn't ask her if she was okay as that'd be insensitive and stupid. He leaned up on his elbow as he waited for her to speak.

"Can I come in? Please?" She couldn't stop herself from crying. There was too much pain inside. She walked toward his large bed and stopped beside it. Forcing herself to admit she needed comfort, she asked, "Can I stay with you, just for tonight? Please? I don't want to be alone. I can't... I can't..." Her sobs wouldn't allow her to continue.

With no hesitation, he tossed his blanket back and sat up to swing his legs over the side of his bed. He reached out for her hand and helped her sit down. He asked himself how could he turn away another human being who was going through so much torment?

How could he live with himself if he turned her away in that instant? She was looking for human contact, companionship, comfort. Nothing more than to know she wasn't completely alone.

She leaned against him, tucking her head under his chin as she cried her heart out. He simply wrapped his arms around her and held her, rubbing his hands lightly on her back, trying to avoid her wounds. She cried so hard she choked and had to cough. He was afraid she'd get sick. Her ribs had to be taking a beating as well as her throat.

He didn't know what else to do except to just hold her tight. It was impossible to make her stop so she wouldn't hurt herself further. He felt the softness of her tears and her hair against him as much as he felt the hard heaves and quakes of her body.

When she got what he figured were the majority of her emotions out, gauging by her soul-deep sobs sliding into softer cries and her full-body shakes to quivering shivers, he left the room. He came back with her pillows, a glass of water, the roll of toilet paper, and a couple of damp washcloths.

She put her glasses on the nightstand and carefully wiped her face with the washcloths and blew her nose until it hurt as bad as when it was first broken. He set his little trash can at her side so she had somewhere to toss her makeshift tissues. He handed her the glass of water, which she took a few sips of before handing back to him with hands that were still shaking. He took the washcloths to the bathroom to rinse out and brought them back.

After a brief internal debate, he had her lie down, propping the pillows behind her. Once she was comfortable, he tenderly wiped her face for her this time, moving her hair out of the way. When he was done, he tossed the cloths over the side of the trash can before he put it on the floor. Getting back into the bed beside her, he positioned the other pillows he brought in for himself and finally pulled the covers over both of them. She was still shaking.

He knew she was basically in shock, and there wasn't a whole lot he could do except keep her warm and offer her comfort. He slid his arm over her waist for the contact, worried he'd hurt her if he let it rest too heavily anywhere else he placed it.

She softly cried even as he held her, listened to his soothing voice when the thundering storm outside the window allowed her to hear him. He knew she needed to let it all out, so he simply held her until she finally began to quiet.

When she was able to, she finally spoke, breaking her silence since she'd walked in and fell apart. Her voice still thick with tears, she said, "It's my fault. It's my fault they're dead. I wasn't there to protect them. When they needed me the most, I wasn't there for them."

He adjusted his head on his pillows before saying quietly, "You weren't there because I took you to the hospital. And if I hadn't, you'd have been in bed. Honey, it's not your fault. I know it feels like it. I know because I'm feeling the same way.

"If I hadn't taken you to the hospital, I would've been there. I would've known they were there. Maybe I could have..." His own voice trailed off.

Would he have known though? Channion asked himself. Even if he *had* heard the shots, it would've already been too late.

She turned her head to face him. "No, Channion. It's not *your* fault. They were *my* horses. *My* kids. *I* was the one who was supposed to take care of them, not you."

Her voice hitched, and she tried to control it. "You did right by taking me to the ER. Even the doctor said that, remember? It was your job to protect me, and mine to protect them. Only I failed, and you didn't."

"Honey, that's not—" he began before she interrupted him.

She whispered, "And all of this, it's not happening to you. It's happening to *me*. *My* life is the one that's been shattered and is now gone. One day, I'll be gone from yours, and your life will continue just as it was. But I have to start all over because *I'm* the one who started all of this. I'll have to live with it the rest of my life.

"I don't regret saving Bryce. That's the only good thing that's come out of all of this. But all of this is *my* fault. You're just here by default because you were assigned to me. I'm just another case for you to solve in the big scheme of things."

He knew her feelings were all over the board. While he had to admit she had logical points, he also tried to not take offense or get mad at her attitude or her words. He made a split-second decision to be a little firm with her, to not allow her to wallow in self-pity. He could offer her comfort, but he couldn't allow her to sink into a pit of quicksand that'd be even harder to get out of, maybe even impossible.

He said, "You're right. It's not my fault, but it's not yours either. How could you even think that? And yes, Ron and I were assigned to you. But we're *also* assigned to Bryce. *He* didn't cause any of this to happen either. He was just doing his job. Nothing more. Nothing less. It could've been me, Ron, Steve, or Luke that this happened to. It just so happened to have been Bryce.

"It's a risk we all take every time we pull over a person on a traffic stop like this was, or knock on a door to serve a warrant, or even to follow up on a lead.

"While you're right this is happening more directly to you, it's *still* affecting me and Ron. We're people who care about you and Bryce, not a couple of unfeeling robots. And

Bryce's life has been altered forever as well. By God, Raina! Bryce is still in the hospital, still fighting to live. You're not.

"You still have a career while Bryce may not. He may not be able to recover from this, whether mentally, emotionally, or physically. If he can't, for whatever reason, he'll need to find a new purpose in his life. Being a cop is all he's ever done.

"This isn't just about you. Both my uncle and I are putting our lives on the line for both you *and* Bryce. It's not fair at all to say none of this is happening to us. I understand it's not as personal to me as it is to you, but that *doesn't* mean we aren't still affected."

She was immediately chastised. She was both right... and so wrong. She realized what she'd said was basically a slap in his face and hurried to apologize.

"I'm sorry, Channion. I'm so sorry I said that it wouldn't affect you. Of course it will. And you're right. You and your uncle *are* putting your lives on the line for me and for Bryce. I'm so sorry. I'm not thinking straight right now. I didn't mean to insult you. It was wrong of me to say that."

He was mollified, knowing he had to strike a careful balance with her. "I appreciate that. If I were exactly in your shoes, I'd probably feel like you do. Just remember, we're *all* in this together, Raina. None of us are going to be the same person we were at the beginning of this case at the other end of it when it's over. And one day, it will be."

He reached over her to get some toilet paper to wipe away her tears. She took some to blow her nose again, tossing the tissues in the general direction of the trash can.

Leaning over her, he said, "You have the right to fall apart. And Ron and I will be here when you do to help pick you back up." He tenderly brushed her hair back from her face. "You're not alone. Are you listening to me?"

She nodded.

"You better be. Now you rest, and let time work its healing powers on you. It'll take some time, and it'll hurt for a while yet. You mourn when you need to and how you need to. Don't lose your fighting spirit. We'll do what we do as quickly and as thoroughly as we can. And we'll be here to help you begin a new life when this is all over. All right?"

She nodded again.

"Try and let it go, Raina. For tonight, staying here with me, just try and let it go. You're safe here. Let your mind relax and sleep. I'll be right here to watch over you."

Worn out, Raina finally drifted into sleep while he held her close.

When her breathing moved into the deep, even cadences of one who was in a deep—or more accurately, exhausted—sleep, he finally closed his own eyes and allowed himself to join her.

Chapter 27

THE ALARM BROUGHT CHANNION back to reality the next morning. Both of them were simply nearing exhaustion from the stress of their lives being drastically changed in a short amount of time. Neither had slept through an entire night lately without *something* happening.

Channion reached over to hit the snooze button and drifted right back to sleep. When the alarm went off the second time, he again hit the snooze button. It was his personal rule to not hit it more than twice even though there were many times when it was hard not to. Like now. He knew he had nine minutes before it went off again, so he did his best to relish being comfortable, at home, in bed, where it was quiet.

Knowing as soon as he got up his job would take over, he tried to let his mind rest. He could still hear the rain outside, the wind whipping it against the glass like sand.

He listened to Raina's even, deep breathing beside him. She was so worn down not even the alarm going off broke into her sleep. Throughout the rest of the night, he'd felt her twitch and jerk, heard her breathing pattern change and an occasional moan. He'd held her loosely in those moments, prepared even in his sleepy state of mind to stop her from hurting herself if she got trapped in her tormenting memories again.

He finally opened his eyes, looking at her profile. He took his time studying her face as he listened to the sound of her deep and rhythmic breathing. Watching her sleep, he felt an overpowering need to protect her. Her good deed of saving someone's life had backfired on her, bringing her only heartache and so much misery. He admired her as much as he worried about her.

Listening to the rain still pouring down, he really just wanted to stay there in bed and hold her to shield her from the world outside his windows. She needed her rest so she could heal. He needed his so he could protect her and work on their case. He leaned forward on impulse and lightly kissed her temple, then got out of bed. He shut off the alarm, pulled the covers back over her and walked out of the room.

RAINA SLOWLY WOKE UP to the sound of rain being pelted against the window. At an incredibly loud crack of thunder, she was jerked wide awake, her heart pounding. The loud crack sounded like a gunshot.

It took everything she had to not leap out of the bed and hit the floor, or bolt and run for cover. She forced herself to focus on slowing down her rapid breathing. She soon realized she was clenching the bedsheets in her hands. It took her a minute to release her death grip on them.

It took her another minute to realize where she was—in Channion's bed. She knew instinctively he'd behaved like a gentleman, and she greatly admired the man for it. Her trust and faith in the detective were absolute.

As she lay there, she heard faint noises from probably the kitchen. She smiled to herself, wondering if she stayed there long enough, would he serve her breakfast in bed? *His* bed? If he did, what else could it mean? If he didn't, she'd be disappointed even when she knew better.

Better to avoid the possibility of either happening, she told herself.

Although the thought was a pleasant distraction from everything else going on in her life right now, she made herself sit up. She waited for her head to stop spinning before getting out of the bed. Seeing her glasses on the nightstand, she slipped them on. She sighed at the lenses being spotted from her salty tears.

When she saw the used tissues on the floor, she lowered herself to place them in the trash can. Holding onto the bed, she carefully pulled herself back to her feet. Grabbing the pillows, the roll of toilet paper, the trash can, and the used washcloths, she walked out of the room.

WHEN CHANNION HEARD THE water running upstairs, he closed the file folders he'd been going through at his table. He glanced at the clock, a slight frown on his face. He was hoping she'd sleep even longer than she did.

After he'd worked out in his gym earlier, he'd called his uncle and told him she'd had another rough night. The worst yet by far emotionally, as they'd expected.

Ron was no fool. If Raina was having rough nights, so was his nephew. Both of them were in this together even more than he himself was. Ron told his nephew neither one of them were to come to the station unless they felt they needed to. There wasn't much else to do right now, anyway, his uncle reasoned, unless they got more evidence in. He was going to go see Bryce later to check on him.

When Channion told him about Raina's desire to work, both men agreed she needed to rest more. As did Channion. He couldn't protect her if he was too tired to keep his own eyes open. It was safer for her to stay put and out of the public eye, so they decided to order her to stay in. Channion once again called Lorenzo at the studio and asked him to call her students, apologizing for the short notice.

When Raina stopped in the doorway to the kitchen, she felt shy because of the night before. She smelled the eggs and bacon frying and thought how nice he was to cook for her yet again. She figured one of these days, she needed to get up first to do it for him instead.

He was once again at the stove, dressed in what she surmised were his workout clothes, just getting ready to slide the spatula under the eggs to put them on the plates that already held toast.

He smiled at her. "Good morning! Hungry?"

"Good morning. I'm a little bit hungry but not overly. I usually don't get much of an appetite until I've been up a while..."

She gave a small smile when he dramatically shrugged his shoulders, let out a loud sigh, and returned the eggs to the frying pan. She walked over to stand beside him, saying, "But since you're so sweet to cook for an overly emotional woman, the least I can do is eat it."

"You're not being overly emotional," he replied as he slid the fried eggs back onto the plates. He noticed her voice was hoarse. "Frankly, I feel better knowing you aren't ashamed to let it out. Don't be because you're going to be healthier for it.

"And I'm certainly not going to think less of you because you came to me for comfort and cried. Asking for help is what you need to do. Don't try and cope with all of this on your own. Crying isn't always a sign of weakness. It's also a coping mechanism." He turned off the burner and placed the bacon on paper towels to soak up the grease, patting them down.

She tried to keep her tone light to ease her nervousness. "I also wanted to say thank you for last night, for letting me come in your room... and your bed. I'm fairly sure that whole scene wasn't part of the job description when you decided to become a detective."

He quipped, "If it was, I would've done it a whole lot sooner!" Turning to look her directly in the eyes, he said with a serious tone, "And you're welcome. And it's also something we'll keep just between us to avoid any potential ethics issues, all right? Promise."

"Absolutely. Promise."

He put the low-sodium turkey bacon on their plates and motioned for her to take them to the table. She noticed he'd already put the silverware and the bottle of pills on the table. She poured a few into her palm since her head was already hurting.

How long was she going to have to endure these headaches? And her throat was so sore from sobbing, screaming, and more crying, it hurt to talk. Was she *ever* going to catch a break?

Channion noticed her shaking out the pills. Watching her, he opened the fridge. "Milk, water, OJ?"

"Milk, please." She glanced at him. She just had to clear her conscience and talk this out, hoping humor would help settle her nerves. "And thanks for not taking advantage of the situation last night either. As a guy, I imagine that must've been a trial for you."

He poured the milk, saying, "You have no idea. After you went to sleep, I slept in your bed to avoid any temptation." He placed her glass of milk on the table before turning away.

She silently watched him as he walked back across the kitchen to return the milk to the fridge. He still wasn't smiling when he sat down across from her at the table with his orange juice and began eating, not saying another word.

"You did?" she finally asked, surprised.

Was this a good thing, or a bad thing? Honest to God, she didn't know how she felt about hearing he left her alone in his bed. She supposed it was more professional, but still...

Keeping his head down so she couldn't see the laughter in his eyes, he considered toying with her some more, but in the end decided not to. He scooped up some eggs, admitting, "No, I stayed."

"Oh. Well... Thank you." It was an odd sense of relief that washed through her at his remark.

With a wide grin, he finally looked up and into her eyes. "I figured if I left, you'd just follow me anyway."

With a small burst of laughter coming from deep inside, she genuinely smiled back at him. Feeling better, Raina began to eat.

WHILE THEY ATE, HE broke the news to her they needed to stay home. To prevent her from possibly arguing with him, he added he'd already called the studio and let Lorenzo know.

While she wondered if something had happened that he wasn't telling her, she was also slightly relieved. While she seriously needed to work, she was just as scared of putting Channion in danger. If something happened to him because of her, she didn't think she could live with it.

Chapter 28

THE NEXT DAY, THEY stayed in again for safety. Since the rain had stopped the previous day, the bright sun had ample time to begin drying the grass. Working around his house was relaxing to him, so Channion was outside doing yard work.

Raina had slept through most of the night on her own although she woke up a few times from bad dreams. She'd had a bad nightmare near dawn that Channion had to wake her up from. Thankfully, it wasn't as bad as the one at her house.

She was remembering little bits and pieces, but she wasn't sure of any of it. What was real, and what wasn't? As promised, anything new she remembered she told to Channion, who would pass it on to his uncle and the ATF agents working the case with them.

She sat at Channion's table with her personal laptop—which remarkably missed getting smashed apart and survived with just scratches when it apparently fell off the desk. She spent a couple of hours changing her website for more security before tackling her emails.

They'd decided when they got her a new phone a few days prior to also get her a new number. She gave it only to those who needed it for her work. Her old phone she decided to turn off after she checked for messages. Now, she texted a couple of family members with the new number but held little expectations to hear from them. No one had called her old one, so why would they call the new one?

She finally took a break and poured herself a glass of milk so she could swallow more pills. Waiting for her small headache to clear, she watched through the window as Channion competently ran the hedge trimmer across the bushes alongside the house for a while. He was wearing his yard jeans that were covered in grass and dirt stains from some earlier projects. It was relaxing to watch him work and hear the sound of the lawn equipment in the background.

With her laundry being done as she worked, all of these sounds were homey sounds. Comforting sounds. They helped make her feel everything was normal. She did her best to ignore the reason she was doing so many loads of her laundry in a strange man's house. Remembering why most of her clothes were crammed into suitcases and duffle bags led to thoughts of her little house, her life now, and the loss of her kids.

If she thought about her horses, she cried. The feelings were far too raw still. It'd only been a few days after all. Her heart was shattered, and her guilt was eating her alive. She wondered if Channion still had those videos of them on his phone. If he did, would watching them hurt her more or help her? She was too scared to ask and take the chance.

Raina was distracted from watching Channion work when her phone rang. It was her student who had sung in her school's talent show the night before. She hadn't won, but *had* placed third. She said she couldn't wait any longer to call Raina to thank her for all of her help in the lessons. The enthusiastic conversation was just what Raina needed to lift up her spirits.

She tossed her clothes into the dryer, set the timer, started another load in the washer before she headed back to her laptop. She figured she needed to pitch in some money for detergent and his utility bills considering how many loads of laundry she was doing. Not to mention daily showers. With no income, she wasn't sure how much she *could* contribute. She wasn't a freeloader by any means. Maybe they could trade housework for utilities? She decided to ask him later.

When she noticed it was after three o'clock, she took another break and headed to the kitchen. Preparing a small lunch for them, she let herself out the back door, knowing he'd turned off the alarm earlier. She figured being in the backyard was safe enough.

Raina found Channion raking up the hedge trimmings around the corner of the house. The wheelbarrow beside him was half-full. She thought he was more than adorable with his baseball hat on backwards. Trying not to stare at him, she called out, "Hey Scott! Ya hungry?"

He stopped raking, leaning on the rake handle while he watched her walk over to him. He tried to not notice her long legs in those blue jean shorts, or how the breeze blew her hair around her face. Unfortunately for him, cops were trained to be quite observant and into the details.

"You made me lunch? That's awfully nice of you." He leaned the rake against the bushes.

"Yeah. I thought you might be thinking about food by now." Thinking it best to ask, she did. "Is it safe for me to come back here?"

"Hopefully."

"I guess you can't get more honest than that."

He grinned at her dry reply.

Raina said, "I know water would be better for you, but I figured you'd prefer the pop. Hedging my bet, I brought you both."

She followed him to a grassy area in the partial shade of an old maple tree. Sitting on a bench made of wood and metal she guessed his mom had put there, she propped her can of pop between her leg and the bench. He went to wash his hands and came back, sitting down beside her.

In companionable silence, with occasional small talk, they dug into the turkey sandwiches, potato chips, and vegetables. They took turns waving away an annoying fly. When they were done, they leaned against the damp bench, both feeling relaxed and enjoying the peaceful day.

"You forgot dessert," he said after some time. "Don't get me wrong. The main course was pretty good, and I'm grateful for it. But where's the dessert?"

Leaning forward, Raina reached into her back pocket and pulled out some cookies in a Ziploc bag. Smiling, she said, "I was a Girl Scout when I was younger, so I'm always prepared!"

Taking them, he handed one to her before popping a whole one in his mouth. With his mouth full of cookie, he looked at her. "A Girl Scout? Really?"

She could barely make out what he said and grinned. "No, not really. I was too busy with other things to bother with the Girl Scouts." She took a bite of her cookie before saying, "However, I *was* in the Boy Scouts."

He chewed another cookie while he contemplated her. "The Boy Scouts? How could you be in the Boy Scouts if you were too busy to bother with the Girl Scouts? Besides, you *couldn't* be in the Boy Scouts. You're a girl, and you probably had cooties."

She laughed. "Probably."

"Are you lying to me, Stewart?"

"Nope, not at all. I was an *honorary* Boy Scout, and we don't lie to officers of the law." She grinned. "My brother was a Scout. And the leader quit or got fired, I don't know which, and since no other dad would take it over, my mom did."

At the look on his face, she laughed again. "Seriously. She did. And she couldn't leave me at home during the meetings, so I went along. I even helped sell stuff for them, kept up at the newspaper recycling trailer, learned how to make the knots. I can make a slipknot with my eyes closed. I even went to camp with them."

He tugged on her hair at that. "Now I *know* you're lying."

"Am not." She smiled. "I couldn't *stay*, but they let me go in with my brother and mom, and we stayed for most of that first night. We had the bonfire and everything. I guess some other troop leader took over my brother and his pals for the week."

She bit into another cookie, chewed it while she remembered her childhood. She smiled at him as he eyed her as he drank the last of his pop.

"Are all cops this suspicious? For real, sir. I was an honorary Scout for a while. No one seemed to care, at least not that I know about. Then he got out of the Scouts, so I was too.

"But now that I'm thinking about it, I *do* seem to recall my mom telling me once his old den leader had been accused of molesting some kid or something. I don't know if that meant a Scout or someone else, but I'm positive that's what happened. Yeah, it was. I remember now she said that was why *she* became the new leader as no other adult male wanted the responsibility. Horrible stuff like that happens, unfortunately."

"Yeah, it does." He took the last cookie, shoved it in his mouth, chewed it before he washed it down with the water. They sat there for a few minutes more, each in their own thoughts.

He finally stood up, holding his hand out for hers to help her stand. He handed over his plate and the empty water bottle and pop cans. They walked back toward the house in an easy silence before she asked, "Were you ever a Boy Scout?"

"Nah, I was too busy to bother with the Boy Scouts..."

She knew where he was going with it and shoved him. He laughed as he caught back up with her. "Thanks for the lunch, Stewart."

"You're welcome, Scott."

Chapter 29

THE FOLLOWING DAY, CHANNION and Raina went to the station for a while. After speaking with a few officers there, they settled down with Ron at their desks. Contemplating a thought she had on the way over, she decided to ask and see what they said.

"Can I ask you guys for something?"

Ron looked up from sheets full of photographs and stats on guns. "Sure. What do you need?"

"Can I see the video from Bryce's car?"

Channion asked, "Why?"

"So I can figure out what's real, and what's not, in these nightmares I keep having. I'm going to go nuts trying to decide what category these memories go in."

As she expected, both of them shook their heads no.

She pleaded, "Detectives, please. I need to see what actually happened."

"It could taint the case, Raina," Ron explained. "Whatever information you give us needs to come from you freely. We can't be accused of leading or directing your thoughts, memories. In court, it could all be dismissed. It could let a murderer or a weapons dealer go free on a technicality."

She tried another route. "Okay, I get that. I really do. But has it occurred to either of you that by me seeing it, it might *trigger* a memory, some information, you or the ATF could use? Aren't I supposed to be trying to help you guys in any way I can?

"I've already given you all the information you really need anyway. I already gave you my written statement from what I remembered, and you have me on video. Maybe I can add to them. You've cleared me as a possible suspect, right?"

They both nodded. They'd done that first thing. It was standard procedure, of course. Her background and prints were clean. She didn't even have a ticket on record. And her hands tested negative for GSR so they knew *she* didn't shoot Bryce. The video also showed she didn't.

They'd made a list of all of her contacts taken from her phone while she was in the hospital, running them all for possible links to any of their suspects. No link was found between any of them.

She was a real, live, modern-day Good Samaritan. Better yet, she was also a *brave* Samaritan who was at the right place at the right time—and willing to risk her life to save another's. Best yet, it was a police officer she was there for.

Raina knew she had their attention now. "What if there's *part* of something I'm remembering in my nightmares, but I'm missing the whole of it? Detectives, it's been fifteen days since this happened. I can handle it. If not, well, I'm having nightmares anyway. At least I'll know if it's real or not now. I tell you both every detail I remember, but it'd be good if I could place it all inside my own head. Please?

"And what if this actually works as therapy for me? I think the positives are strong here and seem legal to me. I don't see how you guys can let an opportunity like this slip by you."

They left her sitting there to talk it over privately. She tapped her fingers on the desk while she waited for them to return. When they did, she knew she'd won. But now, she was feeling anxious.

They led her into a room that had a camera, video equipment, and a table in it. She sat down, hoping this wasn't a mistake. She turned when another man entered the room and took a seat at the little table. He smiled at Raina in greeting, introduced himself. A minute later, another man came in and took the last seat. He also smiled and introduced himself.

Channion looked at her. "Detectives Diggs and Sawyer are here to show impartiality since the two of us are your bodyguards. We don't want any of our reputations or viewpoints questioned. Agreed?"

After she nodded, he continued, "We also can't show you all of it for the reasons we already gave you. However, there are a few parts we've been wondering about that maybe you could clear up for us.

"Are you *sure* about this, Raina? Are you prepared? It's not pretty. It's going to be worse because it's going to hit home that it's *you* in it, but you could possibly answer a few questions for us."

Firmly, she said, "Yes, I'm sure."

Ron put in the DVD, having her turn away until he got to the part they were willing to show her. Telling her she could watch now, she turned around.

Raina took a breath when the video began to play in real time. She watched herself walking from the police cruiser toward her wrecked truck, smashed up against one of the cars which was also rammed into the first one. She was stumbling around. Watching herself walk back around to the truck, she saw herself slowly reach inside, remove something. She walked around, repeatedly stopping before resuming her odd ritual. After stopping at her truck again, she made her way back to the cruiser. It simply wasn't clear enough, had a wrong angle, or was being blocked for them to tell.

She went out of the camera's view. She waited and waited for something to happen. She saw herself walk around from the passenger side of the cruiser, making her way back yet again to her own truck.

What was she doing? Raina asked herself. It seemed familiar, like on the edge of her mind.

This time, she took a little longer. Staggering back toward the cruiser, she'd stopped and, of all things to do, raised her arm. Then she made her way around the first car that'd been pulled over.

The detectives all watched her, hoping she could tell them what she was doing. They all noticed she kept frowning in concentration as she watched herself on the screen.

They watched the screen now as she made her way back to the cruiser, go out of sight again. After a few moments, the video showed the car driving crookedly onto the road, drive by the wrecked vehicles and head toward town. Channion stopped the video at that point.

After a moment of silence, Ron asked, "You okay?"

"Yeah."

He looked at her hopefully as he inquired, "Can you tell us what you were doing when you were walking around like you were? Were you disoriented?"

Looking at the detectives, their looks expectant, she answered honestly, "I have absolutely no idea."

Ron asked, "Do you feel like this helped you any? Jogged any memories?"

"Kinda… It's like it's on the tip of my tongue…" She looked at the now-blank monitor. "*What* was I doing? What was I *thinking?*"

Ron asked, "Why didn't you just get in the squad car and drive off? Get Bryce to the hospital immediately? That was the logical thing to do, wasn't it?"

"Don't be such a movie critic, Ron," she said, faint humor in her voice.

The men laughed.

Raina sat back in her chair. "I always seem to have a reason for everything I do, so there *must* be something there. I can see why you have questions. Can I see it again? Let me do this, guys, if not for you and the case, then for me and Bryce. Are there other parts you want me to clear up for you?"

Her eyes pleaded with them. How could they say no?

Steve Diggs sat there, his own thoughts churning as his respect for this woman went up yet another notch. Here she was, demanding to help more than she already had, despite everything she was going through. Sawyer shared a similar thought as he looked at their brave witness.

It was beginning to play when Ron paused it, telling Raina any thoughts or questions she had to say out loud, even if she felt like she was speaking to herself. She nodded.

They all wondered what she was feeling. What was going on in her mind as she watched it?

Although she wasn't even watching the beginning, she wondered aloud, "Why on earth did he choose a rifle from his trunk anyway? In my nightmares, I see a long gun, so it must be a rifle.

"I mean, I don't know what other weapons were in his car, but why something so big? Why not a pistol? Something someone driving by probably wouldn't see? Something he could conceal? If I hadn't seen the rifle, or what I thought was one, I *never* would've even thought to turn around!"

Channion thought she'd finally answered his one burning question: *Why did she turn around in the first place?* In the video, they all saw her drive by. But then not too much later, she came driving back like a rabid bat out of hell.

He thought to clarify her statement. "So seeing the rifle is *why* you turned around? That's it? No other reason?"

She looked at him as Ron paused the video. She chewed on her lip as she concentrated. Flashes coming back to her, she tried to grasp them. Speaking slowly, she said, "Yes... I think so. I passed Bryce and drove down the road, seeing the other car pulled over. I was wondering if I should stop and offer help? But something told me not to... I just had a bad gut feeling.

"I saw the black guy at the trunk remove what I *thought* was a rifle. Yes... I drove on a bit more and pulled over to figure out *why* would someone need a rifle right then? That's when it hit me something was wrong..." She looked at Channion. "Did you guys ever wonder why a rifle?"

In truth, they hadn't. Channion hazarded a few guesses, saying, "Maybe for intimidation? Maybe at first, they weren't planning on actually shooting Bryce. Maybe it was already loaded, and the others weren't? Maybe he preferred rifles."

She turned back to the monitor, thinking about that, as Ron pushed *play*.

"One man down. Another sprayed. I pepper sprayed the one guy... I remembered that. He was now useless to that other guy, at least for a while, but neither one is there at this moment. Why not? They could, and should, have finished us both off with no problem. They left? They left..."

Raina considered, speaking slowly, talking only to herself. "They left because Bryce shot at them. His gun was at his side when I finally got to him. Yeah, that makes sense. If they'd known..." She visibly shivered, realizing how exceedingly close she and Bryce had been to death.

Detective Diggs sat there quietly, not wanting to interrupt at all, but he finally asked softly, "Do you maybe remember what you were *feeling*? Sometimes remembering how you *felt* can help trigger more memories or put them into perspective.

"All of your senses were probably recording information in your mind. Try to remember them. Forget the logical, the obvious... Use your senses."

Ron paused the video again as she nodded, willing to try what he suggested. She tried to think back and pull that from her memory bank. "Alone. I remember feeling absolutely, utterly *alone*. I suppose I was too full of adrenaline or shock to feel true fear at this point because I don't remember feeling *afraid*. Isn't that odd? I surely felt it then, but right now... I don't remember actually feeling it at all."

She paused, pondering that little revelation for a moment. "And wondering why there weren't any other cars. Did I wonder that then... or later?"

The men let her think her way through her memories out loud. Neither man wanted to interrupt her so they remained quiet.

"Bryce... I saw blood around Bryce. I remember now being scared I was too late, and he was dead. I was so relieved when I got to him... When I realized his chest was barely moving... But he was alive." Her eyes welled up with tears. She choked out, "We were sitting ducks! They could've picked us off right then and there!"

The detectives all shared a look of concern but decided wordlessly to let her continue.

After a few minutes, she motioned to Ron to continue. Her focus returned to the screen when she saw herself going back to the truck, around it, and back again.

Shaking her head in confusion, she asked, "What in the world am I doing? Maybe I was just disoriented. Maybe I didn't know what to do? Maybe I was trying to decide about whether or not I could use my truck?" Something else was happening here... But what? She tried hard to remember, but nothing was coming back.

She watched as she stumbled back to the cruiser. "I don't remember actually picking up his gun at all. It's like it just appeared in my hand. But that's it, there in my hand. Rewind it, Ron." He did, then hit *play* again. She leaned forward. "There it is, in my left hand. See when I trip there, my hand swings forward? I have something in my hand... It's the gun. I must've taken it in case they came back or showed up or whatever. It's a good thing they didn't though."

Ron interrupted her, hitting *pause* at the same time, "Were you worried you'd shoot them?"

Raina looked at him through dazed eyes. She'd been so focused and caught in her memories. "What?"

"Were you worried you'd shoot them? Or worried you didn't actually know how to use the gun? You don't seem to be the type of person to be worried at this point about protecting yourself or the fallen officer with his gun if they came back."

Raina contemplated this before answering. "Oh. No, I meant it was a good thing they didn't come back because I doubt very much I could shoot with my left hand. It would've been more natural in my right, but my right was no good to me. I couldn't hold my pepper spray in it, so how could I have held a gun and fired accurately with it? I don't even know *how* to shoot a gun properly.

"It's just a guess, but a gun would've been way too heavy for my wrist to hold, let alone hold up and fire with any accuracy. Aren't guns kinda heavy?"

Ron nodded, understanding. Before Ron could hit *play* again, Sawyer quickly asked, "How do you know you couldn't hold the pepper spray in your right hand?"

The detectives looked at Raina, who looked blank for a moment.

"Because... I..." She paused. Memories came back, rushing in with sudden clarity. "Oh, wow. During the attack with the first guy at my truck, I didn't faint... I've never fainted in my life. He'd knocked my pepper spray out of my hand... So I faked it, and he let me go... So I *fell down* on purpose to get it. When he was grabbing for me... I remember!

"I couldn't seem to hold it in my right hand... I held it in both hands. But I had to use my left to spray it. I think I almost missed him because I wasn't used to having it in my left hand. I closed my eyes to keep from spraying myself... I think... And I'm pretty sure I kicked his balls into his throat a time or two." She sounded extraordinarily proud of that feat.

The men just looked at her while being eternally and undeniably grateful it wasn't them. It hurt just to think about it.

Ron hit *play* again while Raina concentrated on the screen. "I don't remember what I was doing here at all. Maybe I was seriously experiencing the unexpected effects of head trauma. I'm sure walking all over the place like it." She shook her head, yelling at herself in a soft yet angry voice, "Get in the car, Raina! Get in the car... and *GO!* Get to the hospital! *What* am I doing?"

Despite the circumstances, the men smiled when they heard her berating herself. Obviously so absorbed in the video, she once again forgot they were there. "Man, I'm irritating myself. Just get *in* the car! What else is there to do? Oh my gosh... Get *in* the car! That car right there... Get in it..."

Channion tried to hold back his smile as he looked at his fellow detectives. He was relieved they were finding the humor in it, too, dark though it was.

"Finally. We're moving!" she exclaimed to herself. "I can't believe I took the time to lock my truck. The windows were probably busted anyway! Like locking it would've done any good if someone could just reach through the window. Good grief..." She shook her head. "I'm so crazy about doing that."

"Wait! What'd you just say?" Channion asked while his uncle quickly paused the video. Raina turned to look at him. "What? When?"

Ron now caught it too. He rewound the video a little bit to where he thought the place would be on the DVD.

Channion said, "Just now... Repeat what you just said."

She thought for a moment. "I couldn't believe I didn't get in the car and head to the hospital. I took the time to..." Her eyebrows rose as she realized what she'd said. "Oh... I took the time to stop and lock my truck."

They watched as Ron found the spot they were looking for. They all saw her stop, raise her arm. With her back to the camera, there was no way they could figure out what she was doing.

"I was trying to lock and set the alarm on my truck!" Raina shook her head. "I don't see the lights blinking on my truck though."

"The control box was probably smashed," Sawyer replied. "Or the lights were all busted."

Ron thought back. "But the CSIs said the doors *were* locked when they got there so the locks themselves did work. I don't think anyone ever questioned *how* or *when* they got locked though. Or maybe they didn't think it was important? They got the keys later on from Bryce's car at the hospital."

She looked at them. "Am I really that anal, or was there a reason I locked it? Maybe it was from habit, like muscle memory or something like that?"

Channion asked, "Which do you think is the correct answer?"

She let out a breath before she replied, "I'd like to say number two, but feel it could be a combination of number one and three."

Ron smiled. "You let us know for sure, and we'll buy you a nice dinner that comes with dessert."

With a sigh, she said, "You drive a hard bargain, Lieutenant. Give me some time on that part, okay? Seeing this is bound to ramp up my nightmares, so it'll probably come out sooner or later. Channion, you'd better be prepared."

Chapter 30

LIFE WENT ON AS normally as it could for the next few days. Channion was delegated to be Raina's constant guard unless she wanted to stay at the Kramer's house.

The main reason she *didn't* was because of her unpredictable nightmares. She didn't want to put Ron or Janet through them. She did have another significant nightmare Channion woke her up from, but she couldn't add any new information from it. He again stayed with her until she was calm, wiping away her tears and holding her until she drifted off to sleep before making his way back to his own bed.

Bryce had been moved as a safety precaution, and no one would tell Raina where he was moved to. She wanted to thank him personally for saving her life as well, but they wouldn't take her to him no matter how much she pleaded. They stated it was safer to keep them apart.

As Ron drove her to an appointment one day, she mentioned she thought there was a cop up ahead. Ron caught sight of the marked squad car that was pulled off the road, partially hidden in the grass and shadows, about a mile up the road. When he looked over at her in surprise, she slid her sunglasses down her nose and wiggled her eyebrows at him.

Grinning, she went back to looking at the passing scenery. "I've never been out this way. It's pretty, isn't it?"

The detective didn't know what to make of her. *How* did she do that? he wondered yet again.

When they arrived at the clinic where she was referred to go by Dr. Benson for follow-up care, Ron led her into the welcoming lobby. When he showed his badge to the lady at the desk, she smiled, got up and told them to follow her.

Raina thought it odd that he showed his badge. And why didn't she have to fill out any paperwork? Her instincts were churning as she and Ron were led down a couple of hallways. When the lady stopped at a door, she knocked and waited until she heard the reply. Once she did, she held open the door, waving them in.

Raina stopped in her tracks in pure surprise. A smile spread across her face as she realized who she was looking at. Sitting in a nice, comfortable chair watching TV was Bryce Mitchell.

He gingerly stood up as she walked toward him, a huge smile on his own face. With no hesitation, Raina wrapped him in a bear hug, feeling the officer return it. Ron felt like he was intruding. Considering there was another officer in the room, he knew he wasn't the only one feeling that way.

As the two hugged each other, Ron knew this was a special moment he'd not soon forget. He and Channion hoped her seeing Bryce would help her keep all she was going through in perspective. Maybe it'd help to remind her of the great thing she'd done.

Stepping back, Raina looked him over. Her eyes moist with tears, she finally was able to speak. "Well. You look much, *much* better than the last time I saw you. And taller!" They smiled at each other. "I'm so relieved you're better. I've pestered the detectives to let me see you, but they kept telling me no!"

The wounded man chuckled, his own eyes moist with tears. He reached out and squeezed her hands. "How could they say no to anything you wanted?"

"I know, right? But every now and then, they actually do. It's so rude," she joked.

She helped him sit back down in his chair before sitting in the one next to him. Ron smiled and shook Bryce's hand. "Don't let her fool you, Bryce. We say yes far more than we say no."

The other man standing in the room was someone Raina hadn't met yet. Looking over at him, she smiled. "Hi, I'm Raina." She offered her hand to shake his.

For being a bear of a man, the man seemed a little bit stunned. He automatically shook her hand and smiled back at her. It took him a second to answer her. "It's nice to finally meet you. Thank you for what you did for Bryce, Miss Stewart. It was incredibly brave of you. I'm Deputy Chris Patton."

Bryce smiled at the awestruck deputy. "Chris! You can pick up your jaw when you're done staring at her. Don't be so rude to my guest."

Raina rolled her eyes. "Another one? I'm just me so don't be looking at me like that." Looking at Bryce now, she said, exasperated, "If I'm going to be gawked at like a celebrity, I want the money they make!"

The men smiled as Chris said, "Well, I don't know what I was expecting, but it wasn't you. You have a nice shock value, Miss Stewart."

She laughed. "Well, thank you. Call me Raina if you think you can manage it. Are you a visiting friend or on the protection detail?"

Chris replied, "Protection detail first. Friend second."

Nodding in approval, she turned back to Bryce, saying, "I see that they couldn't find you a nice attractive female cop. I was offered one, but I said no way. Did you say no too?"

They all laughed as Bryce leaned back to get more comfortable. "No, and I wouldn't have as long as she was good at her job. Now Chris here, he does all right. He's good company, if nothing else. It looks like we both got saddled with guards, doesn't it?"

"Yes, we sure did. But hopefully not for too much longer." Turning serious, she asked, "Have they updated you at all?"

"Yeah, Ron's been good at that. I've told them all I could which isn't much more than they already surmised. I never would've guessed all this would happen for simply doing a routine pull-over on a speeding car that was also driving all over the road."

He sighed. "I was coming off a domestic dispute call out that way, otherwise I never would've been anywhere near that area. The other officer that was there with me had already left for another call, and I wasn't in any hurry to get anywhere fast, you know? If I wasn't there, none of this would be happening to you, Raina. I'm so sor—"

She interrupted, saying firmly, "No. Don't you dare sit there and apologize, Bryce. While I appreciate it, don't. I think things happen for a reason, and this must be one of them. I was able to do something some people only wonder about doing, and most others don't even do that. I've never regretted what I did that day, Bryce. Not once.

"You were simply doing your job. If it wasn't you, it perhaps could've been someone else. Channion told me that, and he was right. Maybe you were there not really for that domestic call, but to be there to stop that car from hurting or killing someone else if he was driving erratically. If he'd run someone off the road, *he* wouldn't have stopped to help them.

"Or maybe you were there to simply stop the sale of all those weapons, and the aftermath that would've caused." She squeezed his hand. "You were *there* for a reason, Bryce Mitchell. And apparently so was I. Think of me as your backup. I just wish I could've been there sooner for you. I'm sorry."

Ron sat down on the arm of the chair she was in. "She's right, Bryce. It could've been fate. Just the way the dice was rolled that day. And I can confirm with all she's been through over the past few weeks, I've never heard her say she wished she'd stayed home that day. Since she's normally with Channion, you could check with him, but he's never breathed a word about her wishing she'd never been there for you."

She said wryly, "Of course, they tell me I still have head trauma."

Bryce smiled and shook his head at her. He covered her hand with his and squeezed it. "But you were still my bodyguard. And I can never thank you enough. Never."

Raina looked him in his eyes as she said, "You don't need to."

Chris' alarm on his watch began beeping. After turning it off, he grabbed three orange plastic bottles from a locked cabinet and a bottle of milk from the mini fridge. Giving them to Bryce, he said, "You've just been served."

They laughed at his cop humor.

Raina watched as Bryce took the pills and washed them down with the milk. He handed the bottles back to Chris, who put them away. Chris next handed him a big box of crackers which Bryce began eating by the handful.

Bryce looked at Ron and Raina. "Would either of you like a drink or a snack? Mom keeps me supplied so I have plenty. Help yourself, especially if my crunching annoys you like it does Chris. It'd annoy me, too, if I wasn't the one crunching."

Raina glanced at the cabinet. "Maybe. Whatcha got? Any goodies?"

Chris waved her over to look as he swung open both doors to the little cabinet.

"Oh, yeah, you do! You got *lots* of goodies! Are you sure you want to share?"

"Mom's money."

"Tell your mom thanks!" Smiling, Raina took a small container of chips and tossed a brownie to Ron. "Catch!"

He caught it at the last second before it hit him, thankful for his quick reflexes after her unexpected throw. He smiled at her grin.

"Check the fridge, too, Raina," Chris said as he opened a little bag of chips for himself.

Not shy, she did. She pulled out a bottle of water for Ron and a can of orange pop for herself. Sitting back down beside Bryce and Ron, she opened the chip container and the can of pop.

Curious about the pills she saw him take, she asked, "Antibiotics and pain pills? Do they make you nauseous?"

"Yeah, in a terrible way. Getting sick on them is as bad as why I was in the hospital in the first place. They nearly killed me the first time I got sick. I wished they had for the pain they caused me. Cop humor there..." he added when he realized what he'd said.

Raina smiled as she patted his shoulder. "I understand. Channion's taught me a bit about it."

He shook the box of crackers to loosen them up inside before he grabbed another handful. "I found these help settle my stomach when I take them. It's also better with the milk than water. I guess I need something to soak them up."

She nodded in understanding as she chewed her chips. "Are these drugs also the addictive kind?"

"Yeah. That's why I have Chris here in charge of them. I don't think I'd go nuts with them, but one never knows. I've known guys before on the force that got addicted to them, and I seriously don't want to go down that road." He put down the box of crackers, hoping he'd eaten enough. He drank more milk.

Raina looked at the wounded officer for a while as she ate before she ventured, "So if they've kept you updated, or maybe you even knew yourself, you actually saved *my* life that day too. *Thank you*, Bryce, for being there for me too." She squeezed his hand.

He squeezed it back, saying, "You're welcome, Raina. Actually, I don't remember that part all that much. I was out of it, but for whatever reason I came back to consciousness and... I don't know... I just drew and fired.

"I guess I heard you... I don't really remember. It's more of a miracle that I actually even hit the guy and not you... Or even not just firing at the sky or the dirt. As you said, maybe some things happen for a reason."

They were all quietly thinking until Raina said in a genial voice, "Well, let's think of the positives here—besides you not hitting me, I mean. I was new to the area and didn't know many people outside of my work. Now, though, I personally know a whole lot of people in the medical field. It's always handy to know people like that.

"Not to mention the police force! I think I've met a whole troop or two of you guys. Mainly city cops and not so much you county ones, but I *have* met some of you too." With a grin, she mused, "I wonder if I ever did get pulled over, if I ever get another vehicle of my own, will I get a ticket?"

They all smiled at her again.

"Ask for a Courtesy Card or two. They allow you a freebie although you don't seem like the type who needs one." Bryce looked at her as he took another drink of milk. "No car yet?"

Kramer answered, "Not until we know this is over, she has a guard—"

"Babysitter," Raina interjected with a smile.

"—that does all the driving anyway. When it's over, she'll get to go truck shopping." Ron smiled at her as he pulled gently on her ponytail.

"I was thinking about maybe getting a car this time. Something that's better on gas. And now that I don't have my horses..." Her voice immediately trailed off into silence.

Bryce took hold of her hand again and said softly, "I heard about that too. I'm *truly* sorry about that, Raina. Mom and Bethany cried and cried when they heard."

She looked at him, tears misting her eyes. "Thanks. I appreciate that. I miss my horses so much every single day. It's still too hard to believe they're gone. If it wasn't for Detectives Scott and Kramer here, I would've lost my sanity there. I owe them an immense amount." She patted Ron's knee as she smiled up at him.

Chris watched as she tried to get her composure back. He didn't know what they were talking about, but he knew instinctively it wasn't good. He was about to ask about the horses, but Ron cut him off by asking Raina, "What kind of car?"

"I don't know, but maybe something along the lines of an Outback or a Forester. I want four-wheel drive or all-wheel drive this time."

Chris saw Ron mouth the word "Later" to him as Raina was talking. Chris understood and nodded.

Ron and Raina stayed for half an hour or so before he said they needed to go. Raina could also tell the powerful pain pills were kicking in because Bryce was getting groggier. She hugged him before she left and shook Chris' hand again. "Thanks for taking care of him, nurse. Stay sharp as a needle!"

Chris grinned at her as she headed toward the door with Ron.

As they were driving back toward home, she asked, "So Dr. Benson was in on this? He didn't refer me to go there for myself?"

Ron smiled. "It *is* a follow-up clinic for you, if needed. It's just pretty far away. But we decided to let you see him for yourself once he was healed enough to receive visitors. He hasn't been here very long at all. The safest way to conceal his whereabouts in case we're being followed was to make it look like a simple doctor's appointment. No one would be the wiser he was there."

"That was pretty smart thinking." They drove for a couple of miles before she asked, "Do you think we're really being followed or even watched?"

He sighed. "It's too hard to tell. We've all changed our routines so many times, our schedules, our driving routes, where we shop, it's hard to say one way or another. If we are, we must be doing it right because as far as we know, no one knows where you are. But we sure won't let our guard down until this is all over. We can't forget for a second that they know who you are, where you lived.

"So we keep up with the varying routines. Janet will keep shopping for you guys to keep you out of the public eye. The fact you're staying mainly at home is key. I'd still prefer you stopped working entirely. It's a risk, Raina. Right now, we don't think they know where you are. We're praying we're right, but we aren't depending on it."

She nodded. "Do you think it's safe for me to be around your family this weekend for the reunion? It won't hurt my feelings to be shifted onto someone else for a few days. Anyone but Luke. I'd hate to think I'd put anybody in danger."

Changing lanes, he replied, "We've thought of that, but we're pretty confident all will be fine. It'll be nice for all of us to relax and unwind for a bit. The bulk of our relatives are in law enforcement or the justice system in general. Anyone who crashed this party would regret doing so pretty quickly!"

Looking at the clock on the dash, she said, "I'd say Channion should've picked up Ty at the airport by now. Taking the red-eye like he did to arrive so early today, I'd be sleeping all day if I were him. Channion was sure excited to go get him, wasn't he?"

Ron laughed. "As always! Those two are best friends and long-lost brothers. They have a deep, tight bond. I imagine you'll like Ty as he's pretty easy-going. You can trust him with your life. However, I don't envy you being stuck in the same house with the two of them!" Throwing a humorous look her way, he asked, "Are you sure you want to stay at Channion's while he's here? You're more than welcome at our place."

She laughed. She'd been warned about practical jokes and the like since Ty called a few days earlier, saying he'd stay at Channion's like he normally did. They already had his room ready for him. "You're my reserve, Ron. But if I can't handle two men, I have no business singing in crowded bars full of them!"

Chapter 31

RAINA JOKED THAT THE male bonding should be over by now since Channion and Ty had about six hours all to themselves, unless Ty was catching up on his sleep. Ron grinned as he turned down the road that led to his nephew's.

"Deer..." Her sixth sense clicked on, and she looked for them. "I don't see them yet..."

About half a mile up the road, Ron saw them and applied the brakes. But the two deer were unconcerned and kept walking calmly about twenty feet from the road. He began laughing as he turned to look at her after they'd safely passed them.

"Have you ever thought about bottling up that sixth sense of yours and selling it? You could make a fortune!"

She grinned, saying wistfully, "If only I *could!* Just wait until November."

"November?"

"Yeah. My powers go haywire then. Most deer hits are in November because they're so active. I guess that's also how some people go hunting for their holiday meal. It seems like an awfully expensive and dangerous method to me for a piece of meat, but boys will be boys."

He pulled into Channion's driveway, stopping beside his nephew's truck. As she was opening her door, he asked, "Are you ready?"

Raina grinned as she got out. Stopping halfway to the front door, she said in a frazzled voice, "Geez, *Ron!* You've made me nervous now to meet him! See what you've done to me? Didn't you think I was enough of a mess already?"

He laughed, lightly took her elbow as he steered her forward. "Just think of him as one of your students, and you'll be fine."

The front door opened as they neared it. A tall, black-haired, tanned, and muscular man stood there, smiling broadly at them. Raina, totally surprised, stopped for a second. Think of him as one of her students? That was *so* not gonna happen! Not in a million years.

Recovering quickly, she quipped, "Oh look, Ron! Channion went and hired a cute butler while I was away!"

Both men laughed as Ron ushered Raina inside, letting Ty shut and lock the door behind them. She watched as Ron and his tall nephew hugged each other tightly. No manly slap on the backs in this family, she thought.

Ron held Ty at arm's length and looked him over. "It's so good to see you, Ty! You're looking better than ever. It seems that desert air agrees with you!"

Did it ever, Raina thought to herself. He looked better in person even in his swim trunks and a faded t-shirt than all of those photos on the walls. Wow. This was her new housemate? Now she was stuck with *two* handsome men? Maybe she *should* consider staying with Ron and Janet!

Ty grinned. "I think so." He looked his uncle over again. "You're looking well yourself. You haven't changed a bit since I saw you last."

"A little more gray, but that's it," Ron replied, smiling. "I suppose it's time to introduce you to this lady..."

Looking at Channion's cousin, she held out her hand. "Hi, I'm Raina Stewart. I've heard a lot about you lately."

Ty shook her hand. Even with the scars on her face and arms that his cousin had told him about, Channion hadn't prepared him enough for her beauty. She had a killer smile and a twinkle in her eyes.

"Ty Stanton. It's great to meet you, Miss Stewart. Chan told me we'd be bunking together for a while. Are you sure you can handle us?"

"It'll most likely be the other way around. And please, call me Raina since we're going to be bunking together for a while."

He grinned. "My pleasure, Raina. Call me Ty."

"I already planned on it."

Ty grinned at her quick comeback, wondering where his cousin was so he could pummel him for the joke he was playing on him.

As if she were reading his mind, she asked, "Where's Channion?"

"Miss me?" His voice, filled with humor, came from the kitchen.

With a twinkle in her eyes, she called out, "Not at all. I was just hoping me and Ty would be all alone once Ron left. Chaperones are such killjoys!"

Ty grinned at her.

Ron shook his head. "Oh, I can only imagine the fun you're going to have here, Raina. Don't forget what I told you."

"I think I can handle them. Are you leaving now?"

He nodded. "We'll see you three later for dinner. Janet's expecting you guys by six, half after at the latest. Don't disappoint my girl."

Ty smiled. "Never. We'll be there."

He held the door open for his uncle, then shut and locked it again. She noticed he set the alarm once the door was locked.

When Ty turned around, she said, "Well, I'm going to head upstairs. Is your room all right for you? Is there anything we forgot?"

He smiled. She sounded like she and Channion were living together, and she had the run of the house. But in a good way. He tilted his head. "If you did forget something, what would you do about it?"

She saw the sparkle in his brown eyes. "I'd ask Channion to get it for you." She smiled as she passed him on the way to the stairs. "After all, it's *his* house!"

Ty laughed as she made her way up to her room. When he entered the kitchen, Channion was leaning against the counter, a big grin on his face, an opened beer at his side. Ty looked at him with a *What the hell?!* look on his face.

Channion chuckled. "She upstairs?"

"Yeah." Ty grabbed a cold beer from the fridge, unscrewing the cap with a quick twist of his wrist. He tossed the cap into the garbage can. He was beginning to speak when she walked in.

"Make sure it's all good when you two start talking about me now that Ty's met me," she said. Shaking her head at the two men, she said, "Some cops you two are. You didn't even hear me come down here, did you?"

She walked to the cabinet to get a cup. She held her smile as she poured some filtered water from the pitcher in the fridge before adding a few squirts of lemon juice.

Ty asked, "Who told you I'm a cop?"

"*Ex* cop." Raina looked at him, thinking. "Hmm. Either Ron or your cousin here. Maybe Janet. Or they alluded to it... I'm not sure. Either way, you just confirmed it." She smiled at his surprised look. "They thought it might be something I'd need to know for my peace of mind. For *your* peace of mind, I'm going to be in my room answering emails before we leave. This also lets you know how long you can talk about me behind my back."

She smiled at them as she left.

Ty said, "She's got a great sense of humor!"

Channion grinned. "Yeah, she does. But she also likes to eavesdrop at times."

"I do not. Don't listen to him, Ty!" Raina said as she walked back in. At their raised eyebrows, she defended herself. "I forgot my water." She grabbed the cup. "*Now* I'm going upstairs." And out she went again.

She came right back in, looking directly at Channion. "You said that on purpose, didn't you?" At his unrepentant grin, she laughed. "You saw the water glass still on the counter?"

"I *am* a detective, if you'll remember. I get paid to notice the details."

"Don't count on it. Your fly's open." And out she went again.

Automatically, Channion looked down and laughed. So did his cousin. She got him on that one. His fly *wasn't* open, but she *did* make him look.

Ty looked at his cousin. "So she's single, huh?"

Chapter 32

LIFE WAS A GAMBLE. They'd hotly debated letting Raina sing at Picacho's Bar, concerned word would get out she was still in the area. Giving private music lessons and singing in a crowded public bar were two vastly different situations. Playing the odds, they decided to let her work.

Channion took her to a band rehearsal first to make sure she could handle the noise, using their cover story when her band expressed concern at seeing her wounds and hearing about her "accident." Satisfied she could handle it, Channion gave the final approval.

Raina had called the owner of Picacho's earlier that week, warning him there was a big family reunion in town for the weekend. She told him she'd heard through the grapevine many would be coming to the bar. Besides ordering extra of everything, he did exactly what she figured he'd do when they knew there were large groups in town: He called in the troops.

When Raina, Channion, and Ty arrived at the bar early that evening to set up, she wasn't disappointed. The lead bartender Sammy had three extra bartenders stocking everything they'd need. She noticed the extra waitresses, some rolling silverware in napkins to put in silver bins. The sliding doors to the adjoining room that expanded the dance floor and seating area were open, and the tables were already set up.

"C'mon, I'll introduce you guys. Sammy's great!" Raina happily led the way to the bar, making introductions all around. Looking at Sammy, she said, "Treat these guys like royalty, all right? If you don't, I'll never sing another country Cajun song on your birthday again. You can just scoot on back to New Orleans if you want one."

Sammy laughed. A tall, built black man with a charming smile and sparkling eyes, Sammy's Cajun accent was apparent when he answered her. "Aw, Raina, don't do me like that! I've done you no wrong."

"No, you haven't. Just don't start it with these two." Her bright smile made Sammy grin.

Her band was coming in, so she went over to help set up. She more or less watched and handed them things, but they were also discussing the songs and such as they worked.

Channion and Ty went to the far end of the long bar to talk privately, sitting where they could see Raina and the door. Sammy walked down to them, leaned against the bar. "Since I had to walk all the way down here, you two had better make it worth my while. Why'd you two sit so far away from me? I stink?"

They saw the humor in his eyes and smiled back at him.

Channion said, "Nah. We just wanted the best view." His head tilted toward Raina.

Sammy chuckled. "Fair enough."

With his cousin there, Channion felt comfortable having one drink. "I'll do a Captain Morgan. Could you use either Pepsi or Dr. Pepper instead? I'm just not a fan of Coke. Thanks. Ty?"

Ty ordered his usual bottled Corona.

Sammy quickly returned, sliding their drinks across the bar to them on little paper coasters with the bar's logo on them. As he set a basket of bar mix in front of them, he asked, "Are you fine gentlemen running a tab this lovely evening?"

Smiling at his formal tone, Channion said in kind, "Probably later, my good man. But I'll pay for these now."

Grinning, Ty stopped him and bought them instead. "Keep the change, Sammy."

"Thanks! I knew I'd like you two. That girl has the greatest friends!" His smile was dazzling as he headed back to the register.

They drank for a moment, watching the band set up, before Ty asked quietly, "Did you know none of her family has called her until this morning?"

Channion looked at him in surprise. "Seriously?" He shook his head in disgust. "She's got a rotten family, I'd say. I knew they hadn't called her before, meaning when she was in the hospital. I thought maybe they'd called since then, but she didn't mention it to me. Why would she? I'm with her when she gets her mail, or get it for her, and I've never seen anything resembling a card or a letter. I thought maybe they sent an email.

"She's only mentioned her family one or two times since I've known her—with the exception of her mom. She was in high school when her mom was killed by a drunk driver. It sounded to me like they were close."

He paused before saying, "I didn't know about this morning's call. Was that why she'd been crying in the back room when I came in on you two?" At Ty's nod, he sighed. "How long has it been now? And she *just* got a call?"

Since Ty was just informed Raina lost her mom when she was a teenager, it occurred to him Channion was a teenager when he lost his dad. And both deaths were sudden and senseless: One being killed in the line of duty, and the other by a drunk driver. He wondered if this was something that bonded Channion and Raina, for he felt the bond between them. They probably had felt and experienced the same emotions and trials going through something major like that in their young lives.

But maybe that bond he sensed was because of her case and being practically inseparable. Ty guessed it was both, with her case being more probable as it was a daily weight they shared.

Ty replied, "She said nineteen days. You came in shortly after I walked in there myself. She looked beyond sad, Chan. Just walking by the doorway, I swear I could *feel* the sadness. Her sadness. I meant to quietly leave her alone, but she saw me and invited me in.

"She's also particularly worried, maybe more scared, about where she's to live after the case is closed. Or if it keeps on going, will you ask her to leave until it is? She said she's worried you might want your privacy back but that she doesn't have anywhere to go. She said she can't return to her house because of the memories there, even if it wasn't dangerous.

"Raina seems to be living day to day, waiting for the other shoe to drop. She reminds me a bit of a skittish cat, always ducking down, ready to bolt." He blew out a breath, shaking his head. "She's got an awful lot on her plate. Her stress level has to be sky high, but she seems to be handling it all well enough. And she's still not fully healed, I take it?"

Channion shook his head. "No. Physically, her wrist is almost fine now, but her ribs are still an issue at times. One rib got broken but seems to be healing well enough. Her skin wounds are healing.

"She refuses to see a shrink, but one day she might give in. She still has headaches but not nearly like before. They might just be due to all the stress more than the concussion she had. Her nightmares are still pretty consistent. Some are worse than others. She's handling them in her own way, but I often have to wake her up from them. That's why I leave my door open."

Channion took a drink. "All these broken nights are beginning to wear her down. Me, too, in all honesty. But we're getting through them. It helps we're home more often than not right now.

"She's dropping weight. Aunt Janet had us over for dinner a couple of times to help keep an eye on her. We're all trying to keep her grounded, letting her know she's not alone in all of this. Raina eats... Just not nearly enough.

"As far as I can tell, the only escape she has is working. We haven't gone on the road yet, but she has some concerts lined up. Whether giving lessons or singing here, work is the only thing she has left to have a normal life. It's the *only* reason we're all even letting her continue doing it.

"And it's a fair bet we're going to need to pull her from working at all soon for safety's sake. She's been warned it could happen, so she's partially prepared for it. If, or when, we ship her out, I'll probably go with her since she's comfortable with me, and I live alone. Obviously, Ron has Janet. We have two female officers on standby, ready to go at a moment's notice if we hear any chatter out there about her."

Ty blew out a breath, realizing this woman was in a deep, deep hole. He took a drink of his beer, running his cousin's words through his mind.

Channion glanced over at her. She and the band members were sitting on the side of the stage, talking. "But she's tough. It's a daily battle for her, and I know she dreads nights now more than anything. She naps during the day because she's exhausted from the nightmares. Her doctors tell us her mind isn't done tormenting her yet. Something *is* hidden in there.

"But the nightmares are letting us know her memory is maybe returning. For better or for worse, we don't know. At the very least, the doctors we talk to are telling us it's healthy for her to have us to talk to when she has them.

"It's a long healing process. It's no secret she has a long road in front of her. I only hope Ron, Janet, and I can stay in her life long enough to help her navigate it. Bryce, the deputy she saved, has his family, and they're pretty close. Plus he has the police force and friends for support. But she's completely alone here."

Ty asked after a moment, "What does she do in her spare time for distractions? Watch TV, read, a hobby?"

"Originally, she had her horses. I told you what happened there. Reading gave her headaches, so she stopped. Movies and TV seem all right. We like some of the same stuff, so we tend to spend our time doing that. We've played cards a couple of times."

Channion glanced at her again. "She's also been doing all of the housework lately, saying it was the least she could do since she's staying there. We do our own laundry, but everything else she's basically taken over. She told me she doesn't want to be a free-loader. I appreciate that.

"I know it helps keep her mind occupied, and it makes life seem more normal. I take care of the outside, and she has the inside where it's safer. She hates feeling caged, but it helps she feels so comfortable at my house. I think it gives her some real security. Ron and I hope feeling that way will help her mind relax to let her memories come easier.

"She likes to cook, so we've recently begun taking turns on that. She doesn't eat much of it, but she'll cook it. She's actually a pretty good cook... Thankfully!" Both men chuckled before Channion continued, "She doesn't complain or whine. And as you've heard, she has somehow retained a good sense of humor. I think she uses it purely as a coping mechanism at times. In all honesty, I admire her for even still having one." He took a sip of his drink.

Ty looked closely at his cousin before he asked outright, "You care for her, don't you?"

Knowing he could trust his cousin, he said softly, "It's impossible not to. I've tried a hundred times to ignore it, but the more I'm around her, the more I see. Her courage has no bounds.

"I'd never break ethics or honor, you know that. But sometimes, I wonder about maybe after her case is done? I'm certainly still objective with her, so I figure as long as I'm that, all's fine. If that time ever comes, me and Ron can switch houses."

They grinned at each other.

Ty thought a minute before seriously offering, "Just in case the need arises, and it sounds like it might, you know you can send her out to me, right? It's far from here, and my place is set up for security like yours, as you know. If you can get her out there, she'd be safe.

"I bet Morgan would be a great person for her to be around too. You know how she is. They've a few things in common that I can see so they could bond, give Raina a friend. Either just her, or both of you, are more than welcome. Maybe she'd even want to stay out there, start fresh where she's an unknown."

Channion nodded before he finished his drink before the ice melted too much and ruined it. "We have a few safe houses in mind, but I'll mentally add you to the list. I really like your idea, and I'd feel good about it. And Morgan might be good for her, like you said. The horse thing might be an issue. They might be too much for her right now. On the other hand, maybe they'd help?"

He paused, thinking a moment. "As of right now, she wants to stay. Raina is anything but a runner! For better or for worse, she's insisted on staying put. Of course, with her horses gone now, there's not as much holding her here."

"Well, keep my place in mind. Between me, Morgan, and Josh, I think she'd be able to relax and maybe start fresh."

"Who's Josh?"

Ty studied his cousin. "Morgan's husband. I told you she got married, didn't I? It's been quite a while now, and I was sure I told you."

Channion looked absolutely surprised but also happy. "No, you didn't! At least, not that I remember. No kidding? Morgan got *married?*"

Ty laughed, his eyes sparkling. "Don't let her hear you sound so surprised. She might shoot you. She's still extremely accurate, by the way."

Channion laughed. "That's great to hear—being married, I mean! Wow. Morgan getting married... And to someone else."

Ty shook his head. "Not you too! We're just friends, Chan. That's it."

"I still don't see how that's even possible, but okay." He grinned at the exasperated look his cousin shot him. "So, tell me about this Josh. He must be something if *she* married him. He's legit?"

"Yeah, more than. They're a perfect couple if I've ever seen one. He's also become a good friend of mine as well as a couple of his friends. We hang out fairly often.

"If you ever get yourself out there again and meet him, you'll see. You two would easily get along. He gets along with about everybody, but he's no pushover. He owns a construction company. He's done some stuff at my place and does excellent work. Since I met him first, I put him through the paces before I'd let him anywhere near her, of course."

"He doesn't mind you and Morgan being so close?"

"Doesn't seem to." He grinned at Channion's raised eyebrows. Firmly, he said, "No, he doesn't. He doesn't need to either. And he knows that too."

They sat on their barstools, not saying a word for a minute. They watched the band members and Raina as they went through some books now. Ty assumed they were full of song lists or sheet music. He finished his beer, licked the lime juice from his finger. He asked quietly, "Has she let loose yet? Had a meltdown?"

"Not yet. She fell completely apart when her horses were killed. They were great horses. And like her kids—like how Morgan sees her own. It tore me up something awful too...

meaning them being killed. *And* her crying because it came from the very depth of her soul."

Channion shook his head, remembering that crushing day. "It was like her heart had been ripped out. She could barely breathe. She could barely even function for a bit. It was one of the worst things I've seen or heard in my life. That night, she fell apart again. In times like that, there's nothing to do but offer comfort. It made me feel a little helpless, but I did what I could to be there for her."

Ty glanced over at Raina and studied her for a moment. His own heart ached for this woman he barely knew. He surmised, "But not the meltdown she's bound to have?"

Channion shook his head, spun around the bar mix basket as he thought. "Ron and I have been waiting for her to explode or wilt. As much as she fell apart from Aspen and Rodeo being killed, I still don't think it was her meltdown. That was intense mourning and grief. We both feel she'll explode. At some point, *something* is going to trigger her, and we've tried to be prepared for what it could be. We can't stop it... and don't want to... but we'd just like to be prepared."

Ty nodded. "She seems to me the kind of person where it's all or nothing. When the pressure hits its boiling point, and that little something tips her over the edge, I really think she's going to blow. I agree that she's not going to wilt into a depression. I'd think if she was, she would've hit that point already when she lost her horses."

He paused before predicting firmly, "No, she's going to explode." Attempting to lighten their moods, he added, "If you're lucky, though, she may have a few smaller eruptions to help you gauge the big finale!"

They smiled, even over the desolate subject matter. Channion joked, "With a bit more luck, I won't be around at all. Just let Uncle Ron be in her path when her emotions come to terms with one another. *That'd* be the perfect scenario."

Ty chuckled. "Yes, he could handle her with no fuss. It seems to me Ron is smitten with her too." He paused, grinned. "You're right. She *is* something else! I really like her. It's a good thing I like you as much as I do."

Channion laughed. "Thanks. I'd do the same for you if the situation were reversed. But the thing is, Ty, there *isn't* anything between us like that. It *could*, I think. But I'd say she fully respects that trust, and the professional relationship we have—and need. She knows above all else, I have a job to do. And *she's* my job.

"If it wasn't for this case, we'd probably have never met. But she is someone I'd enjoy seeing on a personal level. Maybe once it gets wrapped up, we could go out and see.

"On the other hand, without the stress of being involved in her case, it's a sure thing all the dynamics will be different. Besides, I don't know how she feels about me in that regard. And I'm not about to ask her. It'd make it complicated or would create a conflict of interests. Both actually.

"And she *has* said being in a relationship with anyone is the last thing on her mind, so there's that too. We joke around some, but she's not out to distract me. Not seriously."

Ty nodded. "Well, I say let things go at their own pace. Once her case is wrapped up, you'll be free to explore any other avenues. Give it plenty of space and time. Maybe she'll just always be a person you protected once upon a time. Maybe you two can stay as friends. Or maybe there'll be more between you two later on.

"But just keep it professional now. Don't take the chance of ruining your reputation, your career, the respect of your fellow officers, or getting the case thrown out for some bogus reasoning from an overpriced lawyer. If it's in your cards, it'll wait."

Channion sighed. "I agree with you, on all points. Like I said, she's my job. She knows it. I know it. I'd say we're forging a nice friendship, but we're professional with humor mixed in. I'm good with that."

Sammy ambled over and took their empty glasses. He leaned on the counter. "It looks like your conversation has lightened up some. Heavy conversation can be as bad as heavy drinking. But since I'm here, do you guys want another?"

Respecting Sammy's comments, Channion replied, "Just a Dr. Pepper for me."

Ty was impressed by Sammy's notice of them and his professionalism as well. "Same. We'll be here a while, so we'll just take it easy. No rush on them."

As Channion prepared to hand him some bills, Sammy shook his head. "Nah, it's all good. No need to pay for these. Ain't no alcohol in 'em, so it ain't no biggie."

"Thanks, Sammy," he replied. "But take a dollar at least for a tip for your long walk down here?"

Sammy smiled broadly. "Make it two, and you got a deal."

"Double or nothing? Fine." Smiling, Channion handed him two dollars.

Ty laughed as the jovial bartender tucked the bills in his pocket and walked away.

When Raina finally climbed on the stage to warm up, Ty noticed many of the patrons in the bar turned around to watch her. She must be something if she can distract grown men from a sports channel in a bar!

He heard the notes play, and then she opened her mouth.

He was more than a little surprised. He looked at Channion with raised eyebrows. His cousin smiled and nodded. And this was her warming up? Ty listened as she ran through different songs, listened as she and the band made changes. When she laughed, he noticed almost everyone else in the bar smiled.

Sammy delivered their drinks. Glancing at Raina and the band, he said, "She's the best thing about this place. She alone has brung in more regulars than I can remember. The girls say their tips have gone up too. You just wait until she actually performs!" He wiped down the bar in front of them with his towel before he left.

Picking up his beverage, Ty thought it was a *really* good thing he loved his cousin like a brother!

Chapter 33

SINCE THEY GOT HOME from Picacho's close to two in the morning, all three of them slept in late on Saturday. Raina had to take a shower before heading to bed because she was so sticky from sweat, but the two cousins hit their beds almost immediately.

She heard the shower running the next morning and went back to sleep. She sensed someone coming into her room, waited to see what they'd do. She figured it was one of the guys seeing if she was sleeping or not. Her gut was telling her to turn over and even though she was still basically sleeping, she did. When she opened her eyes, she screamed. She saw the two hands grab her by the hair and pound her head into the ground. She kicked and punched, but she couldn't get away.

Channion nearly had heart failure when she screamed. Bounding instantly out of bed, he headed straight for her room, flipping on the hallway light as he passed the switch. Ty was just opening his door. "Nightmare!" Channion called out.

He entered Raina's room, flipping on the light. Ty stood at her door, listening to her screams as he watched her fight viciously against an invisible, unknown adversary.

Channion, having learned from past experience, laid on top of her while he called out to her to wake up. It wasn't easy to hold her down. His fingers laced with hers to hold her hands when she ripped her wrists away from him, landing a solid hit to his shoulder. He kept calling out to her to wake up.

He felt the viciousness in this fight—it was different from the others. This was an all-out attack. Her screams rang in his ears. He had no choice but to yell over them to be heard. He barely moved away in time before she sank her teeth into his skin. That was new. She'd never tried to bite him before.

When Ty first saw Channion cover her body with his, he wondered about that method. But he assumed his cousin knew what he was doing. Didn't most people slap or shake someone to wake them up?

He couldn't believe how hard she was fighting. His cousin could actually be injured if she wasn't caught up in the sheets. He quickly realized that's exactly why Channion chose that method. She must be re-living an actual attack, he realized. His heart hurt just watching her, knowing she had to be tormented inside to a great degree to be having nightmares this intense. He saw Channion roll away just before she bit him.

It took long minutes, but she finally dragged herself through the haze and back into the fringes of reality. Channion kept talking to her, soothing now. He felt her fingers squeeze his as she clawed her way back to the surface. Once he felt her breathing was under control, he carefully rolled off her. He sat beside her, studying her. Her eyes were still glazed over. He kept one of her hands in his, using his other to rub her arm.

Ty asked quietly, "Do you need anything, Chan? Water?"

"If you wouldn't mind... Maybe even warm it up a bit? Her throat's got to be raw, and it might help soothe it. This was a really bad one. She's just coming out of it now. It'll be another few minutes before she's really awake though."

As he spoke, he brushed her damp hair back from her face. She was covered in sweat. Her shudders were like aftershocks from an earthquake. He heard Ty head downstairs.

"It's okay, Raina. You're safe here. I'm here... You're okay..." His soft voice calmed her as she became more aware. His warm hands rubbed her arms and shoulders, brushed her hair back again. He'd found contact seemed to help her best.

She looked up at him, tears in her eyes, while taking deep breaths. Her eyes were still not quite focused. He patiently waited, knowing it just took time. He pondered the severity of this nightmare compared to the others. Although she'd had some bad ones while at his place, this one was epic. She hadn't had one this bad since the night he'd rushed her back to the ER. He thought this one was actually worse.

Finally, she whispered, "This one was too real, Channion."

Noticing she was fully aware now, he let her go. He straightened out the sheets over her before he reached over to toss a warmer blanket on her, giving her time to compose herself. She pulled it closer in a bid to stop the chills racking her body. She wiped tears from her cheeks as she looked at him.

In a concerned voice, he said, "You were fighting me really hard. And it took you longer to come out of this one. Did you hurt yourself?"

She shook her head. "I don't think so. I think I'm okay." Whispering again, she said, "I'm sorry, Channion. I'm so sorry."

"Don't be silly. There's no reason to apologize, you know that." He reached over for her glasses, knowing she hated not being able to see clearly. He grabbed some toilet paper from the nightstand beside her, wiped away her tears first.

She saw Ty come in, set the glass of water on the nightstand. She could faintly smell the lemon juice he'd added, knowing she liked it that way. That little detail warmed her insides.

Her voice was still whisper-soft when she said to him, "Thank you, Ty. I'm so sorry I woke you... I'm so embarrassed..." A tear slid down her cheek and dropped down onto the sheets.

Ty shook his head, saying gently, "There's no need for apologies, Raina. And don't feel embarrassed either. There's no need. How are you?" He sat down at the foot of the bed on the opposite side from Channion so she didn't feel crowded.

"I'll be all right in a minute." She wiped another tear from her cheek before it ran into her ear.

Channion finally ordered her to sit up, watching her to see if she flinched from pain. When she didn't, he handed her the glass of lukewarm water when she got situated. He waited until she drank some, and then placed it back on the nightstand. He brushed her hair back from her face, tucking it behind her ear, as he said tenderly, "This one was different, Raina. Do you know why?"

Her voice was shaky when she answered in a raspy voice, "It was more... *real*. It wasn't just the one nightmare, but it was... It started off in the *now*, like in this present time. It somehow wasn't just in the past like before, but moved up to now. Like as in this morning... When we *would* have gotten up. They blended together perfectly. Every detail was crystal clear... I could hear sounds, and I knew I was here, in your house, in this room. It was like I was awake... I honestly thought I was." She took off her glasses and covered her eyes, trying to hold back the tears.

Both men noticed her hand over her eyes was shaking. Channion pulled the heavier blanket up higher to cover more of her to help ward off the chills. He tucked it around her shoulders. Both men waited for her to speak again when she was ready.

"It was morning, and we all slept in because we got home so late. I could hear the shower running, like for *real*, and I decided to go back to sleep. But I sensed something in the room... Or rather *someone*. I was thinking it was one of you checking to see if I was really asleep or not.

"But my gut ordered me to turn over, sensing something wasn't right. So I did, and he was there. No, not *there*... But *here*... As in this room... But yet, not here. The scene... It all merged together. I can't describe it any better. He grabbed me here in bed, but my head hit the ground. I saw *and* felt him grab my hair and begin pounding my head into the pavement. I was trying to fight him off... But we know how that part goes already..."

Channion grabbed a piece of toilet paper from the nightstand, wiping the tears that were running down her cheeks again. She put her glasses back on before he gave her some more so she could blow her nose. She tossed the tissues in the wastebasket beside the bed.

"*Look* at me! I'm shaking like a leaf in a windstorm..." She pulled the warm blanket even closer to her body, all the way up to her chin.

Ty silently watched, understanding now that Channion being here like this for her was one reason their bond was so strong.

As Channion rubbed his hands up and down her arms over the blanket, he was wondering what else happened. This nightmare *had* to have something else hidden in it. "Do you ever see where he goes in your nightmares? Does he ever *leave* before you wake up? Do you ever see *anyone* leave?" Channion asked softly.

That thought had just come to him. What if she'd seen him leave after her attack but didn't know it? Yet.

She sat there, shivering, thinking about it. "I... I don't know. I think I usually wake up before..." She had a confused look on her face now as she thought about it.

He nodded in understanding. His voice still soft, he inquired, "Was there anything else you remember? Any other details that came through from the actual attack?"

With this bad of a nightmare, there *had* to be something trying to break free, he thought again. But *what* could be there that they didn't already know from the video?

Ty sat there, not making a sound or a move. He didn't want to distract her. Obviously, they'd been through this more than once.

Her lips quivered as she made herself go back. She heard Channion whispering to her, "Take your time, Raina. You're safe here. Me and Ty are here to protect you, so there's no one who can hurt you. If you start to get scared, tell yourself you're safe, okay? Maybe that will help. Think back..."

She slowly nodded, closing her eyes to replay it in her mind. Minutes went by. She felt there was *something*... just beyond her reach. Her breath hitched when she almost had it. Channion and Ty saw her brows furrow together in concentration. Neither one moved a muscle.

She whispered, "A car?" She tilted her head as she mentally searched for what was just beyond her reach. She felt like she was climbing up a slippery, tilted iceberg, trying to reach the top to haul herself over to safety. Her breathing almost stopped as she again mentally tried to catch that one, exact moment she was grasping for. *There!* She heard it again in the deep recesses of her mind. And then again.

Her eyes flew open. She sat forward so quickly, she almost knocked heads with Channion, who'd leaned closer to hear what she was whispering.

"Channion! There was a *third* car! I heard the doors closing. Two doors. Voices." She closed her eyes, replaying it yet again. Her heart was pounding, her chest heaving from excitement and shock. Her hand went up. She raised her fingers when she heard them again in her mind. "One." She waited a bit, her eyes still tightly closed. A second finger went up as she heard it again in her mind. "Two."

Both Channion and Ty had chills now themselves. The hairs on their arms were standing straight up.

She opened her eyes, noticing her raised arm, with two fingers raised up as she'd counted. She stared at her arm, not even remembering raising it. She looked at Ty, then back to her protector.

"Channion! It was a car. I'm *sure* of it. There was *another* car."

"One of the guys, say, the one I pepper sprayed, he got in it... One slam. After Bryce shot at the second, the one banging my head on the pavement, he ran. Remember? *Two!* And I swear I heard voices, male voices. There was a *third* car!" She sat up straighter, grabbing onto his hand. "I need to see the video again!"

Ty interrupted, "You let her see the video of the crime?" He couldn't believe they'd risk a technicality on that. Laws could be flexible in some cases, he knew, but it was still a risk.

Raina answered before his cousin could. "Not all. Just a small part they were trying to figure out." Turning back to Channion, she said again, "I need to see the video."

"Raina, there were no other cars on the video. We've all watched it repeatedly. We would've seen them..." He wondered if she was imagining it? Had his questions triggered this? Was she finally cracking? But she seemed so sure! But there was simply no way for them all to miss seeing a car go down the empty road!

Raina must've been reading his mind, trying not to feel defeated. But then a startling thought popped into her mind, making her gasp.

Ty looked at her, wondering what caused that reaction, but her eyes were locked on his cousin. It was like she was willing him to realize the same thing she just did. She saw it in his face the second it lit up like hers. They looked at each other in wonder.

She confirmed their mutual thought. "The third car was *behind* Bryce's car. It knew not to go in front... Perhaps it didn't need to. Channion, do you know what this means?"

"Do I ever." He grabbed her face with both of his hands, smiling. "Raina, I swear you're the best!"

Turning to Ty, he said, "How about we go down to the station? You want to get back into the game. Just for a little while?"

Ty looked at them, saying without hesitation, "You bet."

Chapter 34

IT DIDN'T TAKE MUCH coaxing on Channion's end to get her to take a hot shower before they left for the station. She was drenched in sweat and chilled. When she shut the bathroom door, Channion quickly stripped her bed of the sheets and pillowcases. Ty understood and helped him. Fresh, dry sheets would be appreciated over rumpled, sweat-soaked ones when they returned.

They both got dressed and headed downstairs to wait for her, discussing the case. Ty made them coffee and her some tea to take with them when they heard the shower turn off. Channion immediately started the washing machine he'd thrown the sheets into. When she came down, her hair was still wet, but she didn't care. She felt better and didn't want to waste any more time. She thanked Ty when he handed her the capped mug of tea as they headed out the door.

They arrived at the police station, almost eerily vacant at that time of dark morning. Once Channion checked out the video from evidence, he led them to the video room. Ty shut and locked the door to be sure they had privacy as Channion flipped on the light and walked over to the video players.

Raina sat down, her hands shaking. What if she was wrong? What if she *was* imagining it? But she was sure. She *felt* it, deep down inside. She trusted her gut. She had to.

"This should be the spot, right around here." Channion had forwarded the video to right after the second man was shot by Bryce.

It was a first for Ty, of course. He was waiting for something to happen on the monitor. Both Raina and Channion leaned forward at the same time, obviously knowing where to focus. But there was nothing.

Then Channion made a change. Glancing at her, he said, "I'm going to play it with audio now, Raina. Are you able to listen?"

"You had audio before? Why didn't you let me listen to it?"

"Raina, the video's bad enough. Audio's a whole other realm. Right, Ty?"

Ty nodded. "Audio makes it exceedingly real and can compound it substantially. Are you sure you can handle it?"

"No, but I have to. We have to know for sure."

Channion hesitated before turning on the audio. When they heard the shots from Bryce's gun, Ty saw her shiver. She intently listened for the noises she swore she heard. She didn't hear anything at all.

Neither did Channion or Ty. Channion rewound it, turned up the volume. Still nothing distinct.

Ty said, "Let's try this. With the static on the disc, or maybe that's wind, it may be muffled. The mic may also just be too far away. If his door or window were open, it may have picked up something though. Let me see if I can isolate it a bit." He knew this equipment well and began adjusting the levers and turning knobs. "Okay, *now* let's listen…"

Their hearts pounded again, waiting. Anticipating. They tried to block out her screams, which was impossible, and heard the two shots from Bryce's gun. After another minute or two that felt like forever, there was a slight noise. Ty adjusted a lever. They all heard it. The heartbeats of the three people in the small room kicked into overdrive as they all realized what they were hearing now.

They heard what could only be the sound of tires on the road, and the unmistakable hum of an engine. It was a car coming to a stop on the loose gravel on the pavement—but not screeching to a stop, so no tire marks. Then… Another sound. It was faint, but they could hear it.

A man's voice, calling out, *"Let's go! Now! We got to get outta here!"*

They heard a car door slamming shut. They continued to listen as their hearts pounded.

What sounded like another man's voice was now urging, *"Get in! Hurry. It's too late! Leave 'em. I said just leave 'em!"*

Soon, there was a second car door slamming shut.

Ty and Channion both turned to look at a relieved, and scared, Raina.

Her voice shook when she said, "Thank you, God. I'm *not* crazy! This puts everything into a different light now, Channion. The car Bryce pulled over was most likely *leaving* a store house, a supplier—whatever you call it—from *up* the road, like toward my house. The other car was most likely on its way *to* the same location. They weren't meeting on the side of the road to make an exchange or whatever. They were coming and going. And on a regular enough basis to know the other's routine."

Ty agreed with her. "That sounds right. It'd make sense. I can give you my professional opinion if I can read through the case and see the evidence. I want to watch the whole video too."

Channion nodded. "I think I'd better call in Ron. He needs to be here." He pulled out his phone, hit his speed-dial.

Ron picked up on the second ring. "Chan? What's wrong?" His voice was amazingly alert... and extremely concerned. Why else would his nephew on a protection detail be calling him at this time?

"We're fine, Ron. We're safe." He knew to state that first. "But Raina had a nightmare and remembered something profoundly significant. We're all down at the station and have confirmed it. I think you should be here for this. We're on our floor in the main video room."

He heard his uncle moving as he talked, "I'll be there right away!"

"It's okay. Take your time because Ty wants to review what we have to give us his opinion. Drive safely."

While they waited for Ron to arrive, Channion got the files for Ty, who sat in the corner where he could concentrate on what he was reading. Channion and Raina didn't speak while Ty used his own talents to put it together from his own perspective. He quickly scanned the file, skimming through the reports. He winced when he saw the photos of Raina right after she was admitted to the hospital. He'd never have recognized her. How did she ever survive that? He couldn't figure it out, except God wanted her around yet.

He was getting ready to watch the video when Ron knocked on the door, called out to them. Channion unlocked the door, letting him in. He'd been getting ready to escort Raina out the door since the video was going to be played from the beginning. They just couldn't take the chance of the case being tainted by letting her stay in there with it playing. Raina smelled Ron's familiar blend of coffee he made from home as he walked through the door.

With a shaky voice, she whispered, "It seems I've had a little breakthrough."

Ron hugged her and squeezed Ty's shoulder before walking back out with her. Since Ron had arrived, Channion said he'd stay to watch the video with Ty. Ron nodded before he and Raina sat down at a nearby desk and spoke in quiet tones.

Watching the video, Ty shook his head. Seeing it happen, knowing he was near the woman who was in the video being brutally attacked, Ty's respect for her skyrocketed. No wonder she had nightmares. He briefly wondered how the deputy was coping.

As they came to the part where she was in the cruiser, Channion said, "The next fifteen, twenty minutes is just the driving. Nothing else happens until she gets closer to town. It's some crazy driving. It's nothing short of a miracle she even made it to the hospital, but she did. He was in critical condition when they got there, so she saved his life for the second time."

Ty shook his head again. "She should be dead, Chan. There's no earthly reason why she's not. None at all. Either one of those assaults should've been enough to kill her, or maybe send her into a coma. No lasting head trauma? No surgeries?"

His cousin shook his head. "No."

Ty exclaimed, "How she managed to live through both of those attacks and *still* get the deputy to the hospital all on her own really is nothing less than a miracle. And that's not even counting the initial crash in her truck."

"Ron and I have watched this video repeatedly. We've always come to that same conclusion. She's tough and has a stockpile of grit and courage. She doesn't know how to quit.

"The way she fought the first guy... She was beating the crap out of him! And that was with her already being injured. The second guy's harder to see, but we can put it together by his motions." He offered a small smile. "See why we're allowing a witness to live with us? She's unique, isn't she?"

"That's putting it mildly."

The two cousins reviewed the file, the video, and the notes. Ty asked several questions, looked through the photos again. "Can you get me copies of your entire case file, and the video, so I can review it while I'm here? Maybe I can help. Just keep me out of the loop."

"Sure."

Ty scanned a few papers that had caught his eye before flipping through the photos another time. He shook his head again, still not believing Raina had even survived. Looking up from the photos of her in the hospital, Ty asked, "You said she refuses a shrink? Are you worried about PTSD?"

"We've offered, but she refuses. We even offered a hypnotist, but that was a definite no from her. The doctors tell us to not push her on it. As long as she's willing to talk to us openly about it, especially her nightmares, we're to let her be. She's moving at her own pace. Overall, she seems to be handling it all quite well, considering the severity. Perhaps she'll change her mind later on.

"We've been watching for more signs of PTSD. She has the typical nightmares, flashbacks, stress, and weight loss. We're keeping a close eye on her. The fact that she's striving to live life in a normal fashion is incredible. Some people simply wouldn't be strong enough mentally or emotionally to get that they needed to move forward as soon as they were able. She *insists* on it."

"Which is why you're letting her work."

Channion nodded. "With modifications and extra security. When we're out, we generally have a tail."

Ty nodded as he went through the file, coming across some more photos. "Wait. What are these?"

Channion grinned, then sighed. "Oh. Those are of me."

"*You?* How did you get these bruises all over your torso? You weren't even there."

"Don't tell her because she doesn't know... Raina did that to me during her first major nightmare. We took them for possible evidence comparisons."

"No means *no*, little cousin!"

Channion laughed good-naturedly before explaining her first major nightmare and how she attacked him, similar to that night's experience. "The only way I can wake her up without being pummeled to smithereens is to use my body weight to hold her down until she wakes up. She still got me a couple of times tonight though. I'll probably have a couple bruises pop up soon. She's got quite a punch even injured. And she nearly took a chunk out of me! That was a surprise as she's never tried to bite me before tonight.

"It has occurred to me that by feeling my weight on her, it might lend credit to her believing she really *is* under attack, and make it worse. But in all truthfulness, it's the only way I've found that works to protect her from herself *and* that protects me."

"I saw that unusual method tonight and did wonder about it." Ty looked at the photos again. "Why didn't you tell her about this?"

"Are you kidding? Her guilt would eat her alive. Besides that noble consideration, I simply don't want her to know she can beat up on me. It'd be like when Morgan kicked my butt that one time."

Both laughed at the memory of Channion sparring against Morgan on one of his visits to Arizona. Ty had warned him to pay attention, but he'd still vastly underestimated her prowess at kickboxing. He'd possibly held back because she was a woman—and Ty's boss.

But Morgan didn't have that luxury. In real life, she had to be ready. A man was still a man. She'd mopped the floor with him.

Both men were still grinning as Ty slipped the photos of Channion back inside the file.

Channion asked, "What's your opinion?"

"I think you've been neglecting your abs."

Channion knew he was being deliberately misunderstood and laughed. Ty grinned over at him again as he put all the papers back in place.

When Ron entered the room with Raina, Ty hugged her tightly. "You're an amazing woman, Raina."

She nodded her thanks and acknowledgement to him. Stepping away, she said, "Well, let's show Ron what we've found."

Cueing the disc, Channion said, "Okay, Ron. We've turned on the audio, and Ty has isolated the background noise. This is what we're hearing now..."

Ron set down his coffee as he leaned forward. When he first heard the sounds, his brows furrowed much like Raina's had when she was first remembering it. "Is that what I *think* it is? Do it again!"

Channion replayed it while Ron listened intently.

"That's a *car!*" Ron exclaimed in excitement and no little shock.

"Oh, that's not all. There's more..." Channion said.

Hearing the voices and the car doors slamming shut, Ron's eyes got wide. "Why, this changes *everything!*"

They all nodded. Channion said, "Both Ty and I think Raina's theory is right on. Those two cars weren't *meeting* on the side of the road..."

Ron knew where he was going and nodded. "They were heading to and from the same place. A supplier most likely." He leaned back in his chair. "This is extremely local. Even the ATF guys were thinking it was out of state, or at least farther away from here. But what's large enough out there to house illegal arms and ammo? Unless it's like a relay station of sorts?"

Channion nodded before giving his theory. "When Bryce was beginning to run the guy's plates and ID, the driver he pulled over was texting the guys coming in. He was warning them that there was a cop *and* that he was pulled over. And, I'd bet, probably exactly where. That's why they stopped where they did and took out the rifle on the way in. How else could they have known? No one ever counted on Raina here doing what she did.

"We think she's right on, too, when she said these have to be precisely scheduled drops and pickups. Otherwise, how else could the first driver know to text the incoming car at *that* time?"

Ty nodded. "I agree. Also, she was attacked quite differently. The first attack was from pure rage. She interrupted their plan of murder, just hit and killed one of their business associates, *and* disabled their cars filled with illegal weapons and ammo. She took them all out of service in mere seconds. He was fighting with rage because it was reactionary.

"Meanwhile, as the guy attacked her—the one she soon pepper sprayed and kneed—the second attacker was probably calling to the supplier, letting him know there was a huge, explosive situation happening. They needed extracted immediately. When she broke free from the first guy, this second guy then jumped her with the clear intention of killing her. She was a witness at that point. *He* was calm, methodical."

He paused, thinking. "My best guess is they figured Deputy Mitchell was close enough to death to not bother with him anymore, or maybe thought he already was dead.

"Note the times here. Assuming we're correct, this third car got to them within what? Less than ten minutes, assuming we're correct on when the call was made. But we'll say ten, maybe even fifteen to be on the safe side to not miss something. Unless this third car was already driving out, we can assume the driver lives extremely close to this whole scene. You need to get call logs for the cell towers in the area, narrow them down. You guys know which numbers to look for yet?"

Ron said, "A couple of good guesses, strong leads. Out there in the boondocks like that, there can't be a whole lot of them happening at these times. With this disc and Raina's testimony, we can narrow it down a whole lot more unless they used burners, which they probably did."

Raina said, "Here's a little something more, something either you haven't had time yet to say, or are stalling on saying. Maybe I need to leave the room because I'm fairly sure I shouldn't be in here right now... But, well..." She sighed and blurted out, "*My* house is between ten or fifteen minutes away from this, so it stands to reason that the weapons supplier lives on *my* road. There are no other houses for miles down, so best guess is mine.

"Let's assume something here. Again, unless this third car was already moving, he couldn't have been driving all that fast because of the curves and hills. He had to be close to get there when he did. He also had to know the local area very well to know where to go so quickly."

She looked at them. "And he, or they, knew I had the horses, and how much I loved them. He'd know what my truck looked like. He'd have known all along who it was that ruined his operation and his day. He's known me the entire time... *That's* how they found me. I think I know who it is you're looking for."

Chapter 35

THEY LEFT HER ALONE for a few minutes, needing to talk in private. When they came back into the room, they locked the door again before sitting down to silently wait. She was holding her head in her hands, her elbows propped on her knees. She wasn't crying. She was thinking. She was trying to put it all together, piece by piece, like working a puzzle.

Living at her house for almost a year now, did she ever pay attention or notice anything odd about the traffic pattern on her road? She was the third house on it, and they were all spread out from each other. She used to sit at her little dining room table, eating breakfast after she fed and played around with her horses. She remembered cars on the road, but they never caught her attention. Why would they? After all, she wasn't the only one who lived on that isolated, country road.

Looking back now, it struck her as odd that the cars always seemed to come around at the same times. There were cars and sometimes an SUV, but rarely were there trucks and stock trailers.

Did any cars stand out to her as she rode her horses through the fields? She never picked up on anything unusual. The day she rode Aspen to the neighbor who had the teenage son, did she notice anything at all that was out-of-sync?

The answer was no.

But that's why they could do it. Nothing was suspicious. Nothing was out of the ordinary to anyone passing by. It was simply a big old farmhouse, remodeled and in excellent shape, on lots of well-cared for land, with immaculate outbuildings and that large barn. Not to mention all that beautiful four-plank black fencing for the cattle and their own horses.

It was a front.

She didn't look up when she said, "Whoever shot my horses knew I had them *before* they came out to kill me. Have you guys thought about that? I highly doubt they'd be seen by anyone at night. Maybe they staked out my place beforehand and saw them. My horse trailer is on the other side of the barn because it's flat there and protected from the weather more. You can't see it that well, if at all, from the road or the house. Besides, that doesn't mean there actually *were* horses down there.

"There was absolutely no reason at all for anybody to go to the barn, looking for me down there at three or four in the morning. No barn lights were even on. For all a stranger would know, the barn was empty. It was pitch black out. Was there even a moon? And Channion, remember the lightbulbs in the pole by the barn were out.

"I doubt my Aspen or Rodeo would've whinnied at that time of night for anybody, even me. The shooter must've gone there just to... do what he did when I wasn't conveniently sleeping in bed so they could kill me. I could be wrong, but that's how I see it."

She rubbed the ache in her chest with her hand. Carefully, she thought it out. "There's also a part of me that's saying that my horses were shot first. Or at least, *not* just because I wasn't in bed. If I was, they would've just shot *me*, right? And Channion, since he was there. I mean, assuming he couldn't protect us... I'm just free-thinking here, okay?"

The men nodded, realizing she was worried about insulting Channion and his abilities to protect her. Channion appreciated her letting him know she was simply tossing out ideas.

"Channion told me they were shot humanely... and quickly. But that doesn't make any sense. If they shot *me* first, why even go to the barn? If they *didn't* shoot me first, why be so humane? I mean, obviously I wouldn't want it any *other* way, except to have not killed my kids in the first place, but..." Her voice trailed off for a second as she aligned her thoughts.

"*Why* would they shoot them anyway? If I was dead, *why* would they care about my horses? They had to have known they were there, no matter what. I doubt they were concerned about their well-being if they can shoot a human in cold blood. Why not just steal my horses at that point? None of this makes any sense to me. I'm missing something..."

The three experienced men all realized she was a natural at this. Her logic, her points, her free-thinking were all extremely valid and on-point. Ty was the most interested in her, especially with his undercover background. She had incredible potential!

Ty offered, "But if they did shoot your horses first, wouldn't they have been worried you'd hear the shots? Unless they used a silencer, which is a possibility. Why would they even take the chance of going to them first? *You* were their target. If they shot your horses *first,* then found out you weren't even home, they'd be tipping their hand. If I were them, I'd have hidden nearby until you got home.

"Was it a warning? Something to prolong your pain? To create mental anguish? What would make them want to kill your horses at all? But you're also right that killing them afterwards makes no sense. There is a big piece missing here. We find that piece, and I bet it'll all make perfect sense."

Ron and Channion agreed.

Channion suggested, "What if there were multiple shooters? Most likely, they sent more than one. I don't think they'd take the chance of not killing Raina this time. They'd have come prepared.

"Let's say more than one shooter to hit both the house and the barn at the same time. But again, we're right back to why kill her horses? That *why* is the piece we're missing. I think the *why* is far more important than anything else here. And the other *why* is why so humanely? Raina's right saying it doesn't add up."

After a few moments, she heaved out a sigh before looking up. Speaking simply from her heart, she said, "I'm so tired of all of this. I want to go back to bed and never get up again."

Ron leaned forward, saying, "Raina, we know. You want your life back..."

"No, that's not it. I mean, yes, of course I do, but no. I'm tired of thinking I know someone, just to have it thrown back in my face. I'm tired of dealing with rotten people. Family members who don't even bother to call me when I'm in the hospital until practically a month later. And now my own neighbor who I actually *paid* to take *care* of my horses *kills* them instead!"

Her fury was rising the more she thought about it. She'd prefer to be beyond pissed so she didn't do the opposite and sink into despair. She stood up, paced in the little room while the men watched her. Neither Channion nor his uncle had ever seen her anywhere near mad before. Ty simply waited... Waited for the inevitable explosion of emotions that needed to be set free. Maybe *this* would be her breaking point.

"Is this room soundproofed?" she asked, fury in her voice.

"No," Channion answered immediately.

Yelling, she said, "Well, why not?"

Channion asked, "Would you like to be put in a soundproof room?"

She rounded on him, yelling, "Do I *look* like I need one?"

He wasn't sure if it was a rhetorical question or not, so he kept his mouth shut.

But Ty decided to nudge her along. "Yeah, you do. You look like you're going to get really loud really soon. Wanna go find one?"

The fury on her face when she looked at him was formidable. "No! I think I have more than earned the right to scream my head off right here, and right now!" And for the first time since the detectives met her, she swore. "Damn it. Damn it. Damn it. *Damn it!* The bastard tried to kill me and *did* kill my horses! Damn him to *hell*. And I hope he has those damn devils for roommates while he burns down there for eternity!

"Let's just bomb his entire property, and then we'll see how he likes *that!* Can we do that?" She stopped, her entire body shaking in her anger. Screaming, she said, "Damn it! I need to hit or kick something!"

With no warning at all, Ty shoved his startled, unprepared cousin at her. Channion nearly knocked her down before pinning her against the wall with a loud thud. Ty said loudly, "*Here! Have at it!*"

The room went dead silent before they started laughing.

Looking down at the wall, she exclaimed, "Shit! There's a hole!"

Her comment had them laughing again.

Channion sat down beside Ty. Straight-faced, he complained, "I think you bruised my arm. She once told me that girls think arms are sexy on a guy, and you just ruined mine."

Ty laughed as he put his arm around his cousin good-naturedly. "Bruises fade. Maybe some girl will kiss it to make it feel better."

Channion made copies of the new information to give to the ATF later. He also made a copy of the video and the computer files he had for the case, putting them on a flash drive he took from his desk. Ty slipped the small device inside his sock for more security. He was far from trusting anything at this point. Ron kept Raina in the breakroom so she wasn't aware of Ty getting copies.

They debated calling the ATF, but the men decided to wait. What could a couple of days hurt? They were having a family reunion after all. This was only the second day of it. If they gave the Feds the information, they'd probably end up working instead. They also wondered if the Feds had heard this isolated audio themselves but didn't tell them for some reason.

Looking at his cousin as he put the files back in order, Ty said, "You know that explosion we were wondering about earlier?"

"Yeah."

"That wasn't it."

"Not big enough?"

"Not *nearly* big enough. That was just frustration boiling over even with me egging her on. She still hasn't had that ignition switch flipped. With her passion and inner fire, that internal engine that is somehow keeping her going, I still predict she'll explode."

"Why are you telling me this?"

"Because that was a minor eruption to what I think she's going to have. When she has it, something tells me she's going to need both you and Ron in her corner, and fast, to help her cope with it. She's going to have her emotions all over the place. I just thought I'd prepare you, but you probably already know that."

"Yeah, I do. And I completely agree with you. She hasn't displayed much in the way of temper or anything. The closest is when she met a fellow officer here who was seriously checking her out the first day we brought her here. She set him in his place, and she needed to.

"Other than that, it's probably only because she's been in poor health and just trying to get through each day. But something tells me she has a worthy temper. I think we'll know the explosion when it happens with no questions."

"I almost hate to miss it."

Channion smiled, understanding his warped humor. "I'll be sure to let you know about it if you're not around to see it for yourself."

"I'll look forward to it."

They grinned at each other before heading to the door. After locking away all of the evidence, Channion led Ty to the breakroom to get Ron and Raina.

They were sitting at a table so Ron could fill out a maintenance request to fix the hole in the wall they'd made. Apparently, Raina was helping him. Waiting outside the door for a minute, Ty and Channion grinned at each other as they listened to them laughing.

It was a great sound to hear.

THEY WERE ALL EXHAUSTED when they returned to Channion's. They figured to sleep in and go to the reunion whenever they felt like waking up. After Channion and Raina went to bed, Ty slipped into Channion's office, shut the door, and booted up his computer. He reviewed some of the evidence again, seeing it play out in his mind in the calm quiet of the early morning hours. With the volume turned low, he watched the video all the way through.

Like the others, he was wondering what Raina was doing as she walked from one car to another. To his experienced eye, she wasn't just meandering around, disoriented. To him, it looked like she had a purpose to what she was doing. But with the limited view, distance, and angle, he couldn't quite tell. She wasn't even opening the car doors to look inside. In fact, she hardly went right up to any of them.

It did appear she had something in her hand, but he couldn't enhance the video from here. And according to his cousin, she had no idea herself. If she was doing something on purpose, it was locked away deep in her mind.

He wondered if she was taking pictures? It was the only thing he could think of that made sense of her movements. If so, where were the photos? He skimmed the file photos again but didn't see anything except those taken by the police. If she had, wouldn't they have put them in the file as evidence? he wondered.

Yawning again, he closed down the computer. Knowing the code to Channion's safe, he put the flash drive inside. He decided to take a shower now instead of later as his mind was still running loose. Remembering the laundry, he went downstairs and tossed the sheets into the dryer.

Lying on his back in his bed looking at the ceiling after taking a shower, he felt the strongest urge to join the case. He knew he had the resources and the contacts that could add to this case to close it far more quickly than the locals. Probably even the ATF and FBI.

And if he could help close it more quickly, that meant Channion and Ron would be safe again that much sooner. Not to mention both Raina and Deputy Mitchell. Their lives would once again be their own.

There was also something familiar about this case that was nagging him. He couldn't quite put his finger on it yet. He figured he was just too tired.

As Ty slid into an exhausted sleep, he was thinking about going back to the covert agency he'd left once but was still active in. He thought about going back to being an undercover agent.

Chapter 36

THE HUGE FAMILY REUNION was unlike anything Raina had seen before. The family connections, the games, the stories, the food, and the land owned by family that meant they could do whatever they wanted was impressive. Meeting Ty's parents and sisters, and Ron and Janet's daughters on top of so many others was incredible. Raina now understood why Ty made sure to come to it every year.

But this Tuesday morning meant going back to reality. Most of the family members had already left or were heading back today to their respective homes, Ty among them. His flight didn't leave until later that evening so they had time to chill out at Channion's. Raina already missed Ty even though he was still sitting right across from her, deciding which card to play. Waiting on Ty to play his hand, she reached over for her phone.

Channion scolded, "What are you doing? You're not calling anyone, Stewart! We're playing cards here!" He set his drink down, reaching over to take the phone away from her.

She kept it out of his reach. "Yeah, I know. And we'll still be here tomorrow since Ty's taking so long. At the rate he's going, we'll need to book him another flight."

He grunted at her, signaling her to be quiet. She laughed, but Ty finally put down his card, looking at Channion to play next. She switched her phone to camera mode before holding it up to take a picture of the guys... and froze.

Ty teased Channion, who was now deciding on the best card to play, "Chan, don't take so long. My flight leaves at..." He looked at Raina with a teasing smile, but it faded the second he saw her face. He slowly reached over to get Channion's attention, pointing to her.

Channion glanced over, saw her face and froze himself. The hairs stood up on his arms.

Her face was blank, like she wasn't really there. Her eyes had a faraway look in them. She wasn't even blinking.

Channion slowly put down his cards, moved his drink out of the way. Ty did the same. She didn't seem to notice them moving.

What was happening? Did she see someone outside the window?

She was remembering something! That thought hit them both at the same time.

The hand holding up the cellphone began to shake as her other hand reached over to steady it. She held this position, not moving.

It was the creepiest thing they'd ever witnessed.

Hoping it wouldn't disturb her memory, Channion finally reached for the hand holding the phone. With his other hand, he lightly touched her shoulder, saying softly, "Raina."

When she looked at him out of dazed eyes, he took hold of her other hand, gently squeezing it. He asked softly, "What did you see? A flashback?"

She let out a breath, tried to gather her thoughts. "I remember..." She looked at her cellphone in her hand. "Oh, I can't believe that I..."

Ty sat forward, never taking his eyes off her face.

Without another word, she jumped up and ran out of the room. Both men stared at each other in bewilderment. They heard her running up the stairs. In unison, they stood up to follow her.

Standing outside her room, they watched her opening the closet door, carefully getting a box off the top shelf. Tossing it on the bed, it bounced before she opened it. She began rummaging through it.

Ty and Channion didn't know what had come over her and stood there in silence.

"I found it!" Triumphantly, she held up her old phone. "Let's see if there's any charge left from..." Her voice trailed off as she sat down on the bed and turned on the phone. "There might be enough... It's pretty low..." She reached for the charging cord and plugged it in.

Knowing what was there now, Raina impatiently slid the screen over to the photos. She scrolled back over and over, nodding as she did so. "Oh... I can't believe..." They heard her softly saying to herself.

She hadn't had any reason to use her phone as a camera simply because she rarely ever used it for that purpose. She preferred her digital camera over the phone's camera because of the annoying time and effort to download images and videos she wanted to keep on her laptop. But there had been a time recently that she *had* used it out of necessity.

Patting the bed, she said, "Come sit by me."

She moved the box over so they could all sit side by side, with her on one end. Silently, she handed the phone to them.

They couldn't believe what they were seeing. In surprise, they watched the video Raina had taken of the men and Bryce... *before* he was shot!

When it ended, she said, "Scroll forward."

Channion did. "What... You got pictures of them all before... I can't believe you have all of this!"

He scrolled through the pictures, came to another video. He and Ty watched it, stunned. They watched it again, scrolled through a couple more photos before they ended. Ty realized he'd been right. She *had* been taking photos because here they were.

Ty looked up at her. "And you just *now* remembered all this was on here?"

She nodded. "I guess when I was going to take a picture downstairs, the motion of holding the phone up, framing the camera screen... I don't know. It all... broke free, and it was like I was literally there again.

"I stood behind a tree, one a bit wider that I could hide behind, and took all that. I was terrified the worst would happen, and they'd all get away. I thought, *maybe*, if I had some sort of proof, evidence... But what I have isn't all that great now because Bryce's car camera got it already, right? Mine is like, what? A back-up? Extra evidence now?"

Both men looked at her, stunned she'd been thinking so clearly and calmly. They now knew why she'd grabbed her own hand that was holding the new phone just a few minutes ago: She was steadying the camera because she *had been* doing that same thing when she originally took it all, shaking in fear.

Scenes began racing through her mind. Taking a deep breath, she said, "And I wasn't reacting to head trauma, and I wasn't disoriented." Seeing their questioning looks, she explained, "Remember after I was attacked and left for dead, I began stumbling all around? All of us were wondering *what* I was doing. Now I *know* what I was doing!

"I was terrified they were still there somewhere. Or they'd be coming back to get the body or the cars themselves. I was actually thinking quite clearly. *How* I have no idea. But I was.

"I didn't want them to get away with attempted murder, or murder already, so I forced myself to go to each car." She pointed to the phone again. "If memory serves correctly, I got each make, model, license plate as well as pictures of the dead guy. Just in case..."

Channion shook his head. "But these are *before*..."

She smiled. "Of course they are. But I locked my truck. I do things for a reason, right? *Why* did I lock my truck?" Unable to sit now, she stood up and faced them. "Because I'd used my *digital* camera to take those *other* pictures. I had my phone and my purse when I got into Bryce's car, right?"

They both nodded.

She mused as the images in her mind led her along what had happened that day. "I left my *digital* camera in my truck. I locked the truck with the hopes no one could get it out. We need to find my digital camera!

"Since I probably wasn't really a suspect by the time the CSIs began processing my truck, doing the cars first I bet because of what was *in* them, my guess is the CSIs didn't think to actually look in my truck. Or at least not scroll through my personal camera for pictures if they found it. Why would they?"

Coming to his conclusion, Ty verified it by asking, "You left the *digital* camera in your locked truck in case something happened to you in the police car? Basically, you didn't want to put all your eggs in one basket?"

She nodded. "I recall thinking, or more *sensing*, they could somehow follow me in the car. I don't know why I would've thought that, but I did. If something happened to me, like being run off the road, shot, blacking out, whatever... They probably would've checked my phone thoroughly since I was driving a police car with a shot cop in the back seat. The CSIs would've had my phone and the evidence on it.

"If I ended up dead, with my truck being registered to me... Wouldn't the police tear it apart? Go through it all with a fine-tooth comb? I imagine they would've found my camera and looked through the camera *then*. Wouldn't they?

"Or maybe my family if they got my belongings, if they even cared to look. But since I wasn't dead, and not a suspect, and the cars were keeping them plenty busy, they apparently just didn't check my digital camera."

Raina took a deep breath, taking relief in the weight that seemed to be lifting from her mind and shoulders with these newest memories. "And if they, meaning the bad guys, took my truck somehow, burned it up, broke in, whatever, and took the digital camera? Well..." She pointed to the cellphone Channion was still holding. "I at least had *those*. I didn't know about Bryce's car recording it too. If I'd known that, I bet I would've just shoved him in his car and taken off for the hospital."

Replaying the video in his mind, Channion admitted it made sense now. "How on earth were you able to do all that, Raina? It defies the possible! But some people do react in incredible ways when faced with an intense life-or-death situation."

As Channion and Raina talked, Ty took her phone from Channion to look through the photos again. He'd make copies of these and put them on the flash drive, he thought as he scrolled to the next photo. Something caught his eye, and he zoomed in. It was a bit blurry but... *Son of a...*

Ty abruptly stood up. "I'll be back in a bit."

Walking out to the garage where he'd have privacy, he made a few phone calls. Once he got the ball rolling, he headed back inside.

Chapter 37

AFTER DISCUSSING THE SITUATION with her the following day, they decided she needed to stop giving lessons. For now, they'd let her still sing at the bar since it was infrequent, and the road shows were allowed since she'd removed them from her website and weren't local. If it was indeed her neighbor, they needed to keep her out of sight as much as possible.

It was a difficult decision to make knowing she needed the normalcy—and the money. But they figured financial matters could be worked out. Death couldn't.

After making this decision, Channion drove her to the studio for the only music lesson she had scheduled. He noticed she was distracted during the lesson. Partly it was her missing Ty now that he was gone, but he knew it was more her uncertain future that was weighing heavily on her shoulders.

She contacted her students to cancel all lessons until further notice, wondering how many she'd lose. She didn't make a whole lot of money now, but she didn't want to dwell on what she'd do with even less. Channion took care of Lorenzo, letting him know she had to be on leave for a while to get some things settled. Lorenzo didn't understand and had questions. But not many people could question Channion and get anything from him he didn't want them to know.

Raina apologized again to Lorenzo before they left, promising she'd return as soon as she was able to. She hoped she wasn't lying to him. She decided to take a chance and left her things there as a sign she'd be coming back. A sign for both Lorenzo *and* herself.

———⊱※⊰———

AFTERWARDS, CHANNION, RON, AND Raina drove to the city to meet the ATF agents, who were excited to finally meet Raina as neither detective allowed them to interview her earlier. Citing her health, security, and possible leaks to her whereabouts, both Ron and Channion refused to let the agents near her.

After a short meeting that included Raina, they set her up in an empty office down the hallway. Occupied with Channion's portable DVD player, a few movies to watch, a blanket for comfort or warmth, and some food, she settled in while they had another meeting. She was allowed to leave to use the water fountain and the restroom across the hallway, but she wasn't allowed to roam the halls without an escort.

In the conference room, Ron and Channion presented the newest information they had to the agents. When the ATF men were told about the third car and their theory behind it, first it was so quiet in the conference room they could hear a pin drop. In the next instant, it was bedlam.

Listening to the audio copy Ty had made for them, the agents in the room were stunned. It definitely put a new spin on the entire case. Next, Channion presented her cellphone and digital camera evidence, and it started all over again. Ron was able to get the evidence bag from her truck that morning and found her digital camera. He'd already made copies of what she took on it. Ron and Channion were adamant about giving Raina the credit for everything they were sharing with them. They knew without her, they'd have none of it.

Agreeing with a suggestion from Ty, who the Feds knew nothing about, Ron recommended they make plans to take Raina back to the original crime scene and re-create it. No one knew if it'd garner new evidence, but they all figured it was worth the shot. For Raina, it was also an opportunity for healing by confronting it in person. But this time, she'd be surrounded by armed men who were there to protect her.

They agreed to meet at the scene the next day. Ron walked away to call in favors with the highway department, scheduling the times they needed all traffic re-routed for her safety. While he was doing that, Channion and the ATF team began planning on how to put surveillance on her neighbor. Channion knew this was more their area of expertise than his and gladly let them take charge of it all. His first priority was protecting Raina, and that's what he planned on doing.

Agent Mark Lyles said thoughtfully, "What we need is to get audio and video inside the property itself. Short of sneaking on the property at night, we need to figure out how to get inside. All the best information will be there. This is the only way we'll know for sure if it's her neighbor.

"We can get photos of all the cars that come and go from there once we figure out where we can do a stakeout from. Record them all, see who returns more often, and maybe even figure out their actual schedules. A drone is too risky."

Channion nodded. "It may be possible for us to use her former home as a stakeout point. It's empty, but it still has all utilities on. It's close, and we can watch the road from that direction. We'd still need to figure out something for any cars coming from the opposite direction."

Mark asked, "Do you think she'll let us use it?"

"Yeah, I do. But we'll need to check with her landlord. He knows she's not in it right now, but the lease is still in her name. We'd need his permission. If anything, it's professional courtesy to ask him."

"We'd certainly need permission to be there," Mark agreed.

Channion had a sudden thought. "That could be a problem right there—meaning you guys even staying at her place. They've already broken in once with intent to kill. Having agents in there might be dangerous for them. If they thought it was her, or figured out it was agents, you could be sitting in an ambush. How do we know this guy wouldn't simply blow up the entire house to make sure he doesn't miss her this time?"

"That's true. We need to come up with a solution to that first," Mark said. "We'll put our heads together on that."

Ron walked up, setting down his notebook. "We're set for tomorrow. The road in that whole section will be closed. All traffic will be re-routed all the way around until we're done. No one but us will be there."

Shaking the agents' hands once they finalized their plans, Ron and Channion left to rescue Raina. When they got into Ron's car, she laid down across the back seat. Channion gave her a sweatshirt and jacket his uncle kept in a bag in the trunk so she could use them as a pillow. Once she got them positioned, he leaned inside the car to pull the blanket up around her shoulders.

When they asked if she was hungry, she said no. They were, so they stopped to get some takeout they could eat on the road. She was sound asleep by the time Ron was pulling onto the highway and heading for home.

Chapter 38

RAINA NOW KNEW FOR a fact that hell indeed could freeze over. She knew because she was sitting in hell at that moment, and she was, in fact, freezing.

She was sitting in the backseat of Ron's car, shivering and shaking like she was in a blizzard. Wrapping her arms tightly around herself, she closed her eyes, mentally warring with herself to regain control. Was she on the verge of a panic attack? How would she know? What would she do if she *did* know?

Ron and Channion were talking with the agents as they made sure the area was clear and safe. Once it was confirmed, she'd begin her tour of the crime scene from start to finish.

Sitting there gave her time to think. It was Thursday. It'd been twenty-five long, sometimes terrifying, days since she first drove past the squad car with its flashing lights and the pulled-over vehicle.

She'd been in a wreck that she'd caused, actually killed a man, was beaten almost to death (twice), saved a man's life (twice), been hospitalized (twice), lost her truck, her home, her two beautiful horses, was risking her career itself, was involved in solving a weapons ring with the local police force as well as the ATF, and was currently living with a complete stranger—who also happened to be her personal bodyguard.

Who knew all this would happen when she decided to ditch the cold corporate world to follow her and her mama's dream of becoming a musician?

By the time Channion returned to the car, Raina was getting herself under control.

"Raina? Are you okay?" His concerned voice washed over her. He'd opened the door to let her know it was safe to get out and took one look at her. Crouching down to her level, Channion put his warm hands over hers, surprised to find them ice cold. "Raina? If you're not comfortable doing this, you don't have to. No one will think less of you."

She nodded, letting him know she heard him. She sat there, feeling his warm hands over hers. Looking into his concerned, warm brown eyes calmed her. They let her know he wasn't there to make her re-live an awful event just because she was a job, a means to an end. He was concerned about her as a person. She could trust him. When had she felt that way about anyone?

In a determined voice, she said, "I can do it, Chan." She used Ty's nickname for him. "It's just all coming back to me. Facing it like this is no less than terrifying for me. The first time I was here, it all happened too quickly for me to think it through. This time, well... This time I have nothing to do *but* think and remember. It's the sole purpose of my being here after all."

Channion would in no way push or force her to do this. He believed she wanted to. She just needed to gather herself together first. So he'd simply give her time and support. His mom had always said the most important things one could give in life were intangible. And he knew these two intangibles were the best things he could give this woman.

A few yards away, Agent Mark Lyles stood with Ron. Both men were watching, wondering what was going to happen.

Mark asked, "Are you sure she's strong enough to do this? It looks like she's having a hard time just getting out of your car."

Ron watched his nephew. "I think she's gathering herself together. Channion knows how best to handle her. He'll let her choose what to do. If we force her, the memories may become distorted or even blocked. If so, then she'll be in even worse shape.

"I refuse to cause her any more pain whether mental, emotional, or physical. She's been through more than enough, Mark. God strike me down if I try to force her to do this. It can't be easy for her to be here. We're just hoping it'll help her as much as us—if not more."

The men watched as Channion scooted in beside her so both were now sitting in the car.

Mark said, "Well, damn. It's working backwards, Ron. Instead of her getting out, he got in!"

Ron knew he was only teasing, trying to lighten the tension around them. The more he thought about it, though, the funnier it got. He shook his head, a wide smile on his face. Mark shrugged his shoulders, but Ron saw the humor radiating from his eyes.

Finally, they saw Channion get out of the car. When he nodded at them, both men felt enormous relief. Once she got out herself, Channion guided her toward Ron and Mark.

Shaking her hand, Mark said, "We want to thank you for doing this, Miss Stewart. Maybe it can shed some more light on your case, but we hope it can help you too."

She said, "Well, I don't know what else I can add. But I'll do my best to help you."
Mark nodded.

She looked at the spot where the cars had been. In her mind's eye, she could see it all. As she walked, she described what she saw and felt twenty-five days ago. The other agents walking with them took notes, stood in places as she requested them to, and she described it all to the best of her ability.

At her request, they got into Ron's car and drove the entire route she took that day. She insisted she drive, as it'd be easier to recall everything. When she sat behind the wheel, she had to take a moment to remember how to even drive since she'd been only a passenger for so long. Channion sat in front with her while his uncle and two agents squeezed together in the back seat.

She drove the car up the road so she could start as if she were coming from her old house. She turned around just before getting to the highway crew's road block. As she drove, she spoke out loud, recalling in detail everything she could think of. Her voice shook at times as the memories and the feelings she'd had that day came back to her. She remembered more details as she went through it all.

Raina even stopped the car and ran back through the trees like she had that day. The men followed her, re-living in peace what she'd lived through in fear and uncertainty.

When she was finished, at the point where she got into the cruiser herself and prepared to drive away, she felt emotionally drained. And free. The suffocating weight seemed to have been lifted. Ty had been right about her coming back here and facing it.

Once she was finished driving it all through from start to finish, Mark had her do it again. But this time, they timed it. He put an agent dressed as a highway crew member in each of the spots the would-be murderers had been in. He then had them make calls and send texts to each other on their cellphones to test signal strength and access.

He even had one of his agents drive to Raina's house, but not to her neighbor's so they wouldn't attract attention. They drove back to the scene to gauge how much time was needed to get there after receiving an urgent call to come quickly. They repeated this driving at different speeds.

It was almost three hours later when she leaned against Ron's car, wiped out.

She got into the back seat, leaving the door open so she wouldn't feel closed in. Resting, she patiently waited for Ron and Channion. They were talking with some of the agents a few yards in front of the car, out of her hearing. She was so mentally tired, she didn't even have the curiosity to wonder what they were talking about.

As she sat there looking around, she thought she saw movement in the trees. Her heart skipped a beat. She narrowed her eyes... Searching. Her ears were straining for any noise. Her senses hyper-aware, she waited. When she saw more movement and a figure, she bolted from the car, sprinting toward the tree line. It never crossed her mind to wait and signal the agents that were around her. She was running on instinct.

The men saw her bolt from the car, racing to the trees.

"Wait! What're you doing?" Mark called out, his face showing his confusion. He looked at Ron and Channion, asking, "Where's she going?"

Ron and Channion didn't waste time with an answer as they took off after her. Mark ran behind them as more agents dressed as highway men quickly joined the chase. Although none of the men knew *why* they were chasing after her, they just knew they *should*.

She never slowed down even when she slid on the loose pine needles. Her arms swung out to her sides to help keep her balance as she ran through the trees. Her lungs protested as they tried to get enough air, her ribs feeling like a vice around them. But she ran on.

She slid down a small hill almost on her rear. Using the momentum, she began to climb the next one. She heard running feet in front of her, branches breaking. When she topped the small hill, she stopped, panting.

From this vantage point, she could see over the fields to the tree line of her neighbor's house in the distance. She stood there, listening intently for more sounds to guide her in the direction she needed to go. Where did the runner disappear to? She turned around and around, searching.

Instead, she heard the sounds of men running behind her. She stood there, bent over a bit, her hands on her thighs as she still tried to pick out sounds in front of her. Nothing. She was breathing heavily.

Channion caught up with her first, breathing slightly heavily but in control. His gun was drawn, but the safety was still on. "Raina! What in the world has come over you?"

She waved her hand at him to be quiet so she could hear. She held it up as she kept searching for more movement. He copied her motion to the men coming up behind them. They all stood quiet, waiting. Channion alternated between watching her and looking around himself, trying to figure out what she was looking for.

She finally gave up. "I saw someone in the trees, watching us. They took off, so I thought I'd follow them. It's nice of you guys to join me."

She was breathing fast, trying to get it under control. Thankfully her ribs weren't screaming at her too much. But they *were* letting her know they were there and not happy with her. She watched as the agents climbed the hill and scattered out.

Mark looked around. "Where? Did you see where they went?"

Raina looked at him, wiping sweat from her brow. "You're not serious, are you? Do you really think I'd be standing here talking to you if I knew where they were? Besides, there was only one. Not too tall with a slender build. Probably a male."

Ron smiled, wrapped his arm around her. "*Raina...!*" He broke off, laughing.

Channion chuckled and shook his head, putting his gun in his holster. "Mark here still hasn't caught on to Raina's nature yet, Ron. He doesn't understand that she doesn't quit, or that she runs on gut and instinct. Trust her, Mark. If she knew where they went, none of us would be standing here chitchatting about it."

Mark smiled. "So, she's like a bloodhound or something? If that's so, why do we need you, Detective Scott?"

The men laughed.

Mark asked, "Are you sure it wasn't just a deer?"

She gave him a look of pure exasperation. Although she didn't think his question deserved an answer, she gave him one anyway. "If it *was* a deer, I'm pretty sure I would've known it was there before it ran."

Her tone was so factual, Mark didn't know how to respond. He looked over at the two smiling detectives. They knew she was referring to her innate ability to sense deer. Since she'd proved it while with them both, they had to believe her.

"Besides, I've got brains enough to be able to differentiate between a deer and a human. Unless this deer was wearing footwear and running on only two legs, it wasn't one." She sounded insulted. "I didn't even have to go to college and graduate to know that."

Channion laughed as he gently took hold of her elbow. "Stewart, let's just let the big guys take over here to see if they can find anything. Come along, Lieutenant Kramer," he teased. "I don't think we're needed here any longer." He was still laughing as he made his way with Raina back down the hill.

As the three of them made their way back toward the cars, she tried to control her breathing from the unexpected run. Perhaps it was time to begin using Channion's downstairs gym. She wondered if she'd even be allowed in the man-cave. She'd never gone down there simply because there was no reason to. She also figured it was his only real personal space.

Mark caught up with them before they got to the road. "Scott! Hold up!"

Ron smiled. "Raina, if you wouldn't mind taking a seat again? If you see something, give us a heads-up this time. Okay?"

"Since I'm a bloodhound now, I'll be sure to bark and point first," she retorted, forcing a smile. She didn't want to admit it, but her body was not happy with her at that moment. She imagined it was only going to get worse in the next few hours.

Mark smiled broadly as he watched her walk away. "She sure is something else!" He looked around for a moment before asking, "What about using her house for a stakeout point? Did you ask her yet?"

"No, I honestly forgot about it. Hang on." Channion headed over to the car.

He spoke with Raina for a while, and when he had her answer he came back. "She doesn't care either way. If we want to use it, it's fine with her. Anything that looks personal, be sure no one takes it. Remember the last time she was there, it'd been ransacked, and her horses had been killed. She hasn't had the time, or the inclination, to go back there.

"My guess is that it's going to be a mess. It should be all clear on our end to enter it. Knowing the shape it's in, you guys could go in as a cleaning service. Carry in all of your equipment with cleaning supplies, boxes, and the like, and leave them in there. Anyone passing by wouldn't think twice about seeing a cleaning company there. Or maybe as a remodeling company?"

Ron agreed. "It'd be a perfect cover to go in under even in daylight hours. If we get lucky, maybe somebody will even stop by and ask questions about her. If so, we need to be sure to get their information to run them."

Channion said, "We still need to check with her landlord. Ron, why don't you call him since you already have a good rapport with him?"

Ron walked away, pulling his phone from its case on his hip. He spoke on the phone for about fifteen minutes while his eyes roamed the area. When he was finished, he walked over and gave Mark the go-ahead. "He's okay with it. Not ecstatic, but willing. You make sure your men treat that house with care. Don't use it as a typical stakeout place, got it? It's still a person's home."

"Understood. I'll stress that to everybody who'll be staying there."

Channion added, "I also think the least you can do is pick up the rent tab while you're there. Add some on for the utilities too. Help out both Mr. Farley and Raina."

Mark thought about it. "I don't see why not. As long as we get a receipt, it's a typical expense. I'd be glad to help them out either way. How much?"

Channion gave him an amount and Mr. Farley's name. Channion told him to overnight the check to him so he could give it to the landlord to pay for the use of his house in advance to show good faith. Mark agreed to do it as soon as he could. The detectives gave him firm looks to reinforce their deal. Channion gave him the spare key from his key ring, telling Mark to not lose it before they headed to their car and Raina.

Having access now to her house, Mark watched as they drove away.

Chapter 39

"Miles? Is it really you?" The tall, older man stood up from behind the wide desk, smiling. Reaching out to shake his visitor's hand, the man couldn't believe what he was seeing. He gripped his agent's hand with both of his and held firmly before letting go. "If I wasn't seeing you with my own eyes, I'd never believe it was you standing here in my office!"

Ty, code name Miles, shook his hand, smiling through his new scruffy beard. "Yes, sir. It's me all right. I'm sure this is a surprise for you. It has been for everyone else I've run into so far!"

"Good surprises I can take—and gladly." He motioned with his hands. "Sit down! Sit down!" Taking a seat himself, he leaned forward. "Goodness... How long has it been?"

"About ten years since I walked through these doors last, Solomon. I was hoping you'd still be here at the Agency since I've never been told anything was different. I always respected you and the way you ran the place. Has much changed since I was in here last?"

Solomon, the only name his agents called him by since he took over the Agency decades before, smiled again. Conversely, he knew each of his agents by their real names but rarely used them. "Thank you, Miles. Since you're buttering me up, I guess I'll *have* to help you now."

Ty smiled back.

"And yes, I'm still here. I may retire one of these days, but I have to be sure I find a suitable successor first, of course. That's not an easy thing to do.

"We're still working globally, doing our best. The only thing that has really changed is how the criminals are running their businesses, and the creative ways they're breaking the law. Things here are adjusting as needed to keep pace, if we can't get ahead of the game. Our IT security department has grown over the years, and the cyber division has tripled.

"And we've been drawn further into the cutthroat world of human trafficking as well." He shook his head. "It's remarkable in this day and age that kidnapping, smuggling, and selling humans is as prevalent now as ever in the past. You hear talk about people wanting reparations for their ancestors, right? Do you think it'll still be happening to current generations a hundred years from now?

"Trafficking and slavery in its many forms have been around since the beginning of time. It's even in the bible! I daresay every single generation of every race worldwide for the past six thousand years is owed... Which means no one really is. Otherwise, everyone would just be paying each other off.

"Besides, the only people who truly deserve the compensation are the ones who actually *were* wronged. Generations later on don't really deserve it. It doesn't matter who it was: ancestral Christians, Blacks, Jews, or the Irish. Men, women, or children. *Everybody* has been affected over the generations. White people have been slaves and are even today highly trafficked, so it's not an exclusive market to any minority or gender. If a person has a pulse, they're fair game. It's wrong no matter who it was or is.

"And what does *money* have to do with anything? It's not freedom for the dead. It's mere money for the living. Those people have been dead for hundreds, even thousands, of years. Descendants don't even know anything about them. Doesn't that seem like a descendant is now making money off the very ancestors they say they're fighting for? That *other* people were making money off of? What? Is this a new form of residual income?

"Nothing happened to these modern people for them to get it. They'd just blow it on a big screen TV, a trip, or a car anyway. That's hardly showing respect to their ancestors!" Solomon sighed and gave a small smile. "I'm going off on a tangent and rambling, aren't I?"

He sat back in his chair. "But back to the original subject, it doesn't matter the age, race, or sex. If it's a person with a pulse, they're fair game."

Ty nodded. "I agree with you. And it does seem to be just as bad now as ever. It used to be basically a secret, but now it makes the news. Posters are on the backs of bathroom stalls and on the doors of travel rest stops. It's become mainstream."

Solomon now eyed his tall visitor again with his mind working overtime. As was his usual practice, he got right to the point. "Now, what brings you here?"

Ty didn't waste any time either. "Sir, I've been gathering some intel for someone I know, and I need to run what I've gathered so far by you. I was hoping I could ask a favor of you. I'd like to have you help me track down a few people. I'm confident it will also benefit the Agency."

"Are you working for someone else—or back for us? I don't remember talking with you about returning full-time." Solomon smiled. "You can, you know. We'd love to have you and your talents back with us. Just say the word."

Ty shook his head, showing a quick grin before getting serious. He knew Solomon would try to recruit him back in on a full-time basis. It's not like he hadn't been trying for years now. "No, I'm still only part-time with you. And I'm still on the down-low where I'm living.

"This is a personal case for a trusted person I know who's in law enforcement. A protected witness has given information about a weapons ring possibly headquartered in the Midwest, and I'm helping them out confidentially. Pro bono, you could say." Ty smiled. "Of course, if this helps out the Agency like I think it will, you *could* throw me a nice little bonus! I even have receipts when I can."

Solomon smiled back. "I'm open to it." In the quiet room, he leaned back, considered. "Give me the situation, and we'll go from there."

They spent the next several hours going over the in-depth information Ty brought with him. Leaning back in his chair, Ty finally asked him directly, "Sir, this is the same person of interest the Agency has been looking for now over a decade, isn't it? We weren't entirely sure he even existed—as in it being a singular person."

He knew his boss knew to whom he was referring. There was one particular case they had yet to completely solve.

Solomon finally asked quietly, "What makes you think that *this* is that man?"

It didn't escape Ty's notice Solomon didn't even ask to who he was referring.

Ty gestured to the information he'd compiled over the past two weeks. He'd been working nonstop to gather intel from old informants and other sources, launching from what he got from Channion's case. "Based on what I've just told you that's verified and current, and from our past information, there are an awful lot of similarities. I'd have to say *too* many to be coincidental.

"I know we got one man in court, getting a solid conviction just within these past few years. I also heard through the grapevine that he was killed in prison not too long after he was put in there. Of course, I didn't shed a tear over the news." He'd had his suspicions about it and still did.

He leaned forward, saying earnestly, "Solomon, unless my gut is wrong, I believe the man my contact is about to arrest and try in court is the *same* man who ordered the hit on our fellow agent, Shane Borden. Am I mistaken in thinking that this is the *same* man who killed Natasha's husband?"

Solomon drummed his fingers on his desk for a moment. Leaning forward, he simply asked, "What do you need?"

LATER, AFTER MILES LEFT with a sizeable amount of cash and the promise of assistance from the Agency he'd been working undercover with for about two decades, Solomon sat in his plush chair. He ran the past few hours through his mind, analyzing what Miles had brought him.

He picked up his phone. Dialing a number from memory, one that was never written down, he leaned back and listened to the rings.

"Hello?"

"Good evening. I've just had a visit from an old friend. A remarkably surprising visit. Unless I miss my guess, I think you need to come in so I can get you caught up. This is going to be worth your while." He paused before adding, "It concerns you."

There was a long pause on the other end of the line. "How soon do you need me there?"

"The sooner the better. It's not an actual emergency, so don't worry about that."

After a pause, the voice replied, "I'll be in by the next couple of days since I'm pretty far out right now. Do I need to bring anything special?"

"We'll probably have what you'll need here. You may want to bring a few of your own. Come on in, and we'll go from there. Travel safely, my friend."

Solomon hung up the phone, letting his hand rest on it for a moment before removing it. Releasing a long sigh, he drummed his fingers on his desk. He watched the clock's minute hand click into place, slightly vibrating before steadying. He heard the quiet *tick, tick, tick* of it in the silence.

Who would've thought it'd be Miles to bring him down? Of all his agents, it'd have to be him. A highly-talented agent, one who'd tried to leave the Agency many years ago but was talked into staying on a part-time basis, had found him. Or rather, a close contact of his apparently found him. He wondered who the witness was his contact was protecting.

He looked through the papers and photos his agent had left with him. He couldn't help but still be impressed at noticing Miles kept all information on his witness completely out of it. Description, location, name... Nothing. Not even if it was a male or female or a guess as to an age. There was also no identifying information on this trusted person he was doing this for. Solomon had noticed that Miles had only said his "contact."

As was his habit, Miles never divulged information that could compromise one's safety so getting the name directly from him just wasn't going to happen, no matter he was Miles' boss. If the information wasn't absolutely, critically needed, he didn't share it.

He'd always admired Miles' unshakeable integrity, he thought with a smile.

It really was a small world after all.

Chapter 40

CHANNION TOOK RAINA TO the station for the day. Noticing Ron wasn't in yet, Raina sat in his chair while she waited. She talked for a while with Detective Diggs and a new patrolman riding along with him for training experience. As he listened, the thought came to Channion most of Raina's social life now was with law enforcement personnel. He wondered how she felt about that turn of events.

It was almost three hours later when Ron made his way to his desk. Raina looked at her watch, then at him. Leaning back in the chair, she said sternly, "What is your reason for being so tardy? And do you have a note?"

"Hey there, sunshine," Ron replied instead. With a smile, he ruffled Raina's hair. "Get out of my chair, girl."

Raina smiled as she got up to sit in the empty chair beside the two desks. "Well? Do you have a note for being tardy?"

"I texted Channion I was coming in later. I had some time on the books I needed to use so I went shopping for my lady." He looked over at his nephew, who obviously hadn't told her.

She asked, "Are you in the doghouse with Janet?" She sounded almost shocked at the concept since they were a perfect couple if she'd ever seen one. "Or are you just being sweet?"

Ron laughed. "No, I'm not in the doghouse. But I sure would be if I forgot her birthday was tomorrow! I figured I'd better go now while I had the time in case something came up."

Channion sighed. "Well, you're better than me because I *did* forget."

Raina leaned forward. "Can we go shopping for her, Channion? I'd like to get her something to say thanks for being there for me, besides it being her birthday."

Ron smiled. "She'd appreciate that. Son, go ahead if you're not busy, and take her shopping. It should be okay. You have time to use too. Technically, you're still on the clock with her. I'll call you if you're needed."

"Sure, there's not much going on here anyway. What we came in for I've about got done. And I bet Raina's a fast shopper. She doesn't strike me as the annoying, browsing type. This shouldn't take too long." He locked his desk drawers and stood up. "Let's go, Stewart."

He hid his grin to mess with her as he began walking toward the elevators, texting their back-up security.

Raina grinned as she rolled her eyes. "Doesn't he make it sound like *so* much fun? I don't know if I can stand the excitement. I might just drag this out."

Ron laughed as he shooed her away. He watched the two of them wait for the elevator door to open, then step in. She must've said something contrary to Channion because he was smiling when he turned around to hit the button to the garage. Ron smiled as he leaned back in his chair, still watching as the doors closed.

As it happened, Raina not only found her gift contribution but also Channion's—and both in record time. After he paid for his gift, she said, "We need to wrap these things too. And get a card."

Wandering around looking for a card store, Raina spotted a deep plum sleeveless blouse she thought would look great on his aunt. She stopped in, found one in what they hoped would be her size and purchased it. "I'm up, two-to-one," Raina teased him. "You're buying the rest."

The two of them finally found a Hallmark store, spending twice as long in there reading all the cards than it took to buy the gifts. They finally decided on the cards they wanted, got wrapping supplies and were heading back to the truck when Channion's phone rang. "It's Ron. Here, hold these."

Raina took the bags from his hand.

"Hello! Are we taking too long?" Channion asked, smiling.

His uncle's voice was full of disbelief on the other end. "You won't believe who just came here. How soon can you be back?"

"We're about twenty minutes out."

"Okay, just get here when you can. It's not an emergency, but you need to be here for this!" Ron hung up his phone.

Looking at Raina, Channion said, "Ron needs me back. Let's go."

They were almost to the main entrance when a tall man passed by Raina. She was walking quickly to keep up with Channion's long stride when she came to a sudden stop. "Wait!" she called out.

What was it about him? There was something...

"Raina! We need to get back..." He saw her face, a perplexed look on it. "Raina?"

She didn't answer, grasping for a memory.

He prodded her shoulder. "We need to go! What is it?"

He wasn't prepared for what she did next. She spun around on her heels, practically running back the way they'd just come, the bags she was carrying banging against her side. He stood there for a second, slightly irritated with her because he was needed back at the station.

"Sir!" He heard Raina calling out to a tall man walking away from them. "Mister, wait up!"

Channion's instincts were on alert now. What was she doing?

"Sir!" Raina caught up with the man, tapped him on his shoulder to stop him. "I'm sorry to bother you, but I smelled you as you walked by me back there."

She smiled at Channion. Reaching over, she grabbed his hand and squeezed it in a silent signal to be patient with her as she saw the irritation in his eyes. "Honey, I know we're in a hurry, but this man smells so good I had to stop and ask him what he was wearing!" Turning to the man, she smiled at him. "Do you mind if I ask what it is?"

The man looked at her, asking in a confused voice, "You mean my cologne?"

"Yes. I think my boyfriend here would like it. I know I do!" She threw a charming smile at the older man. Looking intently at Channion, squeezing his hand again, she tried to relay information to him. "Honey, do you like this scent?"

Channion was catching on—at least that she wanted him to notice this man's cologne and remember it. He played along. "Sweetheart, I'm not much into wearing cologne, but now that you mention it..." He looked at the man. "I have to admit, you do smell nice!"

The older man smiled. "It's *Polo for Men*. My wife prefers it or *Old Spice*. You may want to try that one too."

Raina smiled. "And you can get either of those pretty much anywhere, right?"

"You bet. Almost any store carries one or the other, but usually both. I get mine right here in the mall. There's a store down this way that sells them both at the best prices I've found locally. Go down this way here, then go left at the carousel. It's about three or four stores down on the right."

"Thank you so much." She waited until the man walked away before saying to Channion, "I know we're in a hurry, but this won't take long. Trust me, Channion."

She walked quickly to the department store the man had indicated to them.

Short of making a scene, he had no choice but to follow her. He took some of the bags from her. "Raina, I need to get back..."

"I'm on to something right now. Give me a moment, please? Is it an actual emergency?" she asked, quickly scanning the men's fragrances through the glass doors.

"He said no, but he needed me there as quickly as possible." He took out his phone, texting their security detail so they knew what was going on.

"Okay, so I have a minute here." She bent down as she read labels. "There it is!"

"Raina, why—"

She interrupted him as she tested the door. "Dang it! It's locked. Stay here." She turned, taking off to find a sales associate. Within one minute, she was practically dragging a young girl back with her, saying, "We're in an awful hurry here! Can you please get this one right here for us? We're already late for an anniversary party, and this was the gift we know he wanted the most. It took us longer to find it than we expected!"

The young girl took the coiled key chain off her wrist, quickly opening the sliding glass door. "This one?"

Raina smiled. "Yes, please. Can you ring us up here so we can avoid that line up there? We'd really appreciate it."

"Sure. Follow me." The young girl hurried to the empty register counter, punched in her ID number. Ringing up the sale, she swiped Raina's card, had her sign the slip. Putting the cologne into a small bag and handing her the receipt, she smiled. "I hope he likes it!"

"Oh, he'll love it. Thank you so much!"

Turning to Channion, she said, "Well, let's go."

As they headed toward the truck at a pace just short of running, Channion looked at her. Seeing her face, he knew there was something going on here. He unlocked the truck doors, helping her in before tossing the bags into the back seat before heading around the truck to the driver's side. She hurriedly put on her seatbelt before she opened the box that held the bottle of cologne.

He was preparing to pull out of their parking spot when she said, "Hang on a sec. Smell this, Chan. Come on, smell it!"

He put the truck back into *park* as he sighed. He obediently leaned over to smell it.

"Do you like it?"

"It's not bad."

"Guess who else likes it?"

At his raised eyebrow, she smiled. "Okay, I know. Hurry up." He nodded. "A certain man who tried to kill me about a month ago by slamming me up against my own truck and punching me likes it too."

"*What?*"

"I remember this smell as he was cleaning my clock. It was filling up my nose, so it wasn't just a faint whiff. And when we passed that man in there, the smell was the same, and my mind grabbed onto that memory.

"Remember when Steve told me all of my senses were probably recording information? My olfactory ones apparently were. If we can find the man who beat me up, one way to verify it's him is to see if he likes to wear *Polo for Men!*"

Her voice was overflowing with excitement as her speech grew faster. "I'll donate this bottle so anyone on the case can get a whiff of it themselves. Or you can reimburse me, whatever. And whoever may smell it on a suspect can be aware..." Her voice trailed off when she looked up at him again. "What?"

He looked at her, his eyebrows raised. "And that's proof? Do you know how many men wear that scent?"

"*Geez Louise,* Detective Scott! *Think* about it! Men are like women when it comes to perfume or cologne. Those who actually wear it, once they find a scent that appeals to them—and it's not many that really do—they have a strong tendency to stick with it. I'm willing to bet the man who beat me up wears this cologne more often than not. It's not too overpowering, so he'd be apt to wear it practically daily and not just on special occasions."

Channion still didn't look convinced, but he seemed to be warming up to the idea. She slapped his leg, clearly irked with him. "*C'mon*, Scott! He wore it the day he was simply driving a load of illegal weapons down a country road. Who was he trying to impress that day... A *war lord?*"

With a wide grin, he gave in. She did have a point after all. "It's a long shot, you know. But leave it to you to think of this!"

Because they were in a hurry, he turned on the emergency light bar and siren to make a little better time through the traffic. As they drove, he slid a quick glance at her, asking suspiciously, "Boyfriend?"

"We were undercover, Detective Scott. You did good, by the way." She shot a grin his way. "Don't worry. Getting into a relationship with *any* man right now is the last thing I need. Seriously, I'd rather be shot." When she saw his facial expression, she realized what she'd said and quickly added, "Figuratively speaking."

He laughed. "Then undercover boyfriend it is." As he turned onto the street leading back to the station, he added, "You know what? I think you're picking up on our dark cop humor."

"It'd make sense. You guys are the only friends I've got now, so it was bound to rub off on me sooner or later."

He glanced at her again, giving her a look.

She sighed. "What *now?*"

"You certainly can lie convincingly at the drop of a hat. Those lies back there just rolled right off your tongue as naturally as could be. I'm going to have to remember that about you."

"Well, if it helps to know, I rarely ever lie. And remember, as an honorary Boy Scout, I'd never lie to an officer of the law. Honest."

He smiled as she crossed her heart and held up the Scout sign.

Chapter 41

WHEN THE ELEVATOR DOORS opened, Luke was there waiting for them. Before they were more than a few steps out of the elevator, he said, "Miss Stewart, I need you to come with me." Looking at Channion, he added, "Ron's in room four. He said for you to meet him there. Check in first to get the bearings."

Channion seemed to know exactly what Luke said, but Raina was clueless. Channion handed her the bags he was carrying and left.

"What—" Raina began.

Luke interrupted her, "I see you went shopping." He steered her in the opposite direction of the desks as he spoke. "These are for Janet's birthday tomorrow, I bet? Well, they need wrapped. I see you guys have that covered, so let's find you a place to do that."

"Luke, what—"

"Here's a nice, empty office. Let me go find you some tape. Stay here." With that, he shut the door before she could ask anything more.

About ten minutes later, Steve Diggs opened the door. "Hey, Miss Raina! Luke got caught up in something and asked me to bring you some things." He placed a small plastic container that held some clear tape, scissors, a ruler, markers, pens, and pencils on the desk she was standing beside.

Looking down at it, she could tell it was either a last-minute, thrown-together thing, or someone was quite disorganized when it came to office supplies.

"Mind if I ask—"

He cut her off with a smile, saying, "Sure do." He put a candy bar and a cold can of Pepsi on the corner of the desk. "I got these from the vending machines because I thought you'd like them. Stay in here. If you need anything, call one of us first." He handed her a piece of paper with a few numbers on it. "But wait right in here until one of us comes to get you. *Don't* come out. Got it?"

He paused. "I guess I should ask... Do you need to use the bathroom before I leave?"

She shook her head.

He said, "If you need to, remember to call one of us first, and then you wait for one of us to escort you. Got it? It's important, Raina," he repeated firmly.

Before she could say another word, he shut the door behind him.

CHANNION ENTERED THE INTERROGATION room's viewing area first to get his bearings. He saw Ron sitting in a chair, talking with a kid who looked about sixteen years old. Beside the teenage boy was an attractive woman, who looked to be in her late-thirties or early-forties at the most. Both looked more than a bit nervous.

The door opened beside him. Luke walked in, shutting it behind him. "Figure it out yet?" he asked.

Channion shook his head. "No. I'm assuming they have something to do with Raina's case or else Ron and I wouldn't be in on it. Who are they? I haven't heard names yet. They're just making small talk from what I can tell."

"Ron gets a call from downstairs, and the desk sergeant says there were a couple of people who will speak *only* to either Ron or you. They refused to say about what.

"When Ron gets downstairs, the sergeant's holding a bag. He hands it to Ron, who peeks inside, of course, and sees a gun. The teenager there says his name is Zachary Coleman."

"*Coleman?* As in Raina's-neighbor-that-we're-staking-out Coleman?" Channion asked, completely taken aback.

"The one and the same. This is the son, the only child. The woman is his mom, and the wife of said neighbor, Lori Coleman. It's all being verified as we speak. Anyway, Zach and Lori show up here with a gun that Zach says is the same one used to shoot Raina's horses. He knew their names because he used to feed them when she was away for work."

At Channion's incredulous look, Luke nodded. "It's been tagged, and it's already down with the techs in Fingerprints and Ballistics for comparisons. It's the right size and model from what they determined from the bullets they removed from her horses. Ron hasn't asked these two about that whole thing yet because he's waiting on you.

"We have Lori's ID and are running everything we can right now. Ron told them to take fingerprints from it too. If we get a hit on anything we think you'll need or want while they're here, we'll bring it in."

"What are they doing here?"

"I listened in here for a bit, and it seems they're looking for protection from Mr. Coleman. They're offering evidence of his activities in exchange for immunity and protection. And I guess, maybe escape. Unless, of course, this is just a ruse to get information from us on Raina and Bryce."

Nodding, Channion headed out the door to join his uncle in the interrogation room. Before leaving, he asked, "Raina?"

"Whisked away to a back hallway office so she'll not see or know they're here, and vice versa in case this *is* just a ruse. Our first thought was they're grasping for straws trying to locate her. They don't seem to know we have her. Steve took her supplies to wrap Janet's presents." Luke smiled. "She isn't stupid. She knows something is happening, but she won't learn a detail from me."

Channion flashed a smile. "Don't be too sure of yourself, Luke."

As Luke grinned back, Channion went to join his uncle.

Chapter 42

THEY WERE NATURALLY SUSPICIOUS. When they finally ended the interrogation, Ron had a patrolman escort Lori and Zach downstairs. They had another unmarked car follow them to see what happened after they left.

He and Channion went to the conference room, hammering out details, options, and plans. They needed to get with Mark and fill him in. Calling him, Ron gave him the basics of the interview. They set up a meeting for the following day.

Channion rolled his pen around his fingers, staring out the window. When his uncle hung up the phone, he asked, "Do you feel we need to evacuate Raina? Or stick with it as we are now? Neither Lori nor Zach gave any indication they knew where she is. Zach just said that he saw her with us last week from the trees.

"How Mark's men missed seeing his horse tied up is beyond me! And Zach climbing that tree and listening to us is damn unnerving. But maybe, if they're being truthful, it's a blessing since he heard our names and that's why they came in.

"Can we trust them? Or are they spying for Coleman, using a sob story of abuse to get through to us? Was this all done to flush her out? Not once did they ask how she was even though they knew she'd been in the hospital. And they never once asked about a cop being shot.

"If they *are* looking for her, they're leading up to it. All they really said was to pass along their apologies to her. Maybe since Zach saw her in person, they figure she's okay. It's difficult to know what to believe at this point."

Ron leaned back and blew out a breath. "We don't want to gamble with Raina's safety. She's not giving lessons, so that's one less place they can look for her. They apparently don't know where she is now. Lorenzo still doesn't know she's with you, right? And the people at the bar, her band, don't know either?"

Channion shook his head. "We just said I'm a friend and her ride for now."

Ron rubbed his chin, thinking about the best thing to do. "I think we'd better get her to stop singing at the bar. We've been lucky, very lucky with that, so far. They *have* to know she sings there. How could they not?

"If they asked about her, anyone there could simply say she was with a guy named Channion. But they may also know you're a cop because of the truck. It's an unmarked truck, but it still has the lights in it. They could possibly track you. Is it safe there?"

Channion considered. "It was our family reunion the weekend she worked there, so the place was packed. Plus, we had Ty helping out. On the other hand, maybe they want to avoid taking her out in such a public place since everyone has cellphones and cameras these days. If I were them, I'd look for a more private, secluded opportunity, but we can't rule out anything.

"I think we can keep her here just a little bit longer but warn her again it may be a fast exit. She's got a show on the road next week, so that'll get her out of here for a while. I guess I'm going with her?"

Ron thought it over. "Yeah, most likely. If you're both comfortable with that, go ahead. Normally, I'd say take along a female officer, but by now she's practically family. I feel we can overlook that with her. She hasn't given us any reason to not trust her, and she hardly seems the type to cry sexual harassment over nothing.

"Just watch yourself. Don't get into any compromising situations in case something ever got out. You two have been living together for a month or so now, so it'll just continue. It's geography at this point. But I think we'll have your back-up following as usual in case something gets sprung. They'll keep their distance but will be close enough if you need them, hopefully. That good with you?"

Channion nodded. "The more eyes the better."

Ron ran his hand behind his neck, rubbing it for a moment as he thought. "Yeah, let's keep it the same for right now. No movement, no changes, no tracks. Stay home as much as you can. You still have the cameras on at the house, right?"

"Of course. If anyone comes near, they'll trigger the cameras and be recorded. I tested them again yesterday, and all's working fine. Of course, sometimes a bird sets them off so that lets me know they're working too. I also did another bug check and got nothing.

"That infrared equipment Mark loaned us to use to make sure we're not being watched from somewhere outside comes up as normal. My cameras also haven't picked up any cars just sitting there, watching my place. They apparently still don't know she's at my house.

Only that she's with us, if that. As far as I'm aware, few people know where she's actually staying. We've kept a tight circle around her so no one does.

"And I changed my passwords again yesterday. I'm covering every base I can think of."

Ron looked at his nephew, asking directly, "Do you believe their story about his shooting her horses, and why? Overhearing the men there planning to torture them in rage because they knew she was back? Lori having Zach sneak out in the middle of the night to humanely kill them to save them that horrific fate? And as a warning to her to leave?"

Channion let out a deep sigh. "I'd like to, as much as it disgusts me. How they tried to come up with so many ways to *not* do it, but they didn't realize the simple solution of using a neighbor's or friend's phone to call us to warn us? They said they had less than a day's notice, and that's all they could think of to do..." He shook his head. "They seemed truly sincere. Both even cried, and it looked genuine. If not, they're natural and very talented actors.

"I just don't see how a young kid like him could do it though. But in the big picture, it makes perfect sense. We were all wondering why rage in the house, and humanity with the horses? *This* would fully answer that. It's that missing piece we were searching for. Like Ty said, we find it, and it'd make perfect sense.

"Let's say no silencer. Out in the country, anyone who may have heard two shots wouldn't think much, if anything, of it. Someone could've been shooting at coyotes, or it sounded like a car backfiring. Or even fireworks. Even in town, two shots are nothing to get in a stir about."

Ron agreed. After a while, he said, "Now, about this meeting with the ATF tomorrow... I don't feel good having Raina sit there all day. How about we drop her off with Bryce so they can keep each other company for a while?"

Channion grinned. "I think we'd be torturing poor Chris. From what you told me, he was drooling all over her!"

Ron chuckled. "Yes, he nearly did! Call them to make sure it's okay. He's still in therapy, and we don't want to interfere with that. But if she's there, we know she's safe. And she'll have company besides us for a change. It'll be good for Bryce too."

"Will it taint the case having them together?"

Ron answered, "As long as they don't discuss the case, I think it's fine. What difference would it make at this point with all the video and audio evidence we have? With Chris there, he'd be a neutral person to make sure they don't discuss much."

"True. I'll call and ask."

Ron waited while his nephew made the call. When he hung up, Ron asked, "Good?" At Channion's nod, he looked at his watch. "I think we'd better go get Raina. She's bound to be a mess by now, wondering what's going on."

Channion said, "Well, she'd better have those presents wrapped up nicely by now. She's had enough time."

They were smiling as they went to get her.

WHEN THEY ENTERED THE office where Luke and Steve had stashed her away, they saw the perfectly-wrapped presents on the desk, but Raina was nowhere in sight. They also saw the bottle of cologne.

Seeing it, Channion picked it up. He explained the story behind it to his uncle. "I forgot all about it since I joined you the second we got off the elevator. Here, smell it." He held it out. "You'd better memorize this smell because Raina sure knows it."

After smelling it, Ron was duly impressed. "That woman doesn't miss anything, does she? It's incredible all the details she got while fighting for her life! Speaking of which, where's our girl?"

Another officer saw them as they walked out. "Hey. She's in the breakroom with Steve and his trainee. He took pity on her and offered her lunch from the vending machines." He smiled at them as he kept on walking.

Channion looked at Ron as they walked down the hallway. "We give her fine Italian, and Steve offers vending machines. She'd better prefer ours. If not, I'm kicking her out."

Chapter 43

SHE WAS A WITNESS and a victim, not a fellow detective. Raina knew that whatever had happened the day before at the station she couldn't be told about. And even though it was killing her to not know, she knew better than to ask.

Over breakfast when Channion said they needed to go out of town that day, she again didn't ask questions. She knew there were boundaries, and she had to respect them. They were to have a birthday dinner for Janet that evening at a nice restaurant, so she figured they could work faster during the day without her along.

She was excited, though, when he offered to drop her off to spend some time with Bryce. Her bodyguards walked her into Bryce's room that morning, stayed for only a few minutes, then left almost abruptly.

Sitting down beside Bryce, she sighed. "I feel like I've just been dropped off at daycare!"

Relaxed in his chair, Chris chuckled. "Did they remember to give you lunch money before they left?"

"No." After a pause, she asked, "Do I need any?"

Laughing, Chris shook his head. "Even if you did, I'd treat you. We could order in pizza or subs later, if you'd like. We haven't had any of that here yet. What do you think, Bryce?"

"Sure! We've been eating lots of healthy stuff, so it could be our cheat day."

With a smile, she pulled out her phone, flipped to a screen and began typing. A minute later, her phone signaled a new text message. When she read it, she burst out laughing.

She handed over her phone so Bryce and Chris could read Channion's reply:

Although I don't think so, Ron thinks you're gaining too much weight. Don't kill the messenger. You might want to skip lunch today. Save room for dinner and birthday cake!

Bryce was laughing as he handed the phone back to her, saying, "Channion has always been a classy guy."

His eyes sparkling, Chris added, "It's pretty sweet, too, isn't it?"

Raina grinned good-naturedly at the two men watching her, speculation in their eyes. "Not as sweet as I'm sure Janet's birthday cake will be tonight! And don't be going to that place I can see you're going, boys. He has to be nice so I don't practice any of my new self-defense moves on him when he picks me up later." Looking at Chris, she said, "Speaking of which, I need to practice them. You busy?"

THE TWO DETECTIVES SPENT the bulk of the day with Mark and a few fellow agents. They took a copy of the interrogation with them. None of the agents could believe this dramatic turn of events happened, and like the detectives, were naturally suspicious of Lori and Zach Coleman showing up as they did.

Mark asked, "It seems too good to be true, doesn't it? And how did we all miss there being a horse? I need to look into that to see how we missed something so obvious!" He paused before almost sputtering, "*A horse!* How did my men miss running across a *horse?*"

Taking some professional sympathy on him, Channion offered with a straight face, "Maybe it was a pony."

Mark rolled his eyes, but Channion and Ron both saw the smile fighting to come out. The other agents laughed.

Ron said, "Lori gave us one more big piece of information we didn't have solid evidence on before. We won't find much of anything except ordinary information under Ford Coleman. She said when he does business, he uses a different name. He keeps his two lives separated, remember? I'm wondering if the guy doesn't have split personalities or something. He's run two lives quite smoothly for decades. Anyway, when he does his weapons business, he goes by 'Colt Buchanan.' You guys have that name?"

One of the agents leaned forward. "We do have that name in our files but couldn't find much on him. You're saying that Coleman and Buchanan are the *same* guy?"

Channion explained, "As you heard in the video, Lori said that she and Zach go by what she terms the family name, Coleman. When they have family get-togethers and holidays, it's all Coleman. The mailbox is Coleman. Raina only knows them as the Colemans. No mention of Buchanan at all. So, if some person on property asks where Colt Buchanan is, she immediately knows it's a business associate.

"In terms of Zach, he's a good kid as far as we can tell. We're still checking into that—his school records, clubs, and anything else we can dig up. He and Lori seem tight and loyal to the other, but neither seem loyal at all to Ford or Colt. Which name should we call him by?"

Mark said, "Well, I guess we're after the weapons persona of this guy, so we can call him Colt Buchanan. Leave the Coleman name out of it to maybe protect Lori and Zach?" He looked around the room as everyone nodded in agreement.

Another agent asked, "What are the odds of this happening? But if they *are* telling the truth, it's a prime opportunity for us—and for them. If they *are* telling the truth, how could we just leave them there in the midst of all that?"

Channion said, "That's what we've discussed at length. And *if* they're telling the truth and are willing to help us nail Buchanan, we can't let them slip away. It seems we're all in agreement Buchanan *is* who we want the most?" Everyone nodded. "You guys run your own background on them. You may uncover something we can't, and we need as much information as we can get here.

"And I don't like the feeling I have that we're operating more in the dark here than we may realize. It's crucial we get everything we can so we can protect Raina to our utmost. We've been discussing getting her out of here as we feel we've been lucky so far. We don't want to run out of that luck."

All the men nodded, trying to see the situation from all angles.

Mark asked, "So you have it set up that Lori will visit your Italian restaurant. She'll be given cards with questions we all need answers to like she's filling out a comment card. She then hands it to the server, who in turn gets it to you?"

Ron nodded. "Yes. We obviously didn't tell her who owns it. We just said that it was a good Italian place and quiet. It seemed logical and safe. She appears to be scared out of her mind, as does her son.

"If she is indeed being followed or watched, filling out a comment card at a restaurant would hardly raise any suspicion at all. She signs and dates it like anyone else would do, so we then have it as evidence on top of everything else."

Mark smiled. "I have to give it to you guys. Filling out fake comment cards at a restaurant is brilliant. That's one I've never thought of doing."

Reaching into the briefcase he carried with him, Ron removed some papers. Sliding them over to Mark, he explained, "These are some of the questions we need answered right away, mostly regarding their knowledge about Miss Stewart. She's our number one priority at this moment and will remain so. Bryce has better protection and resources than she does. Without her, and Bryce, none of this would be happening."

Channion smiled. "Plus, we like her."

Mark chuckled. "She certainly does make an impression, doesn't she? It's still hard to believe the other day when she saw the boy in the trees while not a single agent did! And this Zach stated she almost caught him so he ran up a tree. He was right above us while we were talking." He practically shivered. "That scares me more than a little bit. Thank God he wasn't there to pick us off!"

Everyone nodded in complete agreement.

He read through the questions, passing them along to the other agents as he finished a page. The two detectives patiently waited until they were all done reading. "These are good and concise. Anybody watching wouldn't think much about her writing down answers since not all comment cards are multiple choices. When's she coming in next?"

Ron answered, "Tomorrow. That's why we needed this meeting today. Is there anything you can add? Or want us to do? This is a major case, and we want it to be solid."

One of the agents inquired, "She mentioned she'd taken pictures of the weapons in the underground warehouse before. It'd be beneficial to get those. We can make copies of them, or keep the originals. Same with the selfies she said she took when her husband beat her for trying to leave. Is she willing to bring those in?"

Ron nodded. "Yes. That's one thing we said we wanted first off as proof she's serious about this. We're hoping she brings them in tomorrow. She said they were hidden but didn't say where."

Another agent leaned forward. "Okay, let's say she's being true and honest about this. And Zach. What are the odds of us getting them to place our listening devices inside the property? Would they do it? Could they?"

Channion pondered the questions before replying, "I think they could. My concern is that if her husband is as serious as we think he is, would he even consider someone bugging his operation? Would he have bug checks? If so, what would happen if he found them?"

"We need to ask her if they know anything about the security down there. As long as this guy's been in business, I don't see him skipping regular bug checks unless his place is made out of steel or something. They said everything is underground, but that doesn't mean above-ground isn't being watched."

Ron nodded. "Yeah. And she and Zach may not know since they aren't allowed there, but perhaps they could find out somehow."

Channion had an idea pop into his mind. "You know what? Ron and I have the information on the tutor she takes Zach to. She was willing to cover for them when they came to us yesterday. We could meet there at the tutor's because that wouldn't arouse suspicion. That's a normal place for them to go, so if they're being followed, there's no change of schedule. We could talk in person there and record it all. We'd need to get in ourselves, probably earlier than their appointment."

Mark nodded. "That's a great idea. It'd be easier and faster to question her, or them, in person."

Channion looked over at Mark. "How come *we're* the ones coming up with all of the cool ideas and stuff? When are you guys going to start carrying your weight? Ever?"

The others laughed.

Another agent spoke up, saying, "I hate to ask this, but I feel it needs addressed. Since they admitted to killing Miss Stewart's horses, will they be charged for that?"

Ron answered, "You know, that's something we've also been debating. The pros and cons are hard to weigh. If we did, it wouldn't be done until *after* we had Colt. Otherwise, that blows their safety cover and our case. If we did, would it give Raina some closure? Would it help her or make things worse?

"We can't make up our minds on it yet. We both agree she and her horses deserve for them to be charged. While we understand they tried to think of something else, they still didn't have to *kill* them.

"He's also a minor, and he's the one who admitted doing it. Lori would be an accessory. Unless they're lying to save her, hoping we'd be lenient on a minor. How can we weigh the benefits of charging them over the deaths of her horses to this weapons case? It's a difficult issue to come to an agreement on. Any suggestions?"

The agent sighed. "I just feel like... I'm an animal lover *and* a law enforcement officer. I feel her horses deserve some sort of justice. We know who killed them. They even gave evidence of it, so what more do we need there? I don't know Miss Stewart like you do, but in her shoes? Well, I'd want to know *why* they were killed. Otherwise, it could haunt her like they were merely collateral damage. I guess, technically, that's exactly what they are...were."

Another agent asked, "Could we charge them with animal cruelty? Just leave out *whose* animals were killed?"

Channion replied, "Any report requires that basic information though. And if Raina ever heard about that charge and their names, she'd put it together instantly."

Ron agreed.

Mark shook his head. "I also don't like them getting away with killing her horses. On the other hand, is it a risk that's worth it? And is it worth giving them a charge on their records for something they say they did out of compassion and not violence? His record could be sealed as a minor. So he'd be charged, she and her horses could have justice, but his life isn't ruined. But again, we'd still need to wait."

Channion suggested, "Another option is for me, or us, to tell Raina to let *her* decide. They were *her* horses. She loved them like her own kids. No one has as much say in this matter than her. And that's if we tell her about this. Do we want to?"

The men sighed. None of them was sure of the right answer and course to take.

Chapter 44

Sitting in the bar's shadowy back corner, Ty watched as a short man walked in and headed toward the bar. On a small portable device held in his hand, Ty could see outside the bar thanks to the small cameras he'd discreetly placed there earlier. He didn't see anyone or anything suspicious. Flipping screens, he checked the back exit of the bar. All seemed clear.

After a few minutes, the man at the bar glanced in the mirror and saw Ty's slight signal. Grabbing his beer, he walked over to Ty's table and sat down like they were friends and had just noticed each other.

Quietly, Ty said, "It looks clear. You?"

"Same, boss. I checked my back trail all the way to here and didn't see nobody." He slid his beer out of the way.

"Good. What do you have for me? Anything useful?"

This CI, a favorite and highly-valued confidential informant of his, was the last one he was planning on talking with before heading back to the Agency to check in. He'd been gathering quite a bit more information over the past few days. He felt he had enough solid information to give his relatives, and the Agency, to get the guy they were all looking for.

But he was still lacking some specific information, including the actual name of the man. He was a ghost even in the underworld. Either that, or everyone was too scared to say it out loud. Ty had a list of aliases, but he needed more. From what he was gathering, this man was one to be feared for good reasons... as he already knew.

But Ty knew this informant was a gem among gems. If Harley couldn't find what Ty was looking for, it was time to give up and go home.

Ty's only worry talking with Harley was that he dropped his Gs when speaking. Harley had a habit of dropping his Gs so much that Ty actually started doing it once. To him, that was dangerous because that was a direct link to Harley, who was known for it. Ty had found if he repeated those words in his own mind that Harley was dropping Gs on as Harley spoke them, he didn't do it himself later on.

His informant took a sip of his cold beer. "I think I got quite a bit, Miles." Harley knew this man he'd met over many years to share information with only as Miles, unaware it was actually a code name. Not that Harley would've cared much. As long as the pay was good, and he didn't get beat up, he didn't care.

"The information you've been wantin' is makin' the rounds out there! There's a strong rumor of a weapons delivery bein' botched up. But it's still business as usual, and all seems to be runnin' fine. The man in charge has been hard to deal with since then, if what I'm hearin' is true. It seems the buyers wanted their product, and he had almost zip to give 'em. And you know buyers of things like this ain't exactly purrin' kittens.

"It seems the man in charge had to scramble to replace the lost order *and* give a discount. But as powerful as he is, I doubt he felt threatened by the buyers. He was just makin' 'em happy to have repeat customers is all.

"And I also heard a story of a man involved in this delivery gone bad bein' hit and killed that seems solid. The name I got is 'Allen Kindle.' He'd been workin' for this dealer for about eleven years, and I doubt Kindle was his real name. I haven't found out yet what it coulda been since everyone knew him as this as far back as I can tell.

"Anyway, he was a delivery driver of part of that order that got botched up and died while on his way. From what I been told, he got hit by a car or somethin'. I've no clue at all how a man drivin' down a road gets hit by a car, but there ya have it. Details are a little sketchy on that part of the story, but everyone's sayin' the guy's dead."

Ty nodded, his brain already repeating all the words with the dropped Gs, and took a sip of his bottled beer. Ty would *only* order a bottle of beer, never a draft mug or a mixed drink to avoid being dosed with any drug or poison if his cover was ever blown. And the bottle either had to be opened in front of him, or by his own hands.

Harley leaned his elbows on the table. "In regards to another man gettin' taken out, one that's linked to this top guy in question, seems right on too. It seems he got too big for his britches, went off against a woman and a police officer, but got nailed—meanin' shot—by that same cop. I guess he thought he'd killed the cop, but he wasn't dead after all.

"Now bein' wounded, not bein' able to see a doctor without alertin' authorities, it got infected—blood poisonin' most likely. But the other thing was, he also had a bite mark on his arm. I just now remembered that. I guess she took a chunk out of him. That all woulda been pretty suspicious if a doctor saw it.

"Anyhow, when he began to threaten his boss about goin' to get medical care, the boss man pulls a gun and kills him on the spot. He then has a couple other fellas dump the body... Somewhere remote is my guess. End of story. His name was 'Rick Hunt' but went mostly by 'Rio.'"

He looked around, scratched his head absentmindedly. "There was even another man in this mess. The girl defended herself against him, and he wasn't able to do much about it from what I hear. He's been a long-time employee of this man you want to know about, and he's been keepin' *really* low lately."

"He have a name?" Ty asked, taking a small sip of beer.

"Kevin Dreyfuss. He's short on temper and long on business savvy." Harley leaned forward. "From my understandin', if anythin' happens to the main boss, this Dreyfuss could be next in line to take over the whole shebang. *Ruthless* is the word I'd attach to him from what I'm hearin'. Bad news kinda guy."

Ty nodded. "Anything about the woman these men went after? Or the officer? What happened to them? They die?"

Harley leaned back. "Funny thing about that! The woman lived through the attack *and* saved the officer somehow. After that, she seems to have disappeared. They watched her house for a little while but got nothin'. To me, it seems too far-fetched. No woman I know of could live through the attacks Dreyfuss *and* Rio woulda put her through. Rumors have flown about them killin' others before—includin' women—so for her to have lived through *both* attacks? I don't see it."

Harley took a drink. "But *then* I hear that this chick returns home. The boss man hears about it, decides to take her out since she can be a witness against Kindle, Dreyfuss, *and* Rio, who are all a direct link to him. After all, they panicked big time and left all their cargo at the scene! Can you even *imagine* such a thing? What were they thinkin'? Anyway, I heard he went on an epic rampage when he heard that news.

"I tell you, Miles, this man in charge? He sounds like pure evil inside like the devil himself. He'd made plans to have some other men go to her place the followin' night... Or somethin' like that. I'm not exactly sure of the day, but it was soon after he heard she was back around."

His eyes darted around for a moment before his voice lowered to almost a whisper. "Boss! When they got there, she was gone! But they knew she *had* been there earlier because they'd been watchin' the house. They even knew there was another guy there with her. A boyfriend, maybe."

Harley took a drink. "When she wasn't there, they went plumb crazy mad. Tore the place up from what I hear. Of course, that was *big* ass stupid to do because *now* she knows they knew where she lived!

"For being professionals, all these guys ain't been usin' their brains. They screwed up from the get-go, but now even others have just been makin' it worse as they go along. If it were me, I'd take them worthless idiots out. They let her know they knew where she was! Ya talk 'bout showin' your hands! It's like this chick cast some sort of voodoo spell on 'em all. *None* of 'em can do anything right. It's a wonder the head boss guy hasn't taken 'em all out on his own."

Harley grinned before saying, "Ya wanna know what I think?" He waited until Ty dutifully nodded. He grinned again, delight shining in his eyes. "I think this here chick is drivin' 'em all nuts. That's what it is. They can't kill her no matter what.

"Beat her? Nope. Try another beatin'. Not that either. Heard they tried to sneak into the hospital not once but *twice* to get to her. They even went in dressed as cops, but they couldn't even get past the first floor. Break in her house to get her? Nope. Not even home.

"They then try and find this chick, right? She just disappeared again, but then she reappears whenever she wants to. She's pissin' 'em off somethin' fierce, and they can't think straight. That's what I think anyway."

Harley grinned again. "She must be somethin' else, savvy as all get out, or the Lord above is watchin' over her. Ain't no other explanation for how she's still alive. Unless she's a witch or somethin'... I dunno. She's bringin' bad luck to 'em all. They should just leave her be!"

Ty offered a small smile to keep Harley talking, knowing his information was truth and solid as gold. By the grace of God for sure, Channion and Raina barely made it out of her house in time that night! Did they have any clue how close they'd come to meeting these ruthless men head-on? Unless he was mistaken, that was the night Raina had her first major nightmare, and Channion had rushed her back to the hospital fearing she'd hurt herself.

It gave him shivers knowing the odds of Channion protecting Raina, even surviving himself, against these men wouldn't have been good at all. That night could've been the worst night of his life—the night he lost his best friend, his brother, to violent criminals. Just thinking about it made his heart break—and his blood boil.

Re-focusing on the task at hand, Ty took a sip of his beer. "What about the woman now?"

His informant shrugged his wide shoulders. "No one knows! Most guesses are she got the hell outta there. I mean, wouldn't you? She now knew she was in danger, so why would she stick around? She better not of! If she's anywhere 'round there, she better get goin' and not look back!"

Harley took another drink, grabbed a handful of nuts from the bowl on the table. He popped them in his mouth, chewing as he thought about what he'd said. "Yep, she's gotta be long gone by now. I dunno if they could find her too easily if she left. Maybe they could though. They know her name, so it'd have to be changed, y'know? But I just dunno 'bout that."

Ty listened to the loud crunching sounds as the man ate another handful. It was a sound he hated to listen to. The sounds from the televisions weren't loud enough to cover up the sounds coming from the guy seated directly across from him. In an attempt to lessen his annoyance, Ty took a handful too.

Harley continued his same train of thought, saying, "If she's 'round, she'd best not stay there. At least not until they get this guy off the street... If they ever do. But in her case, she just needs to get gone. That man has a solid business set up where he's at, so *he's* obviously not gonna be the one to leave. And he's not goin' to let any of this rest.

"No. That girl is as good as dead. Matter of fact, I'd say she already *is* dead. She just ain't been killed yet.

"Now, I ain't an angel myself, y'know, but I ain't evil neither. Evil is what he sounds like to me. I steer clear of fellas like him."

After discreetly checking his cameras on his handheld device to be sure they were still safe, Ty watched the bar for a moment before asking, "Are they looking for her then?"

"You better believe it! But no one knows where she went. They find her, they'll kill her. Pure and simple."

"What if the head guy got taken out? Do you know of anyone else who'd continue looking to kill her after he was gone? They look *until* she's gone? Or is it a standard contract hit?"

The questions seemed to stump his informant. Harley sat back in the wooden bench seat, his face showing he was really thinking those questions through. It was long minutes before he ventured, "Y'know, I'm not sure. Right now, it's just personal.

"I ain't heard of a contract hit out on her. If the shooter gets paid in full in advance, then he'd go until the job was done. Or, he could keep the money if no one would be the wiser. His reputation would be on the line though.

"On the other hand, most times they don't get paid in full. It's a half-and-half deal. If someone was a hitter, hears the head guy was taken out, he'd have no more reason to finish the job unless he was paid by someone else. Even if he was bored and killed her, he'd not get paid so why take the chance?

"But as far as I know, it's really the head guy, the evil one, who wants her taken out. He's the one with the most to lose if she leads the law to his door. The others can scatter and find work elsewhere. I doubt she even knows who's in charge, but that doesn't make a difference to him! She's to blame, so he's goin' to kill her."

It sounded right to Ty. "You mentioned a cop earlier. What about him? Did she save him, or did he die?" he asked, testing Harley's knowledge.

"He lived too! Can you *believe* that? Dreyfuss, Kindle, and Rio sure made a helluva mess out of everythin' that day! Did they all just get up on the wrong side of their beds or somethin'? It's like *everybody* shoulda just stayed in bed that morning. Last anyone knows, the cop is still in the hospital, so he must've been hurt pretty bad. Maybe he's died by now. No one knows for sure or else they'd be sayin' it. Of course, I think he's still alive."

"What makes you say that?"

"It would've made the news. A cop killed in the line of duty makes headlines. News and every social media site would have *somethin'* on it, but there ain't nothin' going 'round. So the way I see it, he's still with the livin'. Yes, sir. I say he's still alive. Maybe barely, but yet still with us.

"If he *is* alive, then he'll be a target along with the woman, of course. He better get gone, too, in that case. But... maybe not. All I'm hearin' is stuff about *her*... I actually ain't heard nothin' about killin' him. It's just common sense that says he'll be killed too."

Ty wondered about something. "You say when she wasn't home, they tore it up. Do you know if drugs were involved, like meth or something? Were they sober? Or do you think it was just pure rage because she wasn't home? If they're pros, it's hard to see them doing something like that without some sort of reason besides rage."

Harley drummed his fingers on the table. "I can't rightly say, but I ain't never heard 'bout this head guy havin' anythin' to do with drugs. My opinion is he's too tight, too in-control of things, to lose everythin' he's built to a drug. So knowin' that, I don't see him hirin' druggies or addicts of *any* kind. Now, I could be wrong, but I'm just not seein' that happenin'."

Ty considered his next question, his eyes roaming the bar. No one seemed to be paying them any attention as they watched the televisions, drank beer, or played darts. "So, at this woman's place they went to... Did they find anyone or anything else to kill or take? What did they do there besides tear it up? Anything?" He was thinking about Raina's horses.

Harley shrugged. "Nope. As far as I understand, she lives alone. When they got there, she wasn't, so they tore it to pieces. Idiots. *Idiots* are what those guys were!" He shook his head in disgust. "They played their hands like a bunch of pure amateurs!"

Ty tried again. "No... animals? Pets? Nothing like that? Nothing to warn her about what was coming? Anything that'd make her disappear besides tearing up her place?"

Harley shook his head. "Nah. She lived there alone. Now it seems to me if she'd had pets, those men woulda tortured 'em somethin' awful. Maybe not even killin' 'em just to make her suffer. Evil, remember?" He shuddered at the thought of doing that to any animal. "Thank God she didn't have any animals there! If she did, the news ain't floatin' around out there that I'm aware of, so I'm sure it was just her there... Although she actually wasn't."

This news perplexed Ty. *Someone* killed her horses, but who? These men certainly would've taken credit for their deaths, wouldn't they? Something wasn't adding up here.

Ty remained calm and relaxed as he took a small sip from his beer. He scratched at the beard he now sported, asking, "So the man who runs the operation... Who is it?"

Harley leaned back, shaking his head. "He's a man no one wants to cross. Even his own wife and kid don't."

"He's got a *family?*" Ty knew about a probable wife and a son from Channion's reports. He was simply testing Harley's knowledge, hoping to get more information on them.

"Yeah, he sure does. But they go by a different name. Not many people know about his wife and kid. A son. High school age now. From what I understand, this big gun-runner shoots blanks if you know what I mean. How ironic is that? But he wants to please his young wife, right? A man like him, well, he goes out and buys a son for her. Not a girl, but a boy... Probably to follow in his footsteps or somethin'."

"He *what?*" This was something Ty did *not* know!

"Yes, sir!" The man leaned forward again, almost hissing out the information now. "Doctors say he's worthless as a family-makin' man, but his wife wants a kid of her own.

One day he goes out, finds a toddler and buys him. Or just took him. I've heard it both ways, boss."

Shocked, Ty worked hard to conceal it as he asked, "Does his wife know that her son was bought and not adopted?"

"Dunno. If she had any brains, she'd know to get a young kid in such a short amount of time, no lawyers and all that, somethin' wasn't kosher. I mean, it wasn't like an overnight deal. But it took less than a year, and it was fast and hassle-free. And from what I hear, she loves him like her very own."

Harley blew out a breath before saying quietly, "She tried to leave him, her husband, a while back. Took the boy and snuck out in the middle of the night when her husband was supposed to be gone. Only thing was, he wasn't gone all that far, and his men spotted her leavin'.

"When they caught her, brought her back to their boss, he beat the shit out of her. I bet he threatened her with the boy's life because he knew how much she loved him. He's evil enough to do that."

Ty had thoughts racing through his mind. He was thinking about this woman and young boy living in sheer hell, unable to escape. Would the boy grow up like his dad? What would happen when he wanted to leave home when he became of age? Or would he be forced to continue the legacy? Or did he *want* to be a part of it?

Looking at his informant, Ty asked, "Does she know about what her husband does for a living? Surely she does?"

"Dunno." Harley adjusted himself on the hard seat before he continued. "See, ya got to understand her husband. From all I hear about him, he's mean. Pure meanness especially when it comes to business. No one wants to cross him. He's thorough, and he's ruthless.

"But it's also said, when it comes to his wife and that boy, he's a different man." He scratched his head. "It's like he's protectin' 'em from the dark side of his life. Like he's got two lives, and he keeps 'em far apart from each other."

"But you just said he beat her..."

"Sure he did. She challenged and disgraced him in front of his own men! How could he expect to control *them* if he couldn't control his own *wife*. A woman? He *had* to beat her to prove a point to his men."

They sat in silence for a while longer. "What about his guns? Ammo? Have you heard anything about a big shipment? Anything like that?"

"Not yet. He's quiet. Now, as far as I can tell, this man's been doin' this for a long, long time. He's never been caught although he's probably been suspected. He's uncommonly low-key.

"He's not goin' to be easy to get more info on, boss. All this information I'm givin' ya now has been tough to get, but I feel fairly certain it's accurate. I'll try to get somethin' on any shipments, but it may take some time. Well, come to think of it, I did hear he doesn't like to use trucks. He prefers to use regular cars."

"Why? Couldn't he move more faster in a truck?"

"Safety and legal issues." Harley smiled at the irony of a man dealing weapons wanting to be safe and legal. "From what I understand, he uses cars because of several reasons. One, they're faster if they need to get away. And smaller, so they're easier to drive, park, hide, handle.

"Next is, trucks stand out. Cars don't. And with cars, there's far less legal issues. Y'know, weights, balances, truck stations, licenses, and findin' guys who can handle drivin' a big truck. And the center of gravity in a curve goin' fast means that truck will just tip over. And if he loses a car, like recently? He loses far less than if he loses a truck, whether it's a dump truck, movin' van, or a semi."

Ty sat back, thinking about this. Raina was right again. She said she only ever saw cars on her road, never trucks... even in farm and cattle country. This tactic could be one of the reasons he's been in business so long and never been caught. He flies under the radar because he's not flashy. The cars that Raina took out were newer, probably for reliability. Regular, boring, everyday cars that were packed with illegal weapons and ammo.

Ty said, "Give me his name."

Harley studied him. "You must want him awful bad." He paused, his nervousness showing a bit now. "If he *ever* finds out I told..."

"He won't from *me*. How long have we worked together now?"

"True, boss. You've always been real careful like that." He blew out a breath, said in a soft voice, "Okay, his real name is Ford Coleman. But now I hear he goes by a couple of other names too. If you want information on him for weapons stuff, you need to know Colt Buchanan."

Chapter 45

CHANNION WAS MOWING THE lawn when he saw the courier van backing up into his driveway. Not expecting anything, he turned off the mower and cautiously walked over to the driver.

Smiling, she stepped out of her van, holding a package. "Hi! Do you live here?"

Channion nodded.

"What's your name?"

"Channion Scott."

"Without looking at the house or mailbox, what's this address?"

When he gave it to her, she smiled. "Okay. I was just making sure you aren't just the groundskeeper or a brazen porch pirate!"

He raised his eyebrow. "Brazen?"

"Word of the Day. Gotta use it in a sentence to remember it!" She grinned as she got the tablet prepped for him.

He smiled. "Good for you! Thanks for verifying too."

"You bet. Here... You have to sign for it. I'm glad you're home because I couldn't leave it otherwise and would've had to come back."

Checking over the package first, he recognized a familiar symbol on it. Now knowing who sent it, he immediately signed his name. He thanked her as she completed the delivery on her screen before hopping back into her van and pulling away.

Walking to his garage, he opened it. Seeing a burner phone, he simply waited. It didn't take but a couple of minutes before it rang. He figured it had either a tracker or immediate notification of delivery. Probably both.

"Ty?"

"Chan! I was hoping you'd be home when this arrived." With some humor in his voice, he asked, "How's our girl? She still single?"

"Of course she is. Being in protective custody kinda puts a damper on her social life." Channion smiled. "You didn't need to send me a burner to ask me that." He heard Ty laugh. "And she's fine. I thought you said to keep it strictly professional?"

Ty was still smiling. "I did, and you should. But I still see the potential between you two."

"Maybe later." Channion then asked seriously, "What's going on?"

"I know why Raina tried to bite you."

SINCE CHANNION MADE A sudden change of plans from them staying home that day before they left for Picacho's that evening, Raina knew there'd been a break in the case. Since he couldn't tell her what was happening, she felt more anxious than ever.

Working at Picacho's this weekend before leaving for her road trip on Sunday, she'd hoped being kept busy would help her stay calm. This sudden turn of events wasn't helping with that.

Getting the unexpected and extremely useful information confidentially from Ty was like using an AED defibrillator on the case. Confirming their suspicions alone was a relief, but Ty gave them so much more. Channion and Ron had Agent Lyles rush to them to share the information since she had to work that night.

The two topics that came back up were if they should put Raina in Kevlar, and should they let her keep singing at the bar? Hearing that Buchanan was still looking for her added pressure to them making firm decisions.

The ATF agents staying at Raina's house were gathering any information they could. Realizing just how many cars *did* use that deserted country road was now eye-opening on how much business Buchanan could be doing. Being told about the preference of cars over trucks from the detectives' confidential informant was enlightening.

Now knowing the identity of the man who Raina had pepper sprayed and fought with over a month ago, they also knew who to look for while watching her neighbor's house. This new name didn't match to any of the car registrations when they checked it. It was simply yet another alias they added to their reports.

Hearing from Ty's informant that Lori and Zach Coleman had indeed tried to escape before, and what had happened to her, confirmed to the detectives they were being truthful. Looking deeply into her background, family and friends, they couldn't find anything that raised red flags.

Everything about Lori seemed legit... except for the shocking news that Zach was a stolen child. Did she know? Or did she recently find out? If so, was *this* why she was trying to escape?

The men decided the best way to handle it was to discreetly get Zach's prints, and anything else they could lawfully get, and begin a search for any missing child information that could be him. If something reliable was found, they'd cross that bridge at that time.

The one thing they could all agree on was this case was turning into a bigger can of worms every time they turned around. From an attempted cop killing, another attempted murder of a civilian, to illegal weapons, the murder of an associate, spouse abuse, home invasion, killing of animals, and now possibly a stolen child?

No one even wanted to hazard a guess to what could happen next.

LATER THAT EVENING WHEN Ron, Channion, and Raina got to Picacho's, she was pumped up and ready to work. Both detectives knew she was getting restless with no work during the week to keep her busy.

With the exception of the occasional band rehearsal, doctor appointment, or her and Channion going to the Kramer's for dinner, she didn't have much else to do. Channion even made a beginner gym workout schedule to give her some daily structure as well as to aid in her recovery.

Raina had confided to Channion that she was no longer worried about some hit man killing her. When he asked why, she simply replied the stress would do her in first.

They decided she needed to wear a Kevlar vest anytime they were out now until further notice. They simply couldn't take a chance with her. They were hoping Raina didn't realize it'd probably be a head shot if done by a professional. If she had, she didn't mention it. They told her she could take it off if her clothes on stage couldn't cover it, but at all other times she was to go nowhere without it on. Raina readily agreed as Ron helped her slip it on and tightened it.

As the bar filled up with more people, Raina watched from onstage. She wore the vest under her clothes, choosing looser ones to hide it. It made her uneasy to have it on because it was making her *expect* to feel the scary and powerful impact of an actual bullet knocking her down. It took most of her willpower to focus on anything else.

The dance floor was full of energetic couples, the bar was busy, and the music was keeping everyone happy. Raina noticed when Janet came in, watched as she made her way to the table where Ron and Channion were sitting. Waiting for the band to get ready for the next song, Raina looked over toward the bar, noticing a man there. In the dim lights, she couldn't see him clearly, but she just *felt* like he was watching her intently. Was it her woman's intuition... Or something else?

She'd glance at him from time to time as she sang. Later when she called out their break and turned on recorded music, she noticed the man slowly get up with what could've been a cane in his hand. In the crowd and dim lights, she lost sight of him.

Once offstage and after using the restroom, she sat down at their table and smiled at them. "It's nice to be up there again. I actually miss working!"

Janet beamed at her. "You're such a natural, dear! Your voice is so beautiful and strong, I think I could listen to you day and night."

"You think, or you know?" she teased, making them laugh.

Channion smiled. "I agree. Just like I said during your lessons, you're wasting some amazing talent here."

She smiled. "Thank you, guys. I appreciate the hopefully honest feedback!"

As they talked, Raina's eyes kept roving back to the bar, searching for the man she'd seen from the stage.

Channion caught her looking over toward the bar yet again. "Some good-looking guy catch your eye over there tonight?"

Glancing at him, she said, "Sorta. He just seemed to be watching me intently while he sat there. He has a cane, at least I think that's what it was. It's hard to tell with the lighting.

"He wasn't doing anything special to draw my attention. He's drinking like everyone else. It's just... He seemed to be *really* watching me. It's probably just my nerves and senses working overtime, especially with my extra clothing accessory. I'm under a fair amount of stress, you know." She tried to downplay it with a small smile.

Ron and Channion looked at each other. Her nerves were made of steel, and her senses were uncanny. She'd proven both multiple times already.

Janet said, "Ronnie, why don't we go dance?"

"Sure, sweetheart!" Ron immediately got up, holding out his hand to his beloved wife.

Once they stepped onto the dance floor, she said, "Now, dance me on over there so we can see for ourselves."

Ron grinned. "Here I thought you wanted me to hold you close, but instead you're just using me."

Janet laughed. "I'm a multi-tasker. You know that."

He laughed as he pulled her close and two-stepped them away.

As they danced, they could barely see the man. He was in the shadows, a cane propped against the small table in the corner. Even when the colored beer signs blinked on, they could barely make him out. Was that accidental, or done on purpose?

When the song ended, they headed back to their table. Janet said calmly, "He's in the corner underneath the blinking beer signs. He looks like anyone else having a drink and watching everybody."

Channion asked, "Did it look like he was hiding or simply sitting alone?"

Ron answered, "Can't tell. We couldn't stare at him without bringing more attention to ourselves."

Channion nodded. "Do you think he's a customer or someone else?"

Raina's heart skipped a beat as she leaned forward. "You mean... You think he's watching me for *other* reasons?"

Channion replied, "It's *always* been a possibility, and that's why you're never alone. He could like being here listening to you sing because he likes hearing a live band. Or maybe he likes the way you look. Maybe he's from out-of-town and just wasting time. This is a bar after all." Still, he stood up. "I'm going to take a look."

As Channion made his way across the room, he stopped at the bar. When Sammy came over, Channion asked for Raina's usual Captain Morgan and his tea.

While he waited, he casually leaned against the bar, scanning the room.

The man in the corner was gone.

Chapter 46

It was the following Tuesday, while Channion and Raina were still gone for a concert and an extended stay, that Agent Mark Lyles and his men arrested Kevin Dreyfuss. Using Ty's information to locate him, they moved in before he gave them the slip.

Ron listened and watched the agents interrogating Dreyfuss for endless hours at the ATF building. The man was holding out against them, which they'd fully expected. He was hardly a rookie criminal.

Ron felt a surge of satisfaction when Mark commented casually on how nice Dreyfuss smelled. He asked Dreyfuss what he was wearing like he was seriously interested in buying whatever it was for himself.

Dreyfuss looked at the agent suspiciously. In a derisive tone, he answered, "It's '*Polo for Men.*' Are you telling me you Feds have nothing better to do with your time than to pull me in here to ask me what kind of cologne I wear? Is wearing cologne against the law now?"

Mark smiled at the one-way interrogation mirror as he walked around the table. Dang it all if she wasn't right again, Mark thought. That woman was something else all right!

They kept Dreyfuss locked up, wondering why he wasn't requesting an attorney. Did he have an ulterior motive for staying in jail? The agents and Ron discussed the situation at length. One of the agents suggested maybe Dreyfuss was turning the tables on them by finding out how much information they actually had on him. Once he had what *he* wanted, he'd then demand his attorney, get out on bail, and tell Buchanan what the ATF had on them all.

It was such a crazy idea, they all agreed it was probably correct.

THE MAN LEANED BACK in his chair, tapping his cane on the floor absentmindedly. "They've picked up Kevin Dreyfuss. They're not going to release him. And I think he's going to talk real soon, especially once he realizes he's not getting the backing he's probably expecting. He hasn't even asked for an attorney, and he's been there two days."

In the bright and quiet room, Solomon nodded, tapping his fingers on his desk as he thought things through. "Where are Miss Stewart and Detective Scott?"

By process of elimination, they'd finally deduced who Ty was helping. It wasn't easy, and it took some time, but they *were* professionals with resources.

"He escorted her to a concert in Kansas with backup security. They should be back later this week." He paused. "They have her in Kevlar now."

Solomon raised his eyebrows. "They know they're on borrowed time then. The next step is to make her disappear by moving her." He sighed. "Lori and Zach?"

"Still at the house."

"Any differences in either one lately?"

The man placed his cane across his lap. "No. Everything is the same as before. Our men haven't seen anything suspicious about them. Do we wait a little while longer, see what Dreyfuss does or says? Or should we take him out now?"

Looking intently at him, Solomon asked, "Do you think we can get in and out of there without being seen or leaving any traces? We're only going to get one shot at him, so we need to be positive we can do it."

"Yes, sir. I'm confident we can do it."

"We've learned it's ATF in her house. Can we get by *them* without being seen or recorded?"

"Yes. I've been watching them. They're using standard procedures, and I haven't noticed any rogues."

Leaning back in his large chair, Solomon asked, "They've had Dreyfuss two days?"

"Yes. He's tough, but I think he's going to talk soon. With the deputy's and her testimonies, and everything those detectives have on him, he doesn't have a leg to stand on. He's probably running every possible scenario through his mind right now, whittling down to his best option." He ran his cane through his hands, thinking out loud. "He's *going* to talk because there aren't any other choices. He also won't want to take all the blame now that Kindle and Rio are gone. We need to get in there and soon."

"I agree. Let's get this wrapped up as quickly as possible. Let's go over everything one more time. Grab a couple of the men to use fresh eyes on this one. We can't afford to miss him."

TWO DAYS LATER DURING interrogation, Dreyfuss was shown a selected amount of their evidence. After hours of more talking and fencing with each other, the agents were silently wondering what they needed to break him down.

One of the agents, thinking and stalling for time, casually remarked how nice Dreyfuss used to smell, and how it was a smell anybody would easily remember. And it was too bad he didn't smell that way now.

Sitting silently for several minutes, Dreyfuss made the connection this time around. They were referring to his cologne again, but now the lack of it. So, it *hadn't* been an idle question when they first brought him in for interrogation after all. He leaned back in the hard, metal chair, thinking fast.

These cops weren't suckers after all, he thought. Here he thought he had the upper hand, but maybe that wasn't true. He thought he'd been playing them, seeing what they might have on him and Buchanan, but now he wasn't so sure.

It was such a peculiar topic for them to bring up again, it took him a while to put it all together. Why would they care what he smelled like? Who would've even mentioned this bit of trivia to Federal agents? Scenarios rolled through his mind until he landed on it: *That woman.* He swore profusely under his breath.

So, not only was she alive, but she was cooperating with the Feds. She could take them all down. Was this something Buchanan knew? Was *this* why there was no communication from him? *Why* hadn't he taken care of her yet?

Brooding for a while, Dreyfuss ran options through his head. He'd been waiting for Buchanan to send him a signal or message of some kind. Even a lawyer. But there'd been nothing.

Was he being left out to dry? Knowing his boss as he did, this wasn't that surprising. And yet it was. He'd been a loyal associate for years! How *dare* Buchanan do this to him! After all he'd done for Buchanan, *this* is how he was going to be treated? Left on his own with the Feds? Rage burned through Dreyfuss like an inferno.

The two agents noticed Dreyfuss was becoming highly agitated as his fists clenched and unclenched repeatedly, and his face turned red. Thankful Dreyfuss was chained to the table, they tried to remain calm to see what their prisoner was going to do.

Kevin Dreyfuss finally caved and agreed to turn on his boss for leniency.

CHANNION AND RAINA WERE driving back from Kansas when Ron called them with the shocking news. As it happened, Channion had just pulled into a restaurant's parking lot when his phone rang.

Seeing the Caller ID, Raina picked up the phone from the console and answered it after Channion nodded to her. "Hey, Ron. We're stopping right now for lunch. You need to talk to Chan?" She listened to his short answer, sensing something had happened. "Hang on. He's pulling into a spot now."

After Channion pulled the borrowed car to a stop after backing in and putting it in *park*, he took the phone from her. He left the car running for the air conditioning. "What's up?"

The shocked look on his face made her heart begin pounding. Channion released his seatbelt, opened his door. Glancing at Raina, he said, "Stay put for a second!" He got out, shutting the door.

In the mirror, Raina watched him walk away with his phone pressed tightly to his ear. She released her own seatbelt, turning in her seat to watch the detective pacing at the edge of the parking lot. She'd learned that Channion never paced unless he was working off excess energy. He was using hand gestures as he talked. Reading his body language, Raina knew one thing for sure: Whatever had happened was big. *Really* big.

Ten minutes later, Channion returned to the car, getting in behind the wheel. The humidity and the situation had him hot and sweaty, so he adjusted the vents so the air conditioning blew directly on him. He looked at Raina, wondering how best to break the news to her. He blew out a breath, still not believing the news himself.

"There's no way to say it that won't be shocking, Raina."

"Spit it out, Channion! Is someone hurt?" She thought of Bryce first.

"The man we were after the most, your neighbor Ford Coleman aka Colt Buchanan, was found dead early this morning when they went in with an arrest warrant."

The silence was deafening. The car's air conditioning was the only sound they heard as they absorbed the news.

Still not believing what she'd heard, Raina asked, "*Dead?* As in... dead dead?"

Channion nodded. "As in murdered. Someone got to him before we did."

Chapter 47

KNOWING HIS AUNT JANET was heading over to stay with her, Channion left Raina at his house the next morning. He and Ron would work with Mark for the day trying to figure out what exactly had happened with Colt Buchanan. Not knowing how long they'd be, they'd decided she'd be more comfortable at home.

Trusting her, he gave her the code for the alarm system, showing her how to work it for when his aunt arrived. Satisfied she'd be safe there, he left to meet his uncle.

Raina was dusting the bookshelves in the front living room when the doorbell rang. Peeking through the window, she smiled when Janet waved at her. She punched in the code for the alarm and opened the door. Once Janet was inside, she locked the door and punched the code back in. She stared at it for a moment.

"Something wrong?" Janet asked.

"He's never let me do it before, and I'm scared I messed it up. All I do is the code, right? Then this button here?"

Janet nodded before heading into the living room. "Yes, it's fine." She saw the cleaning products out on the coffee table. "Hmm. In a cleaning mood, I see. Do you want help?"

"You didn't come here to clean. Besides, it gives me something to do. Make believe you're on vacation, watch TV or something, and help yourself to the kitchen." She smiled at the older woman as she headed back to the bookshelves. "Otherwise, you can sit there while you tell me more about your family. Would you like something to drink?"

"No, thank you. I'm fine for now." Janet put her purse on a chair, casually kicked off her tennis shoes. "You want to know about our family? Any special reason why?"

"Hang on for just a second. I have to let Channion know you're here." Raina texted Channion that his aunt had arrived, and the alarm was back on. His reply text let her know he got it, so she set her phone down on the coffee table.

Stepping back onto the short stepladder, she sprayed lemon cleaner on a rag made from an old sock. "I guess your family reunion got me interested in your stories. It's a tight family that hangs up pictures of their relatives all over the place." She paused to look at the photos on the walls. "It's a deeply comforting thing, you know? Now then, start talking!"

Janet sat down and got comfortable. She inquired with a smile, "Who would you like me to start with?"

MARK LOOKED UP FROM reading a report on his computer when they entered his office. "Ron, Channion, glad you could make it. To get to the point, do either of you have any idea who did this? Any leads at all?"

Ron said, "Mark, let me tell you that we've run everyone through our minds. We've checked alibis for everyone just like you."

Channion asked, "The better question now is this: Does he, whoever *he* is, pose a threat to Raina and Bryce? Or Dreyfuss? Should she continue to be under our protection, or is it safe enough for her to resume her life? Same for Bryce?"

Mark shook his head. "We just don't know. We've reviewed all our cameras on the outside of the property. He's a ghost.

"Whoever got into Buchanan's building, killed him with one shot, then got out without leaving any trace of evidence has got to be a pro. And he *had* to have known about the cameras and bugs. Who had knowledge of them? Or did he, or they, just assume some would be there?

"Lori and Zach were in the house. Neither one was seen leaving it until the next morning when they went out to feed the animals. Unless there's an underground tunnel we've yet to find, they didn't leave it.

"When we got there with the warrant, Lori seemed to be genuinely surprised—and every bit scared. She didn't even know where her husband was. She said when she woke up, he was already gone."

"But he was there when she went to bed?" Ron asked.

Shaking his head, Mark replied, "No. She said she went to bed alone. He came in for dinner, watched the news on TV for a while, then went into his study. She went to bed around ten, Zach about fifteen minutes later, and that was the last time they saw him. Zach said Colt was reading a book on the couch in his study when he stopped to say good night to him.

"When we went in there, the book was on his desk, closed. A bookmark was placed neatly inside, so it wasn't a hurried thing. There wasn't anything that indicated a struggle in either that room or the house itself. Or anywhere else.

"For a timeline, he was in his study reading a book at around ten fifteen that night and dead beside his barn when we got there the next morning at seven."

Ron asked, "What was he reading?"

Mark answered, "Some new book called 'The Rescues.' It looked like an early release. I read the back cover, and it sounded pretty interesting. Why?"

Ron shook his head. "Just wondering."

Channion rubbed his chin, thinking. "Maybe a rival who got him to go outside, maybe for a buy, got mad about something we have no clue about and killed him? If he was in the house that night, there *had* to have been a reason for him going back out to his building later. Or was it not later that night, but more like earlier that morning? I haven't been told how long he was dead yet.

"And whoever it was somehow avoided all the surveillance equipment at the same time. Is there *anybody* on our radar who's capable of doing this?"

Mark said, "Since the moment we found him, every agent has been working and scouring every lead, even ones that don't look like leads just to make sure. The whole place is taped off and is being inventoried to the last bullet. Considering how large this operation is, we're going to be kept busy for quite a while. It was enough work just to bust this ring, but now there's his murder to deal with. This case will either make us or break us!"

Channion smiled. "This is one job I don't envy you on, Mark. The paperwork alone must be mind-boggling. If you get the credit for solving it, I'm okay with that because I feel bad that you have to do all that paperwork. Better you than me though!"

Mark laughed. "You have no idea. And it seems completely unfair that we get the paperwork, and you get the girl!" Ron and Channion laughed as Mark continued, "There's a bonus being in my position, though, because I can delegate. And trust me, I plan on it. I'd say you guys will get equal credit, if not more. Whoever your CI is, I'd love to have him on my side because his information has been impeccable."

Channion smiled. He'd be sure to let Ty know.

Mark was saying, "And you won't believe that underground warehouse of Buchanan's! Let's head on over there ourselves. I want to see if you have the same shivers run down your back as I had when I first saw it. It's huge, and it's full. It's enough to give us nightmares."

Chapter 48

HE WASN'T SURE IF he was a bodyguard, a roadie, or a chauffeur. Channion figured he was all three when he took Raina on another road trip. Making up the Paducah, Kentucky concert she'd missed, she looked forward to heading back to a great venue. Her smile and jovial mood let him know she was excited about coming back here.

When they arrived at the hotel where she'd made reservations for them, she smiled as he turned off the engine. She patted his knee in an exaggerated motion. "See, sweetheart? We made it here in one piece. Your lack of faith was insulting."

Channion laughed. "Why didn't you sense those deer?"

She gave him a dry, direct look. "It's *not* an exact science!"

He smiled as they got out and headed into the lobby to check in.

She unlocked the door to her room, holding it open so Channion could roll in her suitcase she'd set down to open the door. She laid her garment bag and purse on the bed before she turned on the air conditioner. Pulling back the curtains, she looked out the window to get her bearings.

She said, "Hey, you parked the car right below us. That was a good guess on your part. If we have to jump out the window, we're all set! Just don't forget the keys."

"It was my natural cop intuition, not a guess."

"It was the closest available spot to the door," she countered with a grin.

"That too." He smiled.

She walked to the bed, lifted up the sheets and mattress to look for bed bugs. He'd learned she did this religiously in hotels. Later testing the water pressure in the bathroom, she said, "Not too bad. Let's go check out your room."

She followed him next door, again holding the door open for him as he walked inside. When she once again walked to the window, he innocently asked, "In case we need to jump out my window, how far away's the car? Can you see it from here?"

Realizing she was only one room over, maybe ten feet away from her own window, she laughed. Grinning, she shook her head. "It's just a habit! Everyone looks out the window when they check into a hotel room." She flipped on his air conditioner since she was there.

He walked over to look out the window himself. Deadpanning, he asked, "Anything move in the past minute I need to be aware of for your safety?"

He felt the pillow hit his back, then heard her laughing. He grinned as he bent down to pick it up and tossed it back at her. She caught it, threatened to throw it back. At his raised eyebrow, she grinned.

"I'm not afraid of you, Scott. The most you could do is handcuff me." She put the pillow back on his bed, then checked it for bed bugs. "Since that sounds like fun, maybe we could try that later on."

"*Raina...*" He warned before grinning.

"Kidding. Just kidding!" Raina held up her hands in front of herself, smiling as she headed to the door. "You good to eat in about three hours?"

"Yeah. I'll pick you up at your place. Don't make me wait on you," he teased.

"Never. I'll be ready. Just knock on my door like any polite date should!" she teased back.

Both were smiling as she left his room.

AFTER DINNER, THEY WALKED to the Ohio River. She wanted to show him the murals on the floodwall that lined the shore. "It's called 'Wall to Wall.' Every time I come here, it's like seeing it for the first time. I'll see some new detail, or it'll just strike me differently than before. There's so much to see in each mural. The artists did a magnificent job!"

Channion had to agree. They took their time studying each panel, talking about it. As the evening light faded, the artificial lights came on. For her safety, he wanted her indoors in a controlled environment so they turned back. They'd have to finish the murals another day.

As they headed back to their hotel, Raina felt such deep contentment. She hadn't felt like this in a long time... If ever. And to feel like this while her life was in limbo seemed out of place.

Walking alongside Channion, she allowed herself to play make-believe for just a little while. He was hers, and all was right in her world. She had to fight the sudden urge to reach over and hold his hand. He was her protector, she firmly reminded herself. If only.

Walking beside Raina, Channion realized how much he enjoyed being with her. She brought a certain level of peace and contentment to him. The sense of ease he felt with her surprised him. There was a different feel about her from other women he'd known. She had a certain maturity that surpassed the others.

He had the sudden urge to reach over and take hold of her hand, to pull her close to his side. He knew better, so he resisted. Besides, even if he wasn't her protector, she'd rather be shot than be in a relationship. If only.

LATER THAT NIGHT AS he got into his bed, he prayed she wouldn't have any nightmares. He tried to take comfort in knowing they had all but ended after the one when she recalled the car and voices. Her mind was hopefully done tormenting her.

Although he had a key for her room, too, he was worried he wouldn't hear her or get to her fast enough. It'd surely cause a disturbance for other guests. Would someone call the police if they heard her screaming? He left his bathroom light on so he could see in the unfamiliar room, just in case.

He lay there, looking at the ceiling, wondering if maybe they should've shared a room.

Chapter 49

HER CONCERT THE FOLLOWING night was a roaring success. One energetic performance and two encores later, she mingled with her fans. Afterwards, Channion and Raina had a steak dinner and drinks with the band members and Jason Charles, the event coordinator and Raina's diehard fan.

When they finally returned to their hotel, Raina was still on a little adrenaline rush. Following Channion into her room so he could check it first, she said, "I'm still too wired to sleep. Want to stay and watch TV or something with me for a while?"

"Sure. Anything in particular?" He walked to the window and closed the curtains.

"Whatever's on, I guess." She picked up the remote, flipped on the TV and began scanning the channels.

He noticed the channel numbers were getting higher and higher. "I think you're running way past the movie channels. You're going to end up in the music stations. Try the guide." He noticed her bed had different sheets on it. "How did you get those sheets for your bed?"

She looked over. "I bring my own. You didn't notice that before?"

"I think I did, but I guess they didn't register."

"Well, I don't trust hotel beds. After I look for bedbugs, I remove their sheets and put on my own. And I never keep their comforter on because they get washed only once or twice a year.

"I also bring my own cleaning wipes. Sometimes I bring a spray cleaner. It lets me know what I touch is clean, and how well they clean in these places. This one wasn't too bad.

"But I always bring my own bedsheets and pillowcases, if not my pillows. I sleep better knowing it's all clean. I'm not a germaphobe, as you know. But public beds and rooms? Well, they give me the willies."

Channion thought about it for a moment, seeing the logic. But now he was worried about his own room. "Can I just stay in here?" he half-joked.

"Sure, if you can behave yourself," she teased. After a moment, she walked over and tossed him her canister of wipes. "Feel free to use these, and be *sure* to do the remote!" She paused when a fun country song came on. She looked at him, smiling. "Dance with me, Channion! We've never done that, and this is a good song!"

He smiled, setting down the wipes on the dresser. "We don't really have enough room in here."

"We'll take small steps." She put the remote on the entertainment center below the tv that was bolted to the wall before walking closer to him, placing her hands on his shoulders. "Please, please, please?" She gently poked him with her fist in his shoulder as she cajoled him, "Come on. I *never* get to dance since I'm always on stage. Just a couple of songs? Then we can watch a movie or something."

He wondered what it'd be like to hold her in his arms. He removed his gun and ankle holster, setting them on the dresser after checking the safety was still on. "Okay. I lead, right?"

"A good man always does." She grinned as he took her hand and squeezed it as a silent warning to behave herself.

But with a small smile, he pulled her closer, felt the beat of the song and began to lead her. It was a bit tricky to try to do a two-step in a small hotel room, but he guided her around the queen-sized bed and the desk and chair in the corner. He barely stopped her from hitting the small refrigerator at the end of the song, making them both laugh.

"You're pretty easy to follow, Scott," Raina stepped back, grinning at him. Her eyes were sparkling with simple enjoyment.

"You're easy to lead."

There was still only the one light on, so it cast shadows around the room. He couldn't help but notice how the soft light highlighted her facial features. She was so beautiful, he thought. But she also had strength, courage, humor, and compassion for others. He loved her laugh and her smile. What *didn't* he like about her? he asked himself.

Raina wondered what was going through his mind. He was looking at her, obviously thinking about something. When the next song came on, it was a slow one, and one of her all-time favorites. She also thought it was a seductively beautiful song. She'd always wished she had someone to dance with every time she heard it. Well, lucky her. Here he was.

She stepped closer to him, asking softly in an automatic response to the soft and slow music playing, "One more?"

"Sure." He pulled her closer, listening to the song for a moment. "Ronnie Milsap, I think?"

"Hmm. A man who knows his country? I like that!" Raina grinned up at him. "One of my favorites, 'Lost in the Fifties Tonight.'"

She felt slightly shy holding him so close to her, but she also knew it felt wonderful. When he was with her, she felt so safe and cared for. Not wanting to dwell on it, she let her mind drift as she listened to the slow song.

They danced slowly to the music, alone in a hotel room far from home, away from the pressures, the danger, and worries there. For now, it was just the two of them.

He felt her head rest against his chest as they moved slowly together. He curled his hand around hers, resting it on his chest between their two bodies. Pulling her minutely closer, he could smell the shampoo she used. It was like a perfume to him. She'd been right, he thought. Scents *do* tend to remain with someone and bring back memories. And he wanted to remember this one. He closed his eyes as he breathed in her scent and gently kissed her hair.

She adjusted her head, their cheeks resting against each other's now. She'd felt his soft kiss on her hair, and it made her heart thud in her chest. Knowing it was best to ignore it, she tried to control her thoughts from going somewhere they shouldn't. She sighed in contentment. Yes, like this, she thought. This is how she always pictured dancing to this song. Slow and easy.

She raised her head, looked into his eyes as they continued to sway more now than dance. "Channion..." she whispered. Her heart felt like it was lodged in her throat all of a sudden.

"Shh."

Neither would ever know who initiated the kiss. It was like they just merged together at that one point. She slowly slipped her arms around his neck as she felt his wrap around her waist.

It was a slow, sweet kiss. His mouth then brushed against hers a couple of times. She felt the tiny kisses he placed at the corners of her mouth. Her racing heart soon thudded in her chest. Finally, he captured her mouth again with his. She rose up to meet him as his hot mouth slanted over hers, again and again. He felt his heart begin to thud, his pulse thicken as she responded with no hesitation at all.

He pulled her closer, feeling her tongue meet his. He heard her soft moan as he deepened the kiss. Neither noticed when the song ended and another song began. Her hands sank into his hair while his ran up and down her back as their passion began to run free. Their heartbeats raced as their kiss continued.

There were no thoughts running through their minds. They were simply being led by desire and feelings in their purest forms. They moved together, learning one more thing about the other in this most basic of all human connections.

Her knees hit the bed, causing her to fall backwards and dragging him with her. He landed on top of her, practically knocking the wind out of them both. Once they got their breath back, they began laughing.

Leaning up on his elbows so he wouldn't crush her, he looked into her passion-filled eyes. He ran his hand through her hair, letting the long strands run smoothly through his fingers. He traced his finger around her profile, his touch soft as a butterfly's. She closed her eyes at the feelings that simple caress ignited, sighing quietly.

He leaned back down, kissing the scars on her face that proved she had a warrior's heart. He watched her, loving her responses to his touch. She seemed to revel in each basic, elemental touch he gave her. He moved down to nuzzle her neck and shoulder, then slowly moved up to kiss her ear.

She heard his breathing and felt his warm breath and shivered. Opening her eyes, her gaze slowly traveled around his face, as if in great thought to what she was seeing. Raising her hands, she caressed his cheeks before she ran her hand across his smooth forehead. Her thumbs lightly traced his eyebrows as she looked in his eyes as they watched her intently. Her fingers slid around his neck, toying with his hair. It occurred to her that he'd need a haircut soon, knowing he preferred his hair short and neat so he had minimal requirements in fixing it.

Channion knew they couldn't make love. He was her bodyguard, and he was pretty certain there were rules against that particular activity between them. He was simply still on the job. He knew this because he kept reminding himself. Although she was probably safe, he still couldn't break his code of honor and sleep with her. They shouldn't even be doing this, he thought.

Besides, he rationalized to himself, they didn't have any type of protection. Well, besides the Kevlar vests, he thought wryly. But there was no way they could risk the consequences of making love here and having major regrets soon afterwards. The risks and consequences were far too great just for a night of impulsive passion. He pulled away, reluctant to break the contact but knowing he needed to.

Raina closed her eyes, wishing they could make-believe everything in her life was back to normal, and she was with a guy she cared deeply for. Her pulse was racing, her breathing keeping time with his. She knew they couldn't make love. They both knew it. She opened her eyes again and looked directly into his. They were as full of passion and desire as she knew her own had to be.

She'd never felt this open and vulnerable in her life.

"Raina..." he said softly. "We shouldn't be doing this. I won't apologize for it, but we still can't..."

She cupped his cheek, her thumb across his lips, replying just as softly, "I know, Channion. You know I do. And I won't apologize either. And I wouldn't want either of us to wake up with those regrets we both invariably would have. Not to mention how incredibly complicated it'd make things that already are."

She traced his cheekbones lightly with her fingers before curling her fingers around his neck again. As she pulled him back down to her, she whispered, "Besides, you forgot the handcuffs!"

"Did not."

They were laughing when their lips met again.

Chapter 50

REALITY ALWAYS RETURNS, AND life goes on. Channion and Raina kept their passionate kisses at the hotel that night to themselves. Acknowledging they cared for the other, they also knew they could go no further into any type of relationship until the case was closed. They agreed to remain as they were, mainly because neither had any other choice.

Being adults, they were also aware what they felt for each other now could be because of the situation. Once it was finally over, would they feel anything at all? They'd been thrown together, lived together, and faced danger together. Once their normal realities returned, their dynamic would drastically change. Only time would tell, they decided.

With the main threat gone, Raina was allowed to stay at Channion's on her own now. She saw it as a transition, and a test of her living alone again someday. Baby steps, she told herself. Janet would stay with her on occasion, especially if Raina needed a ride to a doctor's appointment, the store, or to her band rehearsals, causing the two women to bond even more. Janet had such a sweet, motherly demeanor, Raina couldn't help but be drawn to her.

But both Ron and Channion wanted more of the men in Buchanan's organization caught, fearing some of them could be harboring hard feelings against her and Bryce for starting all of this in the first place. Because of their concerns, Raina still wore the protective vest anytime she was in public as a precaution. Since Bryce was still healing, he wasn't even able to go out.

Agents everywhere were arresting people almost as quickly as Dreyfuss turned on them. Apparently, Dreyfuss held grudges against more than a few of them. Maybe he simply refused to take the fall alone. He was for sure pretty pissed, and the angrier he got, the more he talked.

As a tactic, no one told him yet that Buchanan was dead. They figured to let him talk all he wanted to, and they'd share that important piece of information later, if needed. Either way, as a jailbird he sang a nice song.

After decades of business, the Buchanan organization had finally been toppled over and irrevocably broken.

IT TOOK ONLY A piece of paper to change her life. Over dinner with Channion, she mentioned she needed to transfer money from her retirement account to her bank to cover her bills. Fretting over those medical bills she knew were coming made her lose what little appetite she had.

Covering her hand for a moment, Channion left the table and came back with a sealed envelope. Handing it to her, he sat down and waited for her to open it.

"What's this?"

"Conrad and Meredith said to give this to you when I felt you were ready for it or really needed it. It's to let you live stress-free, at least financially, for a while. It's just for you."

Opening the envelope, she stared at the check inside. The amount made her speechless. Her eyes filled with tears while she sat there, feeling overwhelmed by this generous gift. She knew they were quite wealthy, but it was the fact they wanted to help her like this that touched her heart. With all they were going through themselves, they were kind enough to still think of her. She could only nod her head, unable to speak for the lump in her throat.

"It's to cover the insurance deductibles and whatever else needs covered. Any of your personal bills—whatever you need money for. They know it's only money, and it can't bring back your sense of security or your horses. But it *is* something they could do for you.

"They already told me they won't take it back, so you have to deposit it. If you rip it up, they'd just do a direct deposit into your account. They were adamant you keep it. They worried you'd think of it as charity instead of a sincere thank you for saving Bryce. Are you comfortable with this?"

When she felt she could speak again, she said, "It *is* charity, but charity isn't always something to be looked down on. Charity is also love, isn't it? I never even expected anything from them in the first place, so this is just... so incredible. The Mitchells didn't need to do this, but I admit their generosity is readily accepted. I need to find a way to thank them. A gift of some sort, maybe?"

"I have a feeling a simple thank you in acknowledgement would be enough. Remember, it's *their* gift to you. But you do what you feel is right to say thank you."

"How could I ever thank them enough?"

"I'd say that's exactly their feelings toward you." He reached over, briefly covering her hand with his own in support.

After a moment, he also mentioned the ATF was still picking up the tab to cover the rent and utilities for her house. Between them and the Mitchells, her bills were being covered. And Mr. Farley, her sweet, elderly landlord, was still making money that he probably needed too.

Still stunned, she looked at the check again. "How long have you had this?"

He smiled. "Not long actually. I certainly wasn't going to hang on to it forever and cause you more stress. I was simply waiting for a good moment to do it. You gave me the perfect opportunity."

With a smile, she replied, "I wish I'd done it sooner!"

Chapter 51

IT WAS THE FOURTH of July weekend when Channion really worried about Raina. He'd already noticed the recent random and unexpected pops, cracks, and explosions of fireworks around his house would make her jump and sweat.

When his neighbors set off a rocket one night, she almost hit the floor. He knew they were signs of her PTSD as those noises undoubtedly sounded like gunfire. He did what he could for her, but he knew it wasn't much.

That Friday afternoon, Channion stopped by his house to pick her up on the way back to the station. He'd spent the morning in meetings, so he'd offered to take her out to eat later to give her a change of pace since she was still confined to his house. Then they'd stay in the rest of the holiday weekend where she felt more secure.

When he arrived, he wasn't his usual self. Instinctively, Raina sensed he wanted space and silence. Respecting him and his needs, she got her purse and followed him back out to his truck. Giving him space, she looked out the side window as he drove back toward police headquarters.

She knew him well enough now to know he'd tell her whatever it was that was bothering him when he was ready. If he was able to, of course. She wouldn't push or pry. His stress level was pretty high, and she tried to not raise it up any more.

He hit the steering wheel with his hand when they stopped at a red light near the station. She looked over at him, debating whether she should try to get him to open up, or just be patient. His jaw was clenched, so she opted for the latter.

Instead of continuing on to the station, he turned and pulled into a small city park. Stopping under the trees for some shade, he left the engine on for the blessed air conditioning. He unhooked his seatbelt like he couldn't breathe with it on. Raina slowly undid hers, waiting. He sat there, staring out the windshield.

His voice finally broke the silence. "We've been strongly accused of dragging our feet on this case. We've been accused of drawing it out for some sort of perverted publicity even though everything is as quiet as it can be. I personally have been accused of dragging it out to spend more time alone with you. 'Shacking up' was the phrase used." He banged the steering wheel again. He clenched his teeth in frustration and contained anger.

Raina's own temper began to simmer. Like she needed anything else to deal with in her life! Something so petty and so wrong had her blood pressure instantly spike. She took a minute to try and calm herself before speaking. "Who exactly is making these accusations?"

He didn't answer.

"Is it someone I know?" she ventured.

"No."

"It must be someone important and obviously higher up the food chain."

"Obviously."

"ATF? FBI?"

"No. We're on the same page with them."

She looked out the window for a minute, watching the breeze gently lift up the green leaves before letting them fall back into place. "Well, it's someone who hasn't been paying attention to the details. Or the enormous amount of time being spent by you and Ron to protect me... and Bryce.

"You'd also think they'd know if you really wanted to 'shack up' with me, you'd want to close the case faster yourself. Obviously, whoever it is isn't using common sense. It's also very insulting to me to assume something like that. What does that imply about *me?*"

She wondered who it was. Who was rude and ignorant enough to not think this would get back to her? Didn't they realize how it could affect her already-compromised health, whether mental or emotional?

They sat in silence. She looked at him, studying his profile. On impulse, she reached over to take his hand in hers in a reassuring grip. He didn't pull away. She studied him further, reading his body language. She rolled through her mind what she knew of this man.

He wasn't a quitter by any means. He was thorough. He wouldn't stop until he had the solid proof they needed for a conviction, for closure. But more importantly, for her safety. He wouldn't stop unless he was removed from the case. Even then, she doubted he'd stop searching. Not just for her, but for himself. It was in his DNA to do it right. He'd see it through to the end, no matter what that ending was, because it was the right thing *to* do.

In a determined and strong voice, she asked him straight out, "*Are* you dragging your feet for publicity? Or for the chance to spend time alone with me?"

He quickly jerked his head around to look at her. Shock, and even a dash of hurt, shone clearly in his eyes. "What the *hell*, Raina? Of course I'm not. We aren't publicizing it at all. We're certainly *not* dragging our feet! I can't believe you even asked me that. You should know better than to even *think* that."

She looked him in the eyes and firmly said, "Now, so do you."

He looked at her, realizing what she'd done. She'd tricked him into believing in himself because he knew the truth. He saw the trust in her eyes. He squeezed her fingers in his hand.

"You and your uncle are the best of the best in my book. I'm grateful now, and will be eternally grateful, that I have you two as my bodyguards. And for having you two in charge of my case. I want you to stop all of this wondering and doubting of yourself right now. *We* know the truth, and what's right. Forget about them, Channion."

He blew out a deep breath, reining in his frustration. After a moment, he whispered, "You're right."

"I know."

He looked over at her and saw her warm smile. Understanding and faith shone from her eyes. She was his unconditional support, and she didn't even know it.

He sighed. "Unfortunately, I can't forget about them as much as I wish I could. I need to figure out a way around them. Get some outside person to be ready to vouch for us if it becomes necessary? I don't know.

"Ron and I can't figure out why those accusations were even being thought about, let alone hurled at us. They can't even claim the cost as much as they could. Mark has picked up a huge portion of the workload and related expenses since ATF came on board. And that was at nearly the beginning. That alone should rule out budget cuts.

"We even used our normal vacation days for our reunion, so we could technically say we were working for free in regards to you those days. We can't tell if it's more personal or political."

They were both silent for a few moments, lost in their own thoughts. Finally, she patted his hand, getting his attention. "One more thing."

He gave a small smile. "What?"

"For all you've done for me, remember I've always got your back too."

RAINA WAS AS GOOD as her word. When they arrived at the police station, he ushered her in, leading the way to the elevators. As they stepped inside, they heard someone call out for Channion. He pushed the button to keep the doors open on the elevator as Raina slapped her hand against the doors just beginning to close on them.

A man in a white lab coat came running up to them. "I was about to call you or Ron. I have something you may want to see. Got a minute?" The lab tech smiled at her so she smiled back.

"Yeah, sure, Mike. Let me take Miss Stewart up, and I'll come back down. It'll just be a minute or two."

"See you there." Mike turned around and headed back toward the lab.

Raina watched the man walk away. "Perhaps your luck has changed. He looked awfully excited about something."

Channion left her at his desk while Ron was on the phone. Raina sat down at Channion's desk. Fiddling with a paperclip, she waited for Ron to finish his call.

Once he hung up, she whispered, "Channion told me you guys are catching some major flack. You're even being accused of dragging out the case. Seriously?"

He spoke just as quietly, "Yeah, believe it or not. We just want to be sure he stays locked away for good. And we want to get *all* of the bad guys, not just one or two. And for being thorough, we get accusations instead of praise." Ron tossed down his pen in disgust. Still speaking quietly, he said, "It's probably political, Raina. It's hard to fight politics."

Raina was looking around for possible pressure players when a door opened. A tall, slightly overweight, authoritative man barked, "Kramer! Get in here."

Raina had seen the man before a couple of times, but she'd never been introduced to him. She had no idea who he was. She didn't see a name on his door.

Ron took a breath and slowly stood up. "It's time to face the dragon again. Stay put, Raina."

She nodded and watched him walk toward the open office door. Once it closed, she adjusted her purse that hung across her body and walked over herself. Blinds blocked the view inside. It wasn't all that soundproof, thankfully, so it wasn't like she was purposely eavesdropping. Well, not really... She just so happened to be standing there. Her suspicions were aroused. A couple of officers looked at her but didn't comment. The longer she listened, the more her temper began to boil.

Raina had finally heard enough. She was so furious, she saw nothing but red. When she heard the ominous threat of Ron and Channion being removed from her case immediately, she lost all control of her temper. And, she admitted later on, maybe her sanity. For sure all of her common sense and usual people skills. In a nutshell, she just lost it.

She threw open the door so hard it bounced twice against the door stop, hitting her in the arm both times. She stepped directly in front of the man who was tossing threats and accusations at Ron. Standing in front of the desk, Ron was pointing back at the man behind it in an angry gesture, his face red with anger. The air inside the office was so thick with tension she felt she could choke to death on it.

Entering hell *this* time, she was ready.

Chapter 52

HELL HATH NO FURY like a woman who's on the warpath. When Raina burst into his office, the man behind the desk yelled at her, "Who are you? And what in the hell are you doing in here? Who told you to come in here without knocking?"

An enraged Raina signaled Ron to keep quiet with a violent arm thrust in his direction before he uttered a single word. When she spoke, her voice was filled with loathing. "Who are *you?*"

"I'm Chief Coutts. Get out of this office—*Now!*" He pointed to the door with an angry gesture.

"Let me tell *you* something, Chief. I just heard quite clearly you threatening this detective and also mentioning his partner Detective Scott. You threatened their removal from the case they're working on if they don't wrap it up immediately. Is this correct?" Raina looked ready to do battle.

"As a matter of fact, it is!" he bellowed. "Now get *out!*"

"No!" she yelled back. "Why would you do such a thing?"

The chief barked back, "They've had enough time to close it up! I don't know who you think you are, or what right you think you have being in *my* office questioning *me...*"

Raina interrupted by shouting, "*You* don't know who I am?" She turned toward a stunned Ron, asking incredulously, "He doesn't know who *I* am?"

The chief jumped back in, yelling, "And why in all that's holy should I care about who you are?"

Shaking in fury and undisguised contempt, Raina shrieked, "What *right* I have to be in your office?" Turning back to Ron, she shouted, "Is this guy for *real?*"

Trying to diffuse the situation, Ron tried to calm her. "Miss—"

But the chief cut him off. "I am *not* going to say it again! I want you out of my office *now!*" He started to come around his desk.

Before Ron could intervene, she shouted at the chief, "Mister, I think you *need* to know who I am. And if you lay *one* finger on me, just one, you'll regret it for the rest of your life!" She reached for her purse, intending on pulling out her wallet for her driver's license.

Ron immediately thought she was getting her new pepper spray from her purse. "Not the pepper spray!" he called out.

"*What?* I'm not getting out..." She looked stunned Ron would even think such a thing. She instinctively swatted his hand away when he reached for her.

"She's armed with *mace?* The hell she's going to spray me in my own office..." Coutts bellowed at the same time.

Raina's temper was further unleashed at this point. She yelled, "I'm *not* going to pepper spray you!"

"Damn right you're not!" Coutts returned in a roar.

"At least not *yet!*" Raina roared back as she reached back into her purse. "I'm getting my ID so this bastard knows who the hell I am!" Seeing even in her red haze of fury something even better than her driver's license, she grabbed it.

She slapped a photograph against his chest. It was of her while she was unconscious in the hospital. It showed her face. A battered face that was bloody, bruised, pieces of pavement embedded in her skin, skin ripped open and away, and swelling already noticeable.

She roared back at him, "*My* name is Raina Stewart! *Raina Stewart!* Got that? The same Raina Stewart who saved an officer by risking her own life and nearly lost it!" She shoved at his chest, hard. The force of her shove actually made the towering man step back a couple of steps.

The chief was fast realizing he'd just made a grave error.

"Look at the damn picture, you bastard!" She shoved again in her unleashed fury. "I am *the* Raina Stewart who singlehandedly stopped vicious, murdering weapons dealers. *The* Raina Stewart who got your department and the ATF—imagine that, *the ATF!*—evidence against these same vicious criminals that you've been trying to get for how long now? Oh, wait. You never even knew about them!

"*The* Raina Stewart who's being protected around-the-clock by two dedicated, caring, loyal, and professional detectives. Men who have, most decidedly, the most ignorant and un-informed boss in the history of bosses!"

Ron vaguely thought to jump in to stop her, but he was so stunned—and proud—he simply couldn't. He could only stand there and watch her explode. He wished his nephew was there to witness this firsthand. Channion would never believe him when he told him all about this! She was finally erupting like they'd expected her to do sooner or later. He absentmindedly wondered how in the world she'd made it this long.

Good for her, Ron thought. Let it out, Raina! Let it all out!

Raina was on a roll with no sign of slowing down. She yanked the picture back to hold it up in front of the chief's face. She roared on, "*The* Raina Stewart whose life has been uprooted and will never be the same again! *The* Raina Stewart whose beloved horses were shot to death for no reason! *The* Raina Stewart who is still, with all that has happened over the past two months, is *still* willing to testify! *The* Raina Stewart who could never in a million years be able to repay either Detectives Kramer or Scott for all they've done for her! They're actually willing to *die* in order to protect *me*... A complete stranger!"

Stepping back, she yelled in a hoarse voice, "That's who the hell I am, Coutts. As the chief of this ship, anyone with a brain would think you would've invested enough time to know who and what your star witness looks like! *And* be able to recognize her when she walks into your office! And to treat her, or any other woman, with some common respect and decency.

"You ask me what business *I* have here in your almighty office? I'm wondering what business *you* have in this office? You obviously don't know what fine work your officers are doing at all hours of the day and night! Do you have *any* idea of the work Detectives Kramer and Scott have been putting in on this case? Not to mention the ATF? The FBI? Did I mention the FBI yet?"

"Miss Stewart, I—" Chief Coutts began.

"Don't interrupt me because I'm *not* finished yet!" she railed. "You want Kramer and Scott off Deputy Mitchell and mine's case? When hell freezes over! You know what? I've got speed dial on my phone." She snatched it out of the side pocket of her purse. "I think speed dial eight is for the mayor. Maybe that was for the police commissioner... *One* of them is eight!

"Maybe eight is for Deputy Mitchell's very wealthy father who's promised me the world for saving his son. Saving him *twice*, as a matter of fact. I told him no debt like that should ever be held over another and to just be my friend. But he *did* insist on me calling him when I needed a favor. I bet *he's* got some political pull with someone in this department.

"*Someone* is speed dial eight, nine, and ten. I'll bet ten is for the commissioner. Let me just check..." Raina began flipping through the screens to the speed dials.

"No! No... That won't be necessary, Miss Stewart." The chief reached out to stop her.

She paused and looked up at him. A look of calmness came across her face even as her chest was heaving with her accelerated breathing. She studied the chief's anxious face as she tapped her phone against her left palm. "As a witness in a court of law, you'd rightly expect me to tell the truth, the whole truth, and nothing but the truth, so help me God. Is this correct?"

"Of course..."

"Let me practice right now, okay? My honest, truthful opinion of you as chief of a police force is not good. You're egotistical, arrogant, and ignorant of even the most basic of facts. How could you possibly know the details of cases others are living with day to day?" She poked him in his chest with her index finger. "You're also a pompous *ass!*

"You want to earn your officers' respect? Why not try treating them with some of the same? Why not tell them what a fine job they're doing? Why not tell them thanks for working to make an airtight case involving horrible people who're out there walking our streets? Why not say thanks for putting their lives in danger on a daily basis? Why not say thanks for having to put up with me on a constant basis for two months now?

"Detective Scott especially has done everything he could to help me get through my living hell in one piece. That man deserves a medal, not false accusations! Why don't you get out of your air-conditioned office once in a while?"

Her chest heaving, she stared at the man in front of her for a second. In a shout that made her own head ring, she said, "And I'd like to thank you myself. Thank you for giving me yet another damn splitting headache!"

Ron stood there, practically biting his tongue, trying to not smile. As far as he could tell, Raina had forgotten he was even in the room with them.

She looked the chief straight in his eyes. With a voice as menacing and firm as Ron had ever heard, she said, "These two detectives will be *staying* on the case involving Deputy Mitchell and myself until it's closed to *their* satisfaction. And maybe even mine and Bryce's. After all, it's *our* lives on the line here.

"Am I being clear on this?" He apparently didn't answer her fast enough because she roared, "Am I being *clear* on this? They *both* stay on my case?"

"Yes."

A fully chastised Chief Coutts stood in front of her now. He held out the picture toward her. She snatched it from his hand, looking at it. Her hands were shaking she was still so furious. "You know what, Coutts? Keep it. You need it more than I do. I can always get another copy." She slapped the picture down on the chief's desk, face up.

With that, she grabbed Ron's elbow and said, "I think it's time for us to leave as this matter is now closed. Would you mind escorting me out? I'm sure there's work to do."

Ron silently laid his hand on hers that was now looped through his arm. He could feel her vibrating she was so worked up. Without waiting for permission from his superior, he led her out the door.

The *open* door. In her fury, she'd forgotten to close it.

As she and Ron stepped out, there was dead silence in the entire squad room. She heard a distant phone ring a few times before someone answered it. Every officer, clerk, visitor, and felon probably on the entire floor had heard her.

The place had been practically empty when she'd arrived, so where did all these people come from? she wondered. Why weren't they out patrolling, dang it? Wait... Was it shift change? Well, hell.

Looking around quickly, Raina noticed their faces were showing a mixture of shock, disbelief, and a few smiles. She saw more than a few jaws had dropped. She curled her hand around Ron's arm in distress. He patted her hand but uttered not a single word.

She was absolutely mortified at her own behavior. With everyone staring at her, she fervently wished for that mythical hole in the floor to swallow her.

In a loud voice, she announced in a general apology, "I'm sorry for my unladylike outburst. I should've stood my ground in private with your chief, and I'm sorry if I have undermined his authority with any of you. I'm sure he acquired his position through hard work and experience, of which I did not intend to demean in any way." Silence. "Have a nice day. Be safe out there." In a whisper to Ron, she said, "*Please* get me out of here!"

He led her past some smiling officers, and more than a few of the shocked ones, to the breakroom down the hall. It was empty—no doubt because everyone had been called to the recent scene. They sat down at a round table in the center of the room. She sat there, not saying a word. She heard the refrigerator humming in the complete silence. She slipped her phone back into her purse before gripping it until her knuckles hurt.

In the silence, Ron looked at her for a moment. He raised both of his hands and covered his face, rubbing it a few times. He let out a long sigh.

She didn't know what to say or do. Softly, she said, "I'm so sorry, Ron. I was so furious with him I, well, I guess I lost it. I'm so sorry! Can you please forgive me?" She was slowly coming to grips with what she just did. Her hands and legs were still shaking. "I'm sorry I didn't stay put."

He almost laughed at her last comment, but he caught himself in time. Ron lowered his hands, a huge smile spreading across his face. "Good heavens, Raina! I don't know if I've *ever* seen a woman's wrath like yours..." He let out a short laugh, knowing it wasn't funny. But yet, it was. He was trying hard to control his laughter because she was obviously upset.

Not more than a minute later, Channion rounded the corner and quickly walked into the breakroom. "*What happened?* Everybody is in some sort of shock out there. I get off the elevator, and everyone's staring at me. Half of them are pointing me toward here but not saying why. Diggs told me I'd find you guys in here. *What* did you do?"

Since he was looking at her, Raina answered, "What makes you think *I* did something?"

She was incredibly annoyed he looked at her while asking that atrocious question. She immediately realized it was only logical. But still. It was rude. Damn rude.

Ron couldn't hide his smile at the murderous look on her face. He looked to see if Channion was burned to a crisp yet. He wasn't. Ron held back his laugh.

"Raina, dear. Would you mind giving my nephew and me a moment alone? Go back to our desks." At her downright pleading look, he said, "It'll just be a moment. Go on, now... No one will bite you."

She got up reluctantly. At a snail's pace, she walked toward the door. She was hoping he'd change his mind about sending her out there alone. As she neared the doorway, he added with a chuckle, "They wouldn't dare!"

She didn't appreciate the jest. Everyone, of course, *had* to watch her as she silently made her way to Channion's desk and sat down. She scooted the chair all the way up, primly tucked her hair behind her ears, and removed her purse. And waited.

Her hands and knees were actually shaking. She concentrated on stopping them, but she couldn't.

Every now and then, one of the cops would stop by and quietly thank her for the day's entertainment. Some thanked her for taking on the prick they apparently had for a boss, and for being who she was. And for standing up for not only Ron and Channion, but for *all* of them. She nodded before apologizing profusely in a low voice to them for behaving like she did. They didn't seem to mind.

Chief Coutts cleared his throat as he made his way over to her. He opened his mouth to speak when Raina interrupted him. "No disrespect to you, Coutts, but I really don't want to talk to you right now. I'm a little bit on edge."

That was putting it mildly, she thought.

"I just wanted to apologi—"

"Coutts, see now? You're *still* not listening. If you attempted to apologize right now, it wouldn't carry any weight with me at all. Do it some other time." She watched him nod once and slowly begin to walk away.

"One more thing actually." She waited until he stopped, motioning for him to step back to her. She had to say this last thing before she lost her courage. "By any chance, are you the one who also suggested Detective Scott is dragging his feet so he can 'shack up,' I believe was the term used, with me?"

She watched his face turn red, and he no longer looked her in her eyes. That was answer enough.

She immediately stood up. Her voice was barely controlled in her refreshed anger. "That's what I thought. Let me tell *you* something, Coutts.

"Channion Scott has been *nothing* but professional and caring in regards to me up until this very moment. And if you think I have the time and inclination for 'shacking up'—and all that implies—with everything else I'm going through, you're wrong. Dead wrong.

"How *dare* you make such sinful accusations against me—a woman you can't even recognize and don't even know. If I *ever* hear you speak so disparagingly and downright disrespectful about the reputations and characters of either Detective Scott or myself ever again, I will have your badge. And don't think I can't do it. Do I make myself understood?"

He looked at her with a little bit of fury in his eyes at the threat.

She refused to back down. "I mean it. Am I being *clear* on these serious matters of defamation and slander?"

"Yes."

It wasn't enough for her. "*How* clear am I being?"

"Crystal."

Chapter 53

IN THE BREAKROOM, WAITING until he was sure Raina was out of hearing range, Ron gave Channion a wide smile. "Son, remember we were wondering about her expected explosion? And how bad it could be? That one day, something would set off her emotional trigger, and she'd let loose? And recently we thought, maybe, just maybe, she simply wasn't going to lose it at all?"

At his nephew's nod, Ron blew out a breath. "Well, you just missed the show, and you should've been there! It was absolutely incredible. It'll be the talk of this department for years to come."

Motioning for him to sit, Ron began to give a detailed description of what exactly happened. As a long-time cop, he was not only observant but practically had a photographic memory for details. He tried to not leave out a single one.

Channion was incredulous at what his uncle was telling him. He kept shaking his head, saying, "She did not!"

"Oh, but she *did*. And more. *Then* she said..."

Channion was caught somewhere between anger at his chief, wanting to laugh, feeling some despair, and a whole lot of shock. In disbelief, he retorted, "Not Raina... She'd never be disrespectful to authority like that. There's no way she would've—"

"Son, I don't believe your Raina was thinking clearly or was in control at all. Good heavens, Channion! I was so shocked myself, all I could do was stand there.

"Apparently, she heard his real threats of tossing us off the case, in disgrace basically, and she lost it. That must've been her trigger. In my life I have never seen someone in such a rage, but it was a good rage. Your Raina—"

"A *good* rage? Ron, what exactly is considered a 'good rage'?" he interrupted, exasperated.

"Son, your Raina was on full frontal attack mode, but yet in defense of us all the way. She's a protector by nature. We figured that out long ago. From the instant she felt Bryce in even possible danger, she acted upon her instincts.

"She was like an irate mama grizzly for not only you and me, but for all of us. But mainly, it was for you and me. That means she cares a great deal about us. She wouldn't have lost her control if we rated only a mere hum-drum on her meter.

"Losing the two people who've been with her constantly since this all began, and who know firsthand what she's been going through, was more than she could take. I think *that* was the last straw. It was the one thing that shoved her right over the edge.

"She doesn't consider us as *just* policemen or bodyguards. Otherwise, she wouldn't have cared one way or another if someone else was placed on her case. Instead, she went on the offensive while also being on the defensive. It was beautifully done!"

"Then what? I was gone a while, you know."

Ron happily continued, "She takes a picture of herself, one taken soon after she'd arrived at the ER, and slapped it on his chest. She even shoved him back. That actually worried me, thinking he could see that as assault or something since she was physically touching him, but that's for later.

"Anyway, she was *roaring* at him by now. She'd screamed, yelled, and shrieked. But this was a bona fide roar. No sweet, mellow, rational talking but..." He laughed, he just couldn't help himself as he saw it all again in his mind. "Then she..."

Ron laughed again before trying to get serious so he could finish. Maybe Raina was wearing off on him. He laughed again at that thought.

"Oh, and you're gonna *love* this! She even pulled out her phone and went to speed dial either the mayor, the PC, or Conrad himself—insinuating quite clearly Conrad would fire Coutts on the spot just because she asked him to. She was so furious she couldn't seem to figure out which one to call. Chief panicked and grabbed her arm to stop her!"

"Does she even *have* their numbers?"

"I don't know. The point is, Coutts believed her without question. Fact is, I wouldn't put it past her to actually have them! We know she has Conrad's numbers for sure."

By the time his uncle finished filling him in, Channion didn't know what to think of the woman he'd been living with for two months. He still alternated between shock, disbelief, and pure pride. A smile began to tug at the corners of his mouth.

Even when she had PMS that last time, apparently worse than normal because of her stress level and her body trying to level out, she wasn't this emotional, he thought to himself.

She'd been slightly embarrassed to tell him, a male cop, it was almost her time, but her sudden dark mood had needed an explanation. She'd warned him the doctors had told her this would most likely happen. He remembered he'd also felt a tad uncomfortable, but he'd also realized it was a natural thing. He'd obviously grown up with his mother, had several close female relatives, and had dated women, so it wasn't a shock to him she had a monthly. Why wouldn't she? So both being mature adults, they both got over it.

Ron and Channion sat quietly for a moment to process the situation. They both looked over when Luke and Steve came in. They were grinning broadly, their eyes bright with amusement.

Steve jokingly saluted him, saying, "Hey Scott, you better go get your girl."

"What now?" Channion asked. He was too alarmed to take issue with Steve's choice of words.

Luke grinned. "Chief just came out to give a probably partially insincere apology to her, but she absolutely refused to hear it. She had the balls to tell him to come back another time!" He laughed as Channion and Ron's eyes went wide. "She also threatened to take his badge if he ever suggested again that you and she were 'shacking up' instead of you just working on her case."

Luke watched Channion close his eyes and grimace. He smiled at Ron who was now smiling again as he glanced over at his nephew. "Damn, Scott. She's a mighty tigress!"

Steve added, "Yeah, she said that all right. She even threatened to charge him with defamation and slander." He looked at his friend, saying with pride, "She's at your desk. She's okay. Embarrassed probably to be out there, but she's tough. I swear I'll never forget that as long as I live.

"That's a real woman out there, Scott. You should've *seen* her tearing into Chief Coutts like she did! If I were him, I would've preferred to jump out the window. I've never seen the like!

"She screamed herself hoarse a few times, so her throat has got to be killing her. You might want to bring her something cold to drink when you go back out there." He grinned again as he pulled his wallet from his pants pocket.

Channion shook his head. "Thanks, Diggs. You're really not helping me here though. Do you think we still have a job?"

Steve laughed as he leaned against a chair. "Scott, I swear! Chief couldn't fire you two no matter what you did now for fear of too many witnesses and the backlash sure to follow. After how he treated Raina like a piece of trash and with no courtesy in the least? If he fired you guys, he'd have the entire department ready to tar and feather him."

"It'll be a bit awkward for you guys for a while, maybe... But mainly for her. But like most things, it'll blow over. Eventually."

Luke purchased a Coke from the vending machine, paused for a moment before he handed a dollar bill to Channion. "Get a drink for her. Keep the change." He walked out, shaking his head and laughing.

Steve got a drink for himself, too, giving another dollar bill to Channion. "My donation." With a wave and a smile, he left.

Ron leaned back in his chair, tapping his fingers on the table top. He wondered if his nephew was figuring out why she'd defended him so fiercely. Sure, she'd defended him and the rest of the officers, but he was betting his weekend off that she was defending his nephew more. Did either of them realize they were falling in love?

That's the only true reason Ron could come up with for her instant and incredible reaction to the chief's threats. She cared for them both, sure. They'd become almost family, but even *that* wouldn't have garnered such an emotional response. This outburst of Raina's had a lot of emotion packed into it. That left only one option in his mind.

If he were right, it did make for a delicate situation considering their positions. They needed to get this case closed—and quickly. He had faith in both of them to not do anything that'd jeopardize the case, but new love could only hold out so long. He'd begun to love Raina like another daughter, so he was happy about his conclusions. Sensing their building chemistry, his Janet had predicted this would happen weeks ago, so he felt he was correct.

Channion felt the humor of the situation as it was slowly filtering through. Leave it to Raina to determine the *exact* person to be making the slanderous accusations against them within what? Thirty or forty minutes of him even telling her?

She had an instinct, all right! She'd make an amazing policewoman, and for sure a detective. Or, as Ty had told him privately before he'd left, a hell of an agent. He wondered if she'd ever consider it. She was wasting a natural gift, he thought. On the other hand, her other gift was being a talented musician.

Ron said, "Well, she's bound to be feeling pretty shaken up still. She's had to go out there alone and face the music." He chuckled at his choice of phrase. "I'm sure she'll bounce back with her usual resiliency though.

"But you'd better talk to her yourself to clear this up because I'm sure she needs to talk it out. Take her somewhere private in case she loses it again." He added with a smile, "Someplace soundproof."

Channion nodded. After a moment, he got a thoughtful look on his face and suddenly grinned.

Ron asked, "What?"

"I was just remembering that ferocious look she gave me!"

Ron laughed. His eyes were full of humor when he asked, "I thought she'd burn you to a crisp! Did she?"

"Nope... Just a little singed."

They both laughed as they stood up. Grabbing the dollar bills Luke and Steve had left behind, Channion got her a Sunkist.

As they walked out again, Channion said quietly, "And stop calling her my Raina. She's not mine, Ron."

His uncle smiled broadly and patted his nephew on his shoulder. He replied back just as quietly, "Yes, she is. Whether either of you know it yet, she is. And in case you ever wonder, I approve."

Chapter 54

THE CHIEF'S DOOR WAS closed when they returned to the squad room. Raina was simply sitting at Channion's desk, her hands clasped together. He was inwardly pleased she chose his desk over Ron's. He wondered if there was a reason for it.

"You okay?" Channion asked, handing her the Sunkist.

"Never been better in my life." Raina opened the can and drank some. "Thanks."

A few nearby officers heard her and laughed. One shot a rubber band at her. It landed on the desk. Throwing a wry look at the men, Raina picked it up and tossed it into a small pile.

Obviously, they'd been at it for a while. Channion figured it was their way of helping her cope and making it easier on her like big brothers who tease their little sisters. Raina was apparently becoming like family now to the force. The thought pleased him considerably.

She asked quietly, "Do you think anyone here recorded any of that on their phones? Or would it be on surveillance video?"

Channion thought about it for a moment. He'd bet on it. "Why?"

Her face red, she answered, "I have no idea what all I said in there, and I was wondering... I mean, *some* of it I remember, but most of it..." She sighed as her voice trailed off. "And I need another picture, if you don't mind."

Ron covered his face with his hand so she wouldn't see him smiling. The other officers didn't care and laughed again. Another rubber band came flying through the air at her.

Channion tried hard to not smile himself. "Raina, come with me a moment."

He rolled the chair away from his desk so she could stand up. He motioned for her to follow him as he made his way through the maze of desks. She meekly followed, feeling like every pair of eyes was tracking her every movement... Which, of course, they were.

They ended up in an empty monitoring room attached to an interrogation room. Flipping on the light, he shut and locked the door. He leaned against it while he just looked at her, thinking things through. He wasn't sure where to start so he was taking his time aligning his thoughts.

It never once crossed his mind her explosion would be to his chief! What would Ty think about *that?* Channion wondered, smiling inside. He couldn't wait to call him.

Raina couldn't take the silence for long. "I'm *so* sorry, Channion. I don't know what came over me! I heard him say some disgraceful things about you and Ron. He said he'd make sure you were off the case for good, and that he'd find someone else better at their job. *And* that *I'd* just have to deal with it. And... I *lost* it! I've never been out of control like that before, never in my life. He... He just infuriated me!"

She spoke rapidly, barely taking a breath, while her hands went every which way as she explained herself. When she was done speaking, her hands dropped to her sides.

He saw the tears pooling in her eyes, but he still didn't say a word.

She continued, "If I got you and Ron fired or written up, I won't know what to do. *You* weren't even there! This is all my fault. If they try to fire you two, I'll fight for you guys to get reinstated..." Her voice trailed off.

"Gonna call the mayor and the police commissioner?" he drawled out.

"What? What are you talking about?" she asked in bewilderment. "Why would I..."

Holding back his smile was difficult, but he managed it. He interrupted her by pulling her close and hugging her tightly. "It'll be okay, Raina."

He smiled now as he held her because he knew she couldn't see his face. He rested his chin on top of her head as he held her. He felt such contentment. Was his uncle right, after all? *Did* she care that much for him? Actions spoke louder than words, and she'd never hesitated to act. It was all or nothing with her. Ty had said that about her too.

"Aren't you mad at me? If you want to yell at me, I wish you'd just go ahead and do it. I can take it, but the wait is killing me." Her voice was muffled as she rested her face against his shoulder. She had her arms wrapped loosely around his waist.

As Channion held her, he began thinking back over the past two months. Was it only two months ago when he and his uncle were called in from patrol and sent to the hospital for a case that involved a wounded fellow police officer and a witness? These past two months seemed more like a year, if not longer.

He recalled when he first saw her unconscious in the hospital, and when she woke up and spoke for the first time to them. He recalled her horrific nightmares, her pounding headaches, her trying to help them in any way she could. The memory of her hearing about her horses, her breakdowns and needing simple comfort, and moving into his house for safety. The day she met Ty, and the times they shared between work, the family reunion, and simply having fun at his place.

He knew Ty approved of her, and that alone was saying something. Even if Ty hadn't told him that before he left, he did by his actions by going back undercover and gathering all that intel to help them without them even knowing. He vaguely wondered what he'd told Morgan.

He thought about her giving music lessons to quiet students to performing for loud, enthusiastic crowds. And how people respected her and even treated her like a celebrity although she couldn't see why they would. And he especially remembered that night at the hotel, and how they'd still managed to stay professional after that because they needed to.

He recalled all the meals they'd had together, their numerous talks, the road trips they'd taken, her generosity and humor, and fierce fighting nature. They'd shopped, lived, worked, and traveled together. And they still got along great.

Maybe his uncle was right. Channion knew she cared about and had feelings for him like he did her. But maybe he'd missed on how deep those feelings went, on both sides. In his attempt to remain professional, had he been ignoring the signs, burying his own feelings? It was what he *needed* to do after all. Even Ty had warned him to keep it professional until the case was over, as he'd sensed their bond even then.

Channion gently pushed her away from him. He looked her in the eyes, and without the least bit of hesitation, he leaned down, capturing her mouth with his. He felt her surprise, and then her instant response. He pulled her close again as his mouth ravaged hers.

She gave a little moan as he plundered her mouth, slanting his mouth over hers again and again. She wrapped her arms around his neck and responded enthusiastically. He ran his fingers through her silky hair and cupped her face as he kept on kissing her. Pouring herself into the kiss, she barely felt him turn her, leaning her up against the wall. Trapped between the wall and his strong, lean body, Raina felt the safest and happiest she'd ever been.

He slowly pulled back and looked into her eyes again. Both were breathing rapidly, and he took a couple of deep breaths to try and clear his head. Although he knew he shouldn't have kissed her, he also knew he was ready to do it again. She trusted her gut instinct, and now he had to trust his. Holding her face gently in his hands, he took the final leap.

Looking at her, he whispered, "Somewhere in the middle of everything going on around us, I fell in love with you. I also know it's the last thing you're looking for right now. It's okay if you don't, but I just have to say it. I certainly didn't see it coming, but I love you, Raina."

She looked up at him in total surprise. He waited, his heart pounding, while rubbing his thumbs slowly over her cheekbones. He kissed the scars she'd most likely carry for the rest of her life. After a moment that felt like an eternity to him, waiting for her reaction to his spontaneous declaration, he saw her smile.

"Are you sure it's not lust?" she asked quietly. Her world had once again been spun right out of its orbit with his softly spoken declaration.

"Yeah, I'm pretty sure it's more than that."

"We haven't known each other that long, Channion. And there's been massive stress since we've met. Nothing has been normal. And there's a lot we don't know about the other." She was trying to be practical and rational. But her heart was pounding in anticipation, hoping he didn't agree with her, knowing she'd be horribly disappointed if he did.

He replied, "And we've dealt with that stress awfully well, don't you think? And even people who love and live together for decades don't know everything about the other. You can verify that with my aunt and uncle if you don't believe me.

"But living life is made better by learning about each other as you go along, and as you both change as long as both are open to the inevitability of it happening. That learning curve is what *builds* a real relationship."

He tucked her hair behind her ear. "Honey, there's no posted time limit to know what's real. Look at all we've been through together so far. I'd have to say we probably know more about each other than many people who've dated far longer than we've even known each other. We haven't had to try to impress the other. What we know about each other is the real stuff. The stuff that tells us who we really are."

Nodding, she agreed. They'd had no choice *but* to be themselves from the moment they'd met. But still, she tried again. "So this isn't from loneliness or sheer desperation?"

"It's not either, and for sure not desperation, sweetheart."

"Are you sure you really do, or have I just worn you down?" Her eyes sparkled with humor.

He grinned back at her. "Raina, you *did* wear me down. This puts us, *me*, in a serious, complicated situation. Professionally-speaking, I'm toast right about now."

She reached up to cup his face in her hands. Running her thumbs over his dark eyebrows while she looked deeply into his eyes, she could see his sincerity. She knew he wasn't the typical guy, one who'd say those three words casually, especially in the hopes of getting a woman into bed. Neither one of them fell into that category at all. There was no reason for him to say he loved her unless he truly did.

No, Channion Scott wouldn't say those words unless he meant them. He came from a strong, supportive, and solid family. He knew what he was looking for in his life. The two of them had been living together for two months now and found they were quite compatible with each other. They'd gone through intense situations as well as normal, daily routines. They even shared losing their parents. Heck, she'd also already met his entire family and most of his co-workers. And he'd met her co-workers too.

Along the way, they'd quietly forged a strong friendship founded on humor, trust, respect, compassion, and mutual interests. They both knew the importance of integrity and values. They didn't agree on everything, but they knew they could compromise because they'd done just that on many occasions already.

As Raina looked at him, she marveled at the unexpected twists and turns life took. She didn't question how it happened, but when. *When* had those feelings snuck up on them both? She felt an inner peace inside of her as it all seemed to fall into place. She felt... settled. Although she was desperately wishing she had control back over her own life, *not* having control of who to fall in love with didn't bother her at all.

"Raina? What're you thinking?" he asked softly, running his hands through her hair. She'd gone unusually quiet. Did he just ruin what they had, damage their trusting, professional relationship?

She whispered back, "My mama used to say that sometimes when everything seems to be falling apart, everything is actually falling into place. But we just don't know it at the time. That for sure fits me right now, without a doubt. And either because of, or despite all of it, I'm pretty sure I love you, too, Channion. It snuck up on me, or was simply overlooked with everything else happening, you know?

"But there's also a part of me that doesn't know if I can seriously trust it, or even trust your feelings, with all that's been going on, and still is. But the other part of me is telling me to trust my gut."

"It's not lust, is it?" he teased.

She struggled to keep a straight face. "I don't think so. Although, I've always thought you were an incredibly handsome man. Once your uncle got me my glasses, I mean."

He smiled before asking seriously, "Is it gratitude for protecting you? Or giving you a place to stay? It's not transference, or is it? Could it?"

"I don't feel the same toward your uncle as I do you, and he's done all of those for me like you." She paused. "But yet, there is the *possibility* of it being that. So I can't disregard it even though my gut says otherwise."

"Desperation?"

"Not at all."

"Loneliness?"

She shook her head. "Not in the least. I was fine on my own before I met you."

"Did I wear you down?" He smiled at her as he rested his arms loosely over her shoulders.

"In every imaginable way." She smiled back, resting her hands on his hips, looping her thumbs in his belt. "And right now, the only thing keeping my feet on the ground is this heavy Kevlar vest!"

Smiling, he leaned down and their lips met again. It was a sweet kiss, one that melted her heart. She reveled in the feelings coursing through her body. For this moment, at least, her world felt normal and full of optimistic outlooks. Her entire body felt... alive. And free. She relished the feel of his strong, confident hands running up and down her arms.

They rested their foreheads together as they simply lived in their own quiet moment of peace, both knowing it'd end in another moment as they returned to reality on the other side of the locked door.

Quietly, he said, "We must be professional at all times, Raina. I can't stress that enough... especially after this afternoon's events. Everything stays as it has been until this case is completely closed. This is a serious case for both you and Bryce. We can't risk a technicality on your case because of our personal feelings.

"This could be months yet. It won't be easy for either of us, but this is extremely important for us to do. We aren't going to be sleeping together, or going out on dates. We can't let our feelings show right now, especially right now, as in when I open this door, and we walk out there in front of everyone.

"I still have a job to do. And I hate to make it sound cold, but *you're* still my job. And I can't do it if I'm getting distracted. If we can't, you *will* end up with someone new on the case. Do you understand?"

"Yes, I do. Besides, I'd never risk ruining your career. Not that I didn't just do that, probably!" Raina cupped his cheek, looked into his brown eyes, adding, "And it'll also give us time to make sure, right? This will be a test, won't it? We'll see how we handle any arguments and disagreements off the clock now that our dynamic just changed. Time will tell?"

"Yes, it will. If anything should change between us, no matter what we feel now, it *could* change. Some things most definitely *will*. We need to be aware of this, and know that we'll need to be flexible.

"We promise each other right now that we keep it always on the level between us. And no games, no lies. Ever. No matter what happens, I want us to always be straight-up honest with each other, Raina. I work with liars and criminals for a living, so I *need* the person I love, that I come home to, to be honest with me. Can you promise me that?"

"I promise to at least always try to be."

"Fair enough." He looked at her for a moment before leaning down again and capturing her lips with his. "Sweetheart, we need to get back out there."

"I know, but I don't want to."

He took a breath, blew it out. "In regards to your outburst earlier, we were expecting it to happen at some point. You've been handling your emotions in admirable fashion, and for a long time, but we figured *something* would set you off. Doctors predicted this so don't think you've lost it... or feel guilty. You understand me?

"It'll all blow over in time. No one is mad at you, least of all Ron and I. Quite the opposite is true. I'm sure I speak for everyone you defended out there when I say thank you for being you. Are you okay?"

"I think so. I'm just embarrassed and mortified."

"You naturally reacted to the threat of losing the two people you've been around nonstop since this all happened, sweetheart. Our circle is small and tight. Losing that familiarity, that trust, that feeling of security would've hit anyone like a sledgehammer.

"I'm proud of you, Raina. I love that you're such a woman of courage. I love that you stood up for not only us, but yourself and Bryce. I think he needs that too. And I love that you're brave enough to have my back. *I* need that. Thank you."

His sincere words made her eyes mist, and she blinked back the tears. "You're welcome. And thank you for being here for me, Channion. For all of it so far. It scares me to know something could happen to you and Ron because of me. But I'm also so grateful it's you two who are here with me and not someone else."

"You're welcome. Just keep doing what you're doing, Raina. We'll get your case closed at some point, and your life will be your own again. Only time will tell if there's space for an *us*. Until that time comes, we have to remain professional." He gave her a hug for comfort.

She held onto him, her anchor in her personal storm. Pulling back suddenly, she whispered in consternation, "Does this mean the chief was right, and we *are* shacking up?"

Channion laughed as he held her close.

Chapter 55

THE JUDGE SCHEDULED THE trial for Kevin Dreyfuss to begin in another two months, keeping him in custody. When Mark, Ron, and Channion stopped for a late lunch at the family's Italian restaurant, they got a quiet, private corner booth.

Once the waitress, not a family member this time, took their order and walked away, Ron asked Mark, "Do you guys have anything new on who killed Buchanan yet?"

Mark shook his head. "No. Whoever it was sure knew what he was doing. He's a complete ghost. No fingerprints, no break-in point, no calls on any phones, no real sounds caught on camera mics, no shoe prints, no fibers. You were there. The only things that were there were animal paw prints, and few of those, so unless he got shot by a rogue animal..."

The men smiled in spite of themselves before he continued. "Whoever it was, I'm feeling inclined to just close the case on it and let it be. Of course, there's a part of me that would like to thank him too."

With a thoughtful look on his face, Channion mused, "Maybe you just can't see the horse for the trees."

"I think you meant to say the forest for..." Mark caught the gleam of humor lighting Channion's eyes and saw Ron smiling. "Never mind." He couldn't help but chuckle at his wit though. All three men laughed for a moment. "I'm never going to live that whole thing down, am I?"

Ron replied cheerfully, "It's doubtful."

"Great." But Mark was smiling.

Seriously, Channion said, "Next time, may the horse be with you."

They all laughed again.

Seriously, Ron said, "I say close it too. Although, it may be in our best interests to know who in the world could've pulled off this job. He's certainly a pro. He left nothing for you to go on. The only evidence you have is that there isn't any.

"Your men have combed the place and found nothing whatsoever. We say there's no perfect crime, but this one?" Ron shook his head. "Move on to a case that you can do more good with." He stopped talking when their waitress brought their drinks and salads. Once she left again, he continued, "So what's happening with Lori and Zach?"

Mark said, "She's getting over the shock and looking forward to a new life, I'd say. They aren't being seen as suspects. If they did it themselves, they've got potential in secret government ops. They both act like a huge weight has been lifted from their shoulders. They're seeing life with new eyes and fresh opportunities.

"We let them back in the house. We found nothing inside it. Besides, all the business dealings were in the buildings, not the house. We spoke with both, especially Zach, about what to say at school, to his friends. He's shaken up but handling it well from what I can tell. We also recommended a counselor for them, but I don't know if they've contacted her yet."

He drank some of his tea before continuing, "My guess is once the place is cleared from us, and it all settles down, she'll sell it, take the money, and start fresh somewhere far away from here. She may just do it now and not even wait that long. The lawyers are still hashing out the estate, trying to figure out what's personal that she can have, and what we're keeping from the illegal business operations. I'm betting it's going to take years before it's all settled.

"She has a great lawyer herself to help protect her rights and Zach's. I say let her have the house, animals, crops, the property value. It *has* been her home for a long time after all. And we're also wondering what to do with that huge underground bunker? Leave it, or fill it up? Say it's a tornado shelter?" Mark shrugged his shoulders.

"Does she know about Zach?" Ron inquired before taking a bite of his salad.

Mark said, "I'm just not sure. We didn't want to bring up something that crucial and life-changing so soon after her husband was murdered, assuming she doesn't already know. We sent the information we have, which isn't much, to Missing Persons and the FBI. If they discover it's the truth, that's for them to handle.

"If it's true, may God be with them all, and I mean that seriously. It's a situation I wouldn't wish on anyone. In something like that, I don't know if anyone's a real winner. It could be closure for one family, if there is one, but rips apart another family in the process. And Zach will be caught in the middle.

"It sure would help if we knew the exact circumstances of where Buchanan got Zach, and how. If he was already an orphan, that makes it not so bad. Buchanan probably did a good thing. On the other hand, if he *stole* Zach as a toddler from a loving family? That's an entirely different situation. But so far, no one knows.

"And I've wondered if Buchanan's got another safe somewhere with paperwork in it? We found the one in the bunker. Maybe in the house? Does Lori have a birth certificate for him? Surely she's needed one before for like school, right?"

Channion took a sip of his tea before adding his thoughts, "What if it was part of human trafficking? If so, it'd be nearly impossible to find out where Zach came from. Being that young, he'd have no clue. Even getting his DNA may not help."

Ron replied, "There's a part of me that says Lori knows more than she's letting on. I'm not trying to be a cynic here, but I think she knows, or at least *suspects*, something is not quite up to snuff. She has to wonder maybe getting her son wasn't by completely legal means.

"She almost said as much in our first interview with her. She never went to an agency or a court for it, right?" He shook his head. "Then again, maybe it was done legally somewhere. Surely she signed *some* papers, right?"

Mark added a new thought, "Do you think *Zach* knows? He knows he's at least adopted, but would he get suspicious and ask her? I wonder how she'd reply?"

Channion suggested, pushing his empty plate away. "Well, at this point, I think we just need to focus on the one case. Let the other agencies handle the mystery of Zach. Shoot, how do we expect to solve Zach's puzzle when we can't even solve the puzzle of not seeing a horse in broad daylight?"

His lunch companions burst out laughing again. They soon discussed the case at length again over their meals, feeling that it was about to be wrapped up for good.

TWISTING HIS CANE ON the carpeted floor, the man listened as Solomon talked on his phone. When he hung up, he leaned back in his chair.

Solomon praised him, "Well done, Storm! They still have no trace or evidence of us being there. That's one less weapons dealer we have to deal with. Everyone who needed an alibi had one, so we'll consider this a major victory. We couldn't have done it without you."

Storm shook his head. "Yes, you could have. You would've just found a different way. They found him, and I dispatched him. It's astounding that it took this many years, and that many people, to bring him down! He was a mastermind, wasn't he?"

Solomon nodded in full agreement. "Yes, he was. And I will enjoy saying 'was' over 'is' for a long, long time!" Solomon paused before saying with pride, "You using your robotic animals was genius, you know. No human footprints, no trace of anything."

Storm nodded and smiled.

"Do you want us to notify Miles that Colt Buchanan has been taken care of?" Solomon asked quietly. "He would want to know. And maybe pass it along..."

Storm thought for a while. "No. His cousin is bound to tell him, sooner or later. He might even hear it on the news."

Solomon nodded as he sat back in his chair, rolling a pen through his fingers. "Are we about ready to deal with Dreyfuss?"

"Almost. Since he's in custody, it'll be a bit different to handle. He's given them more than enough to convict the others he's named. And with what we know they found at Buchanan's, the lawyers don't really need Dreyfuss anymore.

"I certainly don't want him out there. And I don't want Miss Stewart or Deputy Mitchell looking over their shoulders for the rest of their lives, wondering if he escaped, or got released early by mistake or design. He has enough clout and power he could easily order hits from prison. It's not that hard to pay off a guard to let something get through.

"We need to keep a close eye on him even now. He doesn't have anything to lose, so authorizing or ordering a hit on either of them is highly likely. We've got trusted guards around him, so we can only hope we catch it if he tries something."

Storm sighed. "It's a shame, though, as he'd be a valuable asset for information. With any luck, the ATF will get more out of him soon."

"You want full closure, and it's understandable. It makes us take the law into our own hands, but the evidence, and his own confessions, have proven Dreyfuss guilty already. We could try and arrange it so he'd be in our custody. We could see what else we could get out of him."

He waited to see what Storm thought about that idea. After he shook his head, Solomon went on, "Okay. We'll get that loose end tied up pretty quickly. We need to do it like the Buchanan job—quietly and correctly. If this means it takes a bit longer, then take the time that's needed. Don't rush it."

Standing up with help from his cane, Storm nodded. "I'll go talk to the team now. We've been running different options around, working on multiple back-up plans. We may have to put it off for a while, but we'll take care of it."

Solomon nodded. "I have no doubt you will."

Chapter 56

THEY WERE STUBBORN AS mules and refused to listen. The Mitchells weren't done helping Raina get back on her feet. Asking Channion to bring her to their country home, they overrode her objections when Bryce announced his own 'thank you' gift idea.

Finally accepting her protests were falling on deaf ears, Raina graciously went truck shopping at their car dealerships.

It took most of the day since she had to do some research before any test drives, but she eventually chose a four-wheel-drive truck with a tow package since she still had her horse trailer. As Conrad paid for it, Meredith paid for a year's worth of full insurance. She said that was *her* gift.

To celebrate, they took Raina and Channion to dinner. When she offered to pay or leave the tip, they ignored her and said dinner was Bethany's gift. They laughed when Raina asked just how many more family members were left so she could be prepared. Raina hugged them all before they left the restaurant, so overwhelmed she could barely convey her thanks in coherent sentences.

The other advantage to the Mitchells buying her a new truck was she could now keep the insurance check she recently got from her own. The way Channion saw it, she was financially better off now than before. She could put it in savings, or maybe invest it.

Watching them hug her, all Channion could think was it was about time things started going her way.

WHEN RAINA AND CHANNION arrived back at his place later that night, she was quiet as she followed him into his house. He noticed her thoughtful look as he took care of the alarm system.

When she sat down in the chair nearest the door, just looking at him, he wondered what was going through her mind. He placed his keys on a key hook before motioning for her to toss her new set of keys to him. He caught them in mid-air and promptly hung them on an empty hook beside his own.

He sat down across from her. When she still didn't say a word, he prompted her, "What's on your mind?"

"Do you want me to move out now?"

He wasn't expecting that at all. "Why would you ask that?"

She shrugged her shoulders. "Well, you got Dreyfuss in custody. Buchanan is dead. The others I could identify are dead. I'll be able to go back to work almost like before fairly soon, according to you and Ron. I probably lost a couple of students, but I'm not really minding that at this point in time.

"Thanks to the endless generosity of the Mitchells, I have my finances back on solid ground—even better than before. And I now have my own transportation again, so you probably don't need to be my chauffer anymore.

"I haven't had a bad nightmare in a while, so you don't need to watch me for those. I stopped wearing the Kevlar last week. In essence, this case is almost closed up. Also, neither Mark, you, nor Ron think I'm in danger now, and *that* was the main reason I was brought here in the first place... For protection. Of course, we don't *know* that for sure, but theoretically...

"So the thought came to me as we were driving home that it might be time for me to move out. It'd be easier for me to ask you than for you to tell me to go. What are your feelings about this?"

Channion was quiet. He caught that she called his place *home*. He'd grown used to having Raina around him. And he'd enjoyed her being there with him. It now felt incredibly odd to even imagine his house without her in it. He didn't want to imagine how empty it'd feel if she left.

She was right. It was home.

He leaned forward, searching her eyes. "Do you *want* to go?"

"No. But realistically, I have to at some point." She reached out to take hold of his hands. "It may also be the wisest thing for us to do on a personal level. We live our normal lives, living on our own like before. It'll give us each space, to make sure of what we're feeling. I'm more sure of my feelings, but what *if*? And if we live in our own places, and we miss the other like crazy, that's a good sign, right?"

He nodded. "And if we don't?"

"Then it's all your fault for telling me you loved me first." They smiled at each other before she looked at their joined hands, saying quietly, "It'd be better to know that now than later. Just *thinking* about being gone makes me miss you, and I'm still here."

Her eyes filled with tears at just the thought of moving out. Not being around him on a daily basis, and leaving his home where she felt so comfortable and safe, was hard to fathom. Somewhere along the line, she'd fallen in love with the handsome detective. She couldn't quite picture her life without him now. But she still felt leaving was for the best.

She tried to explain the rest of her reasoning. "But more importantly, I need to know for myself that I *can* live alone on my own like before. Since all of this began, I've never once been alone or independent like before.

"I need to know I'm strong enough to face the nights by myself, to make a home again for me. I need to know I can function if I hear something go bump in the night, or someone knocks on my front door for directions or a cup of sugar. I need to find the *rhythm* I had before. Does this make sense?"

Would she be able to do it? she wondered to herself. She had to know.

He waited until she looked up at him, noting the tears in her eyes. She looked scared, and he understood why. He reached up, cupping her face with his warm hands. "Yes, Raina. It makes perfect sense. And it's something you must come to terms with on your own, and in your own time.

"For the record, I don't think you're in danger any longer. I can only pray we're not wrong. Also for the record, I still don't want you to go. But I understand and support your decision one hundred percent.

"And I'll miss you too. It won't seem the same here without you." He smiled, a twinkle in his eyes. "And when you just can't live without me, you know where I am."

She smiled. "Yes, I do. We'll still see each other. It's not like we're breaking up, or we'll be thousands of miles apart. It's just living separately for the first time since we met. It's going to feel... strange. And I'm so comfortable here! It's scary to leave," she admitted.

He held onto her hands. "Yes, it will be. But we'll work through it together. Fear can be dealt with, conquered. You're not alone." He paused. "When do you want to go? There's no rush on my end whatsoever. You stay here as long as you need or want to. It's completely your decision. You tell me."

"I don't know. I guess I need to find a place first."

"What about your old house? It's as good a place as any other to face the past, and now to build your future. The lease is still in your name. It's been totally cleaned and refurnished. There have even been other people living there so you won't be the first. You know it was safe for them. They kept an eye out, but nothing ever came up.

"You'll have to face going back there sooner or later, sweetheart. You *need* to go back. Even if it's just to face it, and to know you were strong enough to do that. Mark said the other day they were cleaning up their stuff and heading out soon. They may already *be* gone. I just need to get your key back. Well, we'd put new locks on your doors, anyway, with Mr. Farley's permission."

Her voice shook as she answered, "I swore I'd never go back there, Channion. The memories there, especially the barn."

"I know. But sweetheart, you *will* have to go back. You need to come to terms with everything, and that's the base. It may not be as bad as you think. Look how well you handled the actual crime scene. You're a resilient and courageous woman, and I have such faith in you.

"If you want, I can even stay there with you to help ease you back in. And it'd be good to get an alarm system put in. Ron or I can speak with Mr. Farley about that." He squeezed her hands.

"Channion, I don't know if I'm strong enough. I think I am, but what if I'm wrong? What if I have a panic attack or something?"

"Sweetheart, let's do this. Take a day or two to mull it all over. Take a week. I'm not kicking you out, so you take as long as you need. If you want me to go with you, all you need to do is ask. If you decide to pack up to move to another location, then we'll do that."

"Raina, I still love you." They grinned at his choice of words. "Whatever you decide, I'll be here for you. Are you listening to me right now?"

She nodded. "And I still love you too."

"Just remember who said it first!" he teased before his mouth closed over hers.

Chapter 57

FOLLOWING A LEAD ON one of Luke's cases to help him out, Ron drove down the highway. He glanced again at his nephew, who'd been unusually quiet all morning long.

Finally, he asked outright, "Is there something bothering you? You've barely spoken a word all morning."

"I'm just thinking."

"About?"

"Trust and relationships."

Ron glanced at him again. "Care to go on?"

"Raina and I had a talk last night. Later I had trouble sleeping, so I ended up thinking about Colt Buchanan, and who could've killed him. Whether the person that killed him was killing Ford, or Colt. Which half of his life got him killed? Free thinking to keep all options open, you know?"

Once he'd mentioned Raina's name and his having trouble sleeping, Ron happily thought he knew where this conversation was heading. But Channion switched right back to Buchanan. Maybe not, Ron thought in disappointment. He was just waiting to dispense with his fatherly advice about the two of them.

Channion said, "I'm positive it was the Colt half that got him killed, so I began thinking about the *type* of person who could've pulled off something that big. Someone with the ability to not leave behind *any* evidence.

"I can only think of one person who knew all about Buchanan, this case, what we had, and who had the possible contacts or means to do it."

Ron pondered what his nephew said for a moment. Before he could ask who the person could be, Channion blurted out, "Ty."

"*What?*" Ron asked in shock. "You honestly think *Ty* killed Buchanan?"

"Maybe not Ty himself. But put the pieces of the puzzle together, and it fits if you line them up just right. Ty was an undercover agent for an agency he never once labeled. Why he got out, he's never told any of us. Not even me.

"Something pretty substantial had to have happened for him to have done that. The guy has talent oozing from his pores when it comes to law enforcement and undercover work! You don't just quit that line of work for no good reason."

"He visits for our annual reunion, meets Raina, and learns about her case. Weeks after he supposedly returns home, he contacts me and sends me enough evidence to help bring down a major crime organization. Soon after, Kevin Dreyfuss is arrested by ATF, and Colt Buchanan gets mysteriously killed with no witnesses, no evidence."

Ron pulled over into a nearby roadside stop. "I can't drive with these thoughts racing through my head." He left the engine running so the air conditioner could stay on. "You think Ty went back to his agency to help us, don't you?" He mulled it over. "They're now in the loop, so they decide to take care of Buchanan first. Why wouldn't they just let us deal with Buchanan?"

"Maybe they had more to gain. Maybe they think we're inferior and would screw it up. Maybe they knew something we didn't... and still don't. Maybe it was just personal. It's all just a working theory of mine, but no matter *how* I turn the puzzle pieces, it always ends up the same way."

"I guess you haven't spoken with Ty about this yet?"

"No. I wanted to try and see all the angles first, but it's still the only one that makes sense." Channion looked at his uncle. "Let me call him and see if I can gauge his reaction over the phone."

Ron understood this was part of the trust in his nephews' strong relationship.

In the quiet of the car, Channion pulled out his phone and dialed Ty.

He immediately answered. "Hey, Chan!"

"Hey back! Are you busy, or can you talk for a few minutes?"

"I'm free. Hold on." After hearing someone talking in the background and answering them, Ty got back on. "Morgan says hi, and you'd better get your butt back out here to visit her."

Channion laughed. "Tell her hi back, and I'd love to!"

After he relayed the message, Ty asked, "How's it going back there? How's our Raina?"

"She's doing great. Things are moving along—"

"Does that mean you two got together?" Ty interrupted, his voice full of humor.

Channion was thankful his phone wasn't on speaker. "I'm not going there, Ty. I have a serious question for you."

"I'd be honored to be your Best Man!"

Channion sighed. "I'll keep that in mind should I ever need you for that."

Ty finally relented. "Okay, Chan. What's on your mind?"

"Is this line secure?"

"Yeah, we're secure. I'm outside by the arena now."

Channion didn't waste any time. "By any chance, did you hear that soon after you left here Colt Buchanan was shot and killed?"

Silence. Heartbeats pumping away.

"Really?"

A bit surprised, Channion asked, "That's all you can say? '*Really?*' Did you know, Ty?"

"Okay, I'll change that to a resounding *fantastic!* Best news I've heard in years." He paused, knowing his cousin wanted the words directly from him. "No, I did not hear or know about it until just this moment. Solemn promise, Chan. Who did it?" Ty asked as he walked farther away from the barn.

"Nobody knows. It wasn't us, and it wasn't ATF, FBI, or even the DEA."

"Well, that about covers them all. Maybe it was the IRS. I doubt he was paying proper taxes."

Channion had to smile. "Somehow I don't see the IRS sending out assassins, Ty!"

Ron laughed as he understood what Ty had suggested from listening to Channion's reply.

"I heard they were cracking down so it's possible," Ty deadpanned.

Channion laughed. "I swear I can't tell if you're serious or not right now."

Ty grinned before he asked, "What do you have on it?"

Serious again, Channion replied, "Nothing at all. That's part of the problem. It was a ghost. It was someone who avoided all the surveillance and didn't leave a trace of evidence behind. And I mean not a single trace of anything. Do you know anyone who could've done it? Or *did* do it?"

Did you kill Colt Buchanan, Ty? was what Channion wanted to ask... but couldn't.

Silence again. Ty finally answered, "There are quite a few people who *could* do it, Chan. All they'd need to be is talented and trained. But in answer to your question, no, I don't know who did it. Nor was it me. I was here, depending on when it happened. Check my flights, or ask Morgan if you need peace of mind.

"It's okay, Channion. It won't offend me if you do. Even if I was offended, your peace of mind is more important to me."

"I didn't ask if it was you."

"Not yet anyway. I saved you from having to because you wouldn't be you if you didn't think it."

Ty's mind was racing. Buchanan was dead. *Finally* after all these years!

"Look, Channion. I won't ever lie to you if I can help it. You know that. So rest easy to know that I had nothing directly to do with it, nor do I know who *did* do it. I'm trying to leave all that behind me now, but I did dig in there to help you out. It's not good to live with real danger like that breathing down your neck.

"And Raina is something special. A person like that deserves to have her life completely back. She doesn't deserve to spend it looking over her shoulder for lurking dangers. They'll all be over soon. She'd never be safe otherwise. Trust me on that, okay?

"You two are good together. Maybe I also wanted to help things move along so you two could try it out, see if it's really in your cards. It may not be. But she's a terrific person even if you two *don't* get together."

"I don't need help there, but thanks for the thought," Channion replied dryly.

"Oh? So you *are* together?" he asked cheerfully. "It's okay, cous. I can keep a secret!"

Channion laughed. "You just won't give up, will you?"

"Not when I see a good thing. Anything else I can help you with?" Ty asked, smiling.

"No. You just get back to work. Tell Morgan I said bye, okay?"

"Only if you give Raina a big smacking kiss from me!" Ty said, laughing.

Channion hung up.

Ty stood there for a moment in the hot Arizona sunshine. He propped his boot on the lower panel of the fence as he replayed the conversation in his head. He didn't exactly lie to his cousin as he *didn't* know who killed Colt Buchanan, or even know that he *was* dead.

He was honest enough when he said he wasn't "directly" involved, but he knew going to the Agency was all he needed to do. They'd take it from there, and that's exactly what they did. And they weren't done yet. He was positive about that. He'd warned Channion... If he'd picked up on it. Ty was sure he did.

Buchanan was gone. He for sure wasn't going to lose any sleep over that. In fact, he'd probably sleep even better. But he *did* have his suspicions on who could've done it. But the important things were that Buchanan was dead, Channion knew he himself didn't do it, Channion and Ron were safe again, and Raina and Mitchell were free as well as Lori and Zach.

And now, so was someone else.

As he walked back to the Center's office, he wondered when he should tell her the good news. He knew she'd want to know for her own peace of mind. With a smile on his face as he opened the office door, he knew she'd be overjoyed.

WITH RON LOOKING EXPECTANTLY at him, Channion sighed. "He said he didn't know about it until my call just now, and I fully believe him. However, I also think he does know who did it... or could have. I could almost feel his brain working through the phone. But it wasn't him."

Ron nodded, speaking thoughtfully, "Well, Channion, it's not our case to worry about. It's Mark's, and he's not overly concerned about it. For all of us being enforcers of the law, this could be seen as a bad image on us. But I doubt anyone cares that Buchanan's dead except maybe his customers. But as we know all too well, they'll find another supplier. I'm sure they already have.

"And truthfully, it's better Buchanan was taken out that way. No courts, no fighting lawyers, no reputations being questioned, no taxpayer money wasted. It also means no court dates being repeatedly pushed back over the years, no lifetime sentence, no bail, no flight risk. No fear of him escaping or calling hits from behind bars. No more weapons sales from him to endanger *us*. Plus, Lori and Zach are free from his hold as are Raina and Bryce. Let's just let it be, and move on to the next."

Channion agreed but added, "Ty also said that Raina never would've been safe otherwise. He obviously knows something more that we don't." He wondered about the lurking dangers comment. It wasn't past tense. "But I'll try to let it go even though it'll probably be lingering in my mind for a while yet."

Ron shifted the car into *drive* and pulled back onto the road. "I understand." With another glance at his nephew, he inquired casually, "You and Raina had a talk last night?"

"Yeah." Channion was looking out the window, his mind on Ty's conversation. Would Ty ever deliberately lie to him? If for duty or security, he'd have to. Channion couldn't hold that against him. Rather, he'd respect him for it. Lurking dangers *would* be over soon. Meaning Dreyfuss?

Ron smiled to himself. "About...?"

"What?" Channion was pulled out of his thoughts at the sound of his uncle's voice.

"What did you and Raina talk about last night?"

"She asked about moving out."

Ron was a bit startled at this unexpected news, but it could be for a good reason. "You two have a fight?"

"No, of course not."

"And this conversation kept you from sleeping?"

"Yeah."

Ron shook his head. "Any particular reason why it should do that?"

Silence.

Ron tried again. "Did she say when?"

"It depends on where she ends up going."

Now Ron *was* concerned. "Is she thinking of moving away from this area?"

No wonder his nephew was moping! He himself felt disappointed at the thought of her leaving. He would've sworn she'd stick around and continue her life here. She'd toughed it out so far after all.

"Possibly. But it's more about whether she feels strong enough to return to her house alone and face all the memories there. Or is it better to go somewhere else to start fresh? Somewhere no one knows her, or what happened here."

Ron took the exit he wanted, waiting at the stop sign at the end of the ramp for traffic to clear. Casually, he asked, "What'd you say?"

"I told her I'd support her in whatever decision she made."

Ron pulled out onto the road, following the GPS map now. "Did you happen to tell her why?"

"Why what?"

"*Why* you don't want her to leave, and *why* you'd support her and her decision?"

"Yeah."

Ron smiled again to himself. "Does she *want* to leave your place? Or does she just need to?"

"No, she doesn't want to, but she feels she needs to. She's concerned about being independent, feeling secure on her own again. Being able to live her own life without fear like before."

Ron nodded in approval. Good. They were both thinking like mature adults. He didn't expect anything less of them but hearing it made him feel better.

It was healthy for her to know she needed to be independent again. She knew she had to have confidence in herself... and in her life. She knew she needed to have her complete identity and peace of mind back in place before she made any major decisions. And his nephew supported her.

They'd be fine, Ron thought.

He glanced at his nephew, who was once again looking out the window with his thinking face on. He took another turn as the GPS guided him. "Channion?"

"What?"

"When you told Raina you loved her, did she say she loved you too?"

Chapter 58

When Channion walked into his house that evening, he could hear Raina happily singing along to the oldies music coming from the stereo system. Since it was a bouncy song, he could imagine her bopping to it. It made him inexplicably happy to hear her singing in his house.

She added such life and warmth to the place. Ever since his mom had died, he'd never really noticed how quiet and almost cold the old house had become. Not until he got saddled with an unexpected visitor for a few months.

He went upstairs to change his clothes and put his weapon in his gun safe before joining her in the kitchen. When he walked in, he grinned at the sight before him.

She was wearing her blue jean shorts and a pink checkered tank top. Her feet were bare. He noticed she was wearing an ankle bracelet on her right leg and thought it made her even sexier than she already was. Her ponytail swayed with her movements as she was mixing up the ingredients in a bowl for what he assumed was meatloaf. He saw the large pot on the stove, and the potatoes, peeler, knife, and mixer already laid out in a neat row on the counter, ready for use.

She smiled when she saw him. "I thought I heard you come in. How'd your day go? Catch any bad guys?"

He walked up behind her, wrapped his arms around her waist and leaned down to kiss her cheek. He felt her just lean back into his arms. He kept his arms around her, resting his chin on her shoulder. "My day went fine. We followed some leads for Luke on a case of his. I also talked to Ty. That was from him, by the way."

She turned her head, raised her eyebrow. "Run that last part by me again?"

He laughed, kissed her soundly on her mouth this time and finally released her. "He said to give you a kiss from him. I figured I'd better get it out of the way first thing. He said to give you the second one, but I'm only willing to give him the first."

Raina laughed as he smiled and winked at her.

He washed his hands in the sink, drying them on the towel as he watched her transfer the beef mixture to the loaf pan. He saw the pack of gum on the counter and knew it was to keep her from crying when she chopped the onion. It was a trick she'd taught him. Who knew chewing gum prevented you from crying while chopping up an onion? She did.

She lightly pressed the meat in the pan. "Well, be sure to tell Ty thanks. And that he needs to call more often!"

"I won't." He winked again, and she grinned back. "By the way, he was also fishing for information on us. I didn't tell him anything, so if you talk to him..."

She smiled and nodded.

Taking a breath, he continued, "And it got even more interesting soon after his call."

She put the loaf pan in the oven. "How come?"

"Ron knows."

"Knows what?" she asked as she closed the oven door, checked her watch but still set the timer. She was grabbing a potato when he answered her.

"About us."

She froze. She slowly turned, looked at him, stunned. "You *told* him? Channion, *why* would you tell him?"

"One, I *didn't* tell him. Two, he's family. And three, he's my partner, so he's okay to know. He'd be bound to figure it out anyway, I guess. In the end, it'll be easier not trying to keep it from him and Aunt Janet. They'll keep it to themselves. Heck, I guess we may as well let Ty know too. He'll keep it to himself, except it's more fun to let him wonder!" He grinned at the thought.

"Well, if you didn't tell Ron, how'd he find out?"

"He's a seasoned detective, that's how."

He motioned for her to begin peeling the potatoes while he filled the large pot with water, set it on the stove to boil. He added some salt and spices to the water while he answered her. "I told him you and I had a talk last night about you moving out. I was thinking about that, among a few other things.

"Anyway, one question led to another and another and, well, he's a detective. A slippery one at that. Ron's leading me along like a puppy because my mind was occupied between you, Ty, and the case, and he says, 'When you told her you loved her, did she say she loved you too?' Or something like that. It may have been the other way around. Either way, he was smooth, that's all I can say. He totally blindsided me."

Raina stopped peeling, stared at him a moment. "What'd you say?"

"Yeah."

"Yeah, what?" She saw him grin again. "Wait... *That* was your response?"

At his grin, she burst out laughing. "Wow, you're a true romantic! No wonder I fell for you."

He cut up the potatoes as she peeled them, placing them in the pot. "I'm glad you find it funny. I was shocked he got it out of me like that. If my head was in place, he wouldn't have gotten it out of me so easily, if at all. I swore I was keeping my mouth shut the rest of the day."

She smiled. "Well, it's done, I guess. What'd he say? Are we in any trouble?"

He smiled. "No. He said Aunt Janet had seen it coming all along, that we were thinking like mature adults, and he trusted us to not do anything stupid that could jeopardize the case. I told him we weren't sleeping together, so he didn't have to wonder and worry about us being stupid and reckless in that regard."

"Oh, you *didn't!*" She both sounded and looked appalled. She was embarrassed about him talking to his uncle about their sex life even though there wasn't one. "You guys talk like girls! I thought your species just grunted, raised your fists in the air, and beat your chests, not actually used verbal communication!"

"Isn't that kinda sexist, sweetheart?"

"Factually accurate," she joked.

He laughed. "*My* species? Aren't we *both* of the same species?"

"See how flustered I am? Fine, the male sex of our species..."

"Raina, it's okay. Really. We just need him to know so he's not worrying about it. If he believed we *were* sleeping together, he'd be over here helping you pack. He wouldn't mind in the general sense since we're both mature, single adults and all that, but he *does* care because I'm still officially protecting you. We have to be professional overall to not raise any suspicions that could land me, or the case, in hot water."

"I understand. And I'd never want to have your good name dragged through the mud. Once you lose your good reputation, it's nearly impossible to ever get it back." She peeled another potato. "I suppose it's nice someone we trust knows. Although, having it be our little secret was pretty romantic."

"Well, that's part of *our* romance. Only you and I know we figured it out earlier, not last night. It's *still* our little secret... and always can be."

"That actually makes it all seem a little sexier too." Her heart thudded in her chest, just thinking about it. "Come here, Mr. Scott." Her voice was a little husky.

At the look in her eyes, he gladly leaned over as she leaned up. Capturing his mouth with hers, their kiss was short but hot.

When they broke away, she smiled. "We're going to have such a great time together, aren't we?"

He smiled. He wanted nothing more to do than grab her and sweep her off her feet. It took all his self-discipline to resist. Instead he quipped, "I sure hope so!"

On impulse, he leaned over and kissed her hungrily again. He finally pulled back and saw her dazed look. It was a look that his ego soaked up. Tenderly, he said, "You're an enormous temptation, Miss Stewart."

She could barely talk. "You as well, Mr. Scott." She got an impish gleam in her eyes. "Now get away from me before I throw professionalism out the nearest door and lock it."

He laughed as he stepped back. He grabbed another large peeled potato to focus on something other than her. "I think that's enough potatoes."

"I'm making enough for leftovers."

"Okay."

When the house phone rang, Raina read the Caller ID. "It's for you."

He leaned over, read it, and laughed. "No, baby. *That* one is for you!"

"Who has landlines anymore anyway? This is definitely your call *and* your fault." Quickly rinsing her hands under the faucet and wiping them on her shorts, she picked up the phone. "Hello, Scott residence." She tried to act like she didn't know who it was.

Channion grinned as he shook his head, cutting up the peeled potatoes.

"Oh, Janet! It's so nice to hear from you... Oh, you and Ron have been talking, huh? About..."

Channion laughed because she sounded like his uncle that afternoon.

She listened. "Well, we just figured it out ourselves." She looked at Channion, shaking her head as she listened to his aunt. "Yes, we're behaving ourselves. No, we won't be having sex on the floor, couch, or the kitchen table." She listened again and laughed. "Fine, not on the washing machine either! I was hoping you'd forget about that one."

Channion grinned at the thought. He leaned against the counter to listen to the one-sided conversation.

"No, you're *not* taking the pond away from us, Janet!" she teased again. After a moment, she said, "Yes, I was only kidding. He's still on the job with me. Both of us are exceedingly aware of that inescapable fact. Besides that, he insisted he wasn't easy, and I respect that about him."

Both Janet and Channion laughed heartily at her last comment.

She now leaned against the counter herself, feeling slightly flushed with embarrassment. "We're going to take it one day at a time. We could simply fizzle out. We both realize we haven't really known each other that long. And with the volatile situation we met in, well, that goes without saying. We figured living and working together gave us a jumpstart on seeing if we could stand the other. Only time will tell, as they say."

Channion felt immensely happy, and relieved, she was having "the talk" now and not him. Raina was quiet as she listened to Janet speaking.

"I haven't decided yet. He'll be the first to know." Raina propped the phone on her shoulder so she could keep up with the potatoes as she listened.

She was in the middle of peeling the last one when the phone slipped off her shoulder and fell onto the counter. It bounced twice before she could grab onto it. Channion missed it too. They were laughing as they tried to catch it before it fell to the floor. He at least had the presence of mind to put down his knife first.

She finally got it, holding it back up to her ear. "Janet, I'm sorry! I dropped the phone... You just got me so hot and flustered earlier!" she teased, laughing when Janet and Channion burst into laughter themselves. "No, I'm actually peeling potatoes, and the phone just slipped..."

She tried to stop laughing as she listened again. "Well, no, you can't..." She paused. "Because I'm peeling them, and he's cutting them up, that's why. At this moment, we're both armed!" She laughed again. "Okay, we'll talk again later... Just about something *else*, all right?" She laughed again before saying, "Seriously, don't worry about us. Bye, Janet."

Raina made sure the cordless phone was turned off before speaking. Turning to him with one hand on her hip, she pointed the peeler at him. "She wanted to talk to you too. You owe me one, Chan."

He swung her hand with the peeler away as he leaned over. Just before he kissed her, he teased, "You're my hero!"

Chapter 59

GATHERING HER COURAGE, RAINA decided to move back to her country house again. She'd spoken with Mr. Farley, who was more than happy to have her back out there. Hearing from her directly for the first time in months, his genuine concern made her want him for an honorary grandpa.

Agreeing to split the costs, they made plans for new locks, adding motion lights, and an alarm system. Channion took care of setting it up.

Feeling anxious and nervous to be there alone, she asked Channion to stay with her until she felt comfortable. It seemed so peculiar to her that she used to dread leaving her house, and now she dreaded moving back.

As she drove her new truck to her old house, she kept reminding herself she'd lived there quite happily before, and she could do so again. Even without her horses for company. She still missed them terribly. She wondered how long it'd be before that agonizing ache inside would end, or at least lessen. Ever? Channion had forwarded the last videos of them to her phone. She bawled every single time she watched them.

When she stepped up on her front porch, she noticed her hands were shaking, and her knees felt a bit rubbery. Mentally preparing herself, Raina slid her new key into the front door, silently turning the new deadbolt. The thick wooden door opened easily under her hand as she stepped inside.

After closing and automatically locking the door, she laid her purse and keys down on the new entryway table. Looking around the open space, she was relieved to see all new furniture, rugs, and décor. She noticed the new paint, realizing they'd even thought of that detail. New colors for a new beginning?

Silently walking through her old house, her palms got sweaty. Her heart pounded in her chest because she half-expected someone to pop out in front of her. Room by room she went, getting a feel for it like getting reacquainted with a friend she hadn't seen in a while. She made her way upstairs, stopping in each room as she came to them. She noticed there was an actual bed now in the spare room for Channion. She assumed the agents had needed it.

When she got to her own bedroom, she sat down on the new bed, trying to relax. When she couldn't, she simply got up and walked out.

Stepping out the back door, she debated going to the barn. Channion was going to meet her here soon, so if she was going to go by herself, she needed to go now. After some hesitation, Raina made herself walk to the barn. Before, it'd been no less than a run to get there to see her horses. Now, she got there sooner than she wanted to.

Gripping the metal door handle and taking a deep breath, she slid the door wide open. The tears welled up in her eyes and were running down her cheeks before she could stop the first one. And she hadn't even stepped one foot inside yet. She wasn't sure she could handle this at the moment, so she just stood there. The slight breeze had the dust particles dancing wildly in the bright sunbeam. She wiped her runny nose with her arm.

She finally stepped inside.

ON A HUNCH AFTER not finding her inside the house, Channion looked out the back door and saw her standing in front of the barn. He didn't know if he should let her work it out alone, or if she'd want him there.

He finally decided she went down there on her own, so he'd give her the space she needed to deal with it on her own terms. He imagined she had some pretty rough memories to work through down there. When she finally stepped inside, he waited another moment before he went to his truck to unload the groceries and his things.

Walking through the house, he got his bearings again, appreciating how everything was new. He hoped these differences would help curb her bad memories. He wondered how she felt being back here. It was tough on him, and it wasn't even his own house. But his last memories there were as black as hers were.

Finally, he sat down on the back porch step to patiently wait for her return.

RAINA WIPED HER NOSE with her arm again as memories assailed her. She could still smell traces of her horses. She could smell the grain, the bales of hay and sawdust that were still stacked neatly along the far wall. Scents that were once so naturally comforting and welcoming now made her unbearably sad.

She made her way to Aspen's stall, made herself look inside. Images of her beautiful golden horse on his side, his once-bright eyes now lifeless, filled her mind. She began sobbing and couldn't stop. She held onto the stall door for support as she let her feelings out.

When she got to Rodeo's stall, it started all over again. She slid down the wall to the dusty concrete floor as she cried, sobbing out loud, "I'm so sorry. I'm *so* sorry I wasn't here for you both..."

She wept as her broken heart beat painfully in her chest.

CONCERNED, CHANNION FINALLY WALKED to the barn. Through the open door, he saw her sitting outside Rodeo's stall. Her head was resting back against the wooden wall. She turned to look at him when she sensed his presence. Tear streaks covered her cheeks, and her eyes were red and swollen.

Removing his sunglasses and tucking them in the V of his shirt, he quietly made his way to her. Still not saying a word, he sat down beside her, wrapping her tightly in his arms. She cried all over him. She thought she'd used up every tear her body could produce, but she'd obviously been wrong.

"I want them back! I want my kids back!" Her sobs racked her body.

Channion got tears in his own eyes. Hearing her sobs, holding her against him, he wondered if she'd ever forgive herself. He was betting she was still feeling enormous guilt. He knew he was.

Raina finally emptied her reservoir of tears. She wiped her face and nose again with her shirt. She leaned her head against his shoulder, taking deep breaths. She felt his warm hand slowly running up and down her arm, and his occasional kiss on her hair as he held her. For a long time, they just sat there in the eerie silence. Not even a bird was heard in the barn.

He finally asked softly, "How are you feeling, sweetheart?"

Her voice was choppy and quiet when she answered, "Hollow, numb, exhausted. The memories just came pouring out of everywhere... They simply overwhelmed me. It was like an avalanche. I couldn't take them all at once like that."

"I understand. I'm so sorry, sweetheart. I really miss them too." He wondered what to say, knowing nothing would help. But he wanted to encourage her to talk it out, hoping by expressing herself, it'd be a positive step forward.

"It's so hard to lose a pet because they become family members, don't they?" He felt her nod. "It was like that when I lost my dog. I'd had her since she was a puppy. Honesty and I grew up together. When she was gone, it nearly broke me in two. She didn't die, but she ran off. We looked and looked for her, but we never found her. The memories we made can both make me laugh and feel sad even to this day."

"I've lost pets before, but none were murdered," Raina said quietly. *Instead of me*, she said to herself.

Channion understood. There was a big difference in an animal dying naturally, having to be humanely put down to stop their misery and suffering, and them being killed by accident. She was right. Her horses weren't just killed. They were murdered.

He kissed her temple, pulling her closer. "A loss is still a loss. The pain of them being gone is a sharp stab to your heart. However it was they went, they're still gone. Our pain is a measurement of how much we loved them and still miss them."

After a while, she said, "I've never felt so alone, and so sad, since my mama died as when I walked in here."

"I understand, sweetheart. It was the same with me when my mom died. The first time I went into her room after her funeral, I cried like a baby. A full-grown man who just had to let it out. It sunk in that I was technically an orphan now.

"I didn't have any siblings to talk to about it, so I was alone. I thankfully had Ty, but no real siblings who could understand exactly what I was feeling at that moment. Once that shock and grief wears down, the rest of the healing follows.

"She was my world after my dad got killed, and now she was gone too. The house I'd always loved, that was my boyhood home, actually *felt* empty. It felt as empty as I did." His own eyes got misty as he remembered those overwhelming feelings like it was yesterday. He rested his head against hers. "Is that how you felt in here?"

She nodded. Raina knew he understood her completely. She held onto one of his hands, offering him comfort as he did her.

After thinking for a moment, she said, "I don't think you're any less of a real man because you cried when your mom died, Channion. Men have tears too. In fact, I think only a real man is strong enough to admit he not only can cry, but did."

"Thank you for that, Raina." He kissed the top of her head.

But in her case of loss, she also felt tremendous guilt. And that guilt had lodged itself inside her very being.

She'd tried to reason with herself, but it still boiled down to the fact she was all they had to save them, and she'd failed them in the worst possible way. After all, they were *dead*.

She'd always thought she'd die to protect an animal she loved, do everything in her power to protect them. But when it came time to prove it, she wasn't even there. She didn't share these feelings with Channion though.

She thought back to the day he'd taken her to their graves in a pasture at one of his relative's farms a couple of hours away, hoping it'd give her some closure. Neither was sure it did, but it *had* eased some pain in her heart knowing they weren't dumped at the local landfill or abandoned in some ditch somewhere. They'd been treated with respect. That knowledge *did* make a difference.

Channion wondered for what seemed like the thousandth time if he should, *could,* explain to her that her horses *weren't* shot by Buchanan's men because they couldn't find her. And *why?* Would knowing the reasoning behind their deaths help her heal, or would it make it worse because it was so senseless? But to Lori and Zach, it'd been the only way they could prevent Aspen and Rodeo being tortured? And to warn her to flee?

He, Ron, and Mark had debated it again, but in the end, decided to let the matter rest and hope that time would heal her heart's wounds. As he'd just told her, a loss is still a loss.

But he also had some personal doubts. What if *he* were in Raina's place? Wouldn't *he* want to know the truth? Would she want to press charges against them? They hadn't formally made any deal with Lori and Zach, so Raina could charge them if she chose to.

And more so now since their relationship had become personal, did he owe it to her? Or was this one of the complications of being in a relationship they needed to avoid? An excellent reason why they shouldn't *be* in a personal relationship yet? Personal feelings and professional obligations were often like oil and water.

As they sat there on the barn floor, he wondered if they progressed, stayed together, even possibly got married one day, and this secret came out, how would she, or they, handle it? Would it destroy them? Would she see it as a lack of trust? Withholding such personal information that may have been able to help her cope better when everything else in her world had crumbled? Knowing how much she treasured Aspen and Rodeo, would not telling her the full truth be unforgiveable?

He didn't know what to do about this. Perhaps he should talk with her doctor, a police chaplain, or maybe Janet for a female's perspective.

In the stillness of the barn, they sat there talking, both trying to deal with their own losses. When they decided to head back to the house, Raina closed the barn door herself.

Hand in hand, they walked back to her house together.

As Raina unpacked her things for the second time in the same house, hoping to make it into a home again, Channion set up her alarm system. He taught her how to work it, changed the default code to a new one, and had her practice it until she was completely comfortable with it.

With the company on the line so they knew it wasn't an emergency, he let it go off so Raina could know how much time it took to activate, hear what it sounded like, and how loud it was.

She wrote out the steps for Mr. Farley since he was her landlord and needed to know. She'd have him come out and show him in person soon, she decided. Just not today. She put another copy in a kitchen drawer with the appliance manuals.

Once she was unpacked, she took a shower and a few aspirin for the headache caused by her crying earlier. Feeling better, she made their dinner, eating it at the new table with the new man she hoped to keep in her new life.

Chapter 60

Raina kicked Channion out of her house three days later. Since she did it with a warm smile and a hot kiss, Channion didn't mind so much. She decided she had to face her demons on her own.

She helped Channion carry his bags to his truck early the next morning before he left for work. She walked out in her pajama shorts and a t-shirt, her bare feet picking their way on the already-warm sidewalk. She considered this a wonderful perk of country living. She'd never even consider doing this in a city, surrounded by strangers and nasty sidewalks. She was a country girl at heart.

Stopping in the living room before he left, he turned her to face him. He ran his fingers through her tousled hair, reading her body language: Slightly anxious, but determined. He brushed his knuckles over her cheek.

"You'd better go, Chan. Don't worry about me. I'll stay downstairs so if I fall off the deep end, I won't have as far to fall." She smiled at him in the early morning sunlight coming through her windows.

"Raina…" With a grin, he quickly kissed her. Resting his forehead against hers, he laughed. "You're going to be fine, sweetheart. I'm not worried at all." Stepping back, he stroked her scarred cheek again with his fingertips. "Remember I'm a phone call away unless I can't answer. Leave me a message or send a text, and I'll call you back as soon as I'm able.

"Please remember my job doesn't always allow me to answer or call right back, okay? So if I don't call you back within the next thirty seconds, I'm not abandoning you, my feelings haven't changed overnight, I'm not having lunch with some hot girl I met at some unknown bar, and I'm not punishing you for some unfathomable reason."

"Duly noted." She cocked her head at him. "Why…?"

He grinned. "I'm trying to cover the major accusations I've heard from my ex-girl-friends when they didn't hear back immediately. I just listed the most common ones for sake of time."

"Just how many girlfriends have you had?" She laughed when he shrugged his shoulders. "Maybe you just had poor taste. Either way, babe, that's why *they're* the exes.

"Don't forget I've gone to work with you for the past three months. I know what it can be like. If you don't answer, and I want or need you to call me back, I'll say so in a message. We have our emergency codes, so you'll know if I'm in trouble."

With a solemn face, she added, "If I *don't* leave a message, I'm not mad at you, I'm not plotting your demise, and I'm not punishing you by making you wonder why I called. It's simply not important enough to leave a message. Maybe I even just butt-dialed you."

She grinned and cupped his face in her hands before kissing him soundly, their tongues swirling and dueling with one another. He groaned and pulled her closer, one hand running up her back, behind her neck and into her hair, his fingers sinking in deep to hold her still as his mouth made love to hers. He didn't let her go when she later pulled back, and so she happily dove back in for another long, breathless kiss. He gently bit her bottom lip before he took her mouth yet again.

When they finally broke apart, she rested her head against his chest, feeling his heart racing underneath her cheek. It was keeping pace with hers. It made her smile inside knowing she could turn this man on... And knowing he did the same to her. They both enjoyed the moment, catching their breaths.

Still a bit breathless, she asked, "So are we on the same page?"

He ran his hands over her hair and down her back. He didn't want to let her go, so he didn't. "Yeah, and it's an unusual and very nice feeling. It's great to know you already understand what I do when I'm not actually with you.

"And since I've also gone to your work places, three or four of them now, I also know it works both ways." He kissed and hugged her again before heading toward the door. He turned around once more and smiled. "Don't forget I love you."

"I won't. I love you too."

From her doorway, she watched him get in his truck, sighing as she watched him leave her driveway. She smiled and waved back when he waved at her. Her heart was already aching and lonely.

"Be safe, Channion. And God, please, please, *please* keep him safe." She sent out her softly spoken prayer as she watched his truck go down the road.

After she closed her door and set the alarm, she felt both alone and yet oddly secure. Leaning against the door, she tried to soak in the feeling of being there alone for the first time. That secure feeling came not from knowing she had an alarm now, but from knowing Channion would be there for her if she needed him. It felt odd, but she had a feeling that the alone part would simply pass.

She couldn't wait.

SEEING HIS NEPHEW EXIT the elevator, Ron watched as Channion walked toward their desks, stopping to talk to some of the guys as he made his way over. While his nephew unlocked his desk drawers, he asked, "How's she doing?"

"She'll be all right in time. The first night she was pretty jittery. Judging by what she looked like the next morning, I doubt she slept much at all. She misses her horses something fierce, and she'll start to cry if she even looks at the barn. I'm not sure how to help her with that. It may just be a matter of time to help her deal and heal. I wish I could help her because it's tearing her up something awful."

Ron nodded in understanding as Channion continued, "But she was calmer and more relaxed the next night. She looked much better the next morning. And last night, she informed me while she made dinner she's ready to go it alone now. She kicked me out this morning. She even helped me pack and carry my stuff to my truck."

Ron laughed. "She wasn't carrying out your stuff to kick you out faster. She just didn't want you to be late for work!" They both laughed before Ron said with approval, "And good for her. The faster she gets on her own, the better off she'll be. I figured she'd want the company longer myself, but again, good for her." He tilted his head as he studied his partner. "What about you? How's it feel?"

"Like I forgot something. It's an unusual feeling after having her constantly around for the past few months, that's for sure. Driving over here, I turned to say something, saw she wasn't there in the front seat and almost slammed on the brakes to go back and get her! Like I could've left without her on accident, right? It'll take some adjusting on my end too."

His uncle laughed.

Channion added with a rueful smile, "I'm more worried I'm going to forget I'm *not* supposed to pick her up and end up waiting for her at the studio or the bar. If I do that, please stop me so I don't look like an idiot."

Ron laughed again good-naturedly. "I will, don't worry. It already feels odd to me as well. I guess it's an adjustment for us all. The case is still open, so we'll just see how this transition period goes." He leaned back in his chair, knowing he could tease his nephew since no one was around to hear them. "Who do you think is going to break down and call the other first?"

Channion laughed, shook his head. "Nope, I'm not even going there with you." He changed the subject. "What are we supposed to do today anyway?"

As luck would have it, they got a call from Homicide later that afternoon. They rode to the scene together, leaving Channion's truck at the station. As Ron drove down the interstate, Channion suddenly laughed. "I already miss Raina. If she hadn't moved out or kicked me out, I'd be home soon!"

Ron grinned. "That's true! We wouldn't be running this case if we were still running herd on her. This is all her fault. Be sure to tell her that the next time you talk to her."

Channion grinned. "Consider it done."

Chapter 61

RAINA WAS PROUD OF herself. She'd made it the entire day (so far) without once calling Channion. She'd gone to work, went to the store, and came home. A typical day like everyone else had... Just like *she* used to have.

Relaxing on the couch, on the edge of dozing, she was startled when her phone rang.

Calling to make sure Raina was adjusting well, Janet mentioned that Ronnie and Channion were working a new case. "They won't get back until after midnight, most likely. It's a long drive home from where they had to go," Janet explained. "And after paperwork and stopping to log evidence, it'll be pretty late."

Raina could picture it. "Hey Janet, thank you for calling. I sincerely appreciate it, but I need to go. I don't mean to cut you off at all. Is that okay?"

"Of course. You let me know if you need anything, Raina."

"I will. Thank you again."

Raina was out her door within twenty minutes.

CHANNION BACKED INTO HIS driveway, turned off the lights and the engine. Feeling wiped out, he just sat there for a moment before even unfastening his seatbelt. Knowing Raina wasn't inside waiting for him, he wasn't in any hurry to go into his now-empty house. He felt like he was some lovesick teenager and shook his head.

But he also felt lonely. Very much like how he felt after his mom had died. Knowing the house was once again empty but for him, he fought off the mournful feeling.

Starving since all the small-town fast food places were closed by the time he and his uncle had been able to leave, he'd had to drive all the way home without eating for the past nine hours. They stopped at a small gas station for snacks to get them home.

Channion finally opened his truck door and slid wearily to the ground. He grabbed his bags from the back seat, managing to lock his truck without dropping them.

When he walked inside and turned off his alarm, he noticed the little overhead kitchen light was shining into the hallway. Although he was certain it'd been turned off Sunday morning before they left for her place, they must've left it on by accident. He yawned as he hung up his keys, reset the alarm, and headed toward the bathroom first, then the kitchen.

Flipping on the light, he wondered if he had anything ready to eat. He was in no mood to cook. When he opened the door to the refrigerator to check there first, he smiled broadly. Right smack in the middle where he couldn't miss it was a covered plate of food with a large, bright yellow piece of paper taped on top. He eagerly grabbed the plate and the soft drink he saw right behind it.

His heart flipped over when he removed her note, reading it with a smile.

Hi there, Detective Scott!

I heard you'd be getting in late. (I have my sources.) Figuring you'd be hungry, I decided to share. Try to save some for your lunch tomorrow. The Pepsi is just in case—but you should stick to water this late at night.

I bought you some milk, cereal, eggs, bread, fruit, and turkey bacon. Cook or not cook... Your decision! I used some of my Mitchell Money to buy the food, so no worries.

P.S. Don't forget to set your alarm clock. Sleep well... xo

Channion glanced at the clock on the wall. It was almost two in the morning. He knew she kept her cellphone in her bedroom now, so if he called or texted her, it might ring and wake her up. But he decided it was worth the chance.

Getting a plastic container, he cut the food portions in half... saving some for his lunch tomorrow, as instructed. Impatiently waiting for the microwave to heat it up, he shot her a text. As he began to eat, he realized he wasn't feeling so lonely anymore.

NOT BEING ABLE TO sleep well during her first night alone, Raina was half awake when she heard the special ring for Channion's incoming text messages. She reached over to turn on the bedside lamp, put on her glasses, and picked up her phone. She smiled when she read his text.

Thank you so much! Starving. If I woke you up, go back to sleep. You doing okay?

Raina sighed as she read it again. She wondered if she should reply since it was so late. If they started talking now, there'd be no telling when either one would get their much-needed sleep. But since she *was* awake, she decided to reply. Besides, it might worry him if she didn't. Knowing to keep their texts professional, she replied back:

You didn't wake me, still adjusting. I'm fine, don't worry. You're welcome! Very glad you made it home safely. Don't reply to this. Get some rest.

Even though she just told him to *not* reply, Raina scooted up to lean against her headboard, staring expectantly at her phone. She noticed her heart was beating faster in anticipation. As she waited, she glanced at the chair she'd wedged underneath her doorknob. She'd hoped blocking her door shut would give her more security to sleep, but it wasn't. She heard his text tone and laughed out loud at his message.

Is this a test?? Am I really not supposed to reply?

Grinning and not able to resist, she sent one back over.

No, not a test. LOL Sleep!! You've got to be exhausted. We'll talk tomorrow unless you're too busy. Giving lessons between 12-7.

She promptly got another message.

I'll call you in afternoon to check in. OK?

One more message... But *just* one, she told herself.

Appreciate it. Free at 2. Get some sleep now. Good night!

His next text came right over.

Good night!

Leaning over, she plugged her phone back into the charger before she placed it and her glasses on the nightstand. This time when she turned off her light and slid back down under her covers, Raina realized she felt much, much better. She soon fell asleep with a smile on her face... and a mind that was now at peace.

Chapter 62

IT WAS THAT FOLLOWING Friday evening after work when Raina headed over to the Kramer house for dinner. Ron and Channion were to get there whenever they finished work, and Janet invited Raina over earlier so they could visit while they cooked the meal together.

Raina had just finished setting the table when Ron and Channion arrived. She saw their vehicles pulling up through the large front window. Simply knowing Channion was just outside and ready to walk through that door made her heart beat faster. Her face glowed with anticipation and happiness.

From the kitchen, Janet knew the instant her nephew, and maybe also her husband, arrived. She didn't hear their cars, and she couldn't see the front window... But she *could* see Raina. The older lady leaned against the counter, holding onto the hand towel she'd been drying her hands with. Watching Raina, she smiled at the joy on her face. Young love was so precious, she thought. She remembered the way she'd felt when she first fell in love with her Ronnie.

Now decades later, here she was watching a young lady look at her own nephew, who was like her son, with that same breathless look on her face. The cycle of life just keeps on turning, she thought. The pure and natural beauty of it brought a sheen of tears to her eyes.

She watched a smiling Raina head to the front door, opening it and waiting for Channion to come in. Moving to the corner of the room where she could watch unnoticed, Janet noted the same wide smile on her nephew's face when he spotted Raina. Janet watched in satisfaction as he walked in, wrapped Raina up in a bear hug and gave her a kiss on her cheek. Janet was amused at the chaste kiss, knowing it wouldn't have been if they were alone.

Janet suddenly felt melancholy at the thought of neither her brother nor her sister-in-law being alive to know the woman who finally captured their son's heart. Tears misted her eyes as she watched them. She remembered how alone Channion had felt after his mother died. Janet had tried to keep the promises she'd made to her dear sister-in-law the last time they were together and alone. Now, seeing her nephew so obviously happy eased some pressure from her heart.

Janet quietly slipped upstairs so they didn't see her crying. She was sitting on the bed when her husband walked in their bedroom. Seeing her tears, he quickly shut the door and walked to her.

"Sweetheart! What's the matter?" Ron wrapped his arms around his wife's shoulders.

Leaning into her husband's arms, she shook her head. "Nothing." She sniffled and wiped her cheeks with her hands. "It's just that Raina—" She broke off on a little sob.

"Wouldn't she play with you?" he asked, jokingly.

She snorted on a laugh through her tears. "Ronnie... What?... No... It's just that I saw that look of joy and love on both Channion and Raina's faces when they saw each other just now. It's so sweet and lovely to see, and it pierced my heart. She's the one for him, isn't she? I think she's the one he's been waiting for."

Ron nodded, kissed her hair. "Yes, I think so. She may not be, but that's something for them to figure out. They're being smart about it, taking their time. But she fits right in with us, doesn't she?"

Silently nodding, Janet tried to compose herself. She added quietly, "I wish Jason and Nikki were here to meet her. I think they'd certainly approve of her, don't you?"

Hugging her tightly to his side, he answered, "Yes, they'd love her as much as we do. And I think she'd love them." Helping his wife recover, he changed the subject. "Now, let me change clothes so we can eat because we're starving. You'd better have our dinner ready!" he teased.

"Hey, *we've* been waiting on *you!*" Janet sat on their bed, watching him exchange his work clothes for more comfortable ones.

Grinning, he said, "Honey? You keep watching me like that and those two downstairs will be eating dinner by themselves, wondering what we're doing up here!"

Janet laughed. "We'd be doing what they better not be! And I say we let them wonder all they want." Walking over to him, she wrapped her arms around his neck, leaned up, and kissed him. "But on the other hand, I was just told you're starving." She walked toward their master bathroom to clean up. With a twinkle in her eyes, she said, "But later on, I'll treat you to dessert."

Ron smiled. "It sounds like my favorite kind."

Downstairs, Channion and Raina were wondering where Janet had gone off to. Raina got the salad dressing and put it on the table. "She was in here when you guys pulled up. I don't know where she went."

"She probably just popped upstairs for something." Channion smelled the stew in the crockpot, and his stomach growled. "They'd better hurry up because I'm starving. How long should we wait?"

Raina whispered, "Since we're alone for a moment, how about a proper kiss this time?"

"Sure." Grinning, he swept her into his arms, holding her face still and kissing her thoroughly. He felt her instantly kissing him back.

"That's more like it!" She smiled before she whispered, "You're a fantastic kisser, in case I haven't mentioned that lately."

He smiled. "You haven't. Shame on you." He leaned down and kissed her again. "I'd have to say the same." Quietly, he added, "One day we won't have to be like this, sweetheart. Your case will end sooner or later."

She ran her hands over his hard chest, sighed. "I know. One day."

They were about ready to begin eating on their own when Janet and Ron finally came back downstairs. Humor in his voice, Channion quipped, "It's about time, you two! It's so rude to make your guests wait for dinner." Turning to a smiling Raina, he gestured, "They're here. Let's eat!"

Chapter 63

ALTHOUGH KEVIN DREYFUSS PLEADED guilty and would normally just have had a sentencing hearing, the Feds and the district attorney's office wanted it all on record. Everything was to be laid out for the official report of what transpired that long ago day, and the subsequent results and events. Everyone involved was required to take the stand.

Today was the first day of testimonies. Raina's turn to testify was coming up. She'd been told Bryce was up before her. She figured it all started with them, so it made sense.

Dressed in a burgundy business suit, she presented a look of both professionalism and yet femininity. She possessed a quality that showed her strength but also said she was a woman. Waiting in a secure room with two trusted guards outside the door, Raina patiently sat in the chair, waiting for her time to testify.

As she waited, it occurred to her that everything was going to be recorded in official books. *Her* name, *her* story, were going down into permanent record. She, Raina Stewart, was going down in history.

Would someone in the distant future run across her case in some law book, some newspaper article? Would they wonder if what they read was the whole truth? Would they believe everything that'd happened, especially to her? Would they want to delve into it even more? Would someone be interested in what had gone on in her personal life?

Or would it all just go into public record and be forgotten for eternity? Would everything she and Bryce endured be important only in *their* lifetimes? Important only to those affected directly? Would anyone else even care? *Ever?*

When the two officers opened the door to escort her to the courtroom, she suddenly felt like she needed more time. Trying to compose herself and calm her racing heart, she stood up. Taking a deep breath, she followed them into the courtroom.

She made her way to the witness stand, took the oath, and sat down. She saw Channion, Ron, Janet, Conrad, Meredith, and Bethany sitting on the hard wooden pews. She also saw Nurses Carter and Laurel and smiled at them. She nodded to Chris Patton, Mark

Lyles, and a few other ATF agents there as well as Chief Coutts. He'd been a much nicer person since the day she'd lost her marbles (as she described it) with him. She wouldn't go so far as to call him a good friend, but they *were* on friendlier terms.

As she waited for the questions to begin, she looked directly at Kevin Dreyfuss. He sat there beside his lawyer, watching her. She wondered what was going through his mind. He didn't look scared or nervous. He looked... complacent. Smug.

Her attention turned back to the prosecuting attorney, Mr. Cannon. He'd given her a moment to adjust being on the witness stand, letting her settle. "Miss Stewart, where were you on May fourth of this year?"

She answered the questions as she'd been instructed, using facts and the truth.

She wasn't wholly prepared when the attorney announced the video from the officer's car would be played in its entirety. Why did they need to play it? she wondered, panic coming in a flash.

Channion made eye contact with her, telling her to be calm without saying a word. He'd seen the look of partial panic cross her face at the announcement that the video was to be played. Ron had seen it too. Both men sat there, willing her to be strong like she'd been all along. Both were now glad they'd let her watch some of it before as it wouldn't be as jarring to her now.

Sitting in the witness stand, she sat there in silence as she watched and listened to the video from start to finish for the first time. Her breathing escalated as she watched herself being attacked, heard her own screams of pain and terror. She watched as she tried to get to Bryce... Just to be viciously attacked again. She saw herself moving from one vehicle to another, recording evidence in case she didn't make it out of there alive herself —which she barely did.

She listened to the 9-1-1 call she'd made as she drove the police car to the hospital, miraculously making it there in time to save Bryce's life. She could barely understand her own words and wondered how the dispatcher had.

When the video and the recording of the 9-1-1 call ended, the courtroom was completely silent. Silent except for the sniffles from those who just fully realized what had happened that day.

With a fierce concentration, Raina worked to control her breathing, quickly blinking away the tears. She absolutely refused to give Kevin Dreyfuss the satisfaction of seeing that show of weakness, of showing *any* type of vulnerability. Murderers didn't deserve that kind of victory.

"Miss Stewart, can you confirm for the court that the courageous woman in this video is you?" Mr. Cannon asked.

Her voice was firm when she replied, "Yes, it's me... Raina Stewart."

"Is the man who *attacked* you, who nearly *killed* you, as we all just witnessed in that video, in this courtroom?" Mr. Cannon questioned her, sensing her inner battle to hold herself together. His gaze was firm, trying to give her some of his strength. Because he was so close to her, he could see her shaking. The judge could too.

"Yes." Raina tried to sound firm.

"Can you point him out to us?"

She did. Dreyfuss sent a hard glare at her. She stared back, refusing again to let him have the upper hand.

Ron and Channion sat there, willing her to get through this part. They could tell the video and hearing the 9-1-1 call for the first time had shaken her up, but she was holding her own.

Again, she answered the attorney's questions, clarifying parts in the video for all to understand.

Mr. Cannon brought into evidence her old cellphone and the digital camera, playing the videos, and showing the pictures she'd taken that day. She answered his questions calmly and directly. He asked for other ways she'd helped the authorities identify and confirm Kevin Dreyfuss was one of her attackers. She explained about smelling his cologne and letting the police know, and how she was told once he was arrested, he smelled like *Polo For Men*, just as she'd remembered.

When Mr. Cannon discussed her house being broken into, and her horses being killed, Raina locked it tight inside herself. She tried to see it as someone else, removing herself from the scene as much as she possibly could. For whatever reason, she wasn't wholly prepared for her home being discussed.

She was so focused on the attacks, the video, the hospital stay, her cameras, even the cologne, that she almost forgot the rest had even happened. Was her mind trying to block it out now?

She heard the defense attorney call out, "Your Honor, there is no evidence my client had anything to do with this alleged home invasion taking place, or the alleged killing of her horses. He shouldn't be held responsible as he's never admitted guilt to either of these two alleged incidents."

The judge looked at Mr. Cannon, who asked for a little leeway. The judge granted him what he'd asked. Although this wasn't an actual trial, she supposed his lawyer had to still protect his rights.

Panic hit her with the thought of them showing photo evidence of her house being broken into, and her horses killed. There was no way she wouldn't break down seeing Aspen and Rodeo dead. Her heart rate sped up, and her hands began to sweat. She turned her focus back to Mr. Cannon as he began to speak to her.

They discussed her injuries, her nightmares, her memories, her conclusions. Everything. Even how she'd been put into protective custody. Just not where, when, or with whom. They thankfully did *not* show photos of her house or horses.

When Mr. Cannon finally rested, the defense attorney stood. He looked at Raina for a long moment before saying, "No questions, Your Honor." He promptly sat back down.

The judge nodded before looking at her. "The witness can be excused."

Raina paused to look at Dreyfuss. Something about him wasn't feeling right with her. He was to be locked away now, for a long, long time... until he died of natural causes or a prison riot. He wasn't to have the chance of parole, ever. If he knew this, why was he looking so righteous sitting there? Like it was *he* who'd won? Did he know something they, or she, didn't?

"Miss Stewart? You may step down now," the judge repeated. He noticed her studying the defendant and wondered about it.

Nodding at the judge to show she heard him, Raina still remained seated. In a soft voice, she said to him, "Yes, Your Honor. I just need a minute here."

Although he didn't understand, he nodded.

This was her moment of closure. She wanted to be able to remember it.

Everyone in the courtroom was looking at her, wondering what was happening. No one made a sound. It became eerie as they all watched the lone woman sitting perfectly still in the witness stand, not just *looking* at the man accused of her own attempted murder, but *studying* him.

After a while, she looked directly at Channion and Ron, offering a weak smile and a nod. Fighting hard to hold back her tears, she mouthed the words "Thank you" to them. They both smiled and nodded back, so very proud of her for hanging in there while her entire life was taken away from her.

Channion blew out a breath, so proud of her on so many levels, he couldn't begin to describe his emotions even to himself. If she didn't get off the stand, he was worried *he'd* start crying for her. Ron was so proud of her he thought he might burst. Janet reached over and held tightly to her husband's hand.

Next, she rested her gaze on Dreyfuss yet again. Her unflinching look remained on him for so long, the smirk actually left his face. Only then was she satisfied enough to leave.

Raina stood up and turned to step down from the old, plainly-carved wooden witness stand, praying her shaky legs wouldn't fail her now. She paused at the defendant's table. She said directly to Dreyfuss, "I won. You may have tried to beat me to death, but here at the end? It looks like I beat you."

Dreyfuss lunged forward like he was going to attack her. Hate spewed from his eyes. His lawyer grabbed his arm, holding him back. Raina bravely stood her ground. She never even flinched. The bailiff and a US marshal moved closer toward Dreyfuss in case they were needed.

When the man who'd tried to kill her sat back in his chair, she knew she had the closure she needed personally. She'd stood up to him, and he'd backed down. She was back in control of her life again. She was no longer at his mercy.

Walking down the aisle, not looking at anyone else, she saw another court officer open one of the double doors for her as she neared him. She nodded her thanks as she passed by. She made her way out of the courtroom, sitting down on one of the benches down the hallway. Her knees and hands were still shaking so she concentrated on calming herself down.

Clearing her mind and closing her eyes, she realized the heavy weight she'd been carrying was gone. It was over. She'd done her duty. But most importantly, she'd lived.

Chapter 64

"EXCUSE ME."

Raina opened her eyes to see an older man with a cane looking at her.

He asked, "I've never been here before, but do you know if they have a water fountain near here? It's time for me to take my pills, and I need some water for them."

She scrambled to get her mind back in gear. "Um, yes, sir. I think I saw a couple down this hallway, on the left. Would you like me to go check in case I'm wrong? It'd save you the walking..."

The older man gave her a sweet, genuine smile. "That's awfully kind and thoughtful of you, miss. Thank you, but I could use the exercise. It keeps my joints from locking up on me."

He sighed before saying softly, "The first step is always the hardest with this blasted thing." He looked at her again, almost intently like he wanted to memorize her features. "Thank you for your help again, young lady. It's rare to meet someone like you nowadays. Thank you for taking care of a stranger."

Raina nodded, a bit puzzled by his words. It seemed like he was referring to something else entirely.

He said, "It was a pleasure speaking with you."

Raina had an image flash through her mind, one she couldn't grasp. With a curious look on her face, she asked, "I'm sorry, but have we met before?"

The man looked at her again, a small smile on his mouth. "No, we've never met before. If we did, I don't think I'd forget a lady like you, no matter how old I got."

She smiled.

He paused, looked around for a moment, like he was getting his bearings or making sure they were alone. "May I sit for a moment with you?" At her nod, he sat down beside her. "I've been told I'm a good judge of character. Let's see if I'm right."

He smiled at her before he said seriously, "To me, you seem to be a lady of strength, a woman of great courage. You're kind, doing your best to help others in need. I can sense honesty and loyalty in you too. And a passion for life. You come across to me like you have grit."

As he searched her eyes, he said, "You stay true to your heart, miss. Take it from an old man... You live your life on your own terms. Be willing to take risks and chances that could better your life. Don't put off today what tomorrow may never bring your way again. You understand?"

Raina nodded, impulsively taking hold of his hand. "Yes, I do." She inquired of him, "How about you? It sounds like tomorrow didn't give you back what you wanted most?"

She was perceptive, the man thought. "You're correct, my dear. Tomorrow snatched away the *one* tomorrow I lived for. Tomorrow waits for no man, nor can she. Nor should she."

Raina replied gently, "I bet she was both something and someone ultra special to you."

The man sat there, his gaze fixed on the lovely woman who still held his hand in kindness. Yes, very perceptive. "She was my world, my galaxy, my entire universe."

"I'm so sorry." And Raina was. "To be alone can be hard for some, but to be alone after you've known great love? It's unbearable to even think about."

He heard—and *felt*—the sincerity in her words. "You're quite right." He squeezed her hand before letting it go. His time table was getting shorter, and he needed to move along. "Now you remember what I told you. And thank you for all you've done for me." Pushing to his feet, he stood there and looked at her again. "Thank you."

"You're welcome," Raina replied. As she watched him walk away, she wondered what his life's story was.

It wasn't too long afterward when she saw Bryce coming down the hallway from where she'd sent the older man. She smiled in relief at seeing a familiar face.

Seeing her, Bryce smiled back. Sitting down beside her, he asked, "How're you holding up, Raina?" He reached for her hand, held it gently in his.

She realized this was the first time she'd ever seen Bryce in his uniform since the day she'd saved him. She didn't want to mention that though.

Instead, she replied, "A little shaken. I wasn't expecting them to show the video. I'd never seen it all before or heard the 9-1-1 call."

"Yeah, I know what you mean. They showed just the beginning part of the video with me. Basically up to when you showed up. They obviously kept the best for last, and used it for their best advantage, didn't they?"

He let out a long sigh, still holding onto her hand. They both needed the comfort of a human touch. It helped when it came from one who knew exactly what the other was feeling.

Looking at him, she asked, "How about *you?* Are you doing okay?"

He shrugged his wide shoulders, saying, "I guess it's giving me some closure. He's caught and going to prison. Personally, I'd rather he not be alive because he's not one to be trusted."

He paused. "It's also stirring up some uncomfortable feelings and memories. I told you before I had nightmares. I'm down to just an occasional bad dream now. I hope this doesn't bring it all back, you know? They'd probably make me go through psych testing again or something."

"I was worried about that too." She let out a long breath, admitting to him, "But it's over for me, I think. This was the closure *I* needed. I made it through the Valley of Death, walked and crawled my way through one hell after another to get to this point. Facing Dreyfuss? Letting him know I won? *That* was what I needed.

"I don't know what else will come my way in regards to this case, or my life in general, but this was a big goal. I lived to see that Dreyfuss was caught. And I did what I could by testifying for both you and me. What they do now is beyond my control, I guess."

Bryce nodded in understanding. He admitted softly, "It sometimes gives me comfort to know that if I *hadn't* made it, you'd have been here to tell our story. And you could hopefully get me, and my family, justice. Thank you, Raina. For everything."

"You're welcome, Bryce." After a moment, she said, "You must be fine mentally if they let you back even on light duty, right? They even let you carry a gun again. If they did that, they must think you're strong enough to handle this."

"More or less. I'm not a mental case anyway."

"I've heard rumors," she deadpanned and was rewarded with his smile.

After a moment, he said, "It could be months yet for me to be back on regular duty, but maybe not. The desk duty isn't all that bad, but I'd rather be out on patrol. And I'm still considering the dispatcher position.

"I may have been released from the doctors overall, but I still go to required check-ups. I'm sure I'm fine, and my body is healed well enough. It's probably best to take my time though. And it's more of an insurance issue, I think."

"You think? You still look too skinny for my taste," she teased him, leaning into his side. "You need to increase your intake of donuts! I do believe you're shirking your duty, Deputy Mitchell."

He groaned. "Have you been talking to Mom, Raina? Bless her heart, but she's driving me nuts. Thank goodness I live in my own place again!"

She chuckled, appreciating his feelings.

"But if *you* think I need to eat more donuts, I'm willing to meet you for breakfast. Name the place and time, and I'll be there," he joked.

She chuckled. "I'll let you know." She looked closely at him before saying seriously, "You do know if you ever need to talk, I'll always be here for you, right? And it'll stay with me."

Bryce squeezed her hand. "Thank you, Raina. You never know. I might take you up on that."

She hesitated before saying, "I know we met under the most extreme of circumstances, but I'd like it if we could remain friends. You and your family are always welcome in my life. I'd mean that even if you all didn't do what you did for me. You're all just good people."

He smiled. "Thank you. I hope we can stay friends too. Even if we don't, I'll still tell Luke we are just to irritate the jerk."

Surprised, she looked at him. "Aren't you friends with Luke?"

"Loosely. I heard how he checked you out when you went in that first day. How he could do that to you so soon after leaving the hospital, saving my life, almost dying? It still pisses me off."

"Did Ron or Channion tell you that?"

"Neither. I won't say who, but it was from more than one person. It didn't go over very well with anyone. I'm glad Ron and Channion laid into him over it." He noticed her surprised look. "I guess you didn't know that?"

Raina shook her head.

"Oh. It might be better to keep that between us."

"Sure. I always did kinda wonder why he didn't come back for round two. His kind always does when they strike out. Thanks for letting me know."

She fleetingly wondered about the old man. Had he found the water fountains? She figured he'd be back this way soon. The restrooms were there, too, she supposed. Well, it must wrap around, as Bryce had come from there, and she never saw him go there in the first place.

The two of them sat in the hallway for another couple of hours, talking until finally the doors opened and people began filing out. Ron, Channion, and Mark spotted them and headed over.

Mark said, "We're done for the day. A little more tomorrow, and it should be all wrapped up for you two."

Raina and Bryce both nodded, but neither moved.

Channion said, "The nurses had to leave for work but said to pass along their hellos and best wishes." He looked at her. "You okay?"

"Yeah. But why's Dreyfuss looking so smug in there? Is something going on that I don't know about?"

"We noticed that too. Nothing has changed as far as we're aware. He shouldn't be looking like that at all. His life is over, but he sure doesn't act like it." It worried Channion, and he hoped it didn't show.

Ron said, "He's a hardened criminal. He wouldn't be one if he let his emotions show."

Shaking her head, Raina said, "No, I feel there's more to it." A thought came to her. "Channion's right. His life *is* over. That's why he turned on everybody he could. He won't make it long in prison at all. He already knows he's on borrowed time. He won't suffer at all in prison because he won't live long enough to."

The men looked at her. Channion stared at her for a long moment. He thought she hit the nail right on the head. *Lurking dangers* suddenly popped in his head.

Bryce still offered his guess. "It could be a façade. He doesn't want us to think we won. Is it a mind game? Maybe he wants us to *think* he has something up his sleeve we don't know about. I think we'd better be prepared in case he does."

Mark said, "I agree with you, Bryce, on all points. I also agree with Raina. We can't lower our defenses. It might be just what he's waiting for."

Chapter 65

THE NEXT DAY, THEY all watched and listened as the case was being wrapped up. Again, the defendant seemed unaffected by it all.

When he took the stand, Dreyfuss answered numerous questions about Colt Buchanan's organization and many of the people in it. He admitted to attacking Miss Stewart that day. And he didn't deny the break-in had happened this time. He just said he wasn't a part of it, but he did know about it. He nonchalantly gave the names of the men who were involved. All of them were already on his previous lists for his plea deal. But he still denied the shooting of her horses.

Raina was confused and irritated about that. She wanted *someone* to admit to killing her kids! She *needed* that! Her best guess was he knew it—and *that* was the sole reason he wouldn't admit it. It was a sick mind game. He was still trying to control her.

At the end of the long day, the case was basically closed. Raina sat there quietly while most of the courtroom emptied out. The Mitchells hugged Raina before they walked out of the room with Janet, assuming she and the detectives may want a private word amongst themselves.

It dawned on her there were two people she hadn't seen or heard a word about whatsoever... Lori and Zach Coleman. Where were they?

Channion and Ron stayed beside her while Bryce talked to the ATF agents at the back of the room. Ron said, "Raina, it's over. But for a few loose ends for the paper pushers to do, you're free again."

She nodded.

Channion covered her hand with his, giving it a reassuring squeeze. "It'll probably take a bit of time to really sink in. But your involvement is over. The case is more or less closed. But not officially, and that's what *we* need. But overall, yeah, it's done. Everything that happened is now on the record. However, we—"

They all heard screams and yells coming from outside the courtroom. The ATF agents ran out with Channion, Ron, Raina, and Bryce right behind them. They headed toward the commotion, pushing past people who were running against them, trying to get away.

They were stopped by the court officers who weren't letting anybody past them. Mark held up his badge, demanding, "What's happened? What's going on?"

The court officer answered, "We're in lockdown. That prisoner named Dreyfuss got shot! He's dead!"

Channion looked straight at Raina and saw her pale face. Once again, she'd been right.

Chapter 66

THEY WERE BACK PLAYING on defense. For safety, Bryce and Raina were immediately put into protective custody again.

Raina was slipped back into Channion's house, both under orders to stay low and silent. Like Bryce's, her phone was turned off before they even left the courthouse so their locations couldn't be traced. Ron called the studio to get her lessons canceled yet again, and then called Picacho's.

It was the second night at Channion's that he sat her down and told her the truth about Aspen and Rodeo's deaths. That it was Lori's idea to shoot them, and young Zach who did it, completely astonished Raina. She couldn't comprehend what she was being told. It took a long time for the truth to settle in her mind. Her shocked denials and endless questions just drew out the inevitable. Channion held her tightly as she cried.

He also explained why he and Ron hadn't told her previously, but he just couldn't take it himself anymore. The simple truth was, Channion felt she more than deserved the truth about her own kids' deaths. He respected her far too much to deny her that.

The fact she understood why he and Ron hadn't told her before relieved his mind and heart. He was afraid she'd hold it against him, and their personal relationship was too new to withstand the pressure. But she'd told him she understood—but that he'd done the right thing by telling her the truth.

That night, they shared his bed so he could hold her while she slept. Her dreams were dark, and she awoke more than once crying. He was there for her every time, ready to soothe and console her in her fresh heartbreak.

The next decision was hers on whether or not to press charges against Lori and Zach. They debated it, weighing her pain to the mere slap on the wrist they'd get if she did. She felt her kids deserved justice, but she also didn't believe the charges would even matter. But at least she'd be doing *something* for them even if it was too late.

Would filing charges help her heal, or just prolong her pain? Neither of them knew.

"What do you guys have on the Dreyfuss killing?" Channion asked.

It was the first day in over a week he'd been allowed to leave his own home. Raina was still there as he came in to get a case report in person.

Diggs sighed. "Not much at all. We know the possible weapon used, and the assumed trajectory of the bullet even though we have no bullet. We know *when* he was killed since it was witnessed by a whole lot of people. We just don't know the who, how, or the why.

"This was for sure a professional hit. No amateur could've made a shot like that. Whoever it was had to be patient, precise, and know the schedule. He took a head shot, not a body shot. To me, this shows he was confident he could make good on his shot. He only took one, and he made it count. Sniper.

"No one has anything to go on. Not us, the FBI, or ATF. There's been no chatter anywhere that even mentioned the killing of Dreyfuss. There's also been nothing about Raina and Bryce."

Channion wasn't surprised. "Another ghost. Or the same one."

Diggs asked, "You think whoever shot Dreyfuss is the same shooter as Buchanan?"

Channion nodded. "Out of all of this, it's the *only* thing that makes any sense."

"Well, welcome to the club. It's the shared theory amongst all of us."

"At least neither one of us are going to be looking over our shoulders. And we won't be calling the prison on a regular basis just to make sure he didn't get released. Or worrying about hits being put out there. Maybe that's what the shooter's point was... Maybe it's all for safety. Either way, *our* job was to catch him and gather the evidence. It was up to someone else to judge and carry out the sentence."

Diggs leaned back in his chair. "And someone surely did."

Channion nodded. "Yes. Someone."

And he had a good idea who knew.

It was being counted as a victory. Solomon looked over when his door opened. "Come on in, Storm." He turned off the news shows he watched regularly, normally just to see how much they got wrong.

Storm rested his cane beside the chair before taking a seat. After a moment, he inquired, "Do you have any news about the latest?"

"No, nothing new that we've heard. It was clean. Considering the risk level involved, it was a small miracle. It's a shame we had to make it public. On the other hand, it did have a couple advantages.

"I still deeply regret the young woman and the officer had their names and faces put out there though. But we had to factor that in as a calculated risk. In the end, it was worth it." He sighed before asking, "Is their case closed now?"

Storm considered before answering. "As far as our sources can tell, it will be soon. The Feds and locals are still working the case, but they'll just hit dead ends. We didn't leave any evidence behind that they can use to further their investigation. They won't have much choice *but* to close it.

"However, I wish we could let them know that Dreyfuss was the only target. Maybe we could leak that to a CI to let them know. With that one message Dreyfuss got out for a hit on Miss Stewart, it forced us into action sooner than we wanted. It was a very good thing we were watching Dreyfuss like we were because that was a close one.

"We're still pretty sure that was the only one, but we'll keep our eye on her for a while yet. His grudge was apparently against just her as he didn't put a hit out on Deputy Mitchell. I told the team we'll also watch him for a while to be on the safe side. We'll listen to the chatter out there as well, of course. No need for any of us to get too confident or sloppy now."

They sat in comfortable silence for a while before Solomon said, "You look and sound tired."

"I am, but it's winding down now." He offered a small smile. "Don't worry about me, Solomon. You're acting like a worried mommy!"

With a wide smile, he replied, "I'll try to stop." He paused. "Are you heading home soon?"

"No, not yet. Not until I know they're all safe."

Chapter 67

IT WAS THREE WEEKS later when Raina got a call from Chief Coutts, asking her if she could come to the station the following day at two for a meeting. Feeling a bit anxious, she agreed.

The next afternoon, Raina parked her truck in the police station's parking lot. She felt exposed since it was the first time she wasn't in the parking garage to enter the building. She walked inside and saw Channion waiting for her by the high counter and smiled.

With a straight face, he said, "I drew the short straw so I'm your escort."

She grinned at his teasing. "Oh, thanks," she said as he handed her a Visitor's Pass. "I see you're prepared."

His eyes sparkled with humor when he answered, "Of course I'm prepared. I was in the Girl Scouts when I was a boy."

She laughed. He actually remembered the story she'd told him underneath his tree that long-ago day.

When they entered the chief's office, she was surprised to see Bryce and Ron sitting in chairs already, talking. They both smiled at her when they walked in. Taking the two empty chairs, Channion and Raina sat down while they all waited on the chief.

Raina leaned toward Bryce. "Do *you* know why we're here?"

Bryce shook his head and smiled at her. "My guess is it's about closing our case. What *else* would it be?"

"Well, I wasn't sure before because I didn't know you were going to be here. But since you are, let's hope you're right!"

After a few more minutes, Chief Coutts entered his office carrying a mug of fresh coffee. Looking at Raina, he made a point of closing the door. She actually had to smile, realizing the chief may have a sense of humor after all. He nodded to them all before sitting in his large chair behind the desk, setting his coffee mug out of the way. With no preamble at all, he got to the point.

"I've called you four in here today to clear up this case of yours. I've already spoken with Agent Lyles with ATF and with the sheriff's department. We're all in agreement.

"Although everyone has been putting in long hours to find the shooter of both Buchanan and Dreyfuss, we have no more leads to follow. And thanks to the information we received via a reliable CI, we know that Miss Stewart and Deputy Mitchell here are presumed safe. Only Kevin Dreyfuss was the target that day at the courthouse.

"Fortunately, Buchanan and Dreyfuss were the last two main suspects *we* specifically wanted in regards to both Deputy Mitchell and Miss Stewart here. Happily, this is because they killed off their own man that we also wanted and saved us the bother. And now since Buchanan and Dreyfuss have both been taken care of, it seems we're done. If this keeps up, we'll all be out of a job."

He saw their slight smiles as he paused, straightened the papers in front of him. "That being said, I propose that we officially close this case that involves Deputy Mitchell and Miss Stewart here."

Silence filled the room. Chief Coutts could see the relief and satisfaction on all of their faces. He took a careful sip of his coffee, waiting for any questions. He leaned forward, bracing his elbows on his desk. It looked like *he* was going to be the one to ask the questions instead.

"Although I'm leery of asking, I feel I should." Looking directly at Raina, he asked, "Miss Stewart?"

"Yes?"

"Closing your case at this point, does this meet with your approval?" He kept a straight face as he looked at her.

Raina looked surprised. "Of course it does. It doesn't sound like there's any need or reason to continue with it. It seems over. But..."

Coutts sighed loudly while he leaned back in his chair. "But *what?*"

Before she could stop herself, she blurted out, "Why do you care what I think?"

She was genuinely perplexed. Raina glanced at Ron and Channion, noticing they were trying to hold back their smiles. She couldn't see Bryce's face since he was sitting on the other side of Ron.

Chief Coutts grinned because he couldn't help it. "*Why?* Why do you think? *You're* Raina Stewart, remember? I seem to recall a time when you demanded to be consulted on your case."

It took only a second for her to catch on. She blushed in faint embarrassment. "Oh."
She smiled before saying, "Yes, I'm satisfied that everyone has done what they could do,
and there's nothing left *to* do. I'd be happy and quite relieved to know this case is closed.
It's been a long time coming, hasn't it?"

"Yes, it has." Coutts nodded and smiled at her.

Raina asked, with just a hint of hesitation, "So as of right now, we're all free and on our
own again? No ties to this case to hang over our heads? We're done, finished? Forever?"

Coutts looked at her for a moment before answering her. He noticed Channion was
smiling broadly as was his uncle. Was he missing something here? Coutts glanced at Bryce,
who just looked satisfied it was over.

Looking back at Raina, he said, "Yes, the case is officially closed. You're all free to go.
Thank you all for the work you've put in to solve it. Deputy Mitchell and Miss Stewart,
I'm glad you're both still with us and doing much better. I know it's still a road to full
recovery, but I think maybe the hardest parts are behind you both."

He looked at the three men in his office. "I wanted to get you all here together in case
someone"—he looked pointedly back at Raina—"had something to add or contest. But
we're all on the same page? Or does anyone want to add anything?"

Everyone looked at each other before shaking their heads. Channion smiled and said,
"No, sir. I'd say we're all good with the case being closed and put to rest. I'd say everything
turned out for the best."

"Good." Leaning forward in his chair, Chief Coutts smiled. "Now get out of here."

They were all smiling as they filed out the door. A moment later, Chief Coutts barked
out, "Sergeant Scott!"

Channion stopped and shrugged his shoulders. "Raina, go ahead with Ron and Bryce.
I'll meet you at the desks." He turned around and walked back into the chief's office.

"Shut the door."

Channion closed the door, wondering what was going on. Facing his superior, he
asked, "Yes, sir?"

"You've been with this department quite a while, Sergeant. Do you consider yourself
a smart man?"

"Not any more than most, but more than many, sir."

Chief Coutts smiled at his answer before prodding, "Patient?"

"Very much so."

"You think you have the ethics and honor enough to serve in this department?"

"Absolutely," he replied firmly.

Chief Coutts nodded as he studied the man standing before him before asking, "How are you at taking advice?"

Channion hesitated, wondering where this conversation was headed. Finally, he said truthfully, "I guess it'd depend on the advice, and who was giving it. I can take it or leave it."

"Well, I'm going to give you some here. You can do with it whatever you'd like." He watched as the officer in front of him straightened his shoulders and raised his chin, probably unconscious gestures. "That Miss Stewart is a special woman, wouldn't you say?"

Channion only nodded.

"All I'm going to say is women like that don't come around every day. And if you're as smart as you say you are, you picked up on that months ago. And if so, my guess is with your sense of ethics and honor that everyone else around here says you have, you've been keeping your relationship with Miss Stewart professional since you've been working her case."

He abruptly stopped talking. Reaching into his inbox on his large desk, he grabbed a file. He began to read it, flipping through a couple of pages.

Silently, Channion waited for him to continue, but he seemed to be done talking. Not knowing exactly what he was supposed to do—stay or go—he inquired, "Sir? You said something about advice?"

Looking up, the chief smiled. "Sergeant, I told you before. The case is officially closed now. You may go. Why don't you take Miss Stewart out for a celebratory dinner? Charge it to your expense account if you want to. Just this once though."

With a smile, Channion said, "Thank you, sir. I'll do that."

Chapter 68

Late May, seven months later at the Kramer house

"RAINA? YOU IN HERE?" Janet peeked around the bedroom door. Seeing Raina sitting on the bed, she asked, "Can I come in?"

"Of course. Find yourself a seat up here." Raina moved her legs over. She had soft music playing on her CD player, and a small lilac-scented candle flickering on the dresser.

Janet closed the door and sat down on the bed. She held a large brown envelope in her hand. "I was hoping I could find a minute alone with you tonight. I have to admit, I sent your friends and Bethany off with my girls for a while. I told them you needed some time alone, but it was because I really needed to talk to you myself. I have something for you."

Janet handed Raina the envelope and looked down at it. After a few moments of silence, she looked up at Raina, her eyes misty with tears.

"Oh, no. Janet... Stop! For Pete's sake, don't you dare start crying on me now. I thought we passed this phase already! I've been plugging it up myself all day long. I even managed to make it through most of the rehearsal dinner, but if you start..." She quickly grabbed the box of tissues from the bedside table and handed it to the woman she'd begun to think of as an adopted mother as well as a true and wise friend.

"I'm sorry, Raina. Ever since you and Channion announced your engagement, I've been looking forward to this moment. I can't believe it's tomorrow!" She smiled, patting Raina's hand. "I can still see Channion as a bright, energetic young boy running around with Ty and their cousins. And now he's a grown man about to be married!"

Raina smiled back. "I know we set a fast date. We just didn't see the point in waiting months and months to do it. We did wonder if it was too soon. Do we *really* know each other enough? But we decided it's different for every couple, and we both felt comfortable with our decision. With our schedules, we felt it'd be better to do earlier than later. Hopefully we're right.

"I mean, we could wait another year or so, but we decided we're both getting too old. We have to live our lives now and on our own terms. Life's too short, as we all know. And as it turned out, it was exactly one year to the month from when we met. It just seemed right, you know?"

The older woman nodded in understanding. "And you're right. Time doesn't mean the same to every couple. It's what you both feel that matters. Neither one of you are spontaneous in this regard. Both of you have been upfront, responsible, and mature from the get-go.

"You've both been through a lot over the past year, and I think it eliminated the extra time some people would need to know each other better. You two just *fit*, Raina, and not all couples do. If we didn't *feel* that rightness from you two, we might worry. But Ronnie and I aren't worried about the time issue, in case you thought we might be." Looking at her, she asked, "Are you nervous?"

Raina looked at the flickering candle before she said quietly, "No, I'm not nervous. But I'm missing my mama so much right now. I was just now wishing she was here with me. We always had such plans for my wedding. And now it's here, but she's not."

Her chin quivered, showing her fight to not cry. But the tears began to fall, and she couldn't stop them. She felt Janet move to her to wrap her up in a tight, comforting hug. She cried in the older woman's arms. Her broken heart ached because her sweet and supportive mama wasn't able to share this moment with her.

Janet rocked Raina in her arms, her own tears flowing in compassion for her. She knew the one thing that most any woman wanted at her wedding was her mother. She knew she couldn't replace Raina's mother, but she sure wanted to try.

Finally, Raina's tears slowed. She grabbed the tissues back and blew her nose. She grabbed a couple more and wiped her face. Janet did the same to her own, tossing her tissues in the waste basket beside the dresser.

Blowing out a breath, Raina said softly, "You know, I was just fine until you came in here! Now look at the two of us. Do we honestly think we're going to make it through tomorrow?"

Smiling, Janet cupped her cheek. "We'll get through it one way or another!" She picked up the envelope she'd brought in. "Speaking of mothers, Nikki and I were close. One of the last times I ever got to talk with Nikki, we discussed Channion. She loved him so much! She worried about how he'd cope with her death. He'd be all alone but for us."

Janet looked down for a moment before going on. "She asked me to be there for him through thick and thin. Thankfully, Channion made this so easy to do. He was never a burden to us. Anyway, Nikki made me make certain promises to her before she could go with a clear mind." She took a deep breath, let it out.

Raina looked down at the large envelope Janet handed her again. There was a slight bulge in it. On the outside, it read: *To Her, My Daughter-in-Law*. Her breath hitched as she looked up quickly and met Janet's eyes.

"Nikki wrote a letter and asked me to give it to the woman her son chose to be his bride the night before the wedding." Janet's chin quivered in her bid to not cry again. "I've kept it in my safe deposit box all these years. For you, Raina."

Janet slowly got up from the bed, bent down to kiss Raina's cheek. Patting it gently, she said, "I'll leave you alone to read it. I don't know what it says as it was written for you."

Janet headed to the door, looking back again. "Honey, my brother and Nikki would've been so honored and thrilled to have met you. They would've loved you. I have absolutely no doubts about that."

She closed the door, leaving Raina alone with a message from the woman who raised the man who was to become her husband the next day.

Chapter 69

RAINA HELD THE ENVELOPE in her hands for a minute. She wondered what it felt like for a dying mother to write a letter to some unknown woman. A woman who was to marry her only son after she was gone.

When she opened the envelope and pulled out the letter, a lumpy, folded white handkerchief slid out. Unfolding it, she found a silver locket on a braided chain. Opening it, she saw it was empty.

Looking at the letter, she saw handwriting that looked slightly shaky. She imagined it had normally been smooth and beautiful. Holding up the letter to read it, a couple of photographs slid onto her lap.

Raina studied them. One was of Channion's parents on their own wedding day, an excited and happy couple. The other was a picture taken of Nikki and Channion. By the date on the back, Raina judged it to have been taken shortly before she got sick again.

Two ends of her life, she thought. One taken with her new husband, the other taken with their grown son. Nikki and her two best men.

Leaning against the headboard and her pillows, Raina began to read:

My Daughter,

Tomorrow you are to become a Scott... Mrs. Channion Scott! Congratulations, my dear! You're joining a respected and loving family! I was always so proud to sign my new name after my marriage to Jason. I hope you feel it, too.

I'm so sorry and heartbroken to not be there for this moment in my son's life—and in yours. I'd give anything to be there for, and with, you both tomorrow. If my Channion has asked you to marry him, it must mean he loves you very much for he won't marry just anyone. He'll marry only for love and in faith that you'll be his until death parts you.

The locket included in this letter is my gift to you. It was given to me by Channion's father on our wedding day. I feel it proper to pass along this locket to you now for your wedding to our son. Perhaps it will remind you of us, or where your soon-to-be husband came from. I removed our pictures so you could put in new ones of you and Channion... New pictures for a new life together.

I only ask, if for whatever reason you and my son ever find it necessary to go your own ways, that this locket is returned to him. It is very precious to me, and I would ask that it stay in our family. Of course, I hope that will never happen to you.

Marriage will test your love, faith, and strength—and sanity—countless times. Hang in there, my dear! It's so worth it and will make you both stronger! You will both need to remember to truly forgive the other, and to know that beyond every argument, every trial, every setback life will throw at you, there's also a world full of hope and promise waiting for you two.

Remember what you're feeling now—the excitement, the love, the feeling that the two of you can do anything and everything together. For if your love is true, then these feelings will hold true as well. It will not always be easy, but there will be those great times when you feel the world is at your feet to do with as you please. Go and live your lives together to make a new one!

I pray that you're an upstanding woman, one who will see marriage as it should be—to stand by your husband, my son, through good times and bad. And I pray also that you're not one to take the easy and fast road out when things get rough. You stick together. You need to understand that my son and your marriage are your priorities now. And the same applies to him toward you and your marriage together. There should be no greater team than a husband and wife. It may seem like an old-fashioned idea, but let me tell you, it's not.

At this time, my son is a law enforcement officer working toward his Detective shield. If he's still in this career field when you read this, you must already realize it demands a strong woman to stand by him. There will be times your sacrifices for the job will seem more than his own. At times it will be stressful—the not knowing if he's safe, and if he will return home to you. His hours may be long and varied. He has a great love for his job. It is a part of who he is, and what makes him the way he is.

If you love him, you'll know you cannot change this about him. If you have doubts about whether you can be a rock for him, it might be best to postpone the wedding until you are sure, either way. It's better to cause a broken heart now than a broken spirit later.

There are no guarantees in life, my daughter, and we must live our lives to the best of our abilities. Be strong. Be true. Be faithful. Always keep a strong sense of humor! Keep God in your marriage, even if others mock you for it. You need a solid foundation to build on, and you can't get much more solid than Him. When others throw in the towel and separate, you two can stick together and work it out with some help. Don't be afraid, or too proud, to ask for that help.

Tomorrow is your wedding day! I wish I could be here to meet you, to learn about you, to learn why my Channion loves you the way he must. I wish I could see him dressed up in his classy tuxedo, looking sharp like his handsome father did for our own wedding, waiting anxiously for you as you're walking down the aisle in your beautiful gown. I wish I could be there to see you both exchange your vows. I wish I could be there to share in the toast, and to have that mother-son dance at your reception. I wish I could be there to hold my grandchildren (should you have some) and watch them grow. I wish so many things I could never list them all.

You must be such a special lady to have caught his eye and to have captured his heart. I pray you will never break it. And that he never breaks yours. If so, remember there are many things that break that can also be fixed—and a heart is one of the most important things to fix no matter what. It's inevitable that at some time, you'll hurt the other. It's to be expected in any relationship. Just remember to love unconditionally and put pride aside. He's a good man, and he's worth the effort! As I'm sure you are worth the effort for him, too!

Family is very important to my son. I pray that you two have one of your own, if you so wish it yourselves. If you do, please tell them stories about me and Channion's father. Jay and I, we'd love to be remembered in our grandchildren's hearts. Remember they'll be watching you on how to love a man, so please show it to my son as I hope he does to you. Be wonderful role models for your children.

Wishing you all the absolute best as you start your lives together, and with much love,

Nikki Scott

~Mom~

Raina sat there, tears rolling down her cheeks as she read the letter. How painful it must've been to write this! she thought. And how can one put into words all the things she'd like to say to someone she's never met?

Saying a prayer that she could honor Nikki's wishes, Raina could only wish she'd been able to meet her. She sat there, trying to compose herself before her friends and the Kramer daughters came back. She couldn't help but wonder what her own mother might've said not only to her, but to Channion, the night before their wedding.

Chapter 70

THE BOYS WERE HAVING quite the party. Ron walked into Channion's house, hearing music blasting from the stereo and laughter coming from the back. He walked down the hallway, wondering what he'd find at the other end of it.

Smiling, Ty waved him into the room. "There he is! You made it!"

Ron smiled, his eyes sparkling. "It's good to see you all enjoying yourselves."

He eyed the pizza boxes, bags of chips and dips, and the variety of drinks everywhere. Most of the guys were fixated on the new large screen TV they pitched in for as a wedding gift. They were dutifully testing it out by playing video games on it. Ron saw everything except the main man.

"Where's the groom?" Ron asked.

One of his nephews joked, "Probably drowning himself in the pond."

Some of the others laughed as Ron shook his head, smiling.

Ty grinned. "He's downstairs checking on the guys. Their competition was getting a little heated."

Ron sat down on the arm of the couch. "How long are you boys planning on partying?"

Bryce looked over from watching the video game. "What time does it start again?"

Ron grinned. "Two."

"Oh, well, we'll probably be up until that this morning then, at least," he replied cheerfully.

Channion walked into the room and sat down in the only available chair, probably reserved just for him. He smiled at Ron when he saw him.

Marty, one of Ron's many nephews, said, "Sure, Uncle Ron. Once he's a married man, he'll never be able to do this again. He'll be *whipped!* He'll never have the house to himself again. Or have beer and pizza parties with the guys over making a mess of it all. This is his last night of freedom!"

Channion laughed. "Don't bet on it, Marty. Raina will probably be the one organizing the next beer and pizza party! And I'll hardly be whipped."

"Seriously? She'd do that?" another relative asked.

Ron, Channion, Bryce, and Ty all laughed and nodded their heads in agreement.

Channion said to Marty, "And if it's the right woman, you won't feel like you're losing your freedom or feel whipped. That's one of the ways you'll *know* she's the right one."

Ty nodded. "I agree."

Another relative piped up, "You two *always* agree with each other."

"No, we don't!" Both Ty and Channion answered in unison, making the entire room laugh.

Smiling, Ty replied, "When we don't, we just respect the other's opinion even though it's wrong!"

Channion grinned, saying, "I agree!"

They all laughed again.

Ron looked at Channion. His nephew looked relaxed and very happy. With a smile, he motioned for him to come to the kitchen. "I need to borrow this guy for a bit," he called out.

Channion walked to the kitchen and washed his sticky hands as he looked around. "Could be worse, huh?"

They grinned at each other.

"It's in better shape than I expected, to be honest. We'll get it put back to rights by the time you two return. I'll let Raina know she'll still have a house to come back to when I get back home tonight. She sent me over here for intel, you know."

Channion laughed. Leaning against the counter, he asked, "So what really brings you over here?"

"Besides to see how you're doing, I'm on an errand from your aunt. She said I needed to give you something before tomorrow. And I'm to give it to you in private, and you're to read it tonight." Ron handed him the large brown envelope he held. "Here."

Curious, Channion reached for the envelope. He could see a little bulge in it. "What is it?" His heart skipped a beat when he recognized his mom's handwriting.

"It's a letter, I think. Let's go upstairs where it's quiet."

Nodding, Channion led the way upstairs to his bedroom. Closing the door after his uncle, he asked, "This is from Mom?"

"Yeah. Janet told me before Nikki passed away, she gave her some things to take care of and guard over. This is one of them. Your mom told Janet this was to be given to you the night before your wedding. Janet's kept it in her safe deposit box until today.

"She said Nikki never told her what it said or was, and it was sealed when Nikki gave it to her. It's never been unsealed because it's a private message from your mom to you. It's no one's business but yours. It's your gift from your mom."

Channion nodded, emotions swelling in his heart so fast it hurt to even breathe.

"I'll tell the guys to let you be for a while."

"Thanks, I'd appreciate it."

"Channion, I knew I could never replace your own father. I never had a son, but I always enjoyed thinking of you as the one I could've had. You've made both your aunt and I proud, and you've grown into a very fine man.

"We love Raina and couldn't be more pleased that you two found each other. And both Janet and I agree that your mom and dad would've welcomed Raina with both their arms wide open, a huge smile on their faces. We just wish they could be here with you."

Hearing that about his parents made him feel better. "I always thought Mom and Dad would've loved her too." He paused. "Thanks for always being there for me, Ron. I was always thankful to have you and Janet, but especially you, since Dad died. You helped raise me, and I only hope to be as good a father to my kids one day as Dad and you were to me."

Ron felt his eyes burn with tears. "It was a pleasure, Channion, to be there to help raise you, but your mother did most of it. The credit belongs to her and your dad. I know without a doubt she'd be so proud of you. *Both* of them would be. And I know she'd wish she could be here and would wish you the best of all life could give you. She loved you so much."

"Yes, she did. I loved her too. And I love you and Aunt Janet even when I don't say it." He gave a small smile.

His uncle patted his cheek. "We know. We love you, too, Channion." Reaching for the door knob, he said, "Take your time with that. I'll tell the guys to stay downstairs, and you'll come down when you're ready." Opening the door, he said, "I'll be here if you need me for anything."

Closing the door behind him, Ron headed downstairs.

Chapter 71

Away from the noise and activity of his friends and family, Channion sat on his bed. He opened the envelope and pulled out an object wrapped in a bandana. He unfolded it. His dad's watch.

He'd wondered what had happened to it. He'd assumed his mom had buried it with her love. Now he knew. His mom had taken it and put it in a safe place, keeping it for him. He studied it for a moment before placing it beside him.

He slid out the letter and saw the photographs on top. His heart skipped a beat. His parents on their wedding day. His dad looked so young and full of energy! He looked invincible. Transferring his gaze to his mom, he saw how young, beautiful, and happy she was. They both looked radiant.

They had the world at their feet, and they lived in that happy and loving world together for just under twenty years. He and his mom thrived in the bright love that came from his dad until that one horrendous day.

He still recalled how difficult it'd been to accept what they were being told that day. The shock, the disbelief, the denials. Thinking they had it all wrong, and somehow they came to the wrong family, the wrong house. But, unfortunately, they had it all right. But it was anything *but* that.

But they'd made it through the following days, the funeral, and the well-wishers constantly reminding them they'd lost one of their own. He saw in his mind how Ron and Janet, completely devastated themselves, took them both in. How Janet and his mom, both crying, just held each other on the couch downstairs. Janet had lost her big brother, and his mom her devoted husband.

And Ty. *What* would he have done without Ty there as his best friend, his brother?

They were only teenagers, but it didn't matter. Ty was his support in an extremely difficult time. Channion could still remember the day Ty arrived after his mom had called Ty's parents, asking them to please fly Ty in just for him. He was down at the pond, missing his dad so much he couldn't think straight. When he saw Ty come ambling down the hill, he started bawling. And his cousin simply hugged him and let him cry, never once making fun of him for crying like a baby.

With the exception of Ty's beloved black lab Jet dying from cancer that one summer, it was the only time in Channion's memory he could recall Ty crying. He loved his Uncle Jason almost as much as he loved his own dad. But Channion had always felt deep inside that Ty was mourning more for *his* loss of his father than he was for the loss of his uncle. Ty grieved because Channion did.

As a family, they were all able to continue on. That first family reunion was brutal. It took years for him to stop dreading it. He was probably the only kid in school who didn't want summer to come. Summers meant the family reunion was coming. It only made him miss his dad even more.

Now, he suddenly wondered how his mom had felt about the reunions. He'd never once asked her. She'd seemed fine with them. But now, looking back, he wasn't so sure. Were they a comfort or a trial? Maybe Ron and Janet knew? Would it matter? Channion wasn't sure. Then he wondered about how Ron and Janet had felt about them back then.

The other photograph was one of the last taken of his mom and him together before she passed away. He remembered they'd gone on a picnic with Ron and Janet. His mom had wanted to be in the country that day. She'd wanted to feel free and alive with the sun warming her chilled skin and broken heart. She'd sat there smiling while the breeze blew gently around them.

Her indomitable attitude and her fight for her life were admirable. It just wasn't meant to be.

At that precise moment, he realized Raina was quite similar to his mom and that realization shocked him. They shared an inner fight and eternal light, a zest for life, strong spirits and independent attitudes. And both displayed their innate compassion and intense loyalty. Even their senses of humor were similar.

He wondered if Ron or Janet had made the connection themselves? It was odd how he'd unknowingly found someone similar to his mom.

Thankfully, they were also different enough to not make that feel creepy, he thought with some comic relief.

Channion held the letter in his hands, preparing himself to read it. He took a deep, hitching breath as he saw his mom's handwriting, shaky from her illness and, most likely, her emotions. He began to read:

My darling Channion,

Could it be that tomorrow is your wedding day, my son? You have found your girl, the one you've been searching and waiting for then. I'm beyond happy for you, Channion! Congratulations!!

My greatest regret, of course, is that I'm not there with you. Oh, how I wish I could be there for you! My broken heart has been shattered into still more tiny pieces at the thought of not being there with you and your new bride.

As you probably recognized, here is your father's watch. It was my gift to him on our wedding day. For twenty years, he wore this watch. It's been worn, repaired, and loved by one man. And now I pass it along to you. Maybe it'll be a talisman for you in your marriage? Do not feel you need to wear it—I only wanted to give you something of your dad's on your special day. I feel it proper and know my Jay, your loving dad, would approve you having it now. He'd love it being a Wedding Day Watch. Maybe a new family tradition? I trust you'll keep it safe and cherish it.

You're getting married! Oh, I wish I could know her. What's her name? What's she like? What made her fall in love with you? What is it about her that captured your heart? She must be something quite special to have been able to do that! I pray she's the one who will stand by your side for a long, happy, and fulfilling lifetime.

There are so many things I wish to tell you, Channion. I could write a book over a thousand pages with all I long to say. I've tried to be the best mother I could be. Losing your father like we did was the absolute worst thing to ever happen. I miss him so very much as I know you do, too. He loved you a tremendous amount. Never doubt that. And he'd be immensely proud of you—as I am. You were the greatest gift and treasure we could ever have had. We both love you to the moon and back.

As tomorrow is your wedding day, I feel I should give you some motherly advice. I find it a daunting task. What to say? You're a grown man and have found your way, and your bride-to-be, without me, so what would you want to hear from me?

Maybe to tell you that marriage is always a work in progress. Even when you're so deep in new love, there will come those times when you'll probably wish you were still a single, free man. Don't! For at the end of the day, at the end of the road, having someone who loves and respects you, who has your back like no one else ever could, there's no greater gift! And you need to be the same to her, son. She and your marriage are now your priorities.

Remember to be honest and open with her. It's a guy thing to not want to talk, to close up, to not discuss feelings. It's the opposite for a woman, my dear. If you find it hard to communicate with words, then do so with actions. Actions speak louder than words. Don't wait for your anniversary or birthday to send her flowers, or a simple note. Call her on your break, or hers. Treat her like a queen, and she will treat you like her king.

Listen to her, and hear what she's actually saying. And remember, sometimes it's what she's not saying that's the most important thing to hear. Never look down on her as less for she is your equal. She has the same rights as a human as you do! If you doubt her judgment, then you doubt her.

Work through the tough times. They'll come at you both in spades. Remember what you love about her, what makes her more special and unique than any other woman you've known. Respect her, trust her, be faithful to her and your vows, love her unconditionally. I pray that she does the same for you. I pray that she'll never break your heart, and that you never break hers. But hurt is a part of marriage, of any relationship, but so is healing and forgiveness. Remember if a heart gets broken, it needs to be fixed.

Keep God in your marriage, Channion. Don't let others mock you, or tell you God is for fools. He's for everyone. He's for you! And always keep a deep sense of humor!

I wish you both the love that your father and I had. It wasn't always easy, but we worked through it. Looking back, I'd do it all over again. He was, and still is, the love of my life. After he was gone, I never could feel that way toward any other man. I was content to live alone, wrapped in the warm memories of his love. No one could have loved me better, or more, than your father.

I hope you feel the same toward your bride. I hope she feels the same to you. There should be no greater and stronger team than a husband and wife who are committed to each other. It's not an outdated idea, but what true marriage is. But it takes work! Don't be too proud to ask for advice or help.

My blessings will be with you and your bride tomorrow, Channion. Know I'd give anything to be there with you both, but that's not in my power to do. This is the best I can come up with, so I hope it's enough. If you should have your own family, all I ask is that you and your wife—your wife!—share stories about your dad and me with them. We'd love that, son! Let us live on from your heart to theirs.

I already regret that we won't be there to see your children be born, grow up, and see what paths they decide to take. Assuming you two decide to have some children, of course. If you do, remember to treat your wife with respect, love, and care! They'll be watching you to see how to properly love a woman. Be a remarkable role model for them.

And if you do have children, be a full-time dad like you should be. Be sure you know how you two want to raise them... before you have them. You can't go back! Share all of the house chores, the cooking and shopping, the complete raising of your children. From the second they're born, they're as much your responsibility as they are hers. They are half yours, aren't they?

Don't make her have to ask, certainly never beg, you for help! Your father was a huge blessing to me in that he did this on his own. And he took amazing care of me when I was pregnant with you. The difference that a loving and attentive man, husband, father, makes to a woman, wife, a mother, is truly remarkable! It's beyond description! She will love you even more if you do this. And she will also notice and resent you for it if you don't. Be in the moment, my dear.

In closing, my beloved son, I wish you happiness, health, and love! Be strong. Be true. Be faithful. And always remember how very, very much I love you. And how much your dad loved you. You were the light in our lives, Channion. You've grown into a fine, upstanding man, and I couldn't be more proud of you! And your dad would be proud of you, too!

I love you, Channion, my darling son, with all my being.

Wishing you only the best that life can bring you and your bride—

I love you forever and beyond,

Mom

Channion sat there, wiping the streaming tears from his face as he read his mother's final words to him. How hard this must've been for her to do! he thought. How he wished she could've met Raina! He could only imagine the way the two of them would've gotten along. And his dad... He'd have been sunk as he was. And Ron. Even Ty, he thought with a smile.

What would they have thought knowing how brave and courageous she was? That they met because she risked her own life to save another's? Another policeman's, as it turned out? What if his dad had had a Raina? How odd that thought never crossed his mind until this moment. But *what if...?* How different their lives would've been!

He sat there holding his mom's letter for a long while. Even when his tears of grief had stopped falling, he still just sat there, thinking. He finally went to his bathroom to clean up.

Returning to his room, he slipped the letter and photographs back into the envelope. He went to his office, putting it in his safe for protection.

The watch he felt compelled to wear. But not tonight. Tomorrow.

Looking it over closely, he felt waves of nostalgia come back to him. Did he ever know this was his mom's gift to his dad on their wedding day? If he did, he'd forgotten. All he remembered was his dad always seemed to be wearing it unless he was doing something strenuous or wet, like swimming in their pond. Now he knew *why* his dad had protected it and gave it such care. As a young boy, he probably didn't even care that his dad wore a watch.

Now it meant the world to him.

Chapter 72

"YOU READY?" RON, DRESSED in a classy black tuxedo with a royal blue cummerbund and pocket handkerchief, and in black, shiny shoes, looked at Raina. He smiled at her, feeling his own heart beat faster in anticipation.

She grinned, sliding her hands down her wedding gown. "I think so. I'm not nervous at all about marrying Chan, or spending the rest of my life with him. I'm more nervous something will happen to *prevent* it."

Ron patted her hand. "That was beautifully said."

She smiled as they waited for Jack to open the door.

While the music was being ceremoniously played, Raina watched her three friends dressed in royal blue gowns walk down the aisle with the handsome groomsmen dressed in black tuxedos.

Whispering to Ron, holding tightly to his arm, she said, "You know the purpose of bridesmaids is to ward off evil spirits to protect the bride. Maybe I should've found a few more."

Ron shook his head. "Honey, we got rid of the bad guys. Three is all you need, and that's just to share your day with. I'm so glad they're here for you." He patted her white gloved hand resting on his arm. "Now get out there and make me a proud man. Don't you dare cry," he added sternly. "If you start, Janet will too."

"I'll try, but I can't promise you. The only promises I'm making today are to Channion." She took a deep breath and let it out slowly, looking straight ahead.

Ron smiled broadly, so proud of the woman his nephew had found. He had sky-high hopes they'd make it on the long haul to forever.

When Channion first caught sight of her coming through the doorway, he swore his heart stopped. He thought she was sexy in her Western clothes she wore at the bar. He thought her sweet in her cut-off blue jean shorts and tank tops while she helped with yard work. He thought her adorable and cuddly in her winter sweaters and boots.

But when he saw her walking toward him, she was all of that plus so much more. He felt Ty, his Best Man, nudge him. Probably in approval, he thought. Maybe in jealousy, he thought again with a small grin.

Raina transferred her bright smile to her soon-to-be-husband as they made eye contact. He couldn't take his eyes off her. He'd never seen a wedding gown like hers. Leave it to his Raina to have one specially made that'd break the mold of wedding gowns.

Her white satin gown had a pattern that resembled a shield across the bodice. One thin blue strip of satin wrapped around her slim waist, where it continued in the back to form a long, colorful trail like a streamer on top of the long, white train. She heard the murmurs of the crowd as people understood the meaning. Going for simple and elegant, she wore elbow-length white gloves and a sparkling tiara instead of a veil.

She'd intentionally chosen the blue to pay homage to the police force. She was also symbolically relaying how she and Channion had met. Her design was also letting Channion, his law enforcement family, even his fellow officers, know she was knowingly marrying into this life. Her own thin, blue line.

As she stopped beside him and Ron kissed her cheek before turning to sit with his beloved Janet, Channion smiled. He couldn't help it. His happiness glowed from his eyes when he saw her. Glancing down, he caught sight of a small heart-shaped locket that looked to have been cleverly added to the gown. Sitting at the top of the gown just above her breasts, he took another look at it.

Why did it seem familiar? he wondered. In the next instant, his heart skipped a beat. When he realized it was his mom's locket, he looked up into her understanding eyes.

Taking his hand in one of hers, her other hand patted the locket. Raina whispered, "It's as close to my heart as I could get it."

Channion squeezed her gloved hand hard and kissed the back of it. He nodded to her in appreciation. She nodded back in understanding.

She caught Ty's wide smile and returned it. He also recognized the locket and heard her whispered sentiment to his cousin. Her simple statement made his heart swell in love and appreciation once again for this woman who'd caught his cousin's heart. She was worthy, Ty proudly thought again, his own eyes misty.

They turned to face the smiling minister. "Dearly beloved, we are gathered here today..."

Raina was proud of herself. She was getting through it without crying. She was doing fine until she and Channion walked over to light the Unity candle. There she saw for the first time the two small framed photographs set around the candle: Channion's parents and her own sweet mama. The three people the two of them had most wanted to share this day with were the only ones who couldn't.

She looked up at Channion. The look on his face let her know he didn't know they were there either. When they lit the Unity candle together, both of their hands shook. Her eyes misted with tears, but she blinked them back. She glanced up at Channion and saw his eyes were misty too. They stood there as the music played, almost frozen in place. They watched as the vivid single small flame danced in the reflections over their parents' smiling faces.

Before she lost her courage to do so, Raina removed her hand from Channion's. She kissed her fingertips on both hands and gently placed them on the faces of their parents. Channion's heart swelled in love and admiration for her in her show of respect. He could do no less and copied her gesture.

They both heard the soft gasps, *oohs,* and *aww*s from the large audience behind them. And more than a few sniffles.

Trying to get herself together, Raina wiped away the first tear that escaped from her eyes. When another fell, she felt Channion wipe it off for her, then the next one, and the one after that. She was going to lose it if they didn't get away from this spot. She looked up and saw the tears in his own eyes. It took all she had to not break down knowing he was as affected as she was.

Ignoring the fact they were being watched by hundreds of people, she pinched the bridge of her nose in an effort to stop the tears. She thought about everything else she could think of to distract herself. She assumed it was Janet who put out the photos. She couldn't wait to talk to her about this!

Finally, Raina felt she was back in control. For now. She took Channion's hand, squeezed it, and began to back away. As if reading her mind, he led her away and back over to the minister.

They stood there for a moment, wishing the minister would get on with it. Channion held tight to her hand, willing them both to be stoic for a little while longer.

When she sniffled again and wiped another tear away, Bethany, one of her brides-maids, step forward and handed her a tissue. Gratefully, Raina grabbed it and used it instead of her white gloves to dab her tears away. She felt Bethany straighten her gown and train as they waited for the music to end so the minister could continue.

It didn't help either of them when they kept hearing sniffles from the large audience behind them. Raina glanced up at Channion and saw a tear on his cheek. Reaching up, she tenderly wiped it away with her gloved thumb. She swore everyone watching sighed in unison at the sweet gesture. She caught Ty's wide smile and his nod of approval. She gamely smiled back at him, her own eyes still misty.

In an effort to distract both herself and Channion, she did the only thing she could think of: She kicked him. With her flowing skirt, the audience probably didn't realize what she did. If they saw it, they probably thought she was untangling her foot or even lost her balance for a second. When she looked up into Channion's eyes, she saw his surprise.

Softly, Channion asked her, "Did you just *kick* me?"

Her brilliant smile was answer enough.

Ty, Bethany, and the minister all smiled broadly, trying hard to not laugh. Since they were the closest, they were the only ones to hear his question. Bride and groom were also trying not to laugh.

Much to their relief, the minister finally got to the ring exchanges and the "I dos." The smiling minister finally called out, "I now pronounce you husband and wife. You may now kiss your bride!" Quietly, he added, "Note I said *kiss*, not *kick*, your bride!"

Channion and Raina smiled as they turned to each other. Just before he kissed his new bride, Channion whispered to her, "Thank God we're not Catholic!"

She let out a quick laugh before his mouth closed over hers. She wrapped her arms around his neck, kissing him back with all the love she felt for him.

The minister had heard his comment. When they finally pulled away from each other, he was grinning broadly. Over the loud cheers from their large audience, he said, "I'm glad you're not Catholic either. In a few more minutes, *I'd* be crying."

Channion retorted, "*I'd* be black and blue!"

They all laughed as the minister announced to the cheering audience, "Mr. and Mrs. Channion Scott!"

Epilogue

"THEY GOT MARRIED A few days ago?" Solomon asked Storm over lunch.

"Yes. It was a beautiful, touching ceremony. I've never been to a wedding with so many Kodak moments. And the reception was a huge, joyous party. They looked incredibly happy.

"Unlike so many nowadays, I'd say they're taking marriage seriously, and I think they'll make it last. Obviously, it's far too early to tell, but some couples seem to have *that* feeling about them. They do."

He smiled as he handed Solomon some photos he'd taken of the wedding. Storm liked to follow-up on cases when he could to remind himself of why they did what they did. They all needed a positive story for personal motivation. The positive stories were like the bright beams from a lighthouse on a stormy night, guiding these agents who chose this life of secrecy and danger to help the innocents.

"One of the guests told me they'd chosen the holiday weekend for their wedding so they could combine it with their annual family reunion. They even set up babysitters so the wedding itself was kid-free. While they left for their honeymoon, everyone else stayed behind for the reunion that was held over the rest of the weekend. It was all planned out quite well.

"I think this couple will make it through the long haul. Some weddings you just *know* won't last, and sometimes make you wonder why in the world *they* thought they would. One's campfire and the other's microwave. Those don't mix very well for the long term."

Entertained by his agent's description of mismatched people as he looked at the photographs, Solomon grinned. "No one noticed you?" He knew his agent would know who he was referring to.

"There must've been three or four hundred people there, so I blended right in. I made sure to stay away from Miles. He's as smart as a whip, so I didn't want to take a chance on talking to him or even getting too close. If I show up in any photos, my disguise should shield me. He seemed genuinely happy about their marriage."

Solomon smiled. "Weddings are blessed events, or should be anyway. They have certainly changed over the decades." He smiled at a photograph. "Isn't this...?"

Storm nodded. "Yes. Deputy Mitchell was one of the three groomsmen, and his sister was a bridesmaid." He handed his friend another photo. "This is when he and the bride were dancing. Miles came out and gave them sunglasses because of all the camera flashes! It was a wonderfully lighthearted moment."

Both men laughed.

Pointing at another photograph, he explained, "Detective Scott is close with his aunt and uncle. His uncle is his partner as well. For the wedding, they stepped in as their parents since neither had any. Ron walked her down the aisle and did the father dance, and his wife Janet got the mother dance. It was emotional for them all."

Solomon came to a shot that nearly took his breath away. He studied it for a moment, comprehension coming immediately. "Her gown is stunning!"

Storm nodded in full agreement. "I heard her call it her 'Blue Line Gown' when I was walking by. She made sure everyone knew she understood who she was marrying—and the life it entailed. I don't think there was a single person there who wasn't affected when she walked down the aisle."

Storm pointed to the silver spot on the gown. "I was told this was a locket she'd been given the night before. It belonged to her new husband's mom. I heard she passed away about five years ago. Miss Stewart, now Mrs. Scott, apparently sewed it to her gown in honor of her.

"And Detective Scott was wearing his dad's watch that he'd also been given just the night before. Both the watch and the locket were wedding gifts from his parents to each other on their own wedding day. As I said, a lot of Kodak moments!"

Before Solomon could reply, they saw another agent coming toward their table. He carried a large brown envelope in his hand.

"Hunter! It looks like you've got something for us." Solomon said with a smile. "It must be good news! Join us..." He pointed to the empty chair at their table while Storm gathered up the wedding pictures and slipped them into his own envelope to get them out of the way.

The tall, formidable, muscled man with black hair pulled out the lone chair and sat down. Smiling at them both, Hunter nodded. "Hey, Storm. Good to see you again!"

His glance went between the top two men in the Agency as he explained his reason for being there. "We have an update on the mother and son. They're in Kansas. They seem to be fine and are building a new life there. Here are the photos we took." He handed over a file to Solomon.

"It's like Show-and-Tell Day!" Solomon said with humor in his eyes.

Hunter continued as the men perused the photos of a woman and teenaged boy. "She has a job at a nearby hospital, and the boy seems to be adjusting well enough. He's in a good school, and he's joined some sports and clubs. We got a few shots of him at a game..." He shuffled through the photos and pulled out the ones he was talking about.

"No one seems to be the wiser with who they are, or were. She went back to her maiden name. She petitioned a court to change Zach's last name to match hers, which the court granted. It appears she's trying to get as much distance as she can manage between them and her deceased husband.

"We've been monitoring them, and we still haven't seen anyone following them. Our assessment is they're safe and are free from her husband's business. The ATF, FBI, and local LEOs brought in a slew of the ones Dreyfuss turned on, so none of us are foreseeing anyone tracking her down. We also aren't seeing any reason for them to do so."

The two men nodded in approval.

"This is all excellent news! If your team feels they're safe, I'll sign off on removing surveillance on them," Solomon said.

"Yes, sir. I'll notify the team to come in." Hunter smiled at them, glancing at their plates of fresh salad. "What's on the menu today?"

"Sirloin is the special. We just ordered, so if you want to join us, you're more than welcome to," Storm said. "You won't have to wait any longer for your meal than we are."

"Thanks, but I ate already. I should've waited! I'll head on back to the office." He shook Storm's hand, saying, "In case I don't see you before you leave, it was great having you back here. Don't be a stranger."

"Thanks. It's hard to know where I'll be and for how long. You know how it is."

"I do. Well, have a safe trip." He rose, pushed his chair back in. "Sirs." He turned and walked back toward the restaurant's entrance, taking the large envelope of pictures with him.

After a moment, Solomon said, "It's been over now for almost a year, Storm. Everyone who hurt you has been held accountable. There's nothing more for us to do. How do you feel about that?"

Storm thought for a moment, drinking some tea before saying, "I don't feel anything, to be honest. I still feel hollow inside. It feels like a lifetime since I left my wife, not knowing we'd never see each other again. She's moved on with someone new after years of grief. She got the closure she needed and deserved.

"And Miss Stewart, now Mrs. Scott, has it also. I'm relieved she didn't have to go through what my wife did. Those endless years of uncertainty, fear, and doubt.

"But me? No, sir. I don't feel any closure at all. Maybe it's been far too long, so it's all anti-climactic like I mentioned last year when we knew we got him. Or perhaps it still hasn't truly sunk in yet. Maybe too much has happened, and with what I've gone through, my emotions just aren't connecting the dots. Maybe it's because I still lost everything I had and loved. I don't know."

"Yes, your life as you knew it ended. You just need to continue building this new one," Solomon replied softly. "You know I'll be here and help you out in any way I can as long as I can."

"Yes, I know." After drinking some more tea, he said, "And I appreciate it. Without you and most of the guys here, trying to get as far as I have on my own would've been nearly impossible, if *not* impossible."

Solomon leaned forward and looked his agent in the eyes. "I disagree, son. You did a whole lot on your own first. You were able to get yourself back here. We've just helped you take the next steps.

"You are the strongest man I've ever known. Don't ever forget that. The next step is up to you. And you're not alone when you decide to take it."

Nodding, Storm hesitated before saying, "As I've always said, taking that first step is always the hardest. It's the one that requires the most courage with sometimes the least amount of confidence. It's walking into the vast unknown."

He gave a sad, pained smile to his superior and friend. "I've taken a lot of first steps over the past few years, haven't I? But this last one has been different. Everything I've been living for, well, it's all gone now. I could even say my mission is accomplished. Now what?"

Solomon spent their meal asking questions, answering others. He was gauging his friend and agent's mood and attitude. Solomon did it so smoothly, in such a conversational way, Storm probably didn't realize he was being evaluated. If he did notice, he didn't mention it.

As they were leaving the restaurant, Solomon held out his hand. "You take care now, son. I want you to keep in touch. The teams and I will be here for you. Remember you are *not* all alone in this world."

"I will. Thank you. And I'll check in with you later. I promise." Storm stood there for a moment, leaning on his cane.

He watched the closest thing to a friend and family member as he had now walk toward a black car. He waited to make sure Solomon was away safely before he took his own leave.

Walking across the parking lot, he watched as he put one foot in front of the other. And then again. And again. And again.

Review Request

Thank you for reading *The Witness*.
I truly hope you enjoyed the journey of Raina and Channion.
If so, could I humbly ask you to write an honest online review for me? What did you like best? How did it make you feel? Did it make you laugh, cry, etc.? Did you like the suspense, mystery, humor, characters?

Please give me the good stuff so I know what made you like/love it! Be honest. If you didn't like it, please be tactful. (Surely there was *something* you liked?)

Please leave a review anywhere/everywhere my books are sold as reviews are not linked together for others to read.

<u>Thank you so much in advance!</u>

Stay tuned for future releases.

Happy trails,
Jordan

About Jordan Standridge

An avid reader and writer since childhood, Award-Winning and Best-Selling Author Jordan Standridge is joyfully and happily expanding her literary sphere.

Influenced by Walter Farley and Louis L'Amour growing up, and later Julie Garwood, Jordan now creates her own stories. Weaving many of her real-life experiences with her imagination, she infuses them with her humor, love for animals, life lessons, values, and romance. And then she'll probably add a dash of mystery and suspense because she can.

A frequent traveler and mover, Jordan currently lives near Lexington, Kentucky.

Need More?

Additional Resources

In my story The Witness, *I mention in passing a couple of real subjects, and go a bit more in-depth on one. To learn more, or if you need help, I added this information. More information is on the next page. If you know of someone in need, please be their voice. Please seek help if* you *need it. You are not alone.*

Human Trafficking

In case of emergency, call 9-1-1

National Human Trafficking Hotline

1 (888) 373-7888

https://humantraffickinghotline.org/

https://polarisproject.org/understanding-human-trafficking/

Domestic Violence

In case of emergency, call 9-1-1

National Domestic Abuse Hotline

1 (800) 799-SAFE (7233)

https://www.thehotline.org/

PTSD (Post-Traumatic Stress Disorder)

https://www.ptsd.va.gov/

https://www.nami.org/

*DISCLAIMER: The author does not personally endorse any of these resources.

When I went to school to get my CDL-A (the license needed to drive large trucks), one of my classes was on this subject. Truckers can be a vital source of help. Some of this information is from my notes. If from another source, it will be cited.

Some Signs Of Human Trafficking

- A person seems to be controlled by another. They cannot come or go, or do what they want.

- A person is unusually submissive, quiet, fearful/scared, or nervous.

- A person is not left alone. Often, a "bodyguard" is with them so they cannot seek help.

- A person shows signs of abuse. (Physical, mental, or emotional—or all of them)

What Is Human Trafficking?

"Human trafficking occurs when a trafficker uses force, fraud or coercion to control another person for the purpose of engaging in commercial sex acts or soliciting labor or services against his/her will. Force, fraud, or coercion need not be present if the individual engaging in commercial sex is under 18 years of age." *–www.hu mantraffickinghotline.org*

"Human trafficking is the business of stealing freedom for profit. In some cases, traffickers trick, defraud or physically force victims into selling sex. In others, victims are lied to, assaulted, threatened or manipulated into working under in-humane, illegal or otherwise unacceptable conditions. It is a multi-billion dollar criminal industry that denies freedom to 24.9 million people around the world."
-www.polarisproject.org (used with their permission)

Domestic Violence

While most domestic violence cases are against women, it also happens to men.

And it's not always just physical abuse. It's often psychological or sexual. These are situations that may not be seen by another person. Verbal and emotional abuse are also common.

Please seek help if you or someone you know is in an unhealthy, controlled relationship or situation. Help is out there for you.

PTSD

Signs of PTSD can vary by severity and by person. The signs I mention are from people I've met or known over the years who have spoken with me about their own.

Flashbacks, nightmares, anxiety, automatic reactions to certain situations, loss of appetite, 'looking' for something to happen, stress, avoiding certain areas or situations are all symptoms. There are more.

Recovery time, options, and management are different for every person.

If you need help, there are several organizations out there for you.

Book Club Discussion Material

"The Witness"
Book 2: The Women of Strength, Courage, and Hope Series
<u>**Also available for downloading at www.JordanStandridge.com**</u>

1. In the beginning, Raina describes listening to her gut as listening to an angel warning her. Do you agree/disagree?

2. We sometimes hear the tragic news of a LEO being killed in the line of duty. In this instance, Deputy Mitchell had a "guardian angel" looking out for him. Would you consider him having a real angel, or one using Raina in order to save him? Or was it just pure luck? Is luck really an angel?

3. If you saw a LEO in danger, how would you feel about helping him/her in order to save their life?

4. While Raina is in the hospital, she suffers from the beginning of PTSD on top of her injuries. Throughout the story, there's mention of her PTSD. What are some of the symptoms of PTSD? What are some ways you could help them (if you knew or suspected)?

5. Discuss how the detectives/LEOs are portrayed as real humans having compassion, humor, and fears themselves.

6. While in the hospital, Raina wants nothing more than to see her horses, Aspen and Rodeo, again. How are you able to connect with her longing for "her kids"?

7. What are some ways that Raina was taking chances and showing her courage with her life throughout the book?

8. In Chapter 14, Channion talks about "cop humor," and how everyone says something they don't mean to be taken literally. What are some things you say that would fit this idea? Do you agree/disagree when he says if cops didn't have it, they'd snap in no time?

9. In Chapter 17, Raina is introduced to Detective Luke Reinhold. When she feels disrespected by him, she immediately stands up for herself and knocks him down a peg or two. If you're a woman, how have you experienced this? Did you stand up for yourself, or did you just let it go?

10. We learn that Channion's dad was killed in the line of duty, his mom died of cancer, and Raina's mom was killed by a drunk driver. As she said, "One taken so quickly with no warning, and the other suffering, wondering if it would ever end." Which situation do you think would be easier to deal with? Why?

11. In Chapter 20, Raina explains why she doesn't try to go professional with her singing, and talks about the music industry, and armchair critics. Do you agree/disagree with her perspectives?

12. Also in Chapter 20, they have a lighthearted discussion about slang/ terms in different regions of the country (USA, in this case). Grilled cheese vs cheese toasties in particular. Do you say *soda, Coke,* or *pop?* What are some other terms you/we use that mean the same thing?

13. In Chapter 25, Channion offers a policeman's viewpoint on the general public and crime. Do you agree/disagree with his perspective? What would you suggest for solutions?

14. The dynamic between Deputy Bryce Mitchell and Raina evolves and strengthens into a deep friendship. Would you have preferred her to have fallen in love with Bryce over Channion, or do you think her and Channion's love are relatable and justified?

15. It indirectly comes out that Lori and Zach are in a domestic violence situation. While not a recurring physically-violent situation, they are both "held captive" by Ford Coleman. Discuss the different ways a situation is considered "domestic violence."

16. In Chapter 25, Raina describes her reasons for wanting/needing to work. Do you agree/disagree with her decision/need?

17. In Chapters 2 and 18, Raina mentions—or even uses—some of her safety precautions and ways to defend herself as a woman. What are other ways to protect yourself (as a man or woman)?

18. Discuss the relationship between Raina and the Mitchell family. How could you thank someone for saving you/your child/sibling? What was most important to Raina?

19. In Chapter 39, the topic of reparations is brought up. Do you agree/disagree with them?

20. Also in Chapter 39, human trafficking is also lightly mentioned. Unbeknownst to many, this is a dangerously real issue that takes place daily. What are some ways you can protect yourself? Do you know how to recognize the signs of someone who may be trapped? Do you know how to help them? Would you?

21. In Chapter 52, Raina finally has her emotional explosion. What was the reason Ron gave for it? How did you like/dislike this scene/situation? How do you feel about the future relationship between Chief Coutts and Raina?

22. In Chapter 56, what do you think about Raina's reasoning/attitude in regards to moving out and living on her own again? What do you think of the author wanting to portray the reality of a person/a character knowing they need to be strong, confident, and independent? For the female character to not just fall on a male character to support her?

23. In Chapter 63, Raina felt she got closure/freedom from Kevin Dreyfuss. How did she feel she did this?

24. After Buchanan and Dreyfuss get killed, do you agree/disagree with the thoughts the law enforcement officers had? From saving tax payers' money, ending lurking dangers, victims getting closure, etc.?

25. In Chapters 69 and 71, you read the letters that Nikki Scott wrote before she died to her son and to her unknown daughter-in-law. What did you think of

these letters? What would you say if you were in her position?

26. Discuss Raina's "Blue Line gown," and her reasons for designing it.

27. Discuss the differences in family dynamics between Raina's family vs. the extended family of Channion's.

28. Included in this story is the relationship between an older married couple, Ron and Janet Kramer. What did you think about the author adding in a long-term, older-person, love story along with the middle-aged one? What makes the Kramer marriage work?

29. In the shadows, we have a covert agency "protecting the innocents." Do you believe these people really exist?

30. Do you feel like Raina got her self-redemption? Why or why not?

31. What are some examples of foreshadowing? Easter eggs? Discuss the overall theme of the story. Tone, setting, humor, values, issues, thoughts, viewpoints?

Sneak Peek

The Rescues

Book Three
The Women of Strength, Courage, and Hope Series

*Can a cautious woman and an abused horse
put their hope in the same man?*

December 2025

Be sure to visit **www.JordanStandridge.com** for more information, and be sure to subscribe to Jordan's FREE e-newsletter while there. You'll get a FREE character backstory when you do!

Excerpt from The Rescues

By Jordan Standridge

Chapter 1

THEY WERE FRYING EGGS on the sidewalk when she drove by. At least, that was her best guess when she saw the young kids squatting down, staring intently at them. She noticed all of the broken egg shells littering the sidewalk and smiled in amusement.

When she saw the little girl holding a yellow plastic spatula in one hand and a salt shaker in the other, she laughed. She hoped their parents had a sense of humor.

After running errands in town, she'd already decided to stop for lunch at one of her favorite watering holes, The Neon Moon. Seeing the eggs, though, tempted her to head to an IHOP or Waffle House instead. But since she was almost to her original destination, she decided to stay the course.

Cooking for one while her husband Josh was away wasn't all that appealing to her. Letting someone else do the cooking and cleanup definitely was. She figured she'd allow herself at least one freebie while he was away from home.

And this just so happened to be the one she chose.

When she turned into the parking lot of the Western-themed restaurant, she immediately noticed the large two-toned brown motorhome parked in the back of the large paved lot. Noting the tan car still hitched to it, she assumed the owners were inside enjoying the local offerings.

She appreciated the courtesy of the motorhome driver for parking out of the way—and for supporting a local business. She pulled into a spot near the door and put her truck in *park*. Since the Arizona sun was doing its best to melt metal—and fry eggs on sidewalks—she slid her windshield sunshade into place to block it. Rolling down her windows a little, she turned off her truck with a flick of her wrist.

The cool air hit her when she walked through the front door into the lobby. God bless the man who invented air conditioning! she thought. She snapped the carabiner hook that held her keys to her belt loop as she walked through the swinging doors that led into the afternoon dining area. She paused to removed her sunglasses and let her eyes adjust.

A waitress smiled and called out to her as she headed toward the kitchen with some dishes she'd just cleared from a table. "Hey there, girl! Sit where ya want. I'll be right with ya!"

"Will do, Jo!" she called back.

Glancing around, she felt a bit surprised when she didn't see any older people at any of the tables. She assumed the motorhome in the lot was being driven by an older couple enjoying their golden years in style. Or someone tired of expensive mortgage payments.

Looking to her left, she saw a middle-aged man in the corner booth reading on his phone, and a young couple sat at a two-top. Looking to her right, she saw three men laughing over something on one of their phones. Then she saw a lone woman who looked about her age. Sitting at a table by one of the wide windows that showcased the local scenery, she was dunking her French Dip in the little bowl of au jus. The window shade was partially pulled to tone down the bright sunlight over her table.

Remembering where she'd been, in particular the feed store and the vet clinic, she made a detour to the restroom. When she came out, she wandered over to the tall tables along the far wall, choosing one that was a respectable distance from the other woman. Sliding onto the stool, she waited for Jo to come back out. Glancing over, she saw the woman apparently texting somebody, and then her smile at their apparent reply.

Jo came back out, drying her hands on a towel and smiling at her as she walked over. "Hey, Morgan! Sorry about the lag time there. I was showing our new dishwasher how the Hobart worked. Where's your honey?"

"No worries. I'm not in any rush. Josh went camping with Ty and Damien. They left yesterday. Male bonding time," she replied, trying to keep a straight face. "If I'm not mistaken, my Fourth of July Extravaganza wore them out!" She shrugged her slender, muscled shoulders as she added, "It's the only thing I can think of that'd make them want to go camping in the hottest part of the year."

"Well, if they went up into the mountains more, it's bound to be cooler than down here. And it's always good to see *you!*" Jo rested her own foot on a stool rung and leaned on the tall back. "I stopped by that day, but you were so busy I don't know if you saw me. And I swear your event gets bigger and bigger every year! My family and I had an awesome time, by the way. My nephews from Nebraska hated to leave, so I have a feeling they'll want to come back next year."

Pleased, Morgan smiled. "I'm glad you all had fun. And I hope you gave me an amazing online review. They're so crucial in today's world." With a raised eyebrow, she warned, "And don't lie and say you did because you know I can log on right now and check."

Jo laughed before saying, "I *will* write an amazing review for you."

"I'll wait," Morgan deadpanned.

Jo chuckled. "I *will*... Cross my heart and hope to die and all that." She tucked the towel in her back pocket. "So, what're ya in the mood for today?"

"I'll do the blackened chicken sandwich combo. But I'll do a salad instead of the fries, with ranch, no croutons. And an iced tea. No, make that a Pepsi." Remembering she was trying to cut back on her only vice, she amended her order again. "Nope. Better make that the tea."

Twirling her pen in her fingers, the petite blonde grinned at Morgan's indecision. "Cutting back on the Pepsi again, I take it?"

"Trying to."

"Oh, just have one. Treat yourself."

"I'm a Pepsiholic. You should be supporting me in my decision, not encouraging me to fail."

"Sorry!" Jo laughed. "Make the tea half sweet, half unsweet?" At Morgan's nod, Jo said, "Coming right up." She went to the Point-of-Sale station the owner recently upgraded and put in the order. She poured the large iced tea and brought it over to her regular customer and friend. "It'll be a minute or two on the salad. They're being made now."

"Okay."

"Crackers?"

"Nope. Not this time around. Thanks though."

"No croutons. No crackers. No Pepsi. You're off your feed, girl. You sick?"

Morgan laughed and shook her head.

With a drawn-out, thoughtful "Hmmm," Jo gave her a doubtful look before she headed over to her other tables to check on her customers. As Jo chatted with the young couple, Morgan's attention returned to the woman who was now looking around at the Western décor as she sipped her drink. By its color, Morgan bet it was a Pepsi and sighed.

Noticing the lady who had just come in looking over at her now that the waitress had left, the other woman debated with herself for a split second as she set down her drink. Since the woman looked and sounded like a nice person, she decided to strike up a conversation. "Hi! I take it you're a local?" she asked with a friendly smile.

"Sure am!" Morgan replied with a smile of her own. "I take it you're not?"

"Nope. I'm traveling through and saw this place as I was driving by. It looked interesting so I thought I'd turn around to see if it was any good. I prefer to taste the local mom-and-pop type places rather than the chains, you know?"

"Absolutely. And trust me, the owner here appreciates it!" Morgan took a long sip of her tea before asking, "What do you think of it so far?"

"Service is great. Food is terrific. Atmosphere rocks!"

Morgan nodded. "Yeah, you got it all down. You should be here at night because *that's* when you really get to see the flavor of this place!

"We have a live band on weekends, karaoke on Thursdays, and pool tournaments on Wednesdays if enough people sign up, and they normally do. Oh, and line dancing lessons on Monday and Tuesday evenings, and sometimes in the afternoons on Fridays. Sunday is really the only down day here.

"And, of course, there are usually friendly people to chat with. But if you like to sing, come back in a couple of days if you're still here. I'm Morgan, by the way."

"Ripley. Nice to meet you, Morgan."

Book 3: The Rescues will be released

December 2025

Visit www.JordanStandridge.com for more information